Daybreak: A Romance of an Old World

James Cowan

Contents

DAYBREAK: A ROMANCE OF AN OLD WORLD

BY

James Cowan

CHAPTER I.
AN ASTRONOMER ROYAL.

It was an evening in early autumn in the last year of the nineteenth century. We were nearing the close of a voyage as calm and peaceful as our previous lives.

Margaret had been in Europe a couple of years and I had just been over to bring her home, and we were now expecting to reach New York in a day or two.

Margaret and I were the best of friends. Indeed, we had loved each other from our earliest recollection. No formal words of betrothal had ever passed between us, but for years we had spoken of our future marriage as naturally as if we were the most regularly engaged couple in the world.

"Walter," asked Margaret in her impulsive way, "at what temperature does mercury melt?"

"Well, to hazard a guess," I replied, "I should say about one degree above its freezing point. Why, do you think of making an experiment?"

"Yes, on you. And I am going to begin by being very frank with you. You have made me a number of hurried visits during my stay in Europe, but we have seen more of each other in the course of this voyage than for two long years. I trust you will not be offended when I say I hoped to find you changed. I have never spoken to you about this, even in my letters, and it is only because I am a little older now, and because my love for you has increased with every day of life, that I have the courage to frame these words."

"Do tell me what it is," I exclaimed, thoroughly alarmed at her serious manner. "Let me know how I have disappointed you and I will make what amends I can. Tell me the nature of the change you have been looking for and I will begin the transformation at once, before my character becomes fixed."

"Alas! and if it should be already fixed," she replied, without a smile. "Perhaps it is unreasonable in me to expect it in you as a man, when you had so little of it as a boy; but I used to think it was only shyness then, and always hoped you would outgrow that and gradually become an ideal lover. You have such a multitude of other perfections, however, that it may be nature has denied you this so that I may be reminded that you are human. If the choice had been left with me I think I should have preferred to leave out some other quality in the make-up of your character, good as they all are."

"What bitter pill is this," I asked, "that you are sugar-coating to such an extent? Don't you see that I am aching to begin the improvement in my manners, as soon as you point out the direction?"

"You must know what I mean from my first abrupt question," she answered. "To make an extreme comparison, frozen mercury is warm beside you, Walter. If you are really to be loyal knight of mine I must send you on a quest for your heart."

"Ah, I supposed it was understood that I had given it to you."

"I have never seen it," she continued, "and you have never before said as much as is contained in those last words. Here we are, talking of many things we shall do after we are married, and yet you have nothing to say of all that wonderful and beautiful world of romance that ought to come before marriage. Is this voyage to come to an end and mean no more to us than to these hundreds of passengers around us, who seem only intent to get back to their work at the earliest possible moment? And is our wedding day to approach and pass and be looked upon merely as part of the necessary and becoming business of our lives? In short, am I never to hear a real love note?"

"Margaret, I have a sister. You know something of the depth of my affection for her. When I meet her in New York to-morrow or next day, if I should throw my arms around her neck and exclaim, in impassioned tones, 'My sister, I love you,' what would she think of me?"

"She would think you had left your senses on the other side," replied Margaret, laughing. "But I decline to accept the parallel. I have not given up my heart to your keeping these many years to be only a sister to you at last."

"But my mother! Is it possible for me to love you more than my mother loved me? And yet I never heard her speak one word on the subject, and, now that I think of it, I am not sure but words would have cheapened her affection in my mind. You do not doubt me, Margaret?"

"No more than you doubted your mother, although she never told her love. No, it is not so serious as that; but I wish you were more demonstrative, Walter."

"What, in words? Isn't there something that speaks louder than words?"

"Yes, but let us hear the words, too. There is a beautiful proverb in India which says, 'Words are the daughters of earth and deeds are the sons of heaven.' That is true, but let us not try to pass through life without enjoying the company of some of the 'daughters of earth.'"

"I will confess this much, Margaret, that your words are one of your principal charms."

"Oh, do you really think so? I consider that a great compliment from you, for I have often tried to repress myself, fearing that my impulsive and sometimes passionate speech would offend your taste, you who are outwardly so cold. Do you know, I have a whole vocabulary of endearing terms ready to be poured into your ears as soon as you begin to give me encouragement?"

"Then teach me how to encourage you, and I will certainly begin at once. Shall we seek some retired spot, where we can be free from observation, and then shall I seize your hand, fall on my knees, and, in vehement and extravagant words, declare a passion which you already know I have, just as well as you know I am breathing at this moment?"

"Good!" cried Margaret. "That's almost as fine as the real scene. So you have a passion for me. I really think you are improving."

Before going on with this conversation, let me tell you a little more about Margaret and my relations to her.

There was good cause for her complaint. I was at that time a sort of animated icicle, as far as my emotional nature was concerned. But although I could not express my feelings to Margaret in set phrase, I do not mind saying to you that I loved her dearly, or thought I did, which was the same thing for the time being. I loved her as well as I was capable of loving anybody. What I lacked Margaret more than made up, for she was the warmest-hearted creature in all the world. If I should begin to enumerate her perfections of person and character I should never care to stop.

Her educational advantages had been far above the average, and she had improved them in a manner to gratify her friends and create for herself abundant mental resources. She had taken the full classical course at Harvard, carrying off several of the high prizes, had then enjoyed two years of post-graduate work at Clark, and finally spent two more years in foreign travel and study. As has been intimated, I had been over for her, and we were now on our way home, expecting to land on the morrow or the day after.

If you imagine that Margaret had lost anything by her education or was less fitted to make a good home, it is because you never knew her. Instead of being stunted in her growth, broken in constitution, round-shouldered, pale-faced and weak-eyed, the development of her body had kept pace with the expansion of her mind, and she was now in the perfect flower of young womanhood, with body and soul both of generous mold. Her marvelous beauty had been refined and heightened by her intellectual culture, and even her manners, so charming before, were now more than ever the chaste and well- ordered adornments of a noble character. She was as vivacious and sparkling as if she had never known the restraints of school, but without extravagance of any kind to detract from her self-poise. In short, she was a symphony, a grand and harmonious composition, and still human enough to love a mortal like me. Such was the woman who was trying to instill into my wooing a little of the warmth and sympathy of her delightful nature. As for myself, it will be necessary to mention only a single characteristic. I had a remarkably good ear, as we say. Not only was my sense of hearing unusually acute, but I had an almost abnormal appreciation of musical sounds. Although without the ability to sing or play and without the habit of application necessary to learn these accomplishments, I was, from my earliest years, a great lover of music. People who are born without the power of nicely discriminating between sounds often say they enjoy music, but these excellent people do not begin to understand the intense pleasure with which one listens, whose auricular nerves are more highly developed. But this rare and soul-stirring enjoyment is many times accompanied, as in my case, with acute suffering whenever the tympanum is made to resound with the slightest discord. The most painful moments of my life, physically speaking, have been those in which I have been forced to listen to diabolical noises. A harsh, rasping sound has often given me a pang more severe than neuralgia, while even an uncultivated voice or an instrument out of tune has jarred on my sensitive nerves for hours.

My musical friends all hated me in their hearts, for my peculiarity made me a merciless critic; and the most serious youthful quarrel between Margaret and myself arose from the same cause. Nature had given Margaret a voice of rare sweetness and a fine musical taste, and her friends had encouraged her in singing from her youth. One day, before she had received much instruction, she innocently asked me to listen to a song she was studying, when I was cruel enough to laugh at her and ridicule the idea of her ever learning to sing correctly. This rudeness made such an impression on her girlish mind that, although she forgave the offense and continued to love the offender, she could never be induced again to try her vocal powers before me. All through her school and college days she devoted some attention to music, and while I heard from others much about her advancement and the extraordinary quality of her voice, she always declared she would never sing for me until she was sure she could put me to shame for my early indiscretion, so painfully present in her memory. This became in time quite a feature of our long courtship, for I was constantly trying to have her break her foolish resolution and let me hear her. Although unsuccessful, the situation was not without a pleasurable interest for me, for I knew it must end some time, and in a way, no doubt, to give me great enjoyment, judging from the accounts which came to my ears. Margaret, too, was well satisfied to let the affair drift along indefinitely, while she anticipated with delight the surprise she was preparing for me.

During the years she had just been spending abroad a good share of her time had been given to her musical studies, principally vocal culture, and in her letters she provokingly quoted, for my consideration, the flattering comments of her instructors and other acquaintances. She did this as part of my punishment, trying to make me realize how much pleasure I was losing. Each time I crossed the ocean to visit her I expected she would relent, but I was as often disappointed; and now this homeward voyage had almost come to an end, and I had never heard her voice in song since she was a child. Open and unreserved as she was by nature, in this particular she had schooled herself to be as reticent and undemonstrative as she accused me of being.

Our talk on the subject of my shortcomings, that evening on shipboard, had not continued much longer before I acknowledged in plain language that I knew my fault and was ready to cooperate in any scheme that could be suggested to cure it.

"What you need," said Margaret, "is some violent sensation, some extraordinary experience to stir your soul."

"Yes," I answered, "my humdrum life, my wealth, which came to me without any effort of my own, and the hitherto almost unruffled character of my relations with you have all conspired to make me satisfied with an easy and rather indolent existence. I realize I need a shaking up. I want to forget myself in some novel experience, which shall engross all my attention for a time and draw upon my sympathies if I have any."

"But what can one do in 'this weak piping time of peace'? There are no maidens to be rescued from the enchantments of the wizard, and it is no longer the fashion to ride forth with sword and halberd to murder in the name of honor all who oppose themselves. No more dark continents wait to be explored, neither is there novelty left in searching the ocean's depths nor in sailing the sky above us. Civilized warfare itself, the only field remaining where undying fame may be purchased, seems likely to lose its hold on men, and soon the arbitrator will everywhere replace the commander-in-chief and the noble art of war will degenerate into the ignoble lawsuit. So even universal peace may have its drawbacks."

"That is quite sufficient in that line," said Margaret. "Now let us come down to something practicable."

"Well, I might bribe the pilot to sink the steamer when we are going up the bay, so that I could have the opportunity of saving your life."

"It would be almost worth the trial if it were not for the other people," she returned. "Such a role would become you immensely."

"I regret that I cannot accommodate you," I said. "But I have thought of something which would be rather safer for you. How would you like to have me fall desperately in love with some pretty girl?"

"Just the thing," exclaimed Margaret, laughing and clapping her hands, "if you can only be sure she will not return your passion."

"Small chance of that," I answered. "So you approve the plan, do you?"

"Certainly, if you care to try it. Lady never held knight against his will. But have you forgotten that, after the resources of this planet are exhausted, as you seem to think they are soon likely to be, you and I have other worlds to conquer? Perhaps in that work you may find diversion powerful enough to draw you out of yourself and, possibly, opportunities for some heart culture."

I must explain that this was a reference to a plan of life we were marking out for ourselves. Margaret was an enthusiast on the subject of astronomy. I would include myself in the same remark, only the word enthusiast did not fit my temperament at that time. But our tastes agreed perfectly in that matter, and we had always read with avidity everything we could find on the subject. Margaret, however, was the student, and as she had developed great proficiency in mathematics, she had decided to make astronomy her profession.

It was understood that I was to perform the easier part of furnishing the money for an observatory and instruments of our own, and I was determined to keep pace with Margaret in her studies as well as I could in an amateurish way, so that she might be able to retain me as an assistant. We were to be married at sunrise sharp, on the first day of the next century, and to lay the corner-stone of our observatory at the exact moment of the summer solstice of the same year. These were Margaret's suggestions, but even I was not averse to letting my friends see I had a little sentiment.

That night I dreamed of almost everything we had been talking about, but lay awake at intervals, wondering if I could, by force of will, work out the reform in my character which Margaret desired. The night passed, and it was just as I was rising that a thought flashed upon me which I determined to put into execution at the first opportunity. This came early the next evening. As we expected to reach our wharf soon, we had finished our packing, and were now sitting alone in a retired spot on deck on the starboard side. As soon as we were comfortably arranged I said to my companion:

"Margaret, as this is the last evening of this voyage, it makes an epoch in our lives. Your school days are now over, and henceforth we hope to be together. Would not this be a most appropriate time for me to be introduced to a voice with which I propose to spend the rest of my life? Last night you were anxious to think of something which would arouse my dormant heart and draw out in more passionate expression my too obscure affections. Your words haunted my sleeping and waking thoughts until it fortunately occurred to me that you yourself had the very means for accomplishing my reformation. You know how impressionable I am to every wave of sound. Who knows but your voice, which I am sure will be the sweetest in the world to me, may be the instrument destined to stir my drowsy soul, to loose my halting tongue, and even to force my proud knees to bend before you? In short, why not adopt my suggestion, break your long-kept resolution, and sing for me this moment? Is the possible result not worth the trial?" To this long address, which was a great effort for me, Margaret answered:

"You surprise me already, Walter. If the mere thought of hearing me sing can prompt such a sentimental speech as that, what would the song itself do? Perhaps it would drive you to the other extreme, and you would become gushing. Just think of that. But, seriously, I am afraid you would laugh at my voice and send me back to Germany. When you were talking I thought I could detect an undercurrent of fun in your words."

"I assure you I was never more in earnest in my life, and I am sorry you will not sing. Is your answer final?"

"I think I will wait a little longer. We are liable to be disturbed here. And now that you have made a start, perhaps you will improve in manners becoming a lover without any more help."

"No, I shall relapse and be worse than ever. Now is your time to help me find my heart."

Without answering, Margaret sprang up impulsively, exclaiming:

"There! I have forgotten that book the professor borrowed. Men never return anything. I must go and get it, and put it into my bag. And I had better run down and see if auntie wants anything. You stay right here; don't move, and I'll be back in just three minutes."

CHAPTER II.
A FALLEN SATELLITE.

I promised, and then settled myself more comfortably into my steamer chair to await Margaret's return. The three minutes passed, and she did not come. Evidently it was hard to find the professor, or perhaps he was holding her, against her will, for a discussion of the book. At any rate, I could do nothing but sit there, in that easy, half-reclining position, and watch the full moon, which had just risen, and was shining square in my face, if that could be said of an object that looked so round.

I fell into a deep reverie. My mind was filled with contending emotions, and such opposing objects as rolling worlds and lovely maidens flitted in dim images across my mental vision. I loved the best woman on the earth, and I wondered if any of those other globes contained her equal. If so, then perhaps some other man was as fortunate as myself. I was drowsy, but determined to keep awake and pursue this fancy. I remember feeling confident that I could not sleep if I only kept my eyes open, and so I said I would keep them fixed on the bright face of the moon. But how large it looked. Surely something must be wrong with it, or was it my memory that was at fault? I thought the moon generally appeared smaller as it rose further above the horizon, but now it was growing bigger every minute. It was coming nearer, too. Nearer, larger--why, it was monstrous. I could not turn my eyes away now, and everything else was forgotten, swallowed up in that one awful sight. How fast it grew. Now it fills half the sky and makes me tremble with fear. Part of it is still lighted by the sun, and part is in dark, threatening shadow. I see pale faces around me. Others are gazing, awe-stricken, at the same object. We are in the open street, and some have glasses, peering into the deep craters and caverns of the surface.

I seemed to be a new-comer on the scene, and could not help remarking to my nearest neighbor:

"This is a strange sight. Do you think it is real, or are we all bereft of our senses?"

"Strange indeed, but true," he answered.

"But what does it mean?" And then, assuming a gayety I did not feel, I asked further: "Does the moon, too, want to be annexed to the United States?"

"You speak lightly, young man," my neighbor said, "and do not appear to realize the seriousness of our situation. Where have you been, that you have not heard this matter discussed, and do not understand that the moon is certain to come into collision with the earth in a very short time?"

He seemed thoroughly alarmed, and I soon found that all the people shared his feeling. The movement of the earth carried us out of sight of the moon in a few hours, but after a brief rest everybody was on the watch again at the next revolution. The excitement over the behavior of our once despised moon increased rapidly from this time. Nothing else was talked of, business was well-nigh suspended, and the newspapers neglected everything else to tell about the unparalleled natural phenomenon. Speculation was rife as to what would be the end, and what effect would follow a union of the earth with its satellite.

While this discussion was going on, the unwelcome visitor was approaching with noticeable rapidity at every revolution of the earth, and the immense dark shadow which it now made, as it passed beneath the sun, seemed ominous of an ill fate to our world and its inhabitants. It was a time to try the stoutest hearts, and, of course, the multitude of the people were overwhelmed with alarm. As no one could do anything to ward off what seemed a certain catastrophe, the situation was all the more dreadful. Men could only watch the monster, speculate as to the result, and wait, with horrible suspense, for the inevitable. The circle of revolution was now becoming so small that the crisis was hourly expected. Men everywhere left their houses and sought the shelterless fields, and it was well they did so, for there came a day when the earth received a sudden and awful shock. After it had passed, people looked at each other wonderingly to find themselves alive, and began congratulating each other, thinking the worst was over. But the dreadful anxiety returned when, after some hours, the moon again appeared, a little tardy this time, but nearer and more threatening than ever. The news was afterwards brought that it had struck the high mountain peaks of Central Asia, tearing down their sides with the power of a thousand glaciers and filling the valleys below with ruin.

It was now felt that the end must soon come, and this was true, for at the earth's very next revolution the tired and feeble satellite, once the queen of the sky and the poet's glory, scraped across the continent of South America, received the death blow in collision with the Andes, careened, and fell at last into the South Pacific Ocean. The shock given to the earth was tremendous, but no other result was manifest except that the huge mass displaced water enough to submerge many islands and to reconstruct the shore lines of every continent. There was untold loss of life and property, of course, but it is astonishing how easily those who were left alive accepted the new state of things, when it was found that the staid earth, in spite of the enormous wart on her side, was making her daily revolution almost with her accustomed regularity.

The lovers of science, however, were by no means indifferent to the new-comer. To be able at last to solve all the problems of the constitution and geography of the moon was enough to fill them with the greatest enthusiasm. But, while thousands were ready to investigate the mysterious visitor, one great difficulty stood in the way of all progress. It seemed impossible to get a foothold on the surface. The great globe rose from the waves on all sides at such an angle on account of its shape that a lodgment could not easily be made. Ships sailed under the overhanging sides, and in a calm sea they would send out their boats, which approached near enough to secure huge specimens. These were broken into fragments and were soon sold on the streets of every city.

The first to really set foot on the dead satellite were some adventurous advertisers, who shot an arrow and cord over a projecting crag, pulled a rope after it, and finally drew themselves up, and soon the lunar cliffs were put to some practical use, blazoning forth a few staring words. These men could not go beyond their narrow standing place, for the general curve of the surface, although broken up by many irregularities, presented no opportunities for the most skillful climbing.

But it was impossible that, with the moon so near, the problem of reaching it could long remain unsolved. Dr. Schwartz, an eminent scientist, was the first to suggest that it must be approached in a balloon, and at the same time he announced that he would be one of two men, if another could be found, to undertake to effect a landing in that way. Here, I saw, was my opportunity. I had often dreamed of visiting the moon and other heavenly bodies, and now here was a chance to go in reality. I had some acquaintance with Dr. Schwartz, and my prompt application for the vacant place in the proposed expedition was successful. The doctor kindly wrote me that my enthusiasm in the cause was just what he was looking for, and he was sure I would prove a plucky and reliable companion. The matter attracted so much attention that the United States Government, moved to action by the public nature of the enterprise, took it up and offered to bear all the expense of the equipment and carrying out of the expedition. Encouraged by this assistance, the doctor began his plans at once. All recognized that one great object was to settle the question as to the existence of life on the other side of the moon; for, in spite of its rude collisions with mountains and continents before it rested as near the heart of the earth as it could get, it had insisted, with an almost knowing perversity, in keeping its old, familiar face next to us. To solve this problem might take much time, and so we determined to go so well prepared that, if we once reached the upper surface of the moon, we could stay as long as our errand demanded.

It was decided to make the ascent from a town near the coast of the southern part of Chile, and thither we went with our balloon, some scientific apparatus, and a large quantity of dried provisions. We took with us also papers from the State Department showing that we were accredited agents from our Government to the inhabitants of the moon, if we should find any. Our arrangements were speedily made, and on a still, bright morning we bade adieu to our friends who had accompanied us thus far, mounted our car, and set sail.

We left the earth with light hearts, excited with the novel and interesting character of the enterprise, and but little realizing its difficulty and danger. Ordinary balloon journeys had become frequent, and the evolution of the air ship had almost passed beyond the experimental stage, but nothing like our present undertaking had ever been attempted.

Our starting place was far enough from the resting point of the moon to enable us to clear the rounded side, but in order to reach the equatorial line of the fallen globe we would be obliged to ascend over a thousand miles.

The fact that we were not appalled by the mere thought of rising to such a height shows how thoroughly we were carried away with the excitement. But we were better prepared for a lofty flight than might be supposed. For among the recent wonders of science had been the invention of an air-condensing machine, by which the rarefied atmosphere of the upper regions could be converted into good food for the lungs. These machines had been successfully tested more than once by voyagers of the air, but the present occasion promised to give them a much more severe trial than they had yet received. And, indeed, it is impossible to imagine how we could have survived without them. Another important aid to science rendered by this air-condensing apparatus is that in the process of condensation water is produced in sufficient quantities to drink. Our little car was tightly inclosed, and we took enough surplus gas with us to keep it comfortably warm. So, with plenty of food, air, water, and fuel, we were pretty well prepared for a long journey.

Our instruments, placed just outside the glass sides of the car, told us how fast we were rising and what height we had reached from time to time, and as we left the denser atmosphere of the earth we were gratified to find that we continued to rise rapidly. On one side of us we could see the rugged surface of the moon, now, on account of its rounded form, drawing nearer to us every hour as we approached the point where we hoped to land. We thought it best to try to pass the center and land, if possible, somewhere on the upper hemisphere, which was the part of the monstrous object that we wanted to investigate. But when at length we thought we were about to fly past the moon's equator successfully, an unexpected thing happened.

If we suppose the moon was resting, at the bottom of the ocean, on one of its poles, we were going toward the equatorial line, and we thought we should not be able to retain a foothold anywhere below that line certainly. But now, what was our surprise to find ourselves under some mysterious influence. Our balloon refused to obey us as heretofore, and in spite of rudder and sail we were drifting about, and appeared to be going toward the moon's surface sooner than we had intended.

In scientific emergencies I deferred to my companion, and now asked for an explanation of this erratic behavior of our balloon. Instead of replying at once, the doctor stooped and cut a fine wire, which released one of the sand bags suspended for ballast from the bottom of our car, and told me to watch it. We both watched it, and instead of starting with rapidity for the center of the earth, as all well-conducted sand bags have done from the beginning of the world, it seemed to hesitate and float around a minute, as though it were no more than a handful of feathers. And then, slowly at first, but soon more and more swiftly, forgetting its birthplace and its old mother earth, it fell unblushingly toward the moon.

Intent on watching the fickle sand bag, we did not at first notice that our whole conveyance was practicing the same unhandsome maneuver. But we soon became aware that we had changed allegiance also. We had started with the earth at our feet and the moon looming up on one side of us, but here we were now riding with the moon under us and the earth away off at our side.

My fellow in this strange experience now found his voice.

"You doubtless realize," said he, "what has taken place. We are now so far from the earth that its attraction is very weak and the nearer mass of the moon is drawing us."

"That is quite evident," I said, "but you seem as unconcerned about it as if such a trip as this were an everyday affair with you."

"I am not at all indifferent to the wonderful character of this journey," he replied, "but its scientific value swallows up all personal considerations."

I believed this to be true, and I will say right here that in all our future experiences the doctor showed the same indifference to everything like fear, and seemed content to go to any length in the interest of science.

We were now able to govern our movements by the ordinary methods of ballooning, and after sailing over the surface of the moon a few hours, studying its rugged outlines, we began to think of selecting a place for landing. There was no water to be seen and no forests nor other vegetation, but everywhere were huge mountains and deep valleys, all as bare and uninviting as it is possible to imagine.

But it would not do to turn a cold shoulder to her now, and so we descended gracefully to make her close acquaintance, cast out our anchor, and were soon on the moon in reality.

CHAPTER III.
TWO MEN IN THE MOON.

W ell, Doctor," said I, as soon as our feet touched the ground, "the moon is inhabited now if never before."

"Yes, yes," he answered, "and I am glad to find the inhabitants are of such a lively disposition."

"Oh, who can help being light-hearted," I rejoined, "when one's body is so light?"

For as soon as we left our car we began to have the queerest sensations of lightness. We felt as if we were standing on springs, which the least motion would set off and up we would go toward the sky. Everything we handled had but a small fraction of the weight it would possess on the earth, and our great air-condensing machines we carried about with ease. But however high we might jump we always returned to the ground, and whether we were on top of the moon or on the bottom of it, it was pretty certain that we could not fall off, any more than we could have fallen off the earth before we voluntarily but so rashly left it.

My exhilaration of spirit did not last, for I could not help thinking of our condition. The law of gravitation surely held us, although with less force than we had been accustomed to, on account of the smaller size of the moon; and how were we to get away from it?

I again appealed to my companion.

"I do not like the idea of spending the rest of our lives on the moon, Doctor, but can you tell me how we are to prevent it? Can we ever get back within the earth's attraction again?"

"I have been pondering the subject myself," he replied, "and I think I can give you some hope of seeing home once more. If our old measurements of the moon are correct, and if we are, as I suppose, somewhere near the equator, we must be about fifteen hundred miles from the earth, following the curve of the moon's surface. Now, after we have finished our investigations here, we can start for home on foot. We can cover a good many miles a day, since walking can be no burden here, and we can easily tow our balloon along. As we approach the earth, my impression is that we shall become more and more light-footed, for we shall be gradually getting back to the earth's attraction. Somewhere between this point and our planet there must be a spot where the attraction of both bodies will be equal, and we can stay on the moon or drop off and return to the earth in our balloon as we please."

"What a curious idea," I answered; "and yet, considering the strange behavior of our sand bag, I don't know but you are right. And I have only one suggestion to make; that is, that we start earthward at once and try the experiment. Let the investigations go. If there are any inhabitants here they will never miss us, since we haven't made their acquaintance yet. Science or no science, I object to remaining any longer than necessary in this uncertainty in regard to our future. You know very well we couldn't live long in this temperature and with nothing for our lungs but what comes through these horrid machines. And what good would come of our discoveries if we are never to get back to the earth again? I profess to have as much courage left as the ordinary mortal would have, but in the present circumstances I believe no one would blame us for wanting to settle this question at once."

"It would seem a trifle ridiculous," said the doctor in reply to this harangue, "for us to return to our planet without any further effort to accomplish our errand. But I will not deny that I share something of your feeling, and I will start with you right away, on condition that you will return here if we find that I am correct in believing we can leave the moon at our pleasure."

"Agreed," I cried, and we were soon on our way.

So far we had been exposed to the sun and were almost scorched by the intensity of its rays. We had never experienced anything like such heat and would not have supposed the human body could endure it. But now, soon after we had started to find the place where the moon would let go of us, the sun set and, with scarcely a minute's warning, we were plunged into darkness and cold. The darkness was relieved by the exceedingly brilliant appearance of the stars, the sky fairly blazing with them, but the cold was almost unendurable even for the few moments in which we were exposed to it. We secured our car as speedily as possible, climbed into it, and got a little warmth from our gas heater.

These extremes of temperature convinced us that no life such as we were acquainted with could exist a great while on the moon.

We found we could make no progress at all by night. We could only shut ourselves up and wait for the sun to come. In trying to keep warm we would work our air-condensers harder than usual, and the water thus produced we would freeze in little cakes, and have them to help mitigate the burning heat a short time the next day.

The country through which we were traveling was made up of bold mountain peaks and deep ravines. There was no sign of vegetation and not even the soil for it to grow in, but everywhere only hard, metallic rock that showed unmistakably the action of fire.

And so it was with the greatest difficulty that we made our way earthward, although there was so little effort needed in walking. As I pondered the doctor's idea, it seemed to me more and more that he must be right. We were certainly held to the moon where we were by gravitation. It was just as true that near the surface of the earth its superior attraction would draw all objects to itself. Accordingly, if we kept on our way, why should we not in time come to a place where we could throw ourselves once more under the influence of the old earth, now becoming very dear to us?

Thinking chiefly of this subject and talking of it every day, we labored on, and finally were wonderfully encouraged with the belief that we were actually walking easier and everything was becoming lighter. Soon this belief became a certainty, and, since leaping was no effort, we leaped with joy and hope.

And now how shall I describe our sensations as we went bounding along, hardly touching the ground, until we finally came to the place where it was not necessary to touch the ground at all? Now we knew that by going only a little further we should be able to mount our car and set sail for the earth again. But with this knowledge we lost at once much of our desire, and thought we would not hasten our departure. Here we were, absolutely floating in the air, and it maybe believed that the feeling was as delicious as it was unique. Using our hands as fins we could with the slightest effort sail around at pleasure, resting in any position we chose to take, truly a most luxurious experience.

"How shall we make our friends believe all this when we try to tell them about it, Doctor?" said I.

"The best way to make them believe it," he replied, "is to bring them up here and let them try it for themselves. I propose to organize an expedition on our return and bring up a large party. We could manage to land somewhere in this vicinity, I think, instead of going up as far as you and I did. What a place this would be for summer vacations! The moon is a fixture now; it cannot get away. I am sure of that, for the law of gravitation will never release it. So we may as well make what use of it we can, and these delightful sensations will no doubt form the most important discovery that we shall ever make on this dried-up and worn-out satellite. You know many people are willing to put themselves to much inconvenience and to undergo many hardships for the sake of a change from the monotony of home life. If we can induce them to come up here for a few weeks, and if they can endure this rather erratic climate, they will find change enough to break up the monotony for one year, I think."

After enjoying this rare exercise to our content, we began preparing for the night which was now coming on. The doctor had reminded me of my promise to return to our former position on the moon, and we agreed to set out the next day. Having fastened our car securely to the ground, so that we might not drift off toward the earth, we entered it and made ourselves as comfortable as possible.

Our resting place was near the center of what seemed to be an immense crater, and some time before morning we were roused by a violent shaking of the ground beneath us, which startled us beyond expression.

"What's that?" I exclaimed.

"That feels very much like a moon-quake," replied my companion.

I was terribly frightened, but resolved to follow the doctor's example and make light of what we could not help.

So I said:

"But I thought the lunar volcanoes were all dead ages ago. I hope we haven't camped in the crater of one that is likely to go off again."

"My opinion is," answered the doctor, "that there is still water inside the moon which is gradually freezing. That operation would sometimes crack the surface, and this has probably caused the quaking that we have felt."

While we were talking the wind began to blow, and soon, although it was long before time for the sun to rise, we suddenly emerged from darkness into bright sunlight. We sprang up instinctively to look about us and try to discover what this could mean, when what was our consternation to find ourselves adrift!

There, in full view of our wondering eyes, was the whole, round earth, hanging in space, and where were we? Then we began to realize gradually that the trembling of the ground was the grating of the moon against the earth as it left its resting place, and the wind was caused by our motion.

The novelty of the situation took away for a time the sense of fear, and I exclaimed:

"Another scientific certainty gone to smash! I thought you said the moon could never get away from the earth. What are we going to do now?"

"Well," replied the doctor, "this is certainly something I never dreamed of in my philosophy. I didn't see how the moon could be drawn away from the earth when once actually attached to it, but I suppose the sun and planets all happen to be pulling in one direction just now and are proving too much for the earth's attraction. But what concerns us more at this time is covered by your question, 'What are we going to do now?' And I will answer that I think we will stick to the moon for a while. You can see for yourself that we are held here much more firmly than when we were disporting ourselves in the air yesterday, and the earth is now too far away for us to throw ourselves and our balloon within its attraction."

I knew by the feeling of increasing weight that what my companion said must be true, but we could not then appreciate the dreadful nature of our condition, so wrapped up were we in the grandeur of the object before our eyes. To those who have never been on the moon in such circumstances it will be impossible to adequately describe our feelings as we gazed upon our late home and knew that we were fast drifting away from it.

There the round globe hung, as I had often pictured it in my imagination-- oceans and continents, mountains, lakes, and rivers, all spread out before us--the greatest object lesson ever seen by the eye of man. As we studied it, recognizing feature after feature, lands and waters that we knew by their familiar shape, the doctor broke our reverie with these words, evidently with the endeavor to keep up my spirits:

"That looks as natural as a map, doesn't it? You have seen globes with those divisions pictured on them, but there is the globe itself. If our summer tourists could take in this experience also, it would make a vacation worth having. Isn't it grand? I see you are thinking about our personal peril, but I think I know men who would take the risk and put themselves in our place for the sake of this magnificent view."

"If you know of any way to send for one of those friends, I wish you would do so," I replied. "I would willingly give him my place."

It may be believed that we were all this time anxiously watching the earth, and it did not lessen our anxiety to realize that we were traveling very rapidly away from it. I had reached a point now where I did not place much dependence upon the doctor's science, but to get some expression of his thoughts I said to him:

"Well, have you any opinion about our fate? Are we doomed to pass the remainder of our lives circling around our dear old earth, looking upon her face day by day but never to approach her again?"

"I think you have stated the case about as it is," said he, "if, indeed, this rate of speed does not carry us entirely beyond the earth's attraction, out into illimitable space."

The thought of such an additional catastrophe silenced me, especially as I could not deny its possibility. Life on the moon, if we could only keep the earth in sight even, seemed almost endurable now, beside the idea that we might be cast out to shift for ourselves, without a tie save such as the universal law of gravitation might find for us somewhere.

It must not be imagined that our conversation was carried on with ease or that we were half enjoying our novel situation. We were simply trying to make the best of a very bad matter. Not long after we had started the wind had taken away the balloon part of our air ship, and now threatened every moment to tear the car from its moorings and end our unhappy career at once. Besides this impending catastrophe, it was with the greatest difficulty that we could get air enough to fill our lungs, but the cold was so intense whenever our side of the moon was turned away from the sun that we needed the severe labor on our condensers to keep us from freezing.

Meantime, our speed increasing every hour, the planet that had once been our home was growing smaller before our eyes. At length we were flying through space at such a rate that we could not suppress our fears that the terrible suggestion of the doctor's would be realized. We had both made a mental calculation as to how large the earth ought to look from the moon at its normal distance, and as it approached that size we could not hide our anxiety from each other. Without a word from the doctor I could see by his face that hope was fast leaving him, and as we were now going more rapidly than ever I felt that we had nothing to do but accept our fate.

In regard to such intensity of feeling at this stage of our experience, it maybe objected that our condition was hopeless anyway, and it could make no difference whether we remained within the earth's influence or not. But in spite of our desperate situation we had some sentiment remaining. The earth was the only home we had ever known, and I am not ashamed to say that we did not like to lose sight of it; especially as there was not the slightest possibility that we should ever see it again, unless, indeed, our moon should turn into a comet with eccentric orbit, and so bring us back at some future day--a very unlikely occurrence, as all will admit who know anything about moons and comets.

Our speed did not lessen but rather increased as we gradually broke away from the earth's attraction, and the dear old earth was fast becoming a less significant object in our sky. If our situation was lonesome before, it was now desolation itself.

"Doctor," said I, when I could control my emotions enough to speak, "where now?"

"Well," he replied, with a grim attempt at a smile, "my opinion is not worth much in our present strange circumstances, but it seems to me we are on our way either to the sun or one of the large planets."

I did not reply, and we both soon found it wise to expend no unnecessary breath in talking. The ether was now so thin that it took oceans of it, literally, to make enough air to keep us alive.

Our provisions were nearly exhausted, our strength was failing, and I really believe we would not have lived many days had not something occurred to divert our minds and to relieve some of our physical discomforts.

CHAPTER IV.
AND ONE WOMAN.

At the time we tied our car to the rocks, to prevent us from drifting away from the earth, we did not anticipate that the fastenings would receive any very severe strain, but now the velocity of the wind was such that there was great danger of our breaking away. The moon was not a very hospitable place, to be sure, as we had thus far found it, but still we preferred it to the alternative of flying off into space in our glass car and becoming a new species of meteor.

And yet it seemed to be courting instant death to attempt to leave the car and seek for other shelter. We could not decide which course to take. Both were so full of peril that there seemed to be no possible safety in either.

As I review our situation now, and think of us spinning along on that defunct world we knew not whither, with no ray of light to illumine the darkness of our future or show us the least chance of escape from our desperate plight, it is astonishing to me that we did not give up all hope and lie down and die at once. It only shows what the human body can endure and of what stuff our minds are made. I think it would not be making a rash statement to say that no man ever found himself in a worse situation and survived.

But help was nearer than we supposed. From what we had seen of the moon we could not have imagined a more unexpected thing than that which happened to us then. Suddenly, above the roar of the wind and the thumping of our car on the rocks, even above the tumult of our spirits, there came to us the strains of more than earthly music. Whether it was from voice or instrument we could not tell, and in its sweetness and power it was absolutely indescribable. At first we did not try to discover its source but were content to sit and quietly enjoy it, as it fell gently upon us, pervading our whole being and so filling us with courage and strength that we seemed to be transformed into new men.

Then, wondering if we could discover from whence the notes came, we turned and looked about us, when there was revealed to us a vision of beauty which filled and satisfied the sense of sight as completely as our ears had been enchanted with the angelic music.

Not far from our car, with her flowing garments nearly torn from her in the fierceness of the gale, was a young girl, stretching out her hands imploringly toward us and pouring forth her voice in that exquisite song. We soon discovered it was not for herself that she was anxious, but for us; for when she observed that she had attracted our attention she smiled and turned to go back the way she had come, beckoning us with hand and eye to follow her, and still singing her sweet but unintelligible words. Perhaps I flattered myself, but I thought she was looking at me more than at my companion, and I began with great eagerness to unfasten the door of the car.

"Wait!" cried the doctor. "Where are you going?"

I could not stop an instant, but answered with feeling:

"Going? I am going wherever she is going. I'll follow her to the end of the moon if necessary, though the surface be everywhere as bleak as our own north pole."

"Well," he replied, "if it is such a desperate case as that, I'll have to go along to take care of you."

I found that when such a woman beckons and such a voice calls there is but one thing to do. The sirens were not to be mentioned in comparison. Twenty thousand hurricanes could not have prevented me from attempting to follow where she led as long as I had breath.

We reached the ground in safety, and with the greatest difficulty made our way in the footsteps of our guide, leaving all our possessions behind us, to the doctor's murmured regret. And now the words of the singer seemed to take on a joyous meaning, and we could almost distinguish her invitation to follow her to a place where the wind did not blow and where our present troubles would be over. She kept well in the lead but walked only as fast as our strength would allow, looking back constantly to encourage us with her smile and ravishing one heart at least with the melody of her song.

Presently we came to the edge of an immense crater, hundreds of feet deep and as empty and cold as all the others we had seen on the moon. Instead of going around this, our leader chose a narrow ravine and took us down the steep side to the bottom of the crater. We supposed she did this just to give us protection from the wind, and we were very much sheltered, but she did not stop here. Entering one of the many fissures in the rocks, she led us into a narrow passage whose floor descended so rapidly and whose solid roof shut out the light so quickly that in ordinary circumstances we would have hesitated about proceeding. But, although it was soon absolutely dark, we kept on, guided by that marvelous voice, now our sole inspiration.

"Come, come, fear no harm," it seemed to say, and we were content to follow blindly, even the doctor no longer objecting.

How many hours we proceeded in this way, going down, down, all the time, toward the center of the globe, I have no means of telling; but I distinctly remember that we began, after a time, to find, to our great joy, that the air was becoming denser and we could breathe quite freely. This gave us needed strength and justified the faith with which our mysterious deliverer had filled us.

At length we were gladdened by a glimmer of light ahead of us, which increased until our path was all illumined with a beautiful soft haze. Soon the way broadened and grew still brighter, and then we were led forth into an open street, which seemed to be part of a small village. There were but few houses, and even these, although they showed signs of a former grandeur, were sadly in need of care. Not a creature of any kind was stirring, and in our hasty review the whole place looked as if it might have been deserted by its inhabitants for a hundred years. There was one spot, however, so retired as to be entirely hidden from our view at first, which had anything but a deserted appearance. The house was small, but it was a perfect bower of beauty, half-concealed with a mass of flowers and vines. Here our journey ended, for our guide led us to the door and, entering, turned and invited us to follow her.

The doctor and I were tired enough to accept with eagerness her hospitality, and soon we were all seated in a pleasant room, which was filled with the evidences of a refined taste. Now we had a much better opportunity to observe the resplendent beauty of our new friend, and we found, also, that her manners were as captivating as her other personal qualities. At intervals, all through our long walk, her song had ceased and we expected she would make some attempt to speak to us; but being disappointed in this, it struck me after we had entered the house that I ought to end the embarrassment by addressing her. The circumstances of our meeting were peculiar, to say the least, and, of all the thousand things I might have appropriately said, nothing could have been more meaningless or have better shown the vacant condition of my mind than the words I chose.

"It's a fine day," I said, looking square in her eyes and trying to speak pleasantly.

In answer she gave me a smile which almost deprived me of what little wit remained, and at the same time emitted one exquisite note.

I was now at the end of my resources. I had always thought I could talk on ordinary topics as well as the average man, but in the presence of this girl, with everything in the world unsaid, I could not think of one word to say. The doctor soon saw my predicament and hastened to assist me, and the remark which he selected shows again his wonderful self-possession in the midst of overwhelming difficulties. He waved his hand gently toward me to attract her attention and said:

"My friend and I are from the United States and have come to make you a visit. This is your home, I suppose, away down here in the middle of the moon? It is very kind of you to bring us here. I hope you will excuse me for my rudeness, but what time do you have supper?"

This time three little notes of the same quality as before and then a little trill, and the whole accompanied by a smile so sweet that I suddenly began to wish the doctor had been blown off the top of the moon. It was a wicked thought and I put it away from me as quickly as possible, being assisted by the recollection that the doctor had a charming wife already, who was no doubt thinking of him at this very moment.

We were not making much progress in opening conversation, but our charming hostess seemed to understand either the doctor's words or his looks, for, stepping into another room, she called us presently to sit down to a table well supplied with plain but substantial food. She soon made us feel quite at home, just by her easy and agreeable ways. We did not once hear her voice in ordinary speech, and at length we began to suspect, what we afterward learned to be true, that she talked as the birds talk, only in song. Whether she used her language or ours she would always sing or chant her words, and every expression was perfect in rhythm and melody.

The doctor and I hesitated to say much to each other, out of deference to the feelings of this fair lunarian, but he took occasion to remark to me quietly that as she could not tell us her name just yet he proposed to call her Mona[1] for the present. I assented easily, as it made little difference to me what we called her, if she would only remain with us.

It happened that the doctor, who knew everything, was well acquainted with dactylology and the latest sign language, used in the instruction of deaf mutes, and as it seemed likely that our stay in our present abode might be a prolonged one, he told me he would try to teach Mona to converse with us. I could not object, although I secretly wished I could have taken the place of instructor. But it soon occurred to me that I must be a fellow pupil, if we were all to talk in that way; and so, with this bond of sympathy established between us, Mona and I began our lessons.

During the closing years of the century great progress had been made, on the earth, in the method of talking by arbitrary signs and motions. The movements of the body and limbs and the great variety of facial expressions were all so well adapted to the ideas to be represented that it was comparatively easy for an intelligent person to learn to make known many of his thoughts. As our studies progressed day after day it began to dawn on me that Mona, in spite of the disadvantage of not knowing our spoken language, was learning faster than I was. I was somewhat chagrined at this at first, but it finally turned out to my advantage, for the doctor announced one day that Mona had acquired all he knew and could thenceforth teach me if I pleased. Here was a bond of sympathy that I had not looked for, but I was glad enough to avail myself of it, and delighted to find that Mona was also pleased with the plan. With her for a teacher it did not take me long to finish. Her graceful movements made poetry of the language, and the web she was weaving around my heart was strengthened every hour.

As Mona gradually learned to express herself to our comprehension we began to ask her questions about herself and her history. The doctor, being less under the spell of her charms than I was, showed a greater curiosity, and one of the first things

---

1   *Mona* is old Saxon for *moon*.

he asked was:

"When do you expect the other members of your family home?"

Mona was at first puzzled, but saw his meaning as soon as the motions were repeated, and answered with a few simple signs:

"I have no friends to come home. I am alone."

The expression we put into our faces told her of our sorrow and sympathy better than any words, and the doctor continued:

"But these other houses! Surely they are not all empty?"

"Yes," she replied, "their inmates are all gone. I am the only inhabitant left."

And then she told us from time to time that there were no other villages anywhere in the moon and that she was absolutely the last of her race. Our method of conversation was not free enough to allow her to tell us how she had discovered the truth of this astounding information, and there were a thousand other questions for whose answers we were obliged to wait, but not forever.

The doctor and I talked freely to each other now, and playfully said a great many things to Mona, who, though she did not understand them, laughed with us and gave us much pleasure with her easy, unembarrassed manner and piquant ways. And she not only jabbered away with hands and face in the manner we had taught her, but she did not cease also to make life bright for us by repaying us in our own coin and talking to us in her natural, delicious way. With such music in the house life could not be dull.

My infatuation increased as the days went by, and I began to seek every possible occasion to be alone with Mona. I often encouraged the doctor to go out and learn what he could of our surroundings, excusing myself from bearing him company on the ground that I did not think it safe to leave Mona alone. Or if Mona wanted to go out I would suggest to the doctor that I needed the exercise also, and that he really ought to be writing down our experiences while he had leisure, as there was no telling how soon the moon would land us somewhere.

I did not then know whether the doctor saw through my designs or not. I thought not, for I did not suppose he was ever so deeply in love as I was. But if he did he was good enough to take my little hints and say nothing.

On these occasions, whether Mona and I remained in the house or walked abroad, I wasted no time in asking her more questions about the moon or such trivial matters, but spent all my efforts in trying to establish closer personal relations between us. While she was exceedingly pleasant and agreeable, she did not seem to understand my feeling exactly, although I tried in every way to show her my heart. She was not coquettish, but perfectly unaffected, and simply did not realize my meaning. For once the sign language did not prove adequate; and so, as my feelings would not be controlled, I was fain to resort to my natural tongue, and poured forth my love to my own satisfaction if not to her comprehension. I did not stint the words, astonishing myself at the fullness of my vocabulary, and hoping that the fervor of my manner and the passion exhibited in my voice would make the right impression on my companion.

Day after day, as opportunity offered, I returned to the same theme. Mona was sympathetic in her own charming way, but apparently not affected in the manner I was looking for. And still, "I love you, I love you," was repeated in her ears a thousand times. The fact that she did not understand the words made me all the more voluble, and I lavished my affectionate terms upon her without restraint.

One day, after this had been going on for some time, the doctor came in from a walk and found us together as usual. He had a rare blossom in his hand, and stepping to Mona's side he offered it to her with some gallantry. She accepted it with a beaming countenance which set my heart to thumping, and then she burst forth in a strain so sweet that it thrilled my whole being and roused in me again that jealous fear that Mona was learning to care more for the doctor than for me. But how shall I describe my emotions when she suddenly blended syllables of our language with the accents of her song, and, still looking into the doctor's eyes, closed her entrancing melody with the burning words, "I love you"?

I wonder how other men have borne such a shock as that. It seemed to me that by simply living during the next few minutes I was proving myself stronger than others. And I was able to think, too. It occurred to me that perhaps Mona was merely a parrot, repeating, with no perception of their meaning, words which she had so often heard from me. But this idea passed swiftly away when I remembered the warmth of her expression and the ardor of her manner, both of which, alas, she had also learned from me.

As I recovered somewhat from the effects of the blow I found Mona's eyes were fixed on me, and she looked so innocent, so entirely unconscious of wrong, that if I had any anger in my heart it melted away and left me more her slave than ever. There was something in her behavior which I could not comprehend, and it was evident that she had not yet acquired any particular fondness for me, but these were not sufficient reasons to make me cease to care for her. My love was too strong to give her up, even after I had just heard her declare, in such a passionate way, her love for another. These thoughts passed through my mind as she beamed upon me in her radiant beauty, smiling as sweetly as ever, as if to encourage me still to live and hope.

But how did the doctor receive this remarkable love-song? Like the philosopher he was. Being astonished beyond measure at what he had heard, he sat and pondered the subject for some minutes. What chiefly interested him was not the personal element in Mona's words, which was so vital a point to me, but the fact that she could make use of any words of our language. The possibilities which this fact opened up to him were of the greatest moment. If Mona could learn to talk freely she would be able to give us much information that would be of great scientific value. After he had pursued these thoughts a while it suddenly struck him that the expression she had used was a singular one to begin with, and he turned to me and laughingly said:

"You must have taught her those words. I did not."

"I shall have to acknowledge it," I replied, "but I assure you I did not influence her to make such use of them."

"No, I suppose not; but that question is of small account beside the knowledge that Mona has begun to learn our speech. Now let us give all our attention to her instruction."

We did so from that hour, the doctor from high motives of philosophy and philanthropy, while I was actuated by more selfish reasons. Although I had learned that I had been too hasty in my attempt to gain Mona's affections I did not despair of success. I should have to take time and approach the citadel of her untutored heart with more caution. In the pleasant task of teaching her the intricacies of the English language I anticipated many delightful opportunities of leading her into the Elysian fields of romance. If she could learn to understand fully my intense feeling for her I had no doubt she would return my passion. With such a hopeful spirit does the love god inspire his happy victims.

In order to assist in the realization of these rosy fore-thoughts, I suggested to the doctor that each of us should take his turn in Mona's instruction, so as to make it as easy and informal for her as possible. He had no objections to make, and we began a task which proved to be much simpler than we had imagined. Mona had heard us talk so much that she had half-learned a great many words and expressions, and her remarkable quickness of intellect helped her to pick up their meaning rapidly as soon as we gave her systematic aid. Hence it was not long before she began to converse with considerable freedom.

From the first the doctor and I had been curious to know if she would give up the musical tone and simply talk as we did, and we were pleasantly surprised to find that her song was not interrupted by the form of words she used. Whatever the phrase she wanted to employ she turned it into verse on the instant and chanted it forth in perfect melody. So spontaneous was every expression that her very thoughts seemed to be framed in harmony. Her voice was not obtrusive nor monotonous and generally not loud, but was always well adapted to the sense of what she was singing. The tones mostly used in conversation were low and sweet, like rippling water, but these were constantly varied by the introduction of notes of greater power and range.

To have such use made of our rugged speech was a revelation to us, and words, as we employ them, are inadequate to express our enjoyment of Mona's song, when to its former beauty was added the clear enunciation of language that we could understand.

It was through this rare medium that the doctor and I learned, from day to day, something of the history of Mona's race. The surface of the moon had once been peopled, as we supposed, but as the day of decay and death approached the outside of the globe became too inhospitable to longer support life. The interior had cooled and contracted, and as the solid crust was rigid enough to keep its place, great, sublunar caverns had been formed. Into these rushed the water and the atmosphere, accompanied by the few remaining inhabitants. The conditions were not favorable, in such places, to the continuation of the race, although their advanced knowledge in every direction prevented them from melting away suddenly.

Settlements had been formed in many different sections of the moon, and interior communication was established between them. As the people gradually passed away, those who remained naturally drew nearer together until at last the remnant of the population of the globe were all gathered in the little village where we were now living. Here the process still went on, and year after year saw a constantly diminishing number. A few years before our arrival Mona's last companion, a girl of her own age, had died, and ever since then this tuneful creature, possessed of the most sunny disposition we had ever known, had lived alone, with the knowledge that there was not another living being in all the moon.

"So you see," she sang, "I was as glad to find you as you were to hear me."

"But," asked the doctor, "how did you know we were out there, nearly ready to be blown off into space?"

"I didn't know it till I saw you. I went out to try to discover what was the matter with my old world. For some time I had had the queerest sensations imaginable. I was accustomed to being out of doors a great deal, and I first began to notice that I could walk and run more easily than before. I was becoming rather sprightly for one who was so soon to pass off this deserted stage. Then everything I took up seemed to be growing marvelously light, and I began to have a feeling that I must hold on to all my movable possessions, to keep them from getting away. After this unaccountable state of things had existed for a while, there came, one day, a terrible shock, which threatened to crack the moon's skull and rattle its fragments down upon my head. This was followed at intervals by similar or lighter shocks, and it was all so exceedingly unusual that I became very curious to know what was happening. Then all was quiet for many days, but when at length the quakings began again my natural instinct of self-preservation told me I ought not to take the risk of another such siege, and so I started to make my way to the surface by a well-known path. The trouble did not continue as I feared, but I kept on, fortunately for you as well as for myself, and found the outside world too uncomfortable a place for any of us to remain in longer than necessary."

This halting prose represents the meaning of what Mona said, but it gives a feeble idea of the beauty of her poetic expressions, chanted in melodious phrase and in ever-changing, ever-joyous tune.

We replied by explaining to her what had happened to her disjointed world, expressing our gratitude also for her kindness in bringing us to her sheltered home.

CHAPTER V.
OUR INTRODUCTION TO MARS.

Ever since the doctor had been inside of the moon he had not ceased to regret that we had left all our goods in the car of our balloon. He mourned the loss of the instruments and other apparatus which had cost him so much care, and then there were our official papers. Our introduction to Mona had been rather too informal, and we thought we might stand better with her if we could show her our credentials, though, to be sure, she could not read them.

Several times the doctor proposed to me that we should go out and bring in what we could carry if, perchance, we should find the wind had left us anything. But I had my own reasons for preferring to remain where we were. I was happy and was expecting every day to be happier still, and so I put the doctor off by reminding him that the weather was very bad outside and that we had been glad enough to get in with our lives.

I think he would have agreed with me and would have been contented to stay if the question had been left entirely to ourselves. But Mona heard us talking it over one day and said we could go without much risk if we cared to try it, and she would go with us to take care of us.

Although it would be difficult to tell how Mona could help us when we were outside, this idea sounded so assuring that the doctor determined to make the attempt. I was obliged to acquiesce, fearing, in my ignorance of all that was to happen to us, that the trip would keep me too much from Mona's side.

After due preparation we started, and reached the upper end of the long passage without incident. But as we emerged we noticed that the light had a peculiar tinge of red, quite different from its usual tone. Meditating on this phenomenon, and speaking to each other as we could find breath, we ascended the side of the crater, when there burst upon our view a magnificent world, apparently but a little way off. Its ruddy face showed us plainly what had caused the red light, and the doctor made haste to exclaim:

"Aha! let me introduce you to the planet Mars."

"Yes," I replied, "and we may become too well acquainted before a great while if our rapid flight is not checked."

We soon found our car just as we had left it, and were glad to take advantage of its shelter. In the new danger which loomed up before us so threateningly, we all agreed that it would be rash to return into the interior of the moon, to be crushed to death in the shock of the impending collision; and yet, in remaining where we were, the doctor and I felt that no reputable insurance company would call our lives a very good risk.

But now was our opportunity to witness some of the depths of Mona's character. What was there in her nature so entirely different from anything we had ever known? We had seen persons of cheerful disposition before, and had heard of many exhibitions of courage and indifference to danger, but here we had the very personification of fearlessness and contentment. She talked freely of our situation and of what was likely to happen, but appeared to be as light-hearted as ever, and her song was just as cheerful as it had been in her quiet home. When we asked her if she were not afraid, she replied that there was no such word in her language and she could not appreciate its meaning.

"Fear," said the doctor, "is a feeling excited by the apprehension of danger."

"I think I know about the danger we are in," she answered, "but I have not the feeling you are trying to describe. When I was alone in my underground village and thought the roof was about to fall down and bury me there, I had no fear, as you say. I know that whatever has come to me or to any of my race has always been for our good, and I am sure it will be so in the future. I have but a short time to remain as the sole inhabitant of this now useless globe, and the manner of my taking off is not of the slightest moment. This old world's day is now passed, and I realize in that fact the reason for its unseemly behavior, first knocking its toughened crust so rudely against the earth and then coquetting in this manner with Mars. It certainly no longer shows any respect for the race it has nourished, and hence I see that my day, too, will soon be over. Whatever may be your fate you will doubtless see no more of me after this excursion is ended."

In the light of history this seemed extremely probable, and yet Mona was not half as concerned about it as I was. I thought she ought to have shown more anxiety about her future for my sake if not for her own, and I ventured to say, although in a rather doleful tone:

"I hope, Mona, if the doctor and I are freed from this peril that you will escape with us. If I thought there was no hope of that, I am sure I should propose that we return at once to the middle of the moon and be buried together."

She laughed aloud as she sang out in joyous notes:

"Your mournful voice, my ardent friend, makes me think you would not be very happy with the last alternative. But cheer up, we will all stand by each other to the last." It was in her abounding good nature and in her faculty for inspiring us with her own hopeful disposition that we found Mona fulfilling her promise to take care of us.

But now our attention could not be diverted from the planet which was rapidly growing before our eyes. As we approached nearer and nearer every minute, flying at such a terrific rate and aimed, apparently, for a direct collision, it may be imagined that the doctor and I, in spite of Mona's presence, began to be exceedingly anxious lest our journey and our lives should meet an abrupt and common end.

Unless such excursions as ours become more frequent in the future, it will probably always remain a mystery how this one came to a close. I can only relate our experience during the time that we retained our consciousness, and leave the imagination to picture the rest. As we entered the atmosphere of the planet, the rush of air increased till it seemed as if a hundred Niagaras were sounding in our ears. I remember having a dim feeling of satisfaction in the belief that such a violent contact with the atmosphere must impede the moon's progress, and offer us some chance of landing in safety. Then I was bereft of all sense, and when I regained consciousness I was lying in the bottom of our car in perfect quiet and apparently unharmed.

I called aloud for the doctor, but no voice replied. Rising, I looked about me and found I was afloat on a ruddy sea, alone, as far as my senses could inform me, alone in a new world. Such a sensation of homesickness came over me, such a longing for human fellowship, that our former lonesome condition on the moon seemed like a paradise compared to my present wretchedness.

So this was Mars, which we had studied with our telescopes and about whose condition and history we had so often speculated. And now, as I leaned my elbows on the edge of the car and gazed off over the deep, I wondered, with more interest than I had ever before possessed, if the world I had discovered were inhabited. Perhaps because it was such a vital question with me, my naturally hopeful disposition began to find reasons for a cheerful view. There were certainly favorable evidences all about me. I was breathing an atmosphere evidently made for lungs like mine. The air was soft and pleasant, and though I was drenched with water by my fall I was not uncomfortable. I tasted the water and, oh! joyful reminder of home, it was salt. The sun shed a beautiful light around me, and as I glanced upward to see how bright and cheerful the sky was, my reverie was suddenly broken off, for directly over my head, poised as quietly as if it had always been there, was our old moon. It seemed but a few miles away and I gazed at it with mixed feelings, with thankfulness that I had escaped from its inhospitable surface with my life, and with scorn for its present behavior. For there it was, apparently perfectly at home and ready to bear the torch for Mars as faithfully as it always had for the earth, its rightful mistress.

"Inconstancy," I cried, "thy name is Luna."

When the novelty of this sensational discovery was gone, my mind returned to the contemplation of myself, and my situation seemed to me so unique as to remove some of the natural feeling of fear. When one is shipwrecked in the ordinary way his anxiety is caused by the uncertainty that anyone will come to his rescue; while in my case I did not even know there was anyone to come. But when I looked up at the moon and remembered its erratic climate and our wild, unearthly journey, I could not suppress a feeling of satisfaction with my changed condition. If the doctor had only been with me we would have been able to extract considerable comfort from our surroundings. But, as it was, I was very lonesome, and whatever consolation I got from my reasoning about the planet's habitability was increased a thousand fold by seeing a speck upon the horizon, which I hoped might prove to be a sail. I watched it with intense interest, and was not disappointed. I will not try to describe my feelings as this ship of Mars approached me, while I sat wondering what manner of men I should see. The first thing that struck me was the enormous size of the craft, and as it drew near I could see that it was manned by beings proportionately large. I now began to fear I should be run down, but soon I noticed one of the passengers or crew who seemed to be looking at me through a glass. In a little while the vessel slowed up, and a boat was put off in which a number of giants, including the man with the glass, rowed toward me. When they had nearly reached me I heard the latter say to the others:

"Yes, this is surely the little fellow we are searching for."

I could not imagine what he meant by this, although it occurred to me that it was a pleasant thing to have him speak good, plain English; but the other circumstances were so entirely novel that, instead of opening the conversation with some conventional remark, like a sensible person, I burst out with:

"But Proctor says Mars has passed its life-bearing period."

I hardly knew what I said, but it proved that they were just the words to commend me to my new friend, for as he reached over and lifted me into the boat he said:

"Why, how did you know Proctor? You must have misunderstood him, for he would never say such a thing as that."

While I was puzzling over this strange speech he continued:

"I think we have some one in the ship whom you will be glad to see."

I began to fear I should not get on very well in Mars if all the inhabitants talked in such riddles, but I said, as politely as I could:

"I am sure I need not wait to get to the ship to be pleased. I am delighted to see you and your companions here."

While we were returning to the vessel I gave Thorwald, for such I found to be his name, a brief account of our journey on the moon and of my mysterious arrival on their planet. I expatiated on the merits of the doctor, and told Thorwald that he was probably still on the moon or else at the bottom of their ocean.

I was thinking that Thorwald did not show much sympathy with me, when, our boat having nearly reached the ship's side, I looked up and saw the doctor himself standing on the deck, a pigmy among giants. I was soon by his side, and we embraced before our new-found friends without a blush.

"Where's Mona?" were the first words he said.

"Mona!" I replied. "Who's Mona?"

"Who's Mona?" he returned. "Well, you have recovered pretty rapidly."

I now discovered that, although I had found the body of my friend, the best part of him was missing. In the fall from the moon he had evidently lost his wits. I thought I would not let him know too suddenly what was the matter, and so I merely said:

"Yes, I went into the water, but was not much hurt. When I came to my senses I found myself in our car still. Tell me how you escaped."

"Oh, I happened to fall near this ship, fortunately, and they picked me up, and then, at my request, they set out to search for you and Mona."

"Well," said I, "you found me, and I am very thankful for it, but Mona I fear you will never see."

"What was the last you saw of her?" he asked.

I had great difficulty in keeping myself from laughing in the doctor's face at his odd fancy, but the thought came to me with some force that I must not let his mental condition become known to the men of Mars around us; and so, instead of replying to his question, I turned to Thorwald and asked him if he could tell us how the moon had landed us so easily on their planet.

In answer he gave it as his opinion that as the moon came rushing toward them so swiftly it compressed the air in its path to such a degree that it acted as a cushion, preventing a collision and sending the moon bounding back over the path by which it had come. Probably at the moment when it was nearest the surface, we had fallen off into the ocean. The rebound, he supposed, was not sufficient to carry it beyond the attraction of the planet, and so it poised itself and began to make a revolution around Mars in its old-fashioned way.

Thorwald told us we had taken the best possible time to visit them, for Mars had not been so near the earth before in a great while.

Our new acquaintances were from nine to ten feet tall and proportionately large every other way, so that they appeared quite monstrous to us. But they were agile and even graceful in their movements, while in manner they were so gentle and pleasing that we recognized at once their high culture.

The vessel was soon under way and made rapid progress, and though our voyage was not very long, it proved to be an exceedingly profitable one to the doctor and me, for we learned more, through conversation with our new friends, about the history and condition of Mars than we could have gained in any other way. The men were all kind to us and seemed to be all equally able to impart information, but most of our intercourse was with Thorwald. He gave us much of his time, at intervals as he could be spared from work, for every man helped at the service of the ship. There seemed to be no system of leadership, but all appeared to know what was to be done, and did it without orders and without clashing.

As we entered into conversation about the earth and Mars, I was surprised to find the doctor taking his full share in it with his usual intelligence. His questions and answers were all so pertinent that I should have supposed his mind was entirely unaffected, had I not known to the contrary. When I saw he could hold his own so well, I determined to take the first opportunity when we were alone to ask him again who Mona was.

CHAPTER VI
A REMARKABLE PEOPLE.

The conversation with our new friends was not all on one side, for we had many questions to answer about the earth, the Martian mind showing as great a thirst for knowledge as ours. One of the first things Thorwald said after we had settled down to a good talk was:

"But, Doctor, your little head is so full of thought that it seems to me you ought not to have been surprised to find us so large here. You knew before you came that Mars is much smaller than the earth and, therefore, the attraction of gravitation being less, that everything can grow more easily. Things may as well be one size as another if only they are well adapted to each other, and we would never have known we were large or that you were small had we not been brought together. In the sight of Him who made both the earth and Mars, and fashioned one for you and the other for us, we are neither great nor small. In fact, size is never absolute but only relative."

"That is very clear to us now," said the doctor, "and I promise not to be surprised again, even when I walk the streets of your cities and see you in your houses."

"Then, Doctor," said I, "if we had found inhabitants on the moon what great folks they must have seemed to us."

This was an exceedingly foolish remark for me to make, for it resulted in the doctor's almost betraying his condition to our friends.

Of course Thorwald was interested in what I said, and eagerly inquired:

"So you found no inhabitants in the moon?"

"Just one," spoke up the doctor quickly.

"What! you found one and left him there?"

"It was a woman," said the doctor.

This talk had been so rapid that I had not had a chance to interfere, but I saw that I must stop it now for the doctor's sake. When I could see him alone I could tell him his memory was playing him a trick and he must avoid that subject. So, before Thorwald could speak again, I said:

"Let me suggest, Thorwald, that we let the moon rest till we have heard more of Mars, which I am sure is of greater importance. We have told you many things in regard to our planet, and are willing to answer all the questions you may please to ask from time to time, but now we would like to listen a while."

"Yes," said the doctor, "we started on this expedition to add to our scientific knowledge, and we seem in a fair way to accomplish our purpose; so that, if you will find a way to send us back to the earth some time, I think our friends will admit that we have been successful. But first we want to learn all we can about this wonderful world. How long has your race existed? Our astronomers tell us Mars is too old to be inhabited, and, considering some of my own recent experiences in finding my science unreliable, it rather consoles me to discover that they are mistaken."

"They are right," Thorwald answered, "in believing that Mars is very old, and so our race is nearing its maturity. It is impossible to judge accurately of the age of the planet itself, but we know it is exceedingly old from the evidences of changes that have taken place on its surface. Neither can we tell when our race was born, though we have legends and traditions dating back fifty thousand years, and authentic history for nearly half that time."

The doctor and myself now began to realize that we had indeed something to learn from these people, and I remarked:

"These figures astonish us, Thorwald, and you can hardly understand how interested we are. But please continue. From what little I have seen I should think you are much farther advanced in everyway than the inhabitants of the earth."

"We believe," replied the Martian, "that our planet is much older than the earth, and if we are right in that it is but natural that our civilization should be older also. If the tendency of mind is toward perfection, if in your experience you have found that, in the main, men look upward more than downward, what would you expect to find in a world so beautiful as this and where life has existed so long? From what we know of our own history and from what we have learned of the worlds around us, we believe the life-bearing period of Mars has long since passed its middle point, and that both our planet and our race have passed through convulsions and changes to which other worlds, perhaps the earth, are now subjected."

This appeared so reasonable that I said to him:

"We must believe that Mars is an afternoon planet. And now we want to hear whatever you may choose to tell us about your civilization."

"That is a broad subject," replied Thorwald, "but it is something I like to talk about. If I judge rightly of what you have already told me of the earth and its people, I think we were in just about your situation ages ago and that we have merely matured. That is, the causes now at work on the earth are having in us their legitimate effect. These processes are slow but sure. To the Infinite time is of no more importance in itself than is size.

"I know of no better topic to begin with," continued Thorwald, "than the matter of government. You wondered at the peculiar discipline on board this ship. It is but a type of what you will find on land. We have no government in its strict sense, for there is no one that needs governing. We have organization for mutual help in many ways, but no rulers nor legislators. The only government is that of the family. Here character is formed so that when the children go forth into the world no one desires to wrong his neighbor. We know from our histories of all the struggles our ancestors passed through before the days of universal peace and brotherhood. Now we go and come as we please, with no fear of harm. We are all one nation because all national boundaries have been obliterated, and we have a common language. There are no laws of compulsion or restraint, for all do by instinct what is best for themselves and their neighbors."

"Oh, happy Mars!" here broke in the usually prosaic doctor. "That sounds like a story. And yet what is it," he continued, addressing me, "but the effect of perfect obedience to our golden rule? If men should really learn to do to others as they would have others do to them, what a transformation it would accomplish."

"So that is what you call the golden rule, is it?" asked Thorwald. "And are you all trying to live by it?"

"Well," I replied, "that is what many of us profess to be doing, but I must say we fall far, very far short of the mark. I do not know a single inhabitant of the earth, with the possible exception of my companion here, who fully obeys that command."

The doctor's smile was not lost on Thorwald, who replied:

"It was rather too bad of you to bring so far away from the earth the only good man the planet contained; but I am glad to know the golden rule, as you may well call it, has been given to men. We have had the same here, and, oh! if I could make you realize something of the struggle our race has had in working it into life and practice, you would gain some hope for the people of the earth. I mean, the result of this struggle would give you hope, for I am not ashamed to say that we are now living up to the full requirements of this law, and if you should spend the remainder of your lives with us I am sure you would not find my statement untrue. It is only by actually loving our neighbors as ourselves that we are able to live as we do. The law of love has replaced the law of force. It is well for you to understand this at the beginning, for it is the secret of our wonderful success in all the higher forms of civilization."

"It must have helped you greatly," said I, "in the matter of which you have just been speaking, that of government."

"Yes, it has," he replied. "In our histories we have full accounts of the long course of events when we were divided into hundreds of nations, each with its own pride and ambition, and each striving to build up itself upon the misfortunes or the ruins of its neighbors. You can perhaps imagine what a mass of material we have for reading and study."

"We can," spoke up the student doctor, "and it fairly makes my mouth water. But tell us briefly, Thorwald, how you ever passed from those troublous times to the blissful state in which we now find you."

"The transition was exceedingly slow; it seemed, in fact, impossible that such a change could ever be effected. But it began with the establishment of universal peace, which was demanded by the growing spirit of brotherly love, and assisted by commercial reciprocity and a world language. Gradually national boundaries were found to be only an annoyance, and in time--a long time, of course--we became one nation and finally no nation. For now no one exercises any authority over his neighbors, since the need for all artificial distinctions has long since passed away."

"Then," said I, "you have no doubt lost all fear and anxiety over the conflicting interests of capital and labor."

"Yes," replied Thorwald, "for we have no such distinctions in society as rich and poor, workingmen and capitalists. We all work as we please, but there is so little to do that no one is burdened, and one cannot be richer than another because all the material bounties of nature and art are common to all, being as free as the air. I suppose, as this seems to be strange talk to you, that you cannot realize what it is to belong to a society where everyone considers the interests of his neighbor as much as his own. You will find when you reach that point that most of your troubles will be gone, as ours are."

"Our troubles!" said the doctor. "Many of our troubles, to be sure, arise from our passions and appetites--in other words, from our selfishness--and these will no doubt disappear when we reach that blessed state of which you have spoken, a condition prayed for and dimly expected by many of our race. But other troubles of ours come from sickness and severe toil, from accidents, famines, and the convulsions of nature. How, for example, can you have escaped the latter, unless, indeed, God has helped those who have so wisely helped themselves?"

"Your last thought is right," answered our friend. "Nature has certainly assisted us. While the crust of the planet was thin we know the central fires heaved and shook the ground and burst forth from the mountains, causing great destruction and keeping the world in fear. We do not know how thick the crust of the planet now is, but nothing has been felt of those inner convulsions for many ages. One of our feats of engineering has been to see how far we could penetrate into the surface of the globe. A well of vast size has been dug, the temperature being carefully noted and observations made of the many different substances passed through--water, coal, gas, oil, and all kinds of mineral deposits. The work has progressed from one generation to another, and no one can tell when it will be called finished, as it is determined to dig toward the center of the planet as fast as our ever-increasing skill will permit."

"Did you find out how thick the crust is?" I asked.

"No," he answered, "we are not much nearer the solution of that question than before, but we have made valuable discoveries as to what the crust is composed of. The temperature has gradually, though slowly, increased, and we believe the time will come when the work will have to be abandoned on account of the heat. We have gone far enough to know that when the fuel on the surface of our globe is all used up we shall only have to tap the center to get all the heat we want." "What a capital idea that will be," I interrupted, "to throw at some of our pessimistic friends on the earth, Doctor."

"We see now, Thorwald," my companion said, "that your planet is too old to give you any more trouble from earthquake and volcano, but how about other natural phenomena, the tempest and cyclone for example?"

"Well," replied Thorwald, "we have a theory that time, the great healer, has cured these evils also. Let me ask, Doctor, if the earth ever receives any accretions of matter from outside its own atmosphere?"

"Yes, we have the fall of meteorites, foreign substances which we believe the earth encounters in its path around the sun."

"I supposed such must be the case," Thorwald continued. "And now, when you consider the great age of Mars, perhaps you will not be surprised to learn that this new matter, coming to us from the outside, was sufficient to increase the weight of our globe and gradually decrease the rate of speed at which we were traveling through space."

"I am surprised, though," said the doctor, "because the accumulation of meteorolites on the surface of the earth is so exceedingly slow that it would take millions of years, at the present rate, to increase its diameter one inch."

"But perhaps they came much faster in past ages. Let me ask you, Doctor, if it is not a fact that the rate of revolution of Mars around the sun is slower than the earth's? I suppose you are far enough advanced in astronomical science to answer that."

"Yes," replied the doctor, "you are correct. I believe the earth speeds along at nineteen miles a second, while Mars travels only sixteen miles in the same time."

"We know by our computations that our speed is much less than it once was, and our theory is that this has in some way hushed those terrible storms and winds which we know were formerly so frequent."

Here the doctor thought he saw a chance to make a point, and spoke as follows:

"If the meteorites come in quantities sufficient to have caused such changes, it seems to me their fall must be as great a menace to your peace as the evils they have cured. They do not strike the earth in large numbers, but still we have a record of a shower of meteoric stones which devastated a whole village. I suppose all parts of your globe are by this time well populated, and how can you be entirely free from trouble when you are living in constant danger of the downfall of these great masses of rock?"

"But we don't have meteorites now," replied Thorwald.

"Oh, you don't?"

"No, they ceased falling long ago. Mars is going slow enough for the present."

"Very kind of them, I am sure, to stop when you didn't need them any longer," said the doctor; "and I suppose you have some plausible reason to give for their disappearance."

"Yes, we believe that the interplanetary space was well filled with these small bodies, circling around the sun, and when their multitudinous and eccentric orbits intercepted the orbits of the planets, they came within the attraction of these larger masses. Mars has merely, in the course of time, cleared for itself a broad path in its yearly journey and is now encountering no more straggling fragments."

"There, Doctor," said I, "you are well answered. And now, Thorwald, tell us how you have escaped other evils, famine and fire for instance."

"Fire," continued our friend, "was one of the first foes subdued. We quite early learned to make our habitations and everything about us of fireproof materials, and, if I mistake not, you on the earth will not long endure an enemy which can be so easily put down. You will find all materials can be so treated with chemicals as to be absolutely safe from the flames. We have fire only when and where we desire it.

"When you speak of famines you touch a more difficult subject, but here, too, time and skill have wrought wonderful changes. In our histories we read of the time when the weather was chiefly noted for its fickleness, and when some parts of our globe were mere desert wastes, where rain was unknown and no life could exist. And in the inhabited portions one section would often be deluged with too much rain while another would have none, both conditions leading to a failure in agriculture and much consequent suffering. A long time was spent in gathering statistics, which finally proved that if the rainfall were distributed there would be just about enough to water sufficiently the whole surface of the globe. Nature provided rain enough, but it did not always fall where and when it was most needed. It seemed to be left with us to find a remedy for this apparent evil. When I say 'us' in this way I mean our race as a whole, for most of these changes took place many ages ago.

"Our philosophers had seen so many difficulties removed and improvements made in things supposed to be fixed that they began, once upon a time, to assert that rain and snow and the weather in general ought to be subject to our will. They said that in the advanced state of civilization toward which we were progressing it would seem to be an anomalous thing that we should continue to be subjected to the annoyances of so changeable a tyrant as the weather. We seemed destined to gain control of so many of the forces of nature that our future mastery in this department looked to them reasonable. For a long time these views appeared fanciful to the many, but this did not deter a few enthusiasts from study and experiment. As knowledge and skill increased we began, little by little, to gain control of the elements; but do not imagine it was anything less than a slow and laborious work.

"First, as we learned something of the laws which control the precipitation of the moisture suspended in the atmosphere, we discovered a way to produce rain by mechanical means. As this discovery was gradually developed we found we had really solved the problem. For, as there was only a certain amount of moisture taken up into the air, the quantity of rain could not be increased nor diminished, and so when we made it rain in one place it was always at the expense of the rainfall somewhere else.

"Since those early days vast improvement has been made, until now these laws, once so mysterious and so perplexing, are obedient to our service. The whole face of our planet has been reclaimed, and drouth and famine on the one hand and floods on the other are entirely unknown. Each section of country is given rain or snow or sunshine just as it needs it, and there is no uncertainty in the matter."

When Thorwald had reached this point my curiosity prompted me to ask him to tell us in a few words how they could make it rain when they pleased, and he answered that he would be glad to give us details of all these matters if we insisted on it, but he thought it would be better for him to present a general view of the state of their society, leaving it for us to see with our own eyes how things were done, after we had reached our destination.

I readily acquiesced, with an apology for my interruption, and Thorwald resumed:

"The doctor spoke of accidents, sickness, and severe toil as among the sources of your troubles. With us, at the present day, all natural laws are so well understood and so faithfully obeyed that there are no accidents. Machinery and appliances of all kinds are perfect; nothing is left to chance, but everything is governed by law. And as we follow that law in every instance nothing can ever happen, in the old sense of that word. To take a homely example, you have of course learned that it is not well to put your hand into the fire, and so, though you use a good deal of fire you keep your hands out of it. You know what the law is, and you do not tempt it. By our long experience we have learned the operation of all laws, and in every position in life we simply avoid putting our hand into the fire. To be sure, we have been assisted in this by superior skill and by our general steadiness and ripeness of character. If I read history aright accidents were caused by ignorance or neglect of law, and I am sure the people of the earth, when they begin to realize fully how unnecessary they are, will soon outgrow them.

"As for sickness, you cannot understand how strange the word sounds to me. Just think for a moment how useless, how out of place, such a thing as sickness is. Like the subject just spoken of, it comes from disobedience to law, and although I know we were a long time in ridding ourselves of it, it seems to me now that it must be one of the easiest of your troubles to remove. With us the science of medicine became so perfect that it accomplished a great deal of the reform, but more was done by each individual acquiring full knowledge of himself and acting up to that knowledge. In learning to love our neighbors we did not forget to foster a proper love for ourselves. In fact, our creed teaches that self-love is one of our most important duties. When one is instructed to love his neighbor as himself it is presupposed that his affection for himself is of that high quality that will always lead him to do the very best he can for every part of his being. So, as our development continued, we came in time to love ourselves too well to despise or abuse or neglect the bodies we lived in. We studied how best to nurture and care for those bodies, and when that lesson was thoroughly learned we found that sickness and pain were gone, and with them, also, all fear of death. For now we die when our days are fully ended. The span of our life has been doubled since we began to know and care for ourselves, and, at the close, death is anticipated and recognized as a friend."

CHAPTER VII.
RAPID TRANSIT ON MARS.

Here Thorwald paused and said he should be obliged to leave us a short time to attend to some duty in the management of the vessel. When he returned I remarked that neither he nor his companions seemed to have to work very hard.

"That," he answered, "is just the thought I want to speak of next, as the doctor has said many earthly troubles arise from severe labor. Here there is no hard work for us. It is all done by some kind of mechanism. Look at the handling of this ship, in which, as you say, no one is burdened. The hard and disagreeable parts of the work are taken out of our hands and are put into the hand of machinery, which in its perfection is almost intelligent. It is so in all departments of work. Inventions looking toward the saving of labor have closely followed each other for so many years that their object is about accomplished, and all the pain and sorrow accompanying daily toil are things of the dead past. Even our animals are relieved from distressing labor and share with us the blessings of an advanced civilization, every heavy weight being raised and every burdensome load being drawn by an arm of steel or aluminum, which neither tires nor feels. We do not need to pity a machine. Why should flesh and blood, whether of dumb beasts or of more intelligent beings, suffer the agony of labor when the work can be better done by mechanical means?

"While speaking of the lower animals I may as well say here that we have no wild beasts. All have been tamed; not merely brought into subjection, but made the friends and companions in a sense of our higher race. Every animal, large and small, has lost its power and will to harm us. The wasp has lost its sting, the serpent its poison, and the tiger its desire to tear. And not only is their enmity to us all gone, but they no longer prey upon each other. Perfect peace reigns in this realm also."

"What has brought about this highly interesting condition?" I asked. "Was there a natural tendency toward perfection on the part of the beasts?"

"No," replied Thorwald, "I think not. The change has been accomplished by us. Nothing that has life could help being uplifted by contact with our ever-expanding civilization. We believe the chief factor in working this great betterment in the animal creation has been our success in entirely eliminating flesh as an article of food. We early came to see it was not necessary for ourselves and that without it we were much better prepared to assume the higher duties belonging to our advanced life. We then began to experiment with the animals nearest us. It was a slow and discouraging task at first, but finally we obtained results that gave us hope of success. We found in the course of many years that the digestive organs of the animals on which we were experimenting were gradually becoming accustomed to a vegetable diet. We continued the work, extending it to one class of animals after another, until in time all carnivorous instincts disappeared."

This interested the doctor exceedingly, and he remarked that he should think there would have been some kinds of animals that would resist all efforts to work such a change in them; but Thorwald answered:

"I have never read of such cases, but if there were any the species must have become extinct, for now, in all this world, no conscious life is taken to support another life. No blood is let for our refreshment and no minutest creature is pursued and slain to appease the appetite of its stronger neighbor."

"Does this condition extend even to the fish of the sea?" inquired the doctor.

"Even to the fish of the sea," answered the Martian.

"Now that you discover," he continued, "what improvement has been wrought in the lower animals, you can understand that their comfort is an object of our solicitude, and that we take great pleasure in knowing that they are relieved from all hard labor."

"But you haven't told us," said I, "what is the source of the power that does all your work."

"Let me ask," replied Thorwald, "if you have begun to use electricity yet?"

"Yes," I answered, "we are trying to harness it, but it is still far from obedient to us."

"I perceive," said our friend, "from this and other things you have told me, that your development is going on in about the order which has prevailed on Mars. Do not be discouraged in your efforts to bring that mysterious and wonderful agent, electricity, into complete subjection. You will find it your most useful servant, and in connection with aluminum it will enable you to solve numerous problems and remove many difficulties from your path of progress.

"Here we have made full use of both of these valuable helps. Electricity enters into every department of life.

"It runs our errands, takes us from place to place, builds our houses, cooks our food, and even is applied to the growth of our food when we are in haste for any article. Its laws are so well understood that there is no fear of personal injury from its use, and I will show you how familiar an aid it is to us. Here," he continued, taking from his pocket a brightly polished case of metal, "is a compact storage battery, containing, not electricity itself, of course, but elements so prepared that a simple touch will start into motion a powerful current, able to perform almost any task I may ask of it. This case, you see, is so small and light that it is no burden, and yet it contains power enough to serve me for many days. Of course, all our work of a fixed character has appliances with the power permanently attached, and these portable reservoirs are carried about with us only for detached and unexpected tasks."

To my experienced eye the doctor's face looked a little skeptical at this last remark, and he said: "But how can the power be applied in these emergencies? Suppose, for example, it were necessary for you to go from here to the other end of this vessel in half a second, how would the electricity in your box help you do it?"

"If I really thought, Doctor, you wanted to be rid of me I would be tempted to try it; but, as I told your companion just now, you had better learn all you can of our history before you begin to see what we can do.

"I haven't told you half of the wonders performed by this marvelous power. It has long been our chief reliance for rapid traveling. You find us in this ship; but, although navigation is a perfected science, this mode of traveling is tedious, and ships are used only for pleasure and such out- of-the-way trips as this. Journeys from place to place over established routes are made in large tubes, in which the cars are propelled by electricity. These tubes run both on land and water, being suspended in the latter a little way below the surface. Both tubes and cars are air- tight, and the adjustment is so perfect that the cars slide along with the greatest ease. Riding in an air-tight chamber would not be pleasant if much time were to be occupied in that way, but the cars are propelled so swiftly that the time from one station to another is hardly appreciable. At every stop the cars are opened and apparatus set in motion which changes the air completely almost in a moment. Where the tubes run under water shafts for air are put in at the stations. There is always a double line, one tube for each direction. No chance is left for accidents.

"Of course we navigate the air, swiftly and safely. If not in too much haste we always take the aerial passage, and often on a pleasant day the sky over a great city will be as full of air ships, or balloons as we still sometimes call them, as its harbor is of pleasure boats. In this department inventors had a fruitful field, the use of aluminum offering abundant opportunity for the greatest variety of devices, and the development of the flying machine was one of the most interesting features in the march toward our present high civilization. Perhaps the presence of so many electrical machines in the air and the utilization of so much electricity on land and water have, after thousands of years, done much toward freeing us from the thunderstorm, with its deadly lightning. We have fairly robbed the clouds of their electricity and taught it to do our work.

"Swift and economical as our modern electric cars are, there is one mode of traveling sometimes adopted which is more rapid still, and the cheapest and in some respects the easiest way of getting over the surface of the globe ever dreamed of. It was discovered by accident, just before accidents entirely ceased, in the following manner:

"A couple of scientific enthusiasts, of the kind we call cranks--I don't know what you call them on the earth--conceived the idea that they could find something better to take the place of the highly purified and buoyant gases which we used in our flying machines. They observed, in the lofty flights they were accustomed to make into the air, that as they ascended the atmosphere grew lighter, and this led them to think they might go far into the upper regions, collect large quantities of rarefied air, bring it down, and use it for floating flying machines. Of course, they understood that any vessel this thin air was put into must be strong enough to prevent being collapsed by the weight of the denser atmosphere on the surface. But they thought small spherical vessels of very thin metal could be made that would withstand this pressure and still hold enough to float and carry some weight besides. They had a large number of these hollow balls made and started on a trial trip, expecting to bring down only a small quantity each time. But, in their endeavor to obtain the very best quality of lifting material possible, they went much higher than they intended, although this did not cause them as much inconvenience as might have been expected, since they were provided with the latest improved breathing apparatus. The result of their adventure, however, was a discovery of such magnitude that it drove from their minds all thought of their real errand and we never again heard of that project. After remaining at an extreme height a few hours, the surface of the planet being hidden by clouds, they began to descend, and when they were near enough to see the features of the country below them, everything looked strange and unknown. They could not account for this, but continued their fall, fully persuaded that it must be their own world and not some other which they were approaching. But even if they had not been correct in that, they could hardly have been more surprised than they were to find, on landing, that they were almost exactly on the opposite side of the globe from the place where they made the ascent. They seemed to have traveled half way around the world in that incredibly short space of time, when in reality they had remained stationary and the world had traveled around them. The fact is, they had risen above all the denser portion of the planet's atmosphere, and had reached a stratum of extremely rarefied air, which, it seems, does not accompany the globe in its revolution. Of course, the facts were at once heralded to the four quarters of the world, and the two aerial travelers found themselves famous. But they did not wish to let such an astounding discovery rest upon the results of a single experiment, and so they proved themselves worthy of their new fame by going home the way they came. That is, they mounted their flying machine, rose again to the same lofty height, remained there about the same time as before, descended, and were near their home."

Here the doctor asked:

"And has this singular mode of traveling become popular, Thorwald?"

"For long distances east and west it is often resorted to. But I presume you are asking yourself whether you could introduce it on the earth. When you return and begin to think it over you will probably see so many practical difficulties in the way that you will not attempt it. You must have patience. All these things will come to your race in time."

CHAPTER VIII.
THORWALD PUZZLED.

I fear," continued Thorwald, "that I am wearying you with this long talk." We assured him we were enjoying it too much to think of being tired, and hoped he would not stop. But he said he had some duties to attend to, and would take us to his room and leave us by ourselves for a while.

As soon as we were alone the doctor looked at me with a smile and said:

"Why did you act so queerly when I spoke of Mona?"

"Why did you speak so?" I asked in reply. "And how could you tell Thorwald we found one inhabitant on the moon?"

"Did you want to have me tell him a falsehood?"

"Of course not. I tried to catch your eye and keep you from saying any thing on the subject till we could consult in regard to it. If we are going to color our narrative in order to make it more marvelous we must at least make our stories agree."

"My friend," said the doctor, "I am now confirmed in my suspicion that your brain was affected by your fall from the moon."

I saw by this time that I need not hesitate further to tell the doctor the truth. I disliked the task, but I saw it would not be safe to leave him any longer in ignorance of his condition. There as no telling what other preposterous tales he might invent. So I said to him gently:

"Doctor, your last remark makes it easier for me to tell you that the first words you said to me on this vessel showed me that you were not right. I kept it from our new friends here, and I thought I had better tell you how you are, so you can be a little cautious. You talk all right on most subjects, but you will do well to avoid the moon as a topic of conversation. If the others ask any more questions about the moon, you can just let me answer them."

I said all this seriously enough, but the doctor laughed boisterously as he answered:

"Well, if this isn't a joke. You think I am crazy, and I know you are crazy, and I can prove it. I will just ask you one question, which please answer truthfully. Don't you remember Mona?"

"Oh, there is Mona again! Don't you see that only proves your own madness? No, I don't remember Mona, and you don't either."

"I must say," returned the doctor, "I never expected to see you get over your infatuation so quickly."

"What direction did my infatuation, as you call it, take?"

"Marriage, I should say."

"Now you interest me," I returned, "and you must tell me more. Is this Mona of yours the sole resident of the moon, of whom you spoke to Thorwald?"

"Certainly she is, but you surely must be out of your head to call her my Mona--I want no stronger proof."

"How so?" I asked.

"Why, because but yesterday you scarce wanted to have me speak to her. You tried to keep your jealousy from me, but there was not room enough in all the moon to hide it."

"This is very laughable," I exclaimed.

"You did not think so then. But let me try to bring it all back to you by another question. Don't you remember her voice?"

"Most truly I do not. Why, what was the matter with her voice? Was it loud and harsh, or was it squeaky? I cannot imagine anything very pleasant in the way of a voice in such a wild and withered home as the moon would make."

"True," answered the doctor, "as to the outside, but you forget our visit to the interior."

"There it is again," said I. "Now, Doctor, the sooner you get rid of these strange notions the better So tell me your recollections of our stay in the moon, and I will let you know where you are wrong."

"Very well. You remember, of course, when we found ourselves rushing away from the earth so swiftly."

"Yes, and then we remained shut up in the car day after day, more dead than alive

I think, until, fortunately, we were spilled out upon this more favored globe."

"You seem to be sincere," said the doctor, "but if you are, then you forget the most interesting part of our experience. Just as we were about to be overwhelmed with our troubles we heard exquisite music, which we soon found proceeded from a lovely maiden. You fell desperately in love with her at first sight and never recovered till you were plunged in the ocean of Mars. You insisted on following her nod, and she led us at once through a narrow path down into the center of the moon. Here, in her quiet home, we taught her to sing in our language--her only speech was song--and the first words she used were to say she loved me. She did not understand what the words meant, of course, but you looked as if you wished I had been blown away before Mona had discovered us. After that I helped you in your wooing all I could, but although your passion increased every day your suit did not seem to prosper. One day I expressed the wish that I had some of the things we had left in the car, whereupon she led us out to the surface again, where we arrived just in time to be thrown upon this planet. Here we are, you and I, all safe, but where is poor Mona?"

"I am sure it would take a wise man to answer that question," I replied. "And now let me show you, Doctor, how wrong you are. If you will only try to exercise a little of that good judgment for which you are noted, you will be convinced that this is only a pretty little fairy tale which has somehow taken possession of a corner of your brain. Now that the fairy is gone you must try to forget the rest. Just think how unlikely the whole story is. Think of a delicate girl living in such surroundings as we found there; and then, how could we exist down in the center of the moon?"

"Why, don't you remember Mona told us the water and atmosphere had all run down there, making it the only habitable part of the decaying globe?"

"Oh, that's only one of your scientific notions, probably as true as the others that we have disproved. Too much science has turned your head, and I will prove it to you again by showing you how impossible is the part which I play in your romance. I will tell you now, what you doubtless do not know, that I am engaged to be married to the best woman in all the earth, excepting your own good wife, of course."

"Is that a fact?" asked the doctor. "And do you love her?"

"To be sure I do. I love her very dearly, and if I ever see her again I shall tell her so in a manner to make her understand it."

"Why, doesn't she understand it now?"

"Yes, I think so, but she thought I didn't show heart enough in my wooing."

"Well, if she could see you with Mona she would learn that you have plenty of heart when the right one appears to make it spring into life."

"You speak as if you thought I did not love Margaret. You do not know her. Why, I wouldn't once look at another woman anywhere, not even in Mars, and most certainly not in that puckered-up old world that we have just left, happily for us."

"Do you know what I think about you?" asked the doctor.

"No."

"I think you have an exceedingly poor memory. First, you forgot Margaret as soon as the voice of that fair singer fell on your ear, and now you have forgotten the singer again the moment we have lost her. I await with much interest your first introduction to a daughter of Mars."

"You will be disappointed," said I, "if you think I shall be more than civil to her."

"If she be handsome and can turn a tune moderately well, I shall be willing to wager a fair young planet against the moon that you will propose to her in a week."

"I have done nothing to give you so poor an opinion of me. It is only your own diseased imagination, and I do not seem to be curing it very fast. I suppose, because your mind is naturally so strong, it is the more difficult to destroy such an hallucination as has taken possession of you."

"I would give it up," said the doctor. "The story is all true, and not a work of my imagination. Isn't it more reasonable to believe that you could forget the circumstances I have related than that I could invent such a tale?"

"Oh, I never could forget it if I had been false to Margaret. You do not know me. If your vagaries had taken any other direction I might possibly be brought to think you were right."

By this time we both began to realize that the conversation was not proving a great success in the way we had hoped, and so, after some pleasant words and a hearty laugh over the situation, we found our way to the deck again. Here there were various things to attract our attention, different members of the crew being eager to show us about. The doctor asked some question in regard to the system of steering the vessel, and when one of the men had taken him back toward the stern to explain the point, I found Thorwald and quietly explained to him the mental condition of my companion.

"The doctor is all right," I said, "on every subject but one. His head must have been injured a little in his fall, and he imagines and asserts with positiveness that we found a young woman in the moon, the last of her race--a ridiculous idea, is it not?"

"And did you find any inhabitants at all?" asked Thorwald.

"Certainly not. No one could live in such a place. It is indeed marvelous how we existed long enough to get here. The doctor calls this creature of his brain Mona, says she was a great beauty, and plainly intimates that I was rather too attentive to her. You will see what a convincing proof this is of his unsound condition when I tell you I am engaged to the best woman on the earth, and so of course could not show any marked preference for another. I have told you about the doctor so that you may pass over unnoticed any allusion he makes to these subjects."

Thorwald thanked me and said he would be careful not to embarrass us in the matter. And so I flattered myself that in the future Thorwald and I would sympathize with each other in commiserating the doctor. But I afterward learned that the doctor, about this time, had also sought an interview with Thorwald and had confided the following secret to him:

"My friend," said he, "is a fine young fellow, but his head must have been injured in his fall. He has entirely forgotten the best of our experience in the moon. Queer, too, for he fell in love with the only and last inhabitant of that globe, a beautiful, sweet-voiced maiden named Mona, who never talked but she sang."

Thorwald then made the doctor tell him the whole story, and at the close he promised he would not pay much attention to anything I might say on the subject in future conversation.

So it was quite a puzzle to Thorwald to tell which of his visitors from the earth was of unsettled mind and which in his normal condition. He decided to hold the question open and wait for further evidence.

CHAPTER IX.
THORWALD AS A PROPHET.

As maybe supposed, the doctor and I were anxious to hear more about Mars, and it was not long before we were all seated together again, when Thorwald resumed his instructive talk.

"What further can I tell you of our condition and achievements? Every science has made mighty progress in bestowing its own benefit upon us. New arts have been discovered in the course of our development, about which you would understand nothing. The aim and result of all science have been to add to our comfort and happiness--our true happiness, which consists in improvement and the constant uplifting of character. The evils that once vexed our world, both those occasioned by natural phenomena and those brought about by our own ignorance and sin, have, as you have heard, almost completely disappeared. Even mental troubles are gone, and no corroding care destroys our peace, for there is nothing for us to dread; no dark future, filled with unknown evils, awaits our unwilling feet, and no superstitious or unnatural fear disturbs the peaceful quiet of our sleep."

"And are we to understand, Thorwald," I asked, "that you believe all this rest from trouble and wrongdoing is coming to the earth, too?"

"Before replying directly to your question," answered Thorwald, "let me ask you if there is any tendency in that direction. Look back to the earliest days of your history and compare the state of things then existing with that of your own times. Has your world made any progress? Is there any less violence? Are men learning to live without fighting? Are the dark corners of the earth coming to the light?"

"In these and many other directions," I answered, "I think we can see improvement."

"Then," continued Thorwald, "it seems to me you must believe with me that your world will one day come to the condition in which you find us. Have not your holy prophets foretold a time of universal peace both for man and beast, a time when a higher law than selfishness shall govern all hearts and the earth be filled with the spirit of love?"

"They have," I replied, "but most of us are so engrossed in the struggle for existence that we think lightly or not at all of such things. These prophecies have never impressed me as they do now when I see your condition, and reflect that similar words may have been spoken and then fulfilled here."

"Let me assure you," Thorwald made haste to say, "that the earth is still young. I can see by all you say that your age is one of unusual vitality and progress. A firm faith that victory will come and that the golden age is before you will be a great help in your struggle with evil. Lay hold of that faith. It is yours. It needs no prophet to tell you that your race will one day reach our blessed state. First will come the spirit of peace, and as I am sure war must be repugnant to such minds as yours, you will readily learn to put it away from you. Then will begin to cease all bitterness between man and man, and you will be started on the road that leads to brotherly kindness. A world of sorrows will fall away with the passing of individual and national strife, not only the horror of the battlefield and the misery that follows it, but also the more secret and world-wide unhappiness that comes from the petty conflicts over the so-called rights of person and property. Selfishness, that monstrous source of evil, must be dethroned, and then the rights of each will be cared for by all. This will usher in for you a new era.

"And now, when the mighty energy that has been expended in learning and practicing the science of war, the skill that has been given to the art of killing, the treasures of money and blood, the time, the brain and the activities that have been employed in carrying out plans of aggression, large and small, of neighbor against neighbor--when these have all been turned toward the betterment of your condition and the salvation of men from degradation and sin, then will the arts of peace flourish and your day begin. Then will nature herself come to your assistance, molding her laws to your convenience and comfort. It will doubtless be a long time before a man can love and consider his neighbor as himself, and before all of God's creatures on your planet can dwell together in perfect peace, but, believe me, the earth will live to see that time."

"Thorwald," spoke the doctor, "your words are so inspiring that I almost wish my life could have waited some thousands of years for that bright day you so confidently promise for the earth, but I cannot help asking myself if it is altogether a misfortune to live in the midst of the conflict, with something ahead to strive for. Will you pardon my presumption if I ask you practically the same question? You have told us of your wonderful history and that you have now reached a condition of peace and quiet. With no sickness or sorrow in your lives, with no evil passions to rise and throw you, with nothing to fear from without or within, yours must be a blissful condition. But still, is there always content? In our imperfect state we are striving and learning. Our happiness largely consists in the pursuit of happiness. If, some day, we should find all difficulties removed, no obstacles left to contend against, no evil in ourselves or others to overcome, not even our bodily wants to provide for, it seems to me life would lose its zest and become a burden hardly worth the carrying. Can you remove this unhandsome doubt?"

"I will try," answered Thorwald. "I suppose if the people of the earth, with their present capacities and aspirations, should be brought suddenly to such a state of civilization as ours, it would be as you say. As your development continues, your minds and souls will expand and you will be prepared to take up new duties and occupations as they come. I cannot tell you what these are, for at present you would not understand me. You mistake if you think we have ceased to learn. The mind is ever reaching forward to new attainments, and the things which chiefly occupy us now would have been beyond our comprehension in our earlier days. Can you not find an illustration on the earth? Suppose the untutored savage were suddenly required to throw away his spear and arrow and engage in your pursuits, Doctor. Would he be happy? Your mind is full of thoughts that he cannot grasp, your life is made up of experiences and aspirations of which he has no conception. You can see your superiority to the savage. Let me help you to look forward and see your inferiority to the coming man, who, I assure you, will never tire of life while anything that God has made remains to be studied. As the mind expands, new wonders and new beauties in creation will unfold themselves and your race will learn to look back with pity upon your present age, with its mean and trivial occupations."

"But, Thorwald," I asked, "can you not tell us something of these higher pursuits?"

"But very little," he answered. "I might give you one or two hints of some things which I think lie nearest you, if indeed you have not already begun to consider them. I need hardly speak of astronomy, which, from the nature of the case, is the earliest of all sciences wherever there is intelligent life to view the works of creation. You will find great profit in advancing in this study as rapidly as possible. We have not yet ceased to pursue it, and I think it is one branch of knowledge which will never be exhausted, in the present life at least. Our achievements in astronomy have been marvelous.

"Do not neglect to look in the other direction also for evidences of God's power and wisdom. The microscope will almost keep pace with the telescope in revealing the wonders of creation. It will greatly assist you in many of your higher employments.

"One thing that you will doubtless soon undertake is the study of the speech of animals, which will go hand in hand with the development of their intelligence. Both of these will claim much attention, but very inadequate results will be obtained until after you have tamed and domesticated the various species. You will want to discover how far animals can be educated and whether their intelligence can ever be developed into mind. As you progress in this study you will feel the necessity of understanding their conversation and you will learn what you can of their language. These tasks will seem of more importance to you when the lower animals are all reclaimed and become the companions and friends of man. You will try to discover the particular purpose for which each species was created, and you will even be led to inquire, by a long series of experiments, whether they possess the faintest shadow of moral perceptions.

"Then there is the great subject of plant life. Does the sensitiveness of plants ever amount to sensibility or feeling? If so, is it a feeling you are bound to respect? That is, should a wounded and bleeding tree excite in you even the slightest shade of that sympathy you feel with a distressed animal? These are inquiries which you doubtless think of little moment now, but we have spent many years pursuing them.

"These are only a few faint indications of the multitude of questions which lie before you for study. In every investigation which you follow, whether connected with the mysteries of your own complex being or with the unexplored depths of creation around you, a chief source of interest will be the constant discovery of a perfect adaptation in the works of God. Of course you know something of it already, but you will never cease to wonder at the unfolding of this truth, as you come to realize more and more fully that creation is one, and is moved and ruled by one intelligence.

"Oh, do not imagine that in the ages to come there will be nothing to make life interesting. As your civilization advances and you are released gradually from trouble and care, and from those petty affairs which now so occupy you, your minds and souls will grow, and you will see far more ahead of you worth striving for than you now do. Your happiness can still consist largely in the pursuit of happiness."

CHAPTER X
MORE WORLDS THAN TWO.

It was now so late in the day that further conversation was postponed, and after a plain but exceedingly enjoyable supper we were shown to luxurious rooms, where we spent our first night in Mars in great comfort. In the morning Thorwald told us we would reach our port in a few hours, and so we sat down as early as we could after breakfast for a short talk. The doctor furnished the text by opening the conversation with this remark: "It is wonderful to think we should find on this planet a race of people so advanced, when so little thought is given, on the earth, to the idea of life in other worlds."

"What has been the general opinion among you on that subject?" asked Thorwald.

"The subject has not had standing enough to call forth much opinion," the doctor answered. "There is an almost universal indifference in regard to the matter. I think the common notion is that the earth is about all there is in the universe worth considering."

"But what are your own views, Doctor?"

"I have been one of those," he replied, "who believed the notion of life outside the earth to be a beautiful theory without one shred of scientific basis. We knew the earth was inhabited and the moon was not, and there we stopped. We did not know, and thought we never could know, anything that could be called evidence pointing to the existence of life in the other planets or elsewhere, and we held that there was no advantage in speculation. We thought it unwise to spend much time or thought on a subject about which we could know nothing. On coming here and finding you I have learned that Mars is inhabited, but I do not know any more about the other planets or stars."

"Does not the mere knowledge that there are two life-bearing bodies lead you to believe that there are more, among the vast numbers of worlds which you have not visited?"

"I don't see why it should. How can we believe anything without evidence? No one has ever come to us from those distant globes, and they are too far away for us to see what is taking place on their surface."

"It seems strange, Doctor, to hear you reason in that way, but I suppose some of our race were just as narrow, if you will pardon me for using that word, as you are, before our wonderful successes in astronomy. I believe you have not properly considered the subject, for it seems to me you had knowledge enough, before you left the earth, to justify you in holding to a strong probability of life beyond your own globe.

"Let us see what some of that knowledge is. You know, to begin with, that one world is inhabited. Then if you should find other bodies as large as the earth and bearing any resemblance to it, there would be no improbability in the thought that they or some of them were filled with life. The improbability is certainly taken away by the knowledge that one such body, the earth, is inhabited.

"You start, then, without prejudice, on a voyage of discovery, aided by your telescope and your reasoning faculties.

"First you find, within distances that you can easily measure, a small group of dark bodies, which you have called planets, all apparently governed by a common law, in obedience to which they are circling around a large body of quite different character, which gives them light and heat. Of these dark bodies, which shine in the sky only by reflected light, the earth is one, and, you are surprised to find, not the most important one, judging from all you can discover. Some of the others are much larger and are attended by more satellites. In fact, the earth is indistinguishable in this little group. While it is not the largest, neither is it the smallest. It is not the farthest from the sun nor the nearest to it. It is merely one among the number. And how much alike the members of this family are. Your telescopes do not point out any material differences, although each has its individual characteristics. Let us enumerate some of the many points of resemblance. They all turn on themselves as well as revolve around the sun. All see the night follow the day, and in most of them there must occur the regular succession of seasons. To each one the sun is the source of light and heat, many of them have moons, and all can see the stars. Nor does the resemblance stop here. For you have discovered that one has an atmosphere, another is surrounded with clouds, while on the surface of our own globe you see the polar snows increase in winter and melt away in summer. Is it not probable that if you could get nearer to these globes you would find still closer resemblances? And if they are like the earth in so many ways, is it at all unlikely that they may, at some period of their existence, be the abode of intelligent life? For what other purpose were they made, Doctor?"

"They make very pretty objects for us to look at," replied my companion.

"Yes, those that can be seen," said Thorwald; "but is that all? Were those great worlds, some of them hundreds of times larger than your own globe, created merely to add a little variety to your sky, and to give you the pleasant task of watching their movements under the pretty title of morning and evening star?" "Speaking from the knowledge I had when I left the earth," the doctor answered, "I can say I never heard that they were put to any other use. No one ever came down to us from any of them to tell us they were inhabited."

"And do you think," asked Thorwald, "that the myriads of stars were also made simply to delight the eye of man?"

"How do I know that they were not?" the doctor asked in reply.

"Because of the absolute unreasonableness of the thought, if for no other reason," answered Thorwald. "But now let me recall to your mind more of the knowledge possessed by the inhabitants of the earth. I think I know about what that knowledge is, from my acquaintance with the present state of your development. Astronomy has been our master science, and I can remember fairly well the extent of our knowledge when we had reached your stage. If I should fall into the error of attributing to you more than you have already discovered you can easily correct me.

"If, now, you leave the little group of dark bodies which are so like the earth, and go out still further into space, what do you find? At distances so great that only the speed of light can be used as a measuring line, you discover vast numbers of self-luminous bodies, which you call stars. Your natural eye can tell but a small fraction of their number. For example, look at the constellation you have named the Pleiades and you see six or seven stars. View it through a three-inch telescope and you can count perhaps three hundred. Now attach a photographic plate to the telescope, and with an exposure of four hours the light coming from that small patch of sky falls upon the sensitive film with a cumulative effect until you have a picture of more than two thousand three hundred stars."

"Yes," broke in the doctor, "you are gauging correctly the state of our knowledge. Our largest telescopes reveal in the entire sky, it is said, one hundred million stars."

"Then," answered Thorwald, "if the glories of the heavens were made merely to delight the eye of man, why was not the eye created of sufficient power to behold them? As it is, only a small proportion of the stars can be seen without the aid of instruments too costly and too delicate for general use.

"But have you the means of establishing any likeness between the earth and those distant bodies? You have discovered that the law of gravitation is universal and that the motions of the stars resemble those of the solar system. Have you made any discoveries tending to prove the existence of other systems like our own?"

"Yes," replied the doctor, "our recent investigations of the periods of some of the variable stars show irregularities in brightness, period, and proper motion. A close study of these irregularities has convinced some of our astronomers that there are invisible bodies near them, evidently planets circling around a central sun. The theory is that the dark bodies cause slight perturbations in the star, which account for the irregularities in period, motion, etc. So Neptune was discovered by the effect it had upon the observed movements of Uranus. This is the first evidence we have had tending to prove that there are other groups of worlds like ours, and it is considered quite significant."

"I can readily believe it," said Thorwald, "and I know how helpful every bit of evidence is, in your search for knowledge. But if I mistake not you have the aid of another instrument, which is destined to play an important part in your future studies. You get much nearer those distant orbs when a spectroscope is placed at the end of the telescope, and the ray of light coming from sun and star is widened out into a band of color, which tells a marvelous story. That light, that has been for years, and perhaps for centuries, on its way to you, now discloses the very nature of the substances which compose those fiery globes. And what are those substances? It must have been a startling truth to the man who first read from the spectrum of the star he was studying, that it contained matter with which he was familiar, materials of which the earth itself is made. By this science you have learned beyond doubt that many of the commonest elements of the earth's crust exist also in other worlds, and, what is of great significance, that the materials most closely connected with living organisms on the earth, such as hydrogen, sodium, magnesium, and iron, are the very ones which are found most widely diffused among the stars. I think I am not wrong in assuming that you are somewhat acquainted with the spectroscope and have made these discoveries."

"You are quite right," said the doctor. "This branch of scientific investigation has already been carried so far with us, and the results of the experiments are so constant and uniform, that when it is asserted, for example, that such and such a metal is present in a state of vapor in the sun's atmosphere, it is estimated that the chances in favor of the correctness of the assertion are as 300,000,000 to 1."

"You are helping my argument, Doctor," resumed Thorwald. "But now let me call your attention to another field of inquiry, in our search for evidence to establish a likeness between the earth and the other parts of the universe. You told me, a while ago, that you have the fall of meteorites on your globe. Have you considered the striking evidence they bring you? Let us imagine we have a meteoric fragment here. Take it in your hand and think of it a moment. You have few things on your earth as interesting as this piece of metallic stone. What a world of questions it starts! What is its composition? Whence comes it? Once it was in existence, but not here. Where, then, was its home? Out, out in the depths of space, where burning suns roll and comets have their dwelling place. The stars have fallen indeed, and here is one of the pieces. Before it came to us as a messenger from the sky did it have an independent existence, or is it a fragment of a shattered world? How long has it been whirling in its unknown orbit, and what story has it for us from its distant birthplace? If we can discover whence meteorites come, and of what they are composed, I think you will agree with me that they furnish valuable testimony in our inquiry. You have no doubt had many theories as to their origin."

I was just about to make answer to this implied question, when Thorwald rose and eagerly scanned the horizon. After a moment he exclaimed:

"We shall have to break off our conversation for a time, as we are nearing our port. I knew by other means that land must soon appear, and now I can see it."

CHAPTER XI
MARS AS IT IS.

The doctor and I looked in the direction indicated and speedily realized that the superiority of the dwellers on Mars extended to the sense of sight, for we could see nothing. But we were sailing so swiftly that the shore we were approaching was before very long brought within our vision also, and among the alert crew, who were now preparing to bring the vessel into its harbor, there could be none so interested in what was to come as the doctor and myself. We were to see what had been accomplished by a race of whose perfections we had been hearing so much.

As we effected a landing and walked up the streets of the city, we were not nearly so much impressed with the size and beauty of the buildings and the appearance of the people as we were by the spirit of absolute peace and quiet which prevailed. With perfect skill, and without noise or bustle, the ship was brought to its dock and the crew went ashore. The screams and calls, the rattle of vehicles and the babel of sounds we had been accustomed to on such occasions, were all missing. The silence and order were almost oppressive because they were so strange. But there was no lack of activity among the immense creatures who thronged around us. Everyone was busy, knowing apparently just what to do without direction from others, and just the best way to do it. Beings with lungs powerful enough to wake the mountain echoes went about with mild and tuneful voices, and, though each one seemed possessed of a giant's strength, no severe labor was required of any.

The streets and walks were paved with a soft material, yielding slightly to pressure, but so firm and tough that it showed no sign of wear, an ideal pavement, over which the wheels rolled as noiselessly as they would over a velvet carpet. It was, moreover, laid in beautiful patterns of the most varied colors. The vehicles, of which there were many kinds for different uses, were so faultlessly made that they moved with the utmost quiet and apparent ease, the power that propelled them being invisible. There were no tracks or wires, but all were guided in any direction and with any speed at the pleasure of the riders.

Thorwald led me from the vessel, and another stalwart son of Mars took charge of the doctor. After walking a few steps up the street we all stepped into an empty carriage without saying as much as "by your leave," Thorwald touched a button, and we were off.

"This," said Thorwald, "is one of the best illustrations of the manner in which we are applying electricity. You saw them also unloading the heavy freight from the boat by the same power. So all our work is done. No fleshly limb is strained, no conscious life is burdened, by any of the labor of our complex society. This subtle force is so well controlled and its laws are so thoroughly understood that it is equal to every demand."

"I am entranced, Thorwald," said the doctor, "with everything I see. But I would like to ask if you own this comfortable carriage and had it sent to the wharf to meet you."

"I own it," our friend replied, "just as I own the street we are riding over or the house I live in. I own this or any other vehicle whenever I desire to use it. You saw a great number of carriages near the wharf, and there are several over on that corner. Anyone is at perfect liberty to appropriate one to his own use at any time, and when he is through he merely leaves it at a convenient place by the roadside for some one else to take."

"I should think they would be stolen," said I.

Thorwald laughed at my ignorance and answered: "Why, who is there to steal when everybody, either friend or stranger, can use them as often and as long as he likes?"

The talk promised to grow more interesting still, but now our attention was turned to the delightful scene through which we were passing. It will be utterly impossible to describe the beauty of the landscape, where nature and art seemed to be striving to outdo each other. Before reaching land I had imagined that the houses, if they were to be proportioned to the inhabitants, must pierce the sky. But we were surprised to find that they were all comparatively low, of not more than two or three stories. And all, even those near the wharf, were surrounded with ample grounds. Some of the houses were larger than others, some more ornate than their neighbors, and the architecture varied as much as the size and arrangement of the grounds. But all were beautiful beyond description. One thing that appeared very strange to us was that the prevailing color of the vegetation was red, although that shade did not predominate as much as green does on the earth. For instance, after we had admired a stretch of lawn brilliant as a crimson sky, we would come to another which would surprise and please us with a lovely shade of blue. Still another was green, and then one glowed with a variety of colors, whose combination showed a most refined taste. As with the grass, so it was with the foliage of the trees. The richest tints of our autumnal forests were here present in permanence, but with a much greater wealth of coloring. Flowers, too, of every hue and form were to be seen on all sides, and their appearance was so perfectly natural that if they had been set with design then the art itself had concealed the art of their arrangement.

With all this mass of color there were no unpleasant contrasts, no discordant tones. As, amid the bustle of the landing place, our ears had not been shocked with rude noises, so now we received through our eyes only a delightful sense of quiet beauty.

Riding, now slowly and now more rapidly, through such a scene, we could think of nothing better to question our friend about, so the doctor found his voice and said:

"This far surpasses our anticipations, Thorwald, and I am sure this place must be exceptional, even on Mars. I suppose it is a resort where some of your wealthy people have built themselves homes in which to enjoy their leisure months."

"Nothing of the kind," replied Thorwald. "These people live here all the year, they are not wealthy, and there is nothing to distinguish this city above others."

"Why, this seems more like a private park than a city. Where are your crowded streets and houses for the poor?"

"After all I have told you of our high civilization, Doctor, do you not understand that we have long since abolished poverty?"

"Yes," answered the doctor, "I understand that in a general way; but I did not suppose everybody was rich, as it is certain everybody must be to own such palaces as these."

"You are still wrong," said Thorwald. "We have no such distinctions as rich and poor. All our cities are of this character, only there is great variety in the residences and in the way in which the streets and lots are laid out. These places that we are passing are inferior to many, but no houses are built that are at all mean or uncomfortable. Indeed, I think we have to-day passed some of the poorest that I know of. As to the word city, we use it only as a convenient expression. It really means nothing more than a certain locality, for, as I told you at the beginning of our conversation, we have no need of government of any kind. In some sections one city runs into another, so that the whole country is filled with the beauty and delight of the landscape which you see about you."

"But," asked the doctor, "with the population spread out in this marvelous way, is there room for everybody?"

"Oh, yes," answered Thorwald. "All the surface of our planet is brought into use; the waste places are reclaimed, and there is abundant room for all. And now, as this pleasant air and easy motion seem to be agreeable to you, we may as well ride slowly for a while longer.

"In your intercourse with us you will find it is never necessary for us to hurry when, for any good reason, we choose to loiter, and, therefore, if you care to hear me talk, I will take the time to correct another wrong impression you seem to have.

"You spoke, Doctor, about the people owning these houses. No one owns them."

"Do they belong to the state?" asked the doctor.

"There is no state."

"Well, this is a curious condition of affairs," resumed the doctor. "Here is valuable property belonging to no one and no government to claim it. I should think anyone that happened along could take possession."

"Now you are right," said Thorwald. "That is just the state of the case. It is with houses and all other property as I told you it was with this carriage. All the right one has to any object is the right to use it. Everything that has been produced by art and skill is just as free as the bounties of nature, such as air and water and land, which of course no one would ever dream of subjecting to private ownership."

The doctor winced as he heard Thorwald include land among these free bounties of nature, and the expression of his face did not escape the quick eye of the Martian, who exclaimed:

"So you earth-dwellers are still in the habit of buying and selling land, are you?"

"That was the practice when we left home," replied the doctor. "And I cannot understand how we can do differently. Your views of property are so strange to us that I am sure my companion will join me in asking you to explain them more fully."

"I certainly do," I said.

"Property," began Thorwald, "we do not have, but we have many of the rights of proprietorship in the things we use from time to time. And what other benefit than the free use of what we need could be derived from the possession of things? Suppose I, for example, owned a thousand acres of land and a hundred fine mansions. I could cultivate but a small part of the land and occupy but one house at a time, and of what value would the remainder be?"

"Would not such palaces as these on this beautiful street bring a good rent?" I inquired.

"Don't be stupid," replied Thorwald good-naturedly. "You must know by this time that we are not a race of self-seekers, each one taking advantage of the necessity of his neighbor. But I suppose it is difficult for you to appreciate a state of society in which each individual considers the feelings and needs of others as much as his own. With us this principle is not preached any more, but it is actually practiced in all our affairs."

"I will try to keep that in mind," I said, "although it is a fact I can hardly realize. But about this matter of houses I want to make another inquiry. After you have become established in a beautiful home to which you have no more right than anyone else, what is to prevent some other man (I use the word for convenience) coming forward and asking you to give it up to him?"

"Nothing," answered Thorwald. "In such a case I should immediately move out and let him have it, knowing he must be entirely unselfish in the matter and that there must be some sufficient reason for the request."

"But would you go to all the trouble of moving without even knowing his reason?"

"Yes, I would do it to accommodate him, but then the trouble would be nothing. We would merely have to go out and take another house."

"But would you not have to move all the furniture?"

"Oh, no. We could take anything we pleased, of course, but it is not usual to make radical changes. Another house would contain all that was desirable. As a matter of fact, however, such removals are by no means frequent. We usually remain in one place and acquire all the tender associations of home which could be possible under any system. But if a family should increase so that it would be better for them to take a larger house, they could easily find one, or if not they would ask those who are fond of that work to build one to their taste. The moment a thing is made or produced it belongs to the general store, to be used by any and all who need it."

"Under such conditions," said I, "what we call the eighth commandment would be superfluous."

"If that refers to theft," answered Thorwald, "you are certainly right, for it is impossible to steal where everything is free.

"It will be well for you to understand how happily we have solved this question of property, but of course we could not have found such a solution until we had first reached a high spiritual plane and learned the lesson of true brotherhood. From your words I know just about the point in our development which corresponds with the present state of your race, and therefore I know something of the nature of the struggle through which the earth is now passing. I warn you that the unrestricted right of private ownership is a menace to your civilization, all the greater because its evil is probably not clearly seen. We are assured by our historians, who try to point out the causes for all the great convulsions in our career, that excessive individualism in property rights, with its selfish disregard of others, was a potent factor in the downfall of many of the enlightened nations of our antiquity. We have noticed that even our animals have the instinct of possession, and it is certain that the love of ownership and accumulation has been one of the hardest evils to eradicate from our naturally selfish nature. If you should ever return to the earth, do not neglect to signal for this danger."

"But what is the remedy?" asked the doctor. "The system of which you have been speaking might be called the mainspring of our society. I can hardly imagine what we should be without it. With our note of warning, what message of help will you send?" "Doctor," answered Thorwald, "it pleases me to hear you ask that question, and I am rejoiced also that I have so good an answer for you. The remedy is to be found in the law of love. Follow that law as closely as possible. The way will be hard, the progress slow, but every step taken will be a solid advance. It is the only safe road, and you will find that every other will lead to disappointment and disaster."

Whenever Thorwald struck these high spiritual themes he spoke with such enthusiasm and positiveness that our respect for him increased rapidly.

CHAPTER XII.
WE REACH THORWALD'S HOME.

All this time we had been riding leisurely along, enraptured with the delightful country, while the way itself and the estates on either hand offered such variety of landscape that the view never became tiresome nor uninteresting.

But as the day was waning, our friends quickened the pace and showed us a burst of speed. This was most exhilarating, and soon brought us to the station where Thorwald told us we were to take an express train for home, which was about two hundred miles distant.

When we alighted we left our carriage by the roadside among many others, and entered an immense building. Both inside and out there were plenty of people moving around, but without noise or unpleasant bustle. With no delay, and also with no haste, we entered what appeared to be a smaller apartment opening out of the general waiting-room. It had the appearance of an elegant drawing-room, the rich but comfortable-looking furniture being disposed in a careless manner, which helped to make us feel at home, if anything could bring us that sensation. There was a door at each end of the room, and soon these were closed and we felt an almost imperceptible jar. The doctor glanced hastily at Thorwald and said:

"Can it be possible that we are to travel in this apartment?"

"Yes," answered Thorwald, "this is our modern traveling coach, and we are already on our way to the city in which my friend here and I reside."

This latter fact surprised us, for we could not perceive by our senses that we were in motion. But as we sat wondering and trying to imagine ourselves flying through space, the doors opened, a pleasant breeze fanned our cheeks, and the doors closed again, we felt that slight jar repeated, and then we were quiet once more. This occurred every two or three minutes, and, remembering what Thorwald had previously told us, we realized that we were riding in a perfectly tight car in a vacuum tube and that these short but frequent stops were to keep us supplied with fresh air.

Thorwald explained this to us again, and told us that the coaches were of different sizes to accommodate large or small parties, and that one could ride alone if he chose to. The cars started so frequently that it was seldom necessary to wait more than a few minutes. The doctor thought there must be great liability to accident, but Thorwald said:

"No, we do not consider the risk worth taking into account. Let me illustrate with a familiar example. Suppose you had just seen a cable tested with a ton's weight without a strain. Should you fear to take hold of the cable and lift yourself from the ground lest it might break and you should fall? The mechanism of this road is just as sure as that. The force that is driving us forward is no longer mysterious. The laws of electricity are well defined, and its mighty power is under perfect control. Nothing is left to chance, and the result is that there have been no accidents for many, many years, and practically speaking there cannot be any."

When we first entered the coach we noticed that there were no windows, and as the doors had no glass we wondered why it was not dark. The light was good broad daylight, exactly like that which fills a room when there are good windows, but where the direct rays of the sun do not enter; and, as we could see no lamps nor fixtures, we could not understand how the illumination could be artificial. But such it was. We carried an electric battery with us, and the lamps were out of sight, and so arranged that they gave us only reflected light. The system was so perfect that the imitation sunlight was just as good as the real, as far as we could discover.

"This is the way we light all our interiors," said Thorwald, "and of course the apparatus is so governed that we can have any amount of illumination we please, little or much."

The doctor was about to ask some question in relation to this practical improvement, when he was stopped by hearing a little silver-toned bell ring. In an instant the doors opened, and Thorwald rose and announced that we had reached the end of our journey. We could not have been in the car more than fifteen minutes, and the doctor and I supposed our ride of two hundred miles had just begun.

"Well, if you travel at this rate," said the doctor, "I do not wonder you have obliterated all national boundaries, for the ends of the world are right at your doors. And now, Thorwald, I would like to see the great tube through which we have been carried so swiftly."

Thorwald smiled a little and led the way through another superb waiting-room out into the open air. Here the doctor looked in all directions, but could see nothing of the object for which he was searching.

"You have seen all any of us can see," said Thorwald.

"We merely step into the comfortable car, sit a few minutes, step out again, and go home. In the meantime we have been carried under ground and under water, across valleys and through hills, but the way itself, the tube through which the car flies, is entirely hidden from sight. Where it is above ground, trees and shrubbery screen it from view, so that it does not mar the landscape. We think much of this, and should regret exceedingly if it became necessary for any such utilitarian object to interfere with our aesthetic enjoyment of nature."

Thorwald's friend now took leave of us, expressing the hope that he would soon see us again. He had taken some little part in our conversation, but had left the burden of it to Thorwald, who was older, and who was, moreover, our first acquaintance.

It seemed singular to the doctor and me that we had attracted so little attention among the people whom we had encountered since leaving the ship. To give the reason for this, which we afterwards discovered, is to reveal one of the pleasantest peculiarities of the Martian character--that is, the entire absence of a disagreeable curiosity. Our dress and appearance and the rather novel circumstances connected with our arrival on the planet, which must quickly have become known, were certainly calculated to excite their interest, and in a similar situation on the earth there is no telling what might have happened to us from a curious mob. But here all was order and quiet. Everybody went about his own business and treated our party with additional respect, it seemed, because some of us were strangers. We found out later how anxious all these people were to learn everything about us, but they were content to wait till the knowledge should come to them in a proper way.

Thorwald now selected a light, pretty carriage, and after a brisk ride through another charming avenue and up a steep hill, we alighted at the door of a noble mansion whose majestic proportions were in harmony with the wide, open plateau upon which it stood alone. Upon entering, Thorwald was at once affectionately greeted by his wife, and while he was introducing us as natives of another world his son and daughter came bounding toward him from an adjacent room.

These were quite small children, but in a few moments Thorwald brought in from another part of the house a young woman of about my age, apparently, and introduced her as a neighbor. It needed but a glance to tell us that she was beautiful as a dream, and she moved about with that exquisite grace which comes only from the highest culture. She spoke to us with such ease and naturalness that we were at once relieved from whatever embarrassment the circumstances might easily occasion.

"Antonia is our very dear friend," said Thorwald, "and, although she hides her curiosity so well, you will find her an exceedingly interested listener to your history and adventures."

"Yes," said the charming voice of Antonia, "Thorwald has told me just enough about you to make me want to know more. Your moon, which is so much larger than our little satellites, caused a great sensation when it was seen coming toward us so rapidly. The situation was well calculated to cause us anxiety, if we had been subject to such a feeling, but, as usual with us at the present day, it has turned out to our advantage; for it has given us two such worthy representatives of a neighboring race."

"I am sure," I answered, "that the advantage is greatly on our side."

I could not say more, for I was conscious that the doctor was watching closely to see how I was affected by the presence of this royal girl. When he saw I was inclined to be somewhat quiet he felt impelled to say something, and offered the following compromising remark:

"If we had only brought Mona safely off the moon with us, you would have had something more worthy of your interest than we are, and my friend here also would now be in better spirits."

Antonia had a question in her eyes but her perfect breeding kept her from putting it into words, after the final expression of the doctor's speech. Of course, I could not ignore the allusion, and said:

"Mona is a friend of the doctor's whom I have not the pleasure of knowing. I suppose he thinks her cheerful disposition, of which I have heard before, would make our present situation even more enjoyable than it is. Speaking for myself, however, I think that would be impossible."

With that she rose, and, with a pleasant word of adieu to us, told Thorwald she would come in another day after we were well rested.

It was now approaching night-fall and dinner was to be speedily announced. The doctor and I were shown to a suite of dressing-rooms, and as soon as we were alone he said:

"Do you think Antonia is as handsome as Mona?"

"If you will show me Mona I shall then be able to judge. But how did I carry myself on my first introduction to a daughter of Mars? Do you think I am in any danger of putting her in Margaret's place in my heart?"

"Perhaps not," replied the doctor. "You kept command of yourself pretty well; but I think the secret of that is that you have not quite forgotten Mona."

"Excuse my frankness, Doctor, but I must tell you I am getting a little tired of Mona. I wish I might never hear her name again. If I can resist the charms of such an exquisite bundle of perfections as Antonia is, do you think I am likely to be overcome by a mocking-bird of your imagination?"

"If you could only hear the voice of that bird once more," replied the doctor, "you would soon begin to sing another tune. But let us go down if you are ready, and not keep them waiting."

We had looked forward with much interest to our first meal in one of these sumptuous houses, and, moreover, being quite hungry, we were glad to find that we were just in time to sit down. If we had felt any fear lest the absence of meat would make a meager bill of fare, the experience of the next hour relieved us. The dishes were all strange, but highly palatable, and the fact that there was nothing that appeared to be in the least unwholesome did not detract from the delicious savor which every viand possessed. The rich variety of courses and the elegance of the service made it a dinner long to be remembered, and gave a new zest to our life on Mars.

It had been a long day to us, and we were allowed to retire at an early hour, being conducted to adjacent and communicating rooms. But, though our fatigue was great, it is not strange that we lay awake awhile, talking of the wonderful things we had seen and heard. Speaking of the Martian method of rapid transit the doctor said:

"Besides its expedition, there is another feature to recommend their way of traveling."

"What is that?"

"Why, there is no danger of getting a seat just behind a window fiend."

"There is something in that," I answered, "but I am thinking just now of our dinner. We must certainly learn how to cook eggs and vegetables before we return to the earth."

The character of our conversation, judged from these scraps, shows that we had no excuse for remaining awake any longer.

CHAPTER XIII.
A MORNING TALK.

Next morning we arose early, but found the family already up. Thorwald seemed disposed to lose no time in showing and telling us everything interesting, and so invited us at once to the top of the house, to take a view of the country. The sun was just rising, and its pleasant rays lighted up a scene of surpassing beauty. We seemed to be set in the middle of a vast park, whose boundaries extended in all directions as far as we could see. The landscape presented the most varied character, wood and water, hill and plain, and every feature needed to make a most delightful picture. Not the least of its charms, and perhaps the greatest, was the profusion of color, which filled the vision and satisfied the sense of beauty with its contrasts and its harmonies. Some of the hills might justly be called mountains, and yet on the rugged sides as well as on the summit of each were grand mansions surrounded by cultivated fields.

The doctor made some remark about this latter fact, and Thorwald said:

"These situations, which would be almost inaccessible without the aid of electricity, are now the favorite sites for building. This wonderful power levels all hills in the ease with which it does its work. No task is too hard for it and it asks no sympathy, so we may as well ride and carry our freight up hill, if we prefer it, and build our houses on the mountain tops. One characteristic of our nature has not changed, and there is still a great variety of taste, so that plenty of people choose the lower land to build upon. I see by your faces that you both admire this panorama and think we were wise to place our house on such high ground. We like to have our friends take this view in the morning, when the world has been freshened by the night's rain."

"Is it not just as beautiful at sunset after a shower?" I asked.

"Oh," answered Thorwald, "I haven't told you that it never rains in the daytime, have I?"

"No, indeed, that's another surprise for us. But how is it managed?"

"You will remember I told you," said Thorwald in reply, "that it was found that rain enough fell for all parts of the world if it could only be rightly distributed. Then when we had discovered by a long series of experiments how to make the clouds shed their water at our pleasure, we set about devising a means whereby we could give each section the right quantity of rain at just the right time.

"We established a central bureau in each country and let the people in every city or district vote and send in their request for a shower or a long rain ten days in advance. At first it required only a majority vote, but this occasioned no end of trouble, as half the community would often believe they were suffering for want of rain when the other half wanted fair weather. Then the rule was changed so as to make a three-quarters vote necessary, which did not help matters much, for very often the crops would be seriously damaged before so large a proportion of the people could be brought to see the desirability of a rainy day.

"At length the happy thought was conceived of letting it rain over each part of the country every night, and giving the right to vote only on the quantity desired. This keeps everything fresh and has been found of immense benefit to vegetation. Besides, it inconveniences no one, in the present state of our society, however it might have been when the plan was first adopted."

"What of those people," I asked, "whose occupation or pleasure calls them out in the night?"

"We have no such class," replied Thorwald. "We have found by long experience that it is best to follow the indication of nature, and take the day for labor and the night for rest. This practice and the attention devoted to our diet have been chief factors in lengthening the span of our lives. If this line of action is best for one it is best for all, and, as everybody is doing the best he can, it follows that there are literally no people out at night."

"I suppose you would call me stupid again," said I, "if I should ask if you have any such old-time personages as guardians of the peace."

"Indeed I should," answered our friend, "for you ought to know us better. If you will excuse a poor witticism, the peace is old enough on our planet to go without a guardian."

As we smiled at this the doctor was encouraged to try his hand, but, not feeling equal to addressing a pleasantry to the usually august Martian, he turned to me and remarked:

"This would be a pretty poor place for an umbrella trust, wouldn't it?"

As we left our place of outlook and made our way down stairs, Thorwald resumed:

"As I have said before, we have reached our present happy condition through many bitter experiences. We read that at one time people had so much work to do and were so thoughtless as to what was good for their physical welfare that they began to rob themselves of their proper rest. Others found it convenient to follow occupations which obliged them to work all night and get what sleep they could in the day-time. Night was considered about the only time that could be utilized, also, for the activities of social life.

"This condition lasted a long time, with the tendency continually toward the practice of encroaching more and more upon the hours of rest appointed by nature. It was then the period of making many laws, and large and influential legislative bodies began to set a bad example to the rest of the world by holding their sessions mainly in the night. Newspapers thought it necessary to appear full-fledged at the break of day, and the railroads made but little distinction between darkness and daylight in the matter of carrying people hither and thither. The change was slow, but it was in the wrong direction. Darkness was driven out by more improved methods of lighting, and houses and streets were brilliant the whole night long; and it finally became the fashion in both society and business circles literally to turn night into day. For a time that remained the universal custom, strange as it seems to us now, but the practice of sleeping in the day-time never became natural. This means that the whole world was living on from year to year without the amount of rest required to keep the race alive. There could be but one result. A brood of nervous troubles fell upon us; life began to shorten, and we became aware that a serious crisis was before us. As soon as we were convinced that we were bringing all this evil upon ourselves by our disregard of the laws of nature, there was a change; and it is well for us that there was still virility enough left in the race to make a change possible. A gradual reform was instituted which, overcoming many difficulties and delays but with no serious set-backs, brought us, after long years, to our present happy way. Of course, our improvement in every other direction, moral as well as physical, assisted us all along in this reform. Now, looking back on our course, and comparing our present with our former state, we are perfectly sure what is best for us, and he would be a rash man who should intimate that we are not doing right in using the night for rest.

"But this is getting to be quite a long talk for so early in the morning. Let us see if breakfast is not ready."

This meal proved to be as appetizing as the first, although the dishes were entirely different; being made up, apparently, of fruit and cereals.

The doctor and I had been exceedingly interested in the way the dinner of the evening before had been served. We did not understand it, and now we were equally puzzled to see the breakfast courses come and go. No one came in to make any change in the table, and our hostess seemed to have as little to do with it as the rest of us. She presided with great dignity, and, as I watched the changes going on with such perfect ease and quiet, I could not refrain from saying:

"If it is proper for me to ask, will you tell us how this is done, Mrs. ----"

"We do not use those titles now," she interrupted. "Call me Zenith, the name by which I was introduced to you. I suppose Thorwald has told you that electricity does nearly all our work. I arrange things in order before the meal begins, and then by merely touching a button under the table the apparatus is set in motion which brings and takes away everything in the manner you see."

"It is wonderful," I exclaimed. "And if we are to believe all that Thorwald has told us, I suppose you have no servants for any department of work."

"You are not entirely right," she returned. "We have excellent servants. This obedient power, that does our work so willingly, is our servant, and so is the mechanism with which our houses are filled, and through which this silent force is exerted. Many of our animals are domesticated and trained to do light services, but as for servants of our own flesh and blood, no such class exists. We all share whatever work there is, and no labor is menial. Whatever I ask others to do I am glad to do for them when occasion offers. Do not suppose we are idle. There is work for us, but with our abundant strength and continual good health it is never a burden. Then there are the duties connected with our higher life and education, for we are ever seeking to fit ourselves for a still better existence than this."

We had now finished breakfast and were walking through the house. Zenith was a beautiful woman, although, from our point of view, of such generous proportions. She possessed the perfect form and the vigor and health of all the Martians. She was, moreover, graceful, modest, and winning. But Thorwald and the other men that we had seen possessed these latter qualities also, and Zenith exhibited the same strength of mind and the same devotion to lofty aims as her husband. In their equipment for the duties of life and in the ability to do valiant service for their kind they seemed equal. Evidently neither had a monopoly of any class of advantages, either of mind, body, or estate.

CHAPTER XIV.
PROCTOR SHOWS US THE EARTH.

We discovered at once that the Mars dwellers understand what genuine hospitality is, for we found ourselves at perfect liberty to do what best pleased us without restraint from our hosts. With so much to tell us of their own high civilization and with so many questions still to ask about the earth, there was no haste nor undue curiosity. Much less was there any attempt yet by Thorwald to resume the argument about the habitability of other worlds.

But at the same time we were aware that our friends were at our service, and early in the afternoon Thorwald asked us if we could think of anything we should like to see.

"Yes," I answered, "I should like to see the earth."

"No doubt, my friend, but I don't see exactly how I am going to take you there."

"I did not expect that," said I; "but, after all you have hinted about your advance in astronomical science, I thought you might give us a pretty good view of the earth without going any nearer to it than we are now."

"Oh, that's what you mean, is it? Excuse me for being so dull. Is it not singular that I should wait to be asked to show you the wonders of our telescopes? Zenith, let us all go with them to see their home, about which we have so often speculated.

"We have many good observatories," continued Thorwald, speaking to the doctor and me, "some of which are noted for one line of study and some for another. The one that has given the most attention to observing the earth and that has the best instruments for that work is situated on the other side of our planet."

"Then, of course," said I, "we will choose one nearer home for our visit."

"Why so?" asked Thorwald. "It is always wise to get the best when you can."

"Yes, but we do not want you to take the time and trouble to make a journey half around your world just because I said I would like to see the earth."

"Oh, our time is yours, and we will not make trouble of it; we will call it a pleasure trip. We may as well take the children, Zenith; they will enjoy it. How soon can you all be ready?"

"In five minutes," answered Zenith.

"Then we had better get off at once," said Thorwald.

And without further words this remarkable family scattered to different parts of the house and in five minutes were ready to begin a journey of five or six thousand miles, and the only reason they did not start at once was that the doctor and I were not quite so expeditious. We were soon on our way, however, having locked no doors behind us and leaving everything just as if we were to return in an hour.

We took an electric carriage to the station, and from there went by the tubular road to the metropolis. This was a great city whence there was direct communication to all the principal centers of population on the planet. As we had not been in any haste in making the changes necessary to reach this stage of our journey, it was now late in the day, and I began to wonder how we were to continue the trip without being out in the night. When I mentioned my thought to Thorwald, he removed the difficulty in a moment by saying:

"We simply travel west and leave the night behind us. You know the surface of Mars, even at the equator, goes east at the rate of only five hundred miles an hour, and as our modern cars take us much faster than that, it is easy for us to keep ahead of the night by going in the right direction. So in making long trips we try to travel west."

"But suppose you want to go east?"

"Then we go west to get east, and we arrange the speed so as to get to our destination in the day-time."

We left our car and found another just ready to start for the distant city in which our observatory was situated. It was a small car comparatively, and we had it all to ourselves. There were all sorts of conveniences in it, and we composed ourselves for a good rest. After a ride of several hours we reached our destination. It was now about noon, so that we had actually made nearly half a day, besides the time spent in sleep while riding. I know some of my friends on the earth, who say the day is too short for them, would appreciate such an improvement as that if they could have it.

We passed part of the afternoon in riding about the city. The same language was spoken here as was used on Thorwald's side of the globe; but, although communication was so easy, we found enough difference in the architecture and in the general appearance of the people to make travel interesting.

Toward night we all alighted at the door of the observatory, and the doctor and I had the pleasure of making the acquaintance of a man of Mars who had spent many years in studying the surface of the earth. It may be imagined that he was glad to meet us and to get our answers to many questions which had long perplexed him, some of which he had never hoped to have solved.

Proctor, for this was the name by which he was introduced, was one of the oldest men we had seen, and impressed us as one possessed of great wisdom. His manner was so dignified, also, that it seemed quite as inappropriate to address him without a title as it was to call our hostess plain Zenith. But when I asked Thorwald aside what I should call him, he said:

"Call him by his name, just as you do the rest of us. We have but one name each."

"I should think that would be confusing," said I. "For example, how are you to be distinguished from any other Thorwald?"

"There is no other that I ever heard of. There are names enough to go all around."

As night came on we were brought face to face with the great instrument whose work of observing the earth was known far and wide.

Proctor was occupied a short time in adjusting it, and then asked us if we could recognize what was in the field. I motioned to the doctor, but as he insisted that I should take the first view I put my eye to the glass with much trepidation. Instead of the magnified disk of the earth, which I expected to behold, I saw but a small portion of the surface, and that a familiar stretch of coast line. I never knew whether Proctor thought by our accent or by the cut of our clothes that we were New Englanders, but he had so pointed the telescope that our first sight of the earth showed us dear old Massachusetts Bay, with its islands and boundaries. I did not speak till the doctor had looked, and then we told the others of our pleasant surprise.

Proctor made another adjustment, saying he would bring the globe still nearer to us, and we looked and saw a patch of beautiful green country. It appeared to be but a few miles away, and we thought we ought to distinguish large objects. But the appearance was deceptive in this respect, and Proctor told us they had not been able to determine definitely whether the earth was inhabited. They could see important changes going on from time to time; they believed they could tell cultivated from wild land; certain peculiar spots they called large cities; and there were many such indications of inhabitants. But they had not yet beheld man nor his unquestioned footsteps. As to their belief on the subject, they had the strongest faith that the earth was peopled by an intelligent race, and Proctor added that he rejoiced to see that faith so happily justified by our presence. To which the doctor pleasantly replied that he should be sorry to have him judge of the intelligence of the race at large from two such inferior specimens.

One question which Proctor asked was, whether we had ever made any attempt to communicate with the other planets. We told him we had not, but that if we should ever try such a thing it would probably be with Mars; but that it would be useless to think of it with our present astronomical attainments, for if we should succeed in attracting the attention of another world we would not know it, because we could not see the answer.

Proctor said they had sometimes seen moving masses which were not clouds, but which they took for smoke and were not sure but they might be intended for signals. We replied that if it were smoke that they saw it was probably caused by forest fires, but if we ever reached the earth again we would organize a company and try to make some electric signals which they could see.

CHAPTER XV.
A NIGHT ADVENTURE

It was late when the conversation closed, and Proctor said we were to spend the night with him of course, and in the morning he would take pleasure in introducing to us the other members of his household.

The residence buildings, beautiful and commodious structures, adjoined the observatory, and to each of us was given a separate apartment. After Proctor had left us, Thorwald came into my room a moment and I said to him:

"Proctor is a friend of yours, is he not?"

"Certainly," answered Thorwald, "what could he be but a friend? But then I never saw him before today."

"Is it possible? Are strangers always treated so hospitably?"

"I see nothing unusual in his treatment of us. We are always at perfect liberty to stay where ever night overtakes us, and it makes no difference with the quality of the hospitality whether the guests are acquaintances or not."

The memory of that night will remain with me many years. Before falling asleep I let my mind dwell on the singular circumstances in which we were placed and the strange manner of our leaving the earth. I had never experienced anything that seemed more real, and yet I could not make it appear quite reasonable that we were in truth living on the planet Mars. All I could say was that it was an instance where the facts were against the theory, and I knew that in such cases it was always safest to believe in the facts. I could distinctly remember each step of our journey, and there could be no mistake about our present understanding. What settled the question more firmly than ever was this thought: If we were not on Mars, where were we? We must be somewhere.

By the time I had disposed of all my doubts I was becoming drowsy, and then

I began to think of the doctor and his unfortunate condition of mind. This malady would doubtless increase and I should have to look out for him, and at the same time fill the arduous position of the only sound representative of our race in Mars. I resolved to try once more to make my companion see how ridiculous his strange fancy was and realize the danger of clinging to it.

With this thought my brain lost coherence, and I passed over the invisible boundary into dreamland. It was a beautiful evening in summer. I was at home among my friends and we were sitting in the open air. The doctor was there, taking his turn with me in telling the story of our adventures. This went on till our listeners were tired out, and then one of the company gave a little variety to the occasion by singing a capital song.

Here the scene changed to the country. It was morning in the woods. The trees wore their spring foliage, bright flowers spread their beauty and fragrance around us, and the air was filled with the music of birds. The sweet notes of these songsters were by far the most vivid part of the dream. Now loud, now soft, the unbroken melody absorbed our attention and made it difficult for us to understand how our situation again gradually changed, until the air became piercingly cold, the cruel wind beat upon us furiously, and the violent elements seemed bent upon our destruction.

The doctor and I were alone, and the surroundings bore a strange resemblance to the inhospitable surface of the moon. But what are those sweet sounds still ringing in our ears? Sure no birds could live in such a wild place. No, it is not a bird's song. It is more like a human voice. I thought I had never before heard music so pure and rich. But wait--had I not heard something like it once before? There was a mystery about it that enhanced its sweetness. Now I was really thinking, for before I knew how it happened I found myself wide awake. The dream was over, but, oh! wonderful dream, the best of it remained. My sense of hearing, always acute, had waked long before and left my other faculties to slumber on and dream out the unreal accompaniments of a real voice. For now, with my eyes open and my mind released from sleep, I still heard that marvelous, half- familiar song.

Could I be deceived? I determined to know beyond a doubt that I was awake. I rose and, throwing on a dressing gown, turned up the light and walked about the room. I looked in the mirror to see if my eyes were open, and then ate a little fruit from a tempting dish that stood on the table. In one corner of the room was an elegant writing desk. I opened it, found its appointments complete, drew up a comfortable chair, and, choosing pen and paper, determined to record my impressions for future perusal, if by any means my memory should fail me. This is what I wrote:

"I, the undersigned, am in my private room in the house of Proctor, the astronomer, province of ----, planet Mars. It is about the middle of the night, precise date unknown. I am wide awake, in my usual health, appetite good, heart a little fluttering but temperature and pulse normal. I have been awakened from sleep by strains of distant music, which mingled with my dreams but refused to be silenced when the rest of the dreams melted away. Now, while I am writing, the delicious melody fills my ears. I never before heard so sweet a voice, unless, indeed, I have heard the same voice before. In regard to this I can form no present opinion. I must take another time to consider it. Now I cannot think, I am so engrossed in listening to the singer's entrancing notes. The song is so full of light and cheer and sends such beautiful thoughts trooping through my brain that I wish it may go on forever."

I signed my name to this with a firm hand, and then, as I leaned back in my chair to close my eyes and drink in more deeply still this rare enjoyment, darkness seemed to fall suddenly upon my spirit. The voice ceased, and in a moment the last sweet echoes had died away.

I crept into bed as speedily as possible, to try to forget my sadness in sleep. But oblivion would not be forced, and so I took what comfort I could in thinking of that interrupted song, and in trying to feel over again in memory that pleasure which my fleshly ears no longer gave me. I could still recognize a distinct tinge of familiarity in the notes, but when I came to the question of locating the singer I was utterly without a clew. I knew well enough that there was no earthly voice which could enter into the comparison, and so I need waste no time in going over that part of my life. But I had heard no singing of any kind in Mars before this night. How was it possible that I could have experienced that delightful sensation before and not be able to fix the place or time? It was a puzzling question, but I refused to give it up I knew the song, and the memory of it warmed my heart with each recurring flash, but the singer I did not know.

At length I fell asleep, and woke to find the sun of Mars shining pleasantly upon my bed. I recalled at once the experience of the night and confirmed my memory by finding on the desk the paper I had written, and still there was enough suspicion in my mind of the reality of the whole thing to make me anxious to know if the doctor had heard what had so impressed me. But on going to find him I discovered that he had left his room, and so it happened that we did not meet till the family came together in the morning reception room, in preparation for breakfast. Here Proctor presented us to his wife, Fronda, and his daughters, two stately girls, whom he did not name. Thorwald and Zenith kindly helped the doctor and me to answer the many questions which these new friends were so eager to ask, so that, as breakfast proceeded, all became engaged in the conversation. My own mind, however, was somewhat preoccupied. I thought perhaps Thorwald might be in haste to depart for home, and I was determined not to let the company separate till I had made an attempt to discover who my midnight singer was. So, when there came a convenient lull in the talk, I made bold to say:

"Can anyone present tell me who it was that woke me in the night 'with concord of sweet sounds'?"

A general smile passed around the table at this question, while Fronda looked at me and said pleasantly,

"It must have been Avis. She is very fond of singing and considers all hours her own. I hope it did not disturb your slumbers."

"It was no disturbance, I assure you. But is Avis present? I should like to thank her for the great pleasure she gave me."

"No," replied Fronda, "she took an early breakfast and started out for a long walk."

"Then I may as well tell you all about it," I said.

And I related my dream and then read to them all the paper I had written. Everyone listened with the greatest eagerness and showed more interest, I thought, than the circumstances as I had related them called for, but I afterwards learned that they had excellent reasons for it.

When breakfast was over I was glad to find that Thorwald seemed to be in no haste to go home. I began to feel an intense longing to see Avis, and I had planned, if Thorwald should insist on leaving too soon, to propose to Proctor that I would stay a few days and assist him in the observatory.

The doctor and I soon found an opportunity to speak together privately, and he began:

"So the voice of Avis was a little familiar to you?"

"Yes," I replied, "but I am not able to tell from what niche in memory's hall it comes."

"Does it recall anything you heard or saw on the moon?"

"That dreadful place? No, indeed," I replied. "Are you going to bring up Mona again?" "You asked me never to mention that name again, and now you have spoken it."

"Well," I asked, "will you forgive me for that foolish request if I will let you talk to me about her now?"

"I am not anxious to talk about her," the doctor answered, "especially as I know the topic is not a pleasant one to you."

Without noticing this last remark, I asked abruptly:

"Was Mona a good singer?"

"Fair."

"As good as Avis?"

"I think so, though I am not a critic."

"Did I understand you to say she was handsome?"

"Beautiful."

"And I fell in love with her?"

"You had all the symptoms. But why do you insist on talking on such a disagreeable subject? Come, let's go and find Proctor."

"Wait. One question more. Have you seen Avis?"

"Yes."

"Who is she?"

"I believe she is a friend of the family merely."

"Does she live here?"

"She is staying here for the present."

"Is she beautiful, too?"

"I shall leave you to be your own judge of that when you see her. Now, not another question."

"Well," I said, as we started to find some of the others, "if the Mona of your imagination gives you as much pleasure as Avis has given me before I have seen her,

I do not wonder that you cherish her memory."

This conversation left me still more anxious to see Avis, and I looked for her return every moment, but the morning passed and finally the day wore to its close without bringing us together. I did not like to make my strong desire known by asking after her, and, besides, I began to have a slight suspicion that there was some design in keeping us from meeting.

When it was time to retire that night I took the doctor to my room, and I think it was a surprise to both of us when we fell to talking about Mona again. At my request the doctor related at considerable length our experience on the moon, as he remembered it, and set Mona out in most attractive style. I let him go on, without laughing at him as I had formerly done, and the longer he talked the more serious and thoughtful I became. As he told the details of our daily life, recalling many of Mona's words and actions, a new thought flashed through my mind--the thought that possibly the doctor was right after all. At that instant, when my interest was most intense, once more the distant echoes of that happy song fell upon my ear.

That was the magic influence needed for my restoration. At once, and all at once, down fell the walls that had so unhappily obscured my mental vision, and left my memory clear as day. I jumped from my seat, seized the doctor's hand, and exclaimed:

"I see it all now, old fellow. You were right and I was the crazy one."

"Good, I rejoice with you."

With that voice coming nearer and pouring its melody upon us, we could not say more at the time. I threw myself into a chair, let my head fall back, and closed my eyes to enjoy it. The doctor, feeling it to be better to let me think it out by myself, stole away and left me alone.

Alone, but not lonesome, for was not Mona with me? I could see her every look and motion, and experienced with a great throb of the heart that my love had only strengthened with my period of forgetfulness. I remembered her last words, that very likely we would never see her again. But why should not she be saved as easily as we were? What if she were even now afloat in the ocean? But perhaps some one had rescued her. Could she be in Mars and singing for other ears than mine? Singing! Why, who is singing now, right here in this very house? Can it be possible? How stupid I have been. Perhaps I can see her now.

I jumped up and rushed from the room, but was no sooner outside my door than the voice began to die again, and in a moment the last notes had floated away. I could not determine from which direction the song had come and had no clew to guide me toward the singer. It was very late and all the house was quiet. Unable to pursue my quest, I reentered my room, but it was hours before I could compose my mind sufficiently to sleep. The possible joy that awaited me in the morning, the dreadful fear that I should be disappointed, the violent beating of my heart at every thought of Mona, and my anxiety lest she might even now be exposed to danger somewhere, all combined to keep me excited and restless the whole night long. As I lay tossing and thinking, my most serious doubt was occasioned by the reflection that people of such exalted morals would not deceive me by declaring that this singer's name was Avis if it were not true. But then I thought further that the doctor had given Mona the name by which we knew her, and that Fronda would have just as much right to give her a new name. Perhaps her real name after all was Avis.

When the welcome morning came I found the doctor and gave him a hearty grasp to show him that there had been no lapse in my mental condition, but I asked him to say nothing to Thorwald just at present about my recovery. Then we hurried down to the reception room and, early as it was, found most of the household already there. After looking eagerly around and seeing only those whom I had previously met, I inquired, with as little apparent concern as possible:

"Hasn't Avis appeared? I thought she was an early riser."

To which Fronda quickly replied:

"Oh, Avis was up half an hour ago, and asked me to excuse her to the company, saying she was going to spend the morning with a friend she met yesterday."

This was a hard blow for me, and it was with difficulty that I restrained my impatience, but I was a little consoled with the idea that the morning only was to be consumed by this visit, and that we might look for a return by noon.

After breakfast, when Proctor had gone to the observatory and Fronda and her daughters were showing Zenith about the house, the doctor begged Thorwald to resume the talk begun on board the ship, which had been interrupted by the discovery of land. As Thorwald expressed a willingness to comply, the doctor continued:

"You were trying to convince me of the probability of life in other worlds besides the earth and Mars, and in your attempt to show a likeness between the earth and other parts of the universe, you were speaking on the interesting subject of meteorites."

"I remember," answered Thorwald, "I was just asking you what theory you of the earth hold on that important topic."

CHAPTER XVI
AN UNLIKELY STORY

I f the doctor," I said, "will pardon me, I will say, in relation to the origin of
meteorites, that our scientific men have held from time to time many different theories. Some have believed that they are aggregations of metallic vapors
which, meeting in the atmosphere, solidify there and fall, just as watery vapors solidify and come down in the form of hailstones. Others have held that they
are thrown out from the center of the earth by volcanic action; and others still that
they all came from the moon when her volcanoes were active. These latter theories
imply that the meteorites in immense quantities are revolving around the earth, and
that occasionally they become entangled in her atmosphere and fall to the surface.

"And now, Thorwald, I am tempted to repay all your great kindness to us with
an act of ingratitude, nothing less than the relation of a story."

This rather foolhardy speech of mine made the doctor wince, and I am not sure
but he began to fear that my mind was weakening in a new direction. But I had my
own excuse for my action, which I felt that I could explain to him at some future
time. The fact is, I was so disturbed in my mind about Mona and was anticipating
so much from meeting the so called Avis, that I thought I could never sit still all the
morning and listen to a dry scientific discussion. It seemed to me that I could stand
it better if I could do part of the talking myself, and so I took advantage of the subject before us to propose relating an extravagant tale that I once had heard.

In contrast with the doctor's frowns, Thorwald showed a lively appreciation
and insisted that I should be heard.

"Not another word from me," he said, "till we have had the story."

With such encouragement, it was easy for me to proceed.

"I fear you will be disappointed," I said, "for what I have rashly called a story is only a fancy founded on the idea that the meteorites were at some time shot out of the volcanoes of the moon. I had it from a friend of mine, whose mind is evidently more open to the notion of life in other worlds than is that of my companion here. As the story was written long before the moon came down to visit the people of the earth in their own home, the writer did not have the advantage of the discoveries made by the doctor and myself, and it is well for me that the doctor's friend, Mona, is not here to disprove any of my statements.

"On account of the smaller volume of the moon, the attraction of gravitation on its surface is only one-quarter that of the earth, and it is estimated that, if a projectile were hurled from the moon with two or three times the velocity of a cannon ball, it would pass entirely beyond her attraction and be drawn to the earth, reaching it at the rate of some seven miles a second.

"Now we all know--this is the way the story runs--that the moon was once inhabited by a highly intelligent race. They tell us it is a cold, dead world now, not at all fit for inhabitants. But that is because its day is passed. Being so much smaller than the earth it cooled off quicker, and its life-bearing period long since found its end. Men have often speculated on the idea that our race will one day fail and the time come when the last generation shall pass away and leave the earth a bare and ugly thing, to continue yet longer its lonely, weary journey around a failing sun. That day the moon has seen. That direful fate the race of moon men have experienced. Some poor being, the last of his kind, was left sole monarch of a dying world, and with the moon all before him where to choose, chose rather to die with the rest and leave his world to cold and darkness.

"From our own experience we do not know how high a state of civilization can be reached by giving a race all the time that is needed. But we know that before the inhabitants of the moon passed off the stage they had attained to the highest possible degree of intelligence. They began existence at a very low plane, developed gradually through long periods of time--there has never been any haste in these matters--and when they had reached their maturity as a race of intellectual and moral beings, primitive man was just beginning on the vast undertaking of subduing the earth, a task not yet accomplished.

"The incident I propose to relate occurred in antediluvian times, when there were giants in the earth who lived a thousand years. Then matter reigned, not mind. It was the age of brawn. Everything material existed on a gigantic scale, and man's architectural works, rude in design but well adapted for shelter and protection, were proportioned to his own stature and rivaled the everlasting hills in size and solidity. And they needed something substantial for protection, for war was their business and their pass time. They lived for nothing but to fight. It was brother against brother, neighbor against neighbor, tribe against tribe; and the man who could not fight, and fight hard, had no excuse for living. War was not an art, but a natural outburst of brutal instincts. A giant glories in his strength and cultivates it as naturally as a bird its song. But it is pleasant to consider the fact that as man's mental and moral qualities have developed his body has become smaller. As the necessity for that immense physical strength gradually passed away, nature, abhorring such unnecessary waste of material, applied to us her inexorable laws whereby a thing or a state of things no longer useful slowly fades away, and our bodies accommodated themselves to new conditions.

"But in those early times men needed great physical strength and long life to bring the world into subjection, and until that was done they could give little attention to the cultivation of the finer qualities of their incipient manhood. They were handicapped by the fact that the lower animals had had the earth to themselves a few million years, more or less, and no puny race could ever have driven them to the wall.

"At length, when the conflict was well nigh over, with victory in sight, men had abandoned the struggle and were using all their fierce strength in fighting each other. This had been going on so long and with such deadly results that it seemed as if the race must be exterminated unless some superior power could step in from the outside and prevent it.

"We can easily understand that there was no such thing as science then. Men considered the sun, for example, only as a very useful thing which brought them light with which they could see their foe, and the moon as a mysterious object sent to make the night a little less dark. Sun and moon and shining stars were all set in the sky for them, and went through their wonderful and complicated movements solely for their amusement.

"But what was the real condition of things on the moon at that time? Why, there was a race of people there of such intelligence and scientific attainments that they were seeing plainly enough everything that was taking place on the earth. This will not appear very strange when we consider our remarkable success in scanning the surface of the moon at the present day, and remember that the inhabitants of the moon were then nearing the close of their history, and so at the height of their civilization.

"Yes, they had watched the coming of man upon the stage with the deepest interest--with a neighborly interest, in fact--seeing in him the promise of a companion race and one worthy of the magnificent globe which they could see was so much larger than their own. Their powerful instruments enabled them to see objects on the earth as distinctly as we now see through our telescopes the features of a landscape a few miles distant.

"Keeping thus so close an acquaintance with man and all his works, they rejoiced at every success he achieved over the lower forms of life, and grieved at all his failures. Especially were they pained when he tired of the conflict with his natural foe, and began to battle with his own kind. As this inhuman strife continued, the folly and wickedness of it roused to the fullest extent the interest and sympathy of the moon-dwellers, and they began to ask each other what they could do to put a stop to it. They themselves had long since given up war and had even outgrown all individual quarrels, and they could not endure with patience what was then taking place right under their eyes. But they found it easier to declaim against the evil than to suggest any practical method of stopping it. Although so near them in one sense, to the other senses the field of conflict was some two hundred and forty thousand miles away.

"However, of what value is a high state of civilization if it cannot help a neighboring world in such an emergency as this? If they could only communicate in some way with men they could soon make them understand that it would be better for them to cease their fighting and finish their legitimate work of subduing the lower forms of creation. But how to open communication! The problem long remained unsolved, the condition of things on the earth in the meantime growing worse and worse. At last it was suggested that a shot might be fired which would reach the earth. This was a bold suggestion, but it was well known that they had explosives powerful enough to carry a projectile beyond the moon's attraction, and no one could give any good reason why such a projectile, being entirely free of the moon, should not reach the earth under the power of gravitation. It was determined to try the experiment, and after due preparation, which was comparatively easy with their facilities, an enormous shot was hurled forth. It was large enough to be seen by the aid of their powerful telescopes as it sped on its way, and it was with intense interest that they saw it enter the earth's attraction and finally strike the surface of that globe. Now that so much had been accomplished, they saw immense possibilities before them. What they now wanted to do was to use their discovery to make men give up their fighting and turn to the arts of peace.

"How could they do this? Some proposed that they should make hollow shot, fill them with Bibles and other books, and bombard the earth with good precepts till men should learn and be tamed. But from their close observation of mankind the moon-dwellers knew they were too uncivilized to get any good from books, and that they certainly could not learn without a teacher. Hence arose the suggestion that missionaries be sent in place of books. As soon as this idea was broached thousands of volunteers offered themselves, and the plan would certainly have been attempted if there had been the slightest possibility that one could live to reach the earth.

"The next proposal came from the medical profession. Long before this time, when the inhabitants of the moon were sometimes governed by their passions and before the day of peace and good will had fully arrived, it had been discovered that what was known as the pugnacious instinct was only a disease, bad blood in fact as well as in name, and a remedy had been found for it. This was nothing less than the bi-chloride of comet. Small comets, such as we call meteorites, were picked up on the surface of the moon and put to this practical use. This medicine, administered as an hypodermic injection, produced wonderful effects, the patient, although afflicted with the most quarrelsome disposition, becoming as mild and harmless as a lamb. However warlike one might be, a few days' treatment would take the fighting spirit out of him so completely that the mere doubling up his fists and placing them in front of his face would make him feel ill. Peace societies got hold of the remedy and tried it on the soldiers of the standing armies with such success that war had to be abandoned because the men would not fight.

"And now the old recipe was brought out, a large quantity of the medicine manufactured, and bombs made and filled with it, each one containing full directions for its use written in Volapiik. These were fired to the earth, and, strange to say, the simple language was soon learned, and the moon- dwellers had the satisfaction of seeing men rapidly metamorphosed into a peaceable, friendly race. Thus the moon directly influenced and governed affairs on the earth. Looked at from that distance it seems to have been the most remarkable case of the tail wagging the dog that the earth had ever seen.

"But we may as well relate the sequel. The effect of the treatment lasted only a few hundred years, and as it was the moon's policy never to repeat a cure, men in time became as bad as ever again, and so at last the flood had to come and wipe them off the face of the earth."

CHAPTER XVII
THE DOCTOR IS CONVINCED

As I finished the doctor looked somewhat bored, but Thorwald was kind enough to thank me, and then, at our earnest solicitation, he resumed his argument.

"You have told me," he said, "of some of your earlier beliefs about the origin of meteorites. Have you any more modern views?"

To this the doctor replied: "If my friend here has really finished talking for a while I will say, Thorwald, that the theories already spoken of seem to be disproved by the discovery that these stones enter the earth's atmosphere with a planetary velocity. A body falling from an infinite distance--that is, impelled only by the attraction of gravitation--would strike the earth with a velocity of only six or seven miles a second, while the meteorites come at the rate of twenty to thirty miles a second, the earth's rate of revolution being nineteen miles in the same time. It is found that a necessary consequence of these velocities is that the meteors move about the sun, and not the earth, as the controlling body. Our latest study points to the conclusion that they are of cometary origin, and, as comets have been known to divide, some scientists believe the meteorites are fragments of exploded comets. At any rate, they are found in the company of these mysterious bodies, and appear to have similarly eccentric orbits."

"Your studies are leading you in the right direction," said Thorwald. "The meteorites do indeed come from the regions of space, and if they have any story to tell it is a story of those distant parts of the universe about which any testimony is valuable. Let us look again at the fragment we are supposed to hold in our hand. Can we tell of what it is composed, or is its substance something entirely new? I am sure you must have analyzed it down to its minutest particle, and if so you have found it contains nothing foreign to the earth. There is not a single element in the meteorite that does not exist also in the crust of the earth. Tell me, Doctor, how many elements have you discovered in them?"

"Nearly thirty," answered the doctor. "And one interesting fact is, that the three elements most common in the earth--iron, silicon, and oxygen-- are also found most widely distributed among the meteorites."

"That is an exceedingly significant fact," said Thorwald; "and now do you not see how strongly the meteorites confirm the story of the spectrum, and how everything tells us the universe is one in its physical structure? By these two widely different sources of information you find that beyond doubt other heavenly bodies are made of like materials with the earth. Is it not time now to give your imagination just a moment's play and look upon some of those distant orbs as the probable abode of life?"

"There I cannot follow you," responded the doctor. "I am wanting in imagination; probably born so, as some people are born without an ear for music. Let us stick to facts. Among the recent discoveries in the field of which we have been talking was the finding of some small diamonds in a meteoric mass. Upon this some enthusiastic writer, whose imaginative soul would be your delight, Thorwald, built this argument: 'Diamonds being pure carbon, their existence necessitates a previous vegetable growth. Hence vegetable life in other worlds is proven, and if vegetable life, it is fair to presume the existence of animal life also. Of course, then, there must be intelligent life, and therefore the stars, or the planets that revolve around the stars, are all filled with men.' This I call not reasoning, but guessing."

"And still," quickly responded Thorwald, "the discovery of diamonds in meteorites was a valuable link in the chain of evidence which you are putting together. Keep on with your investigations. Some time positive knowledge will come to you as it has come to us. But let me appeal once more to your reason. At an earlier stage of development your race no doubt believed the earth was the center of the universe, around which all the heavenly bodies swept in magnificent circles. You have learned that the earth itself, which was formerly thought to be so important an object, is only one of those heavenly bodies flying through space. You find the earth resembles its nearest companions in being subject to the same laws of motion which govern them, but you have yet to learn that they resemble the earth in the main purpose of their creation. You go into the forest and see thousands of trees. You can find no two alike, and yet all are alike in every material respect. Even the myriads of leaves are all different, and yet all alike. So why may not the millions of stars that fill the sky be like our own sun and like each other, differing in such immaterial things as size and brilliancy, color and constitution, but alike in the chief object of their being, the giving of light and heat, as vivifying forces to dark bodies surrounding them? And why may not these planets resemble the earth in being, at some stage of their existence, the theater of God's great designs?

"Let me try to excite your imagination in another way, Doctor. Suppose you should by and by awake and find this visit to Mars only a dream, and then suppose it should be revealed to you in some superhuman way that man was indeed the only race of intelligent beings in the whole universe; that the other planets and all the stars were of no real use; that not one world from that vast region of the milky way and far distant nebulae would ever send forth a note of praise to its Creator, and that the tiny earth was, after all, the center and sum of the universe--tell me, would you not feel lonesome?"

"When you put it in that way, Thorwald," replied the doctor, "I begin to see how unreasonable my position must appear to you. But, however pleasant the idea, I do not see how I can believe that other worlds are inhabited without more evidence than we now possess. This is speaking, of course, without the knowledge we have gained since coming here. But I do not mind saying that your talk has made me wish I could believe it."

I was glad for several reasons that the doctor acknowledged as much as this. First, for Thorwald's sake; for I had been thinking the doctor's obduracy was proving a poor reward for our friend's great kindness to us. I rejoiced, too, that my companion was beginning to show our new acquaintance that, although he had little imagination, he was possessed of a good heart. And, finally, I was myself so much in sympathy with Thorwald's views that I was glad to see his arguments begin to make some impression on the doctor's mind.

But now it seemed to me that Thorwald had much to tell us from his own experience. He had talked so far on this subject from the standpoint of our earthly knowledge, but had hinted more than once that the inhabitants of Mars had more positive evidence than we had ever dreamed could be possible. So I said:

"Your arguments have been very acceptable to me, Thorwald, but can you not strengthen even my faith by speaking now from the results of your own more advanced studies? We must base our belief in the existence of life outside the earth on mere probabilities, which, however strong, lead only to theory and leave us still in doubt. Have you any certain knowledge on the subject, or, I might say, had you any before we came to see you?"

"Oh, yes," replied Thorwald, "we have long had evidence almost as positive as your presence here, fresh from one of our sister planets. It will give me great pleasure to tell you of some of our marvelous achievements in astronomy. The doctor says he would like to believe in the habitability of other worlds; he must believe in it before I am through if he has any faith in me.

"I would like to say, to begin with, that whatever we have accomplished in this science you on the earth can accomplish. I know enough by comparing your development with our own to feel sure that our present condition foreshadows yours, and that all the knowledge we possess in various directions will come in time to you. Let nothing discourage you in your quest for knowledge. If you seem to have arrived at the limit of possibilities in the telescope, for example, have patience. Difficulties which you think insurmountable, time will remove, and you will be able to penetrate more and more into the mysteries of the universe.

"Our telescopes have gradually increased in power until we have been able to accomplish things that you will no doubt think truly marvelous. But, before you call any achievement in this science impossible, just look back and compare the ignorance of the early inhabitants of the earth with your present knowledge; and do not be so proud of the wisdom already attained that you cannot also look forward to an enlarged comprehension of things you now call mysteries, and to a much closer acquaintance with the works of God.

"To our increasing vision the heavens have continued to unfold their wonders. We have penetrated far into the depths of space only to marvel, at each new revelation, at the power and wisdom of the Creator. The number of stars discovered to our view would be incredible to you, and yet it will be interesting to you to learn that we can still place no bounds to creation. We have, it is true, found the limits of what we call our universe and have mapped out all its boundaries. When this had been done we tried to pierce the surrounding darkness, but for a long time, in spite of our belief that we could not yet see the end, all beyond seemed a void. Recently, however, our faith has been rewarded, for we can now see other universes, buried in far space but revealed dimly to the higher powers of our telescopes.

"But you are doubtless eager to hear of some more definite knowledge gained from this wide domain. Well, we have determined the distances, size, and motions of many of the stars, resolved star clusters and nebulae, solved the mystery of the double and variable stars, and, what is of more consequence than all these things, we have in many instances discovered the secondary bodies themselves, revolving around a central sun. We now know, what we so long suspected, that the rolling stars are suns like our own, giving light and heat to attending worlds. With this knowledge, can you wonder, Doctor, that we acquired the belief that these worlds, resembling so much the planets of our own system, are fit homes for intelligent beings?"

"I cannot see," replied the doctor, "that such a belief necessarily follows your discovery, which, I must own, was an exceedingly valuable one. I can readily believe that each star that shines in our sky is a sun surrounded by dependent bodies so dark as to be invisible through our terrestrial telescopes, but still I presume even your instruments are not powerful enough to find any inhabitants on those distant worlds?"

"No," replied Thorwald, "but for what other conceivable purpose were these bodies created?"

"I frankly acknowledge that I am not able to answer that question," said the doctor. "If you have many more wonderful discoveries to relate I shall soon have to own myself convinced."

"I am trying to convince your reason," resumed Thorwald, "without the aid of positive evidence, but I may as well proceed now to show you what further knowledge we have gained.

"The nearer planets of our own solar system have been naturally the objects of our close scrutiny. As our telescopes increased in power we diligently studied the surface of these globes, searching for signs of life. We mapped out their features, noted the various phenomena of season and climate, and discovered many ways in which they seemed to be like our world. But for a long time we found no direct evidence that they were inhabited.

"At length, however, one ardent philosopher, full of hope, as we all were, that we had neighbors on some of these globes, brought out the idea that if these neighbors were as far advanced in astronomical science as we were, there ought to be some means of communication between one world and another. The thought took at once, and occasioned the most lively interest. We had no doubt, from what we had learned of these planets, that they were fitted to be, at some time, the home of intelligent beings. Our question was whether the inhabitable period of either of them coincided with that of Mars, and, if so, whether the race was sufficiently developed to be able to see us as well as we could see them.

"The first means suggested to attract the attention of such a race of beings was fire. You can imagine that we could get together material enough to make a pretty big blaze, and we did. We lighted immense fires in various places and kept them burning a long time, but without accomplishing anything. We scanned minutely the surface of each planet, but saw no sign anywhere that our effort at communication was recognized.

"Disappointed, but not discouraged, we determined next to try a system of simple hieroglyphics by throwing up huge mounds on one of our plains. We thought, if other eyes were studying Mars as closely as we were searching the surface of our sister planets for signs of life, that they would notice any unusual change in our appearance. Then if they did notice it we hoped some means would be found to let us know it.

"It was decided to try first the figure of the circle, because we knew that the form of all heavenly bodies must be the most familiar to intelligent life wherever it existed. It took years of labor to construct the mound, for it was thought best to have it large enough to give the experiment a thorough trial. And now you may believe we considered ourselves well repaid for all our toil and expense when, soon after the circle was completed, our telescopes showed us a similar form actually growing upon the surface of both Saturn and Uranus. We immediately replied by beginning the construction of a square, and before this was finished both planets began to answer, one with the triangle and the other with the crescent. The latter was made by Uranus, and as soon as it was finished the triangle began to appear beside it, showing to us that Uranus was reading from Saturn also.

"Other signs followed, although, of course, the work was very slow, and the experiments are still in progress. Some slight beginning has been made toward the interchange of ideas. The time and labor required will alone prevent extended communication, which would make it possible to form, in the course of ages, a mutual language. As we were the first to start it we propose to try to control the conversation, but if Saturn and Uranus choose to steal our idea and gossip between themselves, we know of no way to stop them."

As Thorwald proceeded with this marvelous recital, it was interesting to watch the doctor's face. It was so apparent to me that he was fast losing his skepticism that I was not surprised to hear him say:

"Thorwald, one fact is worth more to me than a world of theory, and if you had begun by relating this wonderful experience you would not have found me so incredulous. Who could refuse to believe with such testimony before him? What news this will be to take back to the earth! But you have, doubtless, other discoveries to relate to us. Excuse me," the doctor continued, turning to me, "for interrupting, even for a moment, our friend's most interesting discourse."

"Let me say," resumed Thorwald, "that your interruption has been helpful to me, for now I know you have lost your doubts and believe with us in this matter."

"These efforts at communication have occupied us for generations, and the close study which we have been obliged to give to the surface of the other planets has made us well acquainted with their characteristics. We have found many likenesses to our own world, as well as various points of difference. The succession of the seasons has been an interesting phenomenon. We have watched with delight the ever-changing rings of our neighbor, Saturn, and can show you pictures of them as they were thousands of years ago."

"We have taken great pleasure in observing the round of seasons on the surface of the earth, not dreaming that we should ever have the privilege of talking face to face with its inhabitants."

"Well, now that we are here, Thorwald," said the doctor, "we want to get all the information possible. So please go on and tell us more of your discoveries. How about those bodies that you have found circling like planets around other suns? Have you any evidence in regard to their inhabitants? Your telescopes cannot surely bring any such bodies near enough to enable you to communicate with them."

"True," replied Thorwald, "but this is another instance where nature has lent us her assistance. If you have been surprised at some things that I have already said, you will probably find what I am about to relate equally outside of your experience."

CHAPTER XVIII.
STRUCK BY A COMET.

The most remarkable event in the realm of matter that ever occurred in connection with this planet, of which we have a record, was its collision with a comet. This was many ages ago and it made an epoch in our history, so that we say such a thing occurred so many years before or after the collision. Although the records are rather meager we know enough of the details to have a fair understanding of the wonderful event.

"The comet had no established period, as so many others have, but seemed to be an entirely new-comer, and from its first appearance showed plainly that it was making straight for our planet. The astronomers predicted at once what the inevitable result would be, and you can imagine the consternation of the world as this monstrous, fiery object bore down upon us, increasing in size and splendor every day, until it filled half the sky and threatened to engulf us in flame and destruction. There seemed to be no possible escape, and, in fact, there was to be no escape from a collision, but almost all the harm that followed was the result of pure fright. For as the comet came rushing upon us the whole hemisphere of Mars was filled with its blazing substance, which appeared, however, to burn itself out in our atmosphere, and to leave, in most cases, nothing to reach the ground.

"Perhaps you have seen a shower of falling stars on the earth, brilliant and threatening in appearance, but causing in reality little damage. So the comet came to us. Its immense, fiery volume, which filled us with such dread, was so diffused that it was nearly all consumed by impact with our atmosphere. But there was a great solid nucleus, which struck the ground with immense force, and remains as our largest meteorite.

"Thus not only was our world spared from destruction, but that which threatened to be such an evil proved to be a great acquisition. For the comet, as it is still called, has revealed to us the most astonishing secrets. For a long time the mass of matter lay untouched, superstition and the lack of scientific curiosity tending to preserve it as it fell. But at length the spirit of inquiry proved to be too strong, and within a comparatively recent period the comet has been broken into and explored with wonderful results.

"You must know, to begin with, that this greatest natural curiosity on the face of our planet is no common meteorite such as you are acquainted with. Indeed, if it had struck the earth as fair a blow as it did us I think the shock would have been felt much more severely by your little race, for it is hundreds of miles in diameter and the velocity with which it was traveling was simply incredible. Fortunately it fell upon an uninhabited plain, partly burying itself in the ground, and for several years the mass was so hot that it could not be approached. This helped to make it an object of awe and almost of veneration, so that many centuries of time passed before any critical examination was made of it. Even then nothing was accomplished toward revealing its marvelous secrets. The surface was found to be hard and metallic, with the familiar burned appearance caused by contact with the atmosphere, and the substance, in its chemical composition, resembled, with some variation, other meteoric specimens. Some attempt was made to penetrate into the interior of the mass, but all that was discovered led to the belief that it was of similar structure throughout.

"This was the extent of the knowledge obtained of the interesting object until the beginning of the present age of advanced civilization.

"When we had learned by our successful experiments that some of our sister planets were inhabited, and when our powerful telescopes had revealed what we believed to be planets of other systems, there was intense interest in the search for any evidence of life in these more distant worlds. They were so very far away that we doubted if we could ever know enough about them to tell whether they were habitable, and it seemed as if we could only judge of their condition from analogy with our own solar system. These views prevailed until the brilliant suggestion was made, and it is not known by whom it was first advanced, that perhaps we had, right here with us, the means of discovering what we so much desired to know. It had always been assumed that our comet was of uniform structure, but why let such a matter rest in uncertainty? It is one of the strange things in our history that this question was not seriously asked long before that time. But now that the idea was broached the work was entered into with great earnestness.

"This was the position: Here was this huge mass that had come to us from some unknown region of the sky, almost certainly from beyond the bounds of our solar system, and we were to pry into it to see if it had any story to tell us of its former condition. The advancement of science had given us the means of easily penetrating into the interior of the comet, and it was determined to make thorough work of it. And this feeling was found to be necessary, for the enterprise proved to be discouraging for many years. An immense tunnel was made through the entire mass, and nothing was found to repay the trouble. Many were now in favor of abandoning the work, but after a period of rest another trial was decided upon and a second tunnel begun. Never did perseverance have a more perfect reward; for, before the new excavations had proceeded far, discoveries were made which suddenly changed our comet, in regard to which most people had lost all interest, into the most wonderful object in all the world.

"In short, we now know that we have here a fragment of a former planet. How the planet was dismembered and how this piece happened to come flying to us, we do not know. But could it have come about more fortunately for us if it had all been designed by an over-ruling power? When we had learned all that our expanding but limited intelligence could teach us of the other parts of the universe, and when our minds were ripe for more knowledge, we found this magnificent object lesson, which had been waiting for us all these years. Beneath the uninviting surface of that familiar comet were revealed wonders which, if they had been discovered when the mass first came, would not have been half-appreciated, but which now told us, in answer to our eager inquiries, more than we ever thought to know about the far-distant works of our God."

The doctor and I were amazed beyond measure by this recital, and were quite ready to admit that a superior intelligence had directed the wonderful event. But we were exceedingly anxious to know some of the details of the discovery, and when the doctor had expressed this wish Thorwald proceeded:

"I could talk on this subject," he said, "till night-fall if you desire, but it will be better for you to restrain your curiosity till you can be taken in person to the scene.

Let me tell you in general terms what you will find. The comet fell, as I have said, in an uninhabited plain, but it is now at the door of the largest city on our planet, which has been built there since the discoveries were made. The excavations have left an immense opening, where galleries and chambers of great extent have been dug out. These have been finished off with untold labor, and new ones are being constantly added. Here is our greatest museum, beside which all other collections of natural objects are as nothing, for all that has been found in the comet remains there; nothing has been allowed to be taken away. You will appreciate something of the wonderful character of these curiosities when I tell you that they give evidence of a world many times larger than Jupiter and of an intellectual and spiritual development as much beyond ours as ours is in advance of that of the earth.

"We have exhumed buried cities in our own planet more than once, where volcano or other convulsion had overwhelmed them, and found the relics of past civilization; but here, in our comet, we look not upon the past but upon the future, as it were, and see what has been done in a world much older than our own. The belief that the comet did not originate in our solar system has been verified, for we find that the globe of which it was once a part revolved around an immense sun which had a retinue of twenty- seven planets of various sizes. Whether this great sun is one of the stars of our firmament we can only conjecture; perhaps in some future state of existence we shall know.

"You have wondered if the earth will ever advance to the condition in which you find us, and we are asking the same question in regard to ourselves and the still higher development exhibited in our comet. My opinion is that these very discoveries are to be in a measure the means of our advancement. We are only beginning to make out their wonderful character. As we learn more of them we hope to find out more closely how that people lived, and to be directed in our upward path by their example. In the pursuit of this knowledge we are hampered by our ignorance of their language. All that we know of them and their planet has been gained by their very suggestive pictures and illustrations, for of their written records, which exist in great abundance, we can as yet make nothing. In our former studies of the different languages of our own world we found something common to them all, upon which we could work; but in this case an entirely new principle seems to obtain, and the problem so far baffles all our skill. So you see here is something for us to do, and when we have accomplished the task, as I have no doubt that result will come, we shall then be able to study in detail that remarkable civilization the knowledge of which is wisely kept from us until we can understand and appreciate it.

"You come here from your young planet, representing a race that is still struggling with the lower forms of materialism, and find us so much in advance of your condition that perhaps you imagine we are perfect. We ourselves know we are far from that state, especially since we have been able to compare our development with the higher civilization of the people who once lived on our comet."

Thorwald paused a moment, and the doctor, who showed by every indication that he was engrossed in the subject, took occasion to remark:

"We certainly have harbored the thought you attribute to us, Thorwald. After all you have told us of your freedom from trouble, of the dethronement of selfishness and the reign of love, of your great achievements in every art, and of your ideal life in general, we shall always look upon you as a perfect race. How is it possible to rise to a higher plain? Can you express in terms suited to our comprehension your idea of that advanced state of existence of which you find indications on your comet? What is the character of that development?"

"You will perhaps understand something of its character," answered Thorwald, "if I say it is almost entirely spiritual. While we have made some progress in that direction, our superiority over the earth-dwellers is chiefly in physical and intellectual attainments. In the realm of the spirit we have yet far to go, and as long as we can see imperfections in our nature we feel that there is something ahead for us to strive after. With that example before us of a much more exalted life, we shall not be satisfied until we have learned its secrets and attained to its perfections. In this upward march we shall be sustained and helped by the same divine Power that has thus far led us."

CHAPTER XIX.
I DISCOVER THE SINGER.

We were much impressed by Thorwald's earnest words and manner, and we began to realize that the civilization of Mars was above our most exalted conception. I had been so carried away by the topics which I had feared were going to be uninteresting that I had lost some of the restlessness of the morning, but as our sitting broke up and I noticed it was drawing near noon my anxious thoughts returned. Finding Fronda and learning from her from what direction Avis might be expected to come, I determined to go out alone and see if I could meet her. I managed to get away without the fact being noticed, as far as I could discover, and started down the walk at a brisk pace. The houses were a good distance apart and were all attractive enough to draw out both wonder and admiration, had my mind been in a condition to appreciate their beauty. Occasionally an electric carriage would pass me, but the first pedestrian I met was a woman of noble bearing and about the age of Fronda, I should judge. After all I had heard of the physical and mental perfections of the inhabitants of Mars, I did not expect to see any but good-looking people. In this we were never disappointed, though still there were gradations of beauty even there. This woman whom I had met must have been at one time strikingly handsome, and if time had robbed her of any of that quality it had made it up by giving her a rare sweetness that fully atoned for the loss. As I was about to pass her she looked at me with such a pleasant and agreeable curiosity that I stopped and said:

"Pardon me, but may I ask you a question?"

"Certainly," she answered in a charming voice, "and I shall be very glad to help you in any way. I recognize that you are one of the earth- dwellers, and I have met your companion the doctor."

"Is it possible? I wonder he has not told me of such good fortune. But this is the question I wanted to ask you. As you came along this path did you see a young girl named Avis?"

"I did not, I am sure. I have met no young girl, and I could not see any one by the name of Avis."

"Why so?"

"Because there is no such girl."

"Excuse me," I said, "but probably you do not know her. I have just come from one of the houses yonder, where she is expected about noon, and I came out to try and meet her."

"Do you know her?" she asked.

"No--or, rather, I hope so; I cannot tell till I see her."

"That's curious. Have you ever met her?"

"I am not sure. I hope I have. I cannot explain it to you just now, but the minute I put my eyes on Avis I shall be able to answer all your questions."

"But her name cannot be Avis."

"Oh, yes, it is. It is quite plain that you do not know her."

"I beg your pardon," she returned, "there is but one person in all this country by the name of Avis."

"Then that is the very person I am trying to find."

"You have found her."

"Where?"

"Right here. I am she."

I laughed outright and said:

"Oh, no, you must be mistaken. I do not mean to be disrespectful, but the Avis I am looking for is young, younger than I am--evidently another person of your name, whom you have never met."

"How do you know she is young?"

"Why," I answered, "of course she is young."

And then, when I thought of it a moment, I remembered that no one had told me her age, but I added:

"I know she is young, because I have heard her sing."

It was now my companion's turn to laugh, but although her merriment was at my expense its expression, like all her actions, was exceedingly pleasing. The thought occurred to me that even the most cultured of the earth's inhabitants have still much to learn in the realm of manners.

"Oh, do you imagine," she asked, in the midst of her laughing, "that you can tell one's age in Mars from the quality of the voice? Does this Avis of yours sing well?"

"Excellently well. Until I heard her I had supposed there was but one singer anywhere, in earth, sun, moon, or star, possessed of such a sweet and thrilling voice."

"And where, if I may ask, did you find that one?"

"Oh, the doctor and I discovered her in our travels. I will tell you all about her when I have more time. Now will you excuse me while I continue my search for Avis?"

"You have forgotten," she answered, "what I told you. I am Avis."

"Not my Avis, the singer."

"Yes, the very same, and I can prove it."

"How?"

She answered by turning half around, lifting her head, and sending out on the air one full, rich note. It poorly describes my emotions to say I was astonished. If I had been blind and dependent only on what I heard at that moment, I should have thrown myself at her feet and called her Mona. It brought back to me not only every expression of Mona's marvelous voice, but also every feature and every grace which had formerly so bewitched me. If I had loved her passionately when we were together in the body, it would be difficult to characterize my feelings now that she was present only in memory. These sensations swept over me rapidly, but before I could utter a word my companion spoke again:

"I see you hesitate. Let me complete my proof by saying that you are visiting, with Zenith and Thorwald, at the house of Fronda, and have heard me sing two nights in succession."

"Then," I exclaimed, with sorrow and despair in my voice, "I have indeed found Avis, but, alas! I have once more lost Mona."

"How so?"

"Why, don't you see? I expected to find Mona and lose Avis. I thought Avis was Mona, a thought born partly of hope, I suppose, but it did not seem possible that there could be two such singers. So you are really Avis. I must try and remember that, and not express any more sorrow at not losing you. If Avis could not be Mona it is certainly a great consolation to find her in you. Let me return with you to Proctor's; and now, will you not sing for me as we walk?"

"Are you so fond of singing, or is it because you like to be reminded of Mona?"

"Both, I assure you."

"Does my voice sound like hers in conversation?"

"Oh, no, Mona never talked as we do. Everything she wanted to say she sang."

"You surprise me," said Avis. "I should think she would soon become tiresome to her friends."

"If you had ever known her you would not make such a remark as that."

"I beg your pardon," she quickly returned. "I presume you are right. And now, to atone for wounding your feelings, I will sing till we come in sight of Fronda's house."

"I thank you very much, and I promise you I shall walk as slowly as possible."

She sang some sweet little things for me as we sauntered along, attracting me powerfully and making it easier for me to conceal my great disappointment.

When we reached the house Avis explained, in a few pleasant words, the fact of our acquaintance, and as soon as family and guests were all gathered for the noonday lunch I told them about my peculiar forgetfulness of what had occurred on the moon and then about the manner in which the events had been brought back to my mind. They showed more interest in the latter part of my relation than in the former, and when I was through the doctor said:

"I must confess to you now, my friend, that I told these good people something about your aberration. It was entirely for your own sake, for I wanted their help in bringing about your recovery, and now that we have been successful I hope you will forgive me."

"You know there is nothing to forgive," I replied. Then Zenith said:

"The doctor implies that we have all helped in the happy result, but I can tell you that it is entirely due to himself and Avis. He happened to meet Avis and heard her sing. He was struck at once with the likeness between her voice and Mona's, about whom he had told us, and he conceived the idea that if you could hear it when you were alone, say in the night, and not know who the singer was, it might be the means of bringing the forgotten circumstances all back to you. From what the doctor has told us we have, every one of us, fallen in love with Mona, and I presume when we get your estimate we shall think none the less of her. If I am correctly informed you found her especially attractive."

"In answer to your kind expressions of interest in me, Zenith, I will say that, in spite of my appreciation of what you are all doing for us, I shall never see another really happy moment until Mona is found."

"Then," quickly responded Thorwald, "we must redouble our efforts to find her. I must tell you that ever since the doctor first acquainted us with the loss of Mona we have had parties searching for her in all that part of the ocean."

"How thoughtful you are," I exclaimed. "But why do we not hurry home? Perhaps she is found."

"I regret to add to your sorrow," said Thorwald, "but we should learn of it here as quickly as at home, for I am in constant communication with my friends who are conducting the search. Still, we have been staying here for you and can now bring our visit to a close at any time."

So after lunch we bade adieu to Proctor and his household, and started for home, the same way we went out--that is, by going west again. As we made a leisurely journey and enjoyed a good night's rest on the way, it was just before noon when we arrived at Thorwald's house. Here we found Antonia, who had been advised of our coming by telephone, and had prepared a nice lunch for us. Just as we were all about to sit down to enjoy it, a young man entered unannounced and, without formal invitation, joined us in gathering about the board. This was not an instance of undue familiarity, as we soon discovered, but illustrated again the free and hearty hospitality of these generous people.

"Foedric," said Thorwald, as soon as the guest had been greeted, "let me present you to these two friends from the earth. You doubtless have heard of their arrival."

"I have," answered Foedric, "and I am exceedingly pleased to make their acquaintance." And then turning to the doctor, he said:

"We shall not let Thorwald and Zenith have the monopoly of your company while you are visiting our world. Many others are anxious to see you and to learn something of our sister planet."

"There is not much to learn," said the doctor, "from such an unripe race as we represent, and I must say your people have not exhibited any unpleasant curiosity."

"I am glad you have not been annoyed. We understand too well what is due you as our guests to crowd our attentions upon you, but you will allow me to say that already the main facts in your case are known all over our world, and our scientists are discussing the earth and its inhabitants in the great light of the knowledge which you have brought."

Foedric spoke with ease, and yet with entire absence of youthful pedantry. The doctor and I could but admire his fine face and robust form, as well as his manly courtesy and friendliness. And before the meal was over we discovered that one other person at the table admired him, probably for the same and many other qualities. It seemed to us accidental when Foedric had dropped in upon us and chosen a seat next to Antonia, but it soon became evident that we had not witnessed even that kind of an accident.

What was exhibited to us there, among that highly developed people, was a genuine, old-fashioned, new-fashioned love affair. We rejoiced in our hearts to find that their advanced civilization left abundant room for the development of the tender passion, and that it also seemed not to discourage a plain and sensible exhibition of it. For these two young people made no effort to conceal their happiness. Not the company of their chosen friends nor the presence of strangers from a distant world caused them the slightest embarrassment, as they spoke from time to time their words of love, simple words to other listeners, but full of meaning to themselves.

"Say that again, Antonia," spoke Foedric.

"Why do you ask me to repeat it so often? I have said it so many times and with so little variety of expression that I fear the monotony will tire you. You can tell how strong my devotion is by my every look and action."

"Very well," Foedric responded, "then I, too, will be silent."

"Oh, no; I retract what I have said if it is to have that effect. It is only my own expressions that seem tiresome. I could not be happy without your voice in my ears, though you repeat from morn till eve the old, familiar words."

"Then you must believe the same of me," said Foedric.

As we all happened to be listening to these two at that moment, Foedric looked up to our host and said:

"Thorwald, do you think Antonia and I had better try to reform the customs of the world, and do away with all verbal expression of our attachment, on the ground that it is unnecessary and only a waste of breath?"

"If some cruel master should force such a prohibition upon you, Foedric, what would be your feeling? The heart craves such expression as naturally as the body craves food. Suppose a couple were to start off by saying once for all that they loved each other, and then agree to live the rest of their lives on that one expression. They would argue that all such sentiment was folly, and interfered with the serious business of life, and so, denying a healthy appetite, their hearts would shrivel up and the fair blossom of their love would soon wither and die."

As we smiled at Thorwald's words, Zenith showed her interest by saying:

"The subject reminds me of that epoch in our history of which we read, when all the world went without eating for a time."

"Without eating?" asked the doctor.

"Yes, I will tell you about it. Once science reached that condition where it thought it could make the world over and improve on the first creation in a great many ways. Men began to say that the time spent in cooking and eating was all wasted, that time, being the most valuable thing they had, should be employed in some more useful way than in indulging a mere sensual passion. The appetite came to be looked upon as something too gross for intelligent beings and suited only to the natures of the lower animals. Under the influence of this growing sentiment, science soon discovered a process for condensing our food to wonderfully small proportions. All extraneous matter was rejected, and only those particles retained which were absolutely essential to our nourishment, chemical knowledge having reached a high state. The result was that it finally became possible to subsist a whole day on a single swallow. One pill, taken every morning, contained all the food required, both for the growth and maintenance of the body Science prided itself on such an advanced step, and men looked forward and wondered what further marvels the future would bring forth."

The doctor did not try to hide his interest in this recital, and as soon as Zenith paused he said:

"My friend and myself are most truly thankful that that custom did not continue to the present day. But did it remain long?"

"No," replied Zenith, "of course it could not. At first people thought it an immense gain. Just think of the time and expense it saved in every household, doing away with dining-room and kitchen, with all their furniture and utensils, and reducing the cares of housekeeping much more than half. But it proved to be a costly experiment, and nature soon exerted itself, as it always will in time. Science, not satisfied with what had been accomplished, kept striving after what it called more perfect results, and just as it had made a pellet of such powerful ingredients that it would sustain life for a week, men began to die rapidly of the treatment. This called a halt, but the damage done was serious enough to give the world a good fright, turn it back to the old fashioned habit of eating, and confirm us forever in that indulgence. Since then we have believed that such appetites are given us for a wise purpose and that, rightly enjoyed, they are a means of growth toward a more and more perfect state."

"This lesson from our experience then," said Foedric to Antonia, "is to teach us the plain duty of lavishing upon each other, without measure, our affectionate words, because it is a legitimate, healthy longing of our nature, and I sincerely hope you will take it to heart. Do not undertake to make me exist a week or a day on a single morsel."

As for myself, I was not so much engrossed in this talk as to forget my own condition, which seemed all the more forlorn by contrast with the unalloyed happiness of these joyous beings. I wondered if such affairs always went smoothly in Mars. Was early love always mutual, or did one sometimes refuse to be wooed and prefer another? And did it ever happen that the loved one was lost, as Mona was lost to me, perhaps never to be found?

But in the company of such happy people I felt that my anxious spirit was out of place, and I tried to cast off my forebodings and to seize from the image of Mona present in my memory a portion of her own cheer and hope. That I was not entirely successful my looks must have shown, for as we rose from the table Zenith said to me, with a look of sympathy:

"You are sad--I think I will send for Avis to come over and cheer you up."

This was spoken as if Avis were just across the street and could run over in a minute. But as I did not discourage the idea the invitation was sent, and before night Avis was with us, filling the house with melody. She delighted in her song and was as youthful in spirit as a girl, and this was a quality always noticeable in the Martians. And, moreover, under the influence of Avis the members of our own household found their voices, so that the doctor and I learned that they need not send to the antipodes for singers. Zenith and Foedric were exceptionally good, but no one except Avis possessed the peculiar charm of Mona.

CHAPTER XX.
A WONDERFUL REVELATION.

There was no way by which we could learn so much and so rapidly about that wonderful world as by conversation, so at every opportunity we tried to get Thorwald and the others to give us portions of their history. From time to time my companion and myself compared our impressions, and expressed to each other the pleasure we anticipated in relating all the amazing things we had seen and heard to our friends on the earth. The exceedingly doubtful problem of our ever getting back to our home again did not trouble us then.

We said to each other that the most startling things had probably all been told us, and that we could not be much surprised by anything that they could tell us further. And yet there was that to follow which, if we could fully enter into its significance, would make us forget much of what we had already heard, or at least care but little to recall it. In truth, the new revelation which we were about to receive from the lips of our friend was of so much value, and so different in character from the other subjects Thorwald had spoken of, that we afterward came to look upon all that had gone before as an introduction, perhaps intended to prepare our minds for a much grander truth. Yet it was brought out by a question from me, a question of whose importance I had little conception.

When Thorwald was ready to talk one day I said to him:

"We have heard you several times speak reverently of a God. Will you tell us definitely what your religion is?"

"With pleasure," he replied. "We worship one God, the maker of all things, and his Son, Jesus Christ, who gave his life for us."

"Why, how did you hear of his death, Thorwald?"

"I might better ask how you heard of it. Many centuries ago God saw fit to reveal himself more fully to us by sending his only Son, who came in the likeness of our flesh, dwelt among us, and by cruel hands was slain. He gave himself a sacrifice for our sins, but rose again from the dead, as we, too, shall rise. He ascended into heaven and through him we now have access unto the Father."

"But Jesus died on the earth too, and you but describe his relations to us."

"I rejoice greatly to hear it," answered Thorwald, "and I know now why you were sent to us. This information is of inestimable value to us, for we have spent much thought on the question of the moral government of other worlds that we knew were inhabited. In God's dealings with Mars, lifting up our souls and preparing us for his service and glory, we believed he was working in the very best way. There can be but one best way; and so, considering that there might be many other races of sinful beings needing a saviour, we wondered how God's mercy was revealed to them. This bright news which you bring is worth more to us at the present time than all other possible information about the earth or its people. The fact that the earth is inhabited was no great surprise to us after what we had learned of our larger neighbors, but this--this is news indeed.

"As an example of what our interest in this subject has prompted us to do, let me tell you that in our extremely laborious and limited intercourse with Saturn and Uranus we made the form of the cross. We all feared our work might be in vain and many doubted seriously the wisdom of proceeding with the undertaking, which occupied many years, when it was so probable that those distant people would not know what the sign meant. But we labored on, and before the form was fairly finished it was with the keenest pleasure that we saw the answer growing on the rounded surface of each planet. They worked, they stopped, and then we realized that both had replied to our question with the short straight line which, in our communications, has come to be the affirmative sign, or the 'yes' in the new universal language.

"We interpreted this answer to mean that the great redemption signified by the cross was known to the highly intelligent races that peopled these rolling worlds. But how did that knowledge reach them? To that question we never hoped to get an answer. Did a troop of bright angels issue forth from the gates of heaven and wing their way from one planet to another, as each race was ready for the joyful tidings, and make this glad announcement?--'Peace from heaven to this world! On Mars, your sister planet, a child was born, the Son of God, the Saviour of the universe. He lived a perfect life for your example, he died on the cross for your salvation. Believe in him, love him, follow him!'

"We thought much on this point, wondering reverently how God had wrought. And now you have come to explain all the mystery, to answer all questions. One simple sentence tells it all: 'Jesus died on the earth too.'

"I see it perfectly now. Christ, the Lord of heaven, came to us in the fullness of time, took upon him the likeness of our flesh, lived nobly, was slain, rose again from the dead, and ascended into heaven to prepare blessed mansions for all his followers. So, too, in the fullness of your time, when the earth was ready for the great sacrifice, Christ offered himself again. He appeared in human form and lived among men as he had lived with us, pointing your race, also, to a home of peace and joy above.

"Better than any announcement of angels of what had taken place in some other world was his actual life among you, going about doing good, shedding around him the spirit of love and self-denial, showing you the way to live, the way to die.

"Among the vast multitude of peopled worlds which God has made, there is doubtless great variety in nature and condition. But if there are any others whose inhabitants were ever in our lost condition, let us hope and believe that the same great act of mercy has been shown to them which has so greatly blessed the planets of our own system."

Here, at Thorwald's request, I told him briefly of the Saviour's advent on the earth in the fulfillment of prophecy, of his beautiful life, and then of the marvelous improvement his religion had brought about as it spread in the world.

Thorwald appeared intensely interested, and exclaimed: "Oh! how this truth you have told us does make brothers of us all, and how it will enhance the pleasure of our intercourse. Now in our future conversation we shall be in full sympathy, knowing that, though born so far apart, we are all followers of the same dear Master.

"Zenith," said Thorwald to his wife, who was sitting with us, "this is a happy day for us all. These earth-dwellers, these men who have come to visit our world, are not strangers; they are Christians. Think of it."

At this juncture I could not help studying the doctor's face, for I knew this was the first time he had ever been called a Christian. In spite of the seriousness of the situation, I was obliged to indulge in a quiet smile to think he had to go all the way to Mars to be recognized in his true character. For although he would not acknowledge the divine source of it, he had imbibed a great deal of the real Christian spirit. But he had spent his life in seeking for scientific knowledge in various directions and was content, as he often said, to leave the unknowable without investigation. I wondered whether, in these novel circumstances, he would care to give voice to his agnosticism. But the doctor was honest or he was nothing, and he could not endure that Thorwald should rest under the false impression implied by his closing words. So with some effort, as I could see, he said:

"I dislike exceedingly, Thorwald, to destroy the least particle of the effect of your eloquence, but I feel compelled to say that, as for me, I have never called myself a Christian."

"Not a Christian!" said Thorwald. "I do not understand you. But perhaps you use some other name. You surely do not mean that you turn aside from that divine being who came to the earth to save you."

"I do not know that such a being did come to the earth."

"What!" exclaimed Thorwald, "is there any doubt of it? Has your companion here been deceived? Must we give up our new-found joy?"

"Oh, no, no," answered the doctor hurriedly. "I suppose it is true that a good man named Jesus once lived on the earth and taught, and died a shameful death."

"A good man! Nothing more?"

"I don't know," answered the doctor.

"What do you believe?"

"I do not allow myself to have any belief."

"Well, now, Doctor, you are a thinking being. Considering all you know about Jesus--his noble life, his character and the character of his teachings, and then the claims he made for himself--what do you think of him?"

"Before such mysteries, and in answer to all questions relating to what is called the supernatural, I always say, 'I do not know.'"

"Well," continued Thorwald, "do you think the life and death of a good man could set in motion forces that would so transform the world and give it such a start toward a higher and more perfect state?"

To this the doctor replied:

"In the early part of this conversation my companion told you he thought the condition of man on the earth was improving, or, in other words, that the earth was growing better. In that opinion he has many supporters, but it is only fair that you should know that some of us hold just the opposite view. We see so much evil in the world, evil that is unrebuked and growing stronger from year to year, so many forces at work dragging men downward and such fearful clouds ahead, that it seems to us that the good is overmatched, and that there is but little hope of a happy future for our race. I will also say, in order to be perfectly frank, that even if we should admit that our civilization was advancing, we should not attribute it to the influence of the Jewish reformer."

"Then," said Thorwald, "if I understand your feeling, you have no love, no thanks even, for him who gave his life for you, and no sense of gratitude for the loving Father who sent his Son to die for your sins."

"I think you are hardly just," replied the doctor, "for I am not conscious of living a life of ingratitude. Your words imply a great deal that I know nothing about. I am not aware that anyone was ever sent from heaven to die for me, and I do not even know there is a heaven and a God."

"Did it ever occur to you, Doctor, that your attitude does not alter the facts? In spite of your unbelief, or indifference if you will, there is a God whose steps are heard throughout the universe, whose hand upholds all worlds, and who looks with loving eyes upon all created beings, even upon those who have the intelligence but not the heart to acknowledge him. Oh! it is amazing to me that there can be one such being in all God's dominions."

"Why, are there not any in Mars?"

"In Mars? Not one. Let me tell you, Doctor, that here you will be unique, if that is any consolation to you. When this talk is made public and the facts in your case are spread abroad everybody will want a share in bringing you to your right mind, and we shall see what the result will be with a world full of missionaries to one heathen."

"Please do not use that word, Thorwald. I was born in Boston--you must know where Boston is--of good old Puritan stock, and I am not a heathen because I don't know about some matters that I cannot, in the nature of things, know anything about. You found a while ago that I wanted imagination, and you now see that I am deficient also in faith, which it seems to me is a product of the imagination."

"No," broke in Thorwald, "faith might rather be called the product of reason and of the conscience, enlightened by every revelation which God has made. But with us faith is an instinct. We believe in God as naturally as we trust our parents. Our souls reach after divine things to satisfy their longings, just as our bodies seek the food that shall nourish them. In all this world there is not a heart devoid of love to God, not one that does not own a personal and joyful allegiance to the divine Saviour.

"But I forget that the earth is still young, and that, very long ago, when Mars was in your condition, representatives of our race actually walked the surface of this planet with no more thought of its Maker than you exhibit. Forgive me if, in this talk, I have seemed too positive of things which you claim cannot be known. But here there is no uncertainty in these matters. There is now no open question in regard to the existence of God and his loving care of us."

"But, Thorwald," asked the doctor, "how can you be sure? Help me to see these things as you do. In the matter of the habitability of other worlds you brought me over to your opinion by producing evidence which took away all uncertainty and left me no room to doubt. Is it so in this case?"

"No, my friend," answered Thorwald, "it is not so. The evidence in this case is of an entirely different character. Your companion has told me how God has dealt with men, by what means he has made known his will, and how he has revealed his love and mercy to your race. So has it been with us, only here we have had more time to acquaint ourselves with these blessed truths. If you ask for proofs, I can only say they are the same which have no doubt been reiterated many times in your ears. The voices that come to us from the invisible world are not tuned to the coarse fiber of our physical nature, but are addressed to our spirits, our very selves, and he who does not heed those voices would not be persuaded even though one should rise from the dead.

"Let me induce you, Doctor, to cultivate the spiritual part of your being, evidently undeveloped as yet, for only then will you begin to realize that the evidence in support of these divine truths is more convincing than any possible proofs that could be presented to our outward senses."

"Under your instruction," said the doctor, "and with the example of a world full of spirits of your faith and practice, I will do my best to follow your advice, and try to catch some faint strain from those heavenly voices. If I cannot believe, it shall no longer be because I will not. But now, Thorwald, you have given too much time to me and have been drawn away from your purpose of enlightening us in regard to your wonderful planet."

"Yes, Thorwald," said I, "we must hear more of your interesting history, and I think an account of what the religion of Jesus has done for Mars will help to win the doctor to right views."

"I shall take much pleasure in doing the best I can whenever you are good enough to listen," Thorwald answered. "But we shall now be still more anxious to hear further about the earth."

CHAPTER XXI.
A LITTLE ANCIENT HISTORY.

In the foregoing personal conversation, Thorwald had been uncompromising in look and tone, as well as in word, toward the errors of my friend, but for the doctor himself I was sure he had the kindest feelings. The discovery of the dearth of spiritual perception in the doctor was a greater surprise to Thorwald, I really believe, than our first appearance was. And it was a surprise well calculated to awaken in his finer nature a feeling as near akin to indignation as the Martian mind of that era was capable of experiencing. So we had here the opportunity of observing how a member of this highly civilized race, one endowed with such lofty attributes, would act under severe provocation. The exhibition was instructive. Thorwald certainly resented with all the force of his pure and upright nature all that was evil in the doctor's attitude. Such doubt was entirely new to his experience. He had no place for it; and he could do no less than cry out against it as he had done. But his manner softened as soon as the doctor's mood changed, and it was apparent that he was ready to encourage in every possible way the slightest indication of a change. And from this time Thorwald was particularly tender toward the doctor, evidently desiring to show him that, unbending to everything like disloyalty to God, he recognized his sincerity when he declared that he would no longer set his will against the reception of the truth.

In this mind Thorwald said:

"I perceive, Doctor, that your sturdy self-respect and the fear that you might appear in a false position have compelled you to be unfair to yourself. You believe more than you confess, else why did you repel with such feeling my insinuation that you were a heathen? But if you have ever determined to go through life believing in only what your hand can touch and your eye can see, let me induce you to close your eyes and fold your hands for a while, and with expectancy wait for the coming into your heart of that divine influence which, encouraged however feebly, shall presently show to your inner and better vision, in all his beauty, him whom no eye hath seen nor can see.

"I do not exclude you therefore, Doctor, when I say again that we have all been drawn into close sympathy by the knowledge your companion has imparted, and in what I have to say further I am sure you will both see a great deal to cause you to realize that your race and ours have the same dear Father, who is guiding us to a common destiny.

"At your request I am to give you from time to time, as we have opportunity, an account of the successive steps of our development, and I would like to say at the start that there will be one great difference between what I am to tell you and the rambling talk with which we began our happy acquaintance. Then I gave you a few facts to show our present condition, without intimating that there was any higher force at work than a natural desire in us to make the most of ourselves, and treat our neighbors well. Now, since I have discovered that you can enter into my feelings to a greater or less extent, I shall not hesitate to refer to its true source all that has helped us attain to our present condition, and all that is urging us on to a still higher state."

"We shall he very glad to know what you consider the spring of all the vast improvement in your race," I remarked.

"I did not use the word 'consider,'" replied Thorwald. "That would imply doubt where there is none. It is established beyond controversy that both our material and spiritual development have come only through the personal love and care of God for the creatures whom he has made, exhibited through all our history, but especially through the sending of his Son."

"Some on the earth recognize the same truth in reference to our race," I said. "But, in general, people do not think much of such things, or if they think they do not say much. In fact, religious subjects are not as a rule popular in conversation."

"Why, what reason can there be for that?" Thorwald inquired with eager interest.

"Oh, there is too much indifference in the matter," I replied. "I suppose most men do not think their relations to their Maker important enough to give them any concern. And even the best among us shrink from urging their opinions on others, partly because they know they are not perfect examples themselves, and also from the feeling that their friends are intelligent beings and ought to know, as well as they do, what is best for them."

"Oh, then, my dear Doctor," said Thorwald, "I perceive that I have committed a breach of etiquette in forcing this subject upon you, and in asking you to put yourself in the way of receiving spiritual impressions."

"In the circumstances, I think you are excusable," replied the doctor; "and, besides, I believe I introduced the topic."

"If you stay long with us," resumed Thorwald, "you will become accustomed to religious conversation, for here there is entire freedom in such matters. Our spiritual experiences and the great possibilities of the future state are exceedingly pleasant things to talk about, we think, and we feel no more sensitiveness in doing it than in conversing on the ordinary affairs of life. Being relieved of so many of the cares pertaining to your existence, our minds are the more prepared to occupy themselves with these high themes, and what is more natural than that we should often like to speak to each other about them? As these things become more real to you and the necessity of spending so much time in caring for the body diminishes, you will gradually lose your present feeling. You will also find that, in making these subjects familiar, they need not lose dignity and you need not lose reverence."

"Thorwald," asked the doctor, "could you not give us a brief sketch of your career, so that we may compare it with that of our race?"

"I will do the best I can," answered Thorwald. "I think that is a good suggestion, and after that is done any of us can tell you the history of different epochs as opportunity offers. You are both such good listeners that it is a pleasure to talk to you, but I want you to promise to interrupt me with questions whenever you wish anything more fully explained."

We promised to do so, and Thorwald began: "Our world is very old. The geologic formations tell us of a time when no life could exist--long ages of convulsion and change in the crust of the globe. In time the conflict of the elements subsided and the boundaries between land and water were established. Then came vegetable life, rank and abundant, preparing stores of coal and oil for use in the far future. Animals followed, the first forms crude and monstrous, but succeeded by others better adapted to be the contemporaries and companions of our race.

"The planet was now ready for its destiny, and it was put into the hands of intelligent beings, made in the image of their Creator. This race started in the highest conceivable state, perfect in body, mind, and spirit. The material world was soon subdued to their use, and paradise reigned below. We do not know how long this condition lasted, but in some way sin entered and all was changed. Sorrow and death came, and a thousand ills to vex us. Another period passed, and the race had become so wicked that it could not be allowed to exist. A pestilence swept over the world, and all but one tribe perished. Through this remnant the world was re-peopled, but sin and woe remained, to be driven out at last only by a struggle too great for the arm of flesh alone.

"But the conflict began in hope, a hope inspired by the voice of God. From the very entrance of sin help from above had been promised in the person of one who should conquer evil, and through whom the race might be restored to a much higher position even than that from which it had fallen. Slowly the spirit of good, which is the spirit of God, worked upon the heart, and in all ages there were some who walked in that spirit. By one such soul God raised up a people to whom he committed his message to the race, and through whom, at a later day, he fulfilled the promise. Among this people there arose many faithful ones, and by them, from time to time, God added to his message, acting as the personal guide and defender of his people, and leading them by every path until they finally knew him, in every fiber of their being, to be the only God.

"Prophets, too, there were among them, who, under divine guidance, foretold a time of universal peace, when the kingdom of Christ should come in all hearts and when even the beasts of the field should dwell together in unity."

"Why, we have just such prophecies," said I, "but they are generally interpreted figuratively. Do you really think they will be literally fulfilled on the earth?"

"Well," answered Thorwald, "I have already told you what has come to pass here, and I will leave you to judge from our experience as to what will come of the prophecies that have been made to you. From all you have said at one time and another, I can see plenty of evidence that the earth is traveling the same road with us, and I have no doubt it will one day reach even a higher condition than the one we now enjoy.

"At length, when the time was ripe, God sent the promised Saviour. He, the Lord of heaven, came and lived as one of us. He gathered around him a few faithful souls, he preached his gospel of light and comfort to the poor, and wept over the very woes he had come down to remove. His humility proved a stumbling-block to the selfishness of the world, and his own nation rejected him. He conquered death and returned to his Father's home, but his spirit, which had always been present in some measure, now came with force, and began, through his followers, the task of regenerating the race.

"A feeble church, planted thus amid sin and darkness, took deep root in loyal hearts, grew strong with persecution, and soon kindled a light which pierced the darkness and gradually spread its illumination over all our planet. The history of that church is the history of our development. The race has not come so far toward its maturity without a mighty struggle. The long course of preparation for the present higher condition has had many interruptions and obstructions. There have been dark ages of stagnation and threatened defeat, and there have been ages of hope and advancement. Through all this history the light of the gospel, though often obscured, has never been extinguished, and every step of progress that has been made in our condition is to be traced directly to that light. We have not always been able to realize that; but, now that we understand more fully our wonderful career, we see how true it is that we have been led by a divine hand."

"Do you mean," I asked, "that your vast improvement in material affairs has come through Christianity?"

"Certainly," answered Thorwald. "Our civilization has walked hand in hand with true religion, and in all ages every permanent advance in our condition has come through the influence of the spirit of good, which is always urging us to a higher and better state. In our progress many mistakes have been made, with consequences so serious as to threaten at the time our final defeat; but a higher power has led us through all our troubles to a place of safety, where we can survey with gratitude the field of conflict. If you so desire, I can relate to you at another time some of the mistakes which have at times set us back in our march toward a physical and spiritual superiority."

We were pleased to notice by this last remark of Thorwald's that he had still in reserve many things to tell us, and we so expressed ourselves to him.

CHAPTER XXII.
AGAIN THE MOON.

Days passed and brought no news of Mona. I did all in my power to appear cheerful, but often made a dismal failure of it. No one could help me, and Thorwald, though sympathetic like all the rest, would allow me no false hopes. He said a systematic and thorough search had been made, both on land and water, without result, and he could see no prospect of any success in the future. But, while I could see that Thorwald was about ready to abandon in despair the attempt to find Mona, I would not give up hope. I did not know at the time what excellent reasons Thorwald had for his feeling, for I did not realize how very complete the search had been, but my own faith was not founded on reason. I simply refused to believe that I should never see again the object of such deep love.

While affairs were in this condition, Thorwald said to us one morning:

"I wonder you have not been more anxious to see one of our flying machines. Our system of aerial navigation is one of the most enjoyable of our material blessings, and I shall take great pleasure in giving you a taste of it."

"I think one reason," I answered, "why we have not asked about it is because we have had so many other interesting things to see, and then you know we had our share of traveling in the air in coming to you. However, we shall be delighted to see your method at any time when you are pleased to exhibit it."

"Very well," said Thorwald; "then we will get up an expedition at once. Zenith and Avis will accompany us, I think; and as we shall probably fall in with Foedric, we will send for Antonia to go also."

"That will make a pleasant party," I said.

We found all were glad to go and witness our introduction to a modern air ship, and we were soon off.

Not far from the house we found a luxurious carriage of just the right size for us all. We did not see another like it anywhere about, and I was moved to ask:

"How does it happen, Thorwald, that exactly the kind of conveyance you want is ready without any prearrangement? This sort of carriage does not appear to be very plentiful."

"Things generally 'happen,' as you call it, for our convenience," he said. "Is it not so with you to some extent? If all the people wanted to travel in your cars on the same day and at the same hour, they could not easily be accommodated, but some dispensation divides them up so that there are, I presume, about the same number who find it necessary or convenient to travel each day. This subject has been studied by us, and we believe that even these details of our lives are all arranged by him to whom nothing is small, nothing great."

A pleasant ride of a few miles brought us to a seaport, and to a scene of much activity. It seemed to be a great distributing point, as numerous loads of many kinds of goods were moving about, and immense stores of fruit and vegetables were to be seen. These products of the soil were of bewildering variety and surpassing richness, showing us that agriculture, providing most of the food of the people, must be a favorite science with many, and one that brought rich rewards. It was pleasing to see everything going on in such a quiet, orderly manner, and so many people at work without friction and with no look of fret, hurry, or fatigue. Everyone seemed to be enjoying his work, if that could be called work which looked so much like pleasure.

After riding through several busy streets we drew near an imposing structure, which Thorwald told us was the front of the aerial station. At the same time he directed our attention to the sky, and we saw a number of air ships sailing leisurely along, some just starting out and others apparently returning home. The doctor and I had our interest quickened by this sight and were anxious for a closer view. As the fact of riding in the air was not new to us, we had not been much excited by the prospect of seeing how the Martians did it. But these ships were so different from anything we had ever seen before that we began to anticipate a great deal from our excursion after all.

Going through the building, we came into an immense court or open space, large enough, one would suppose, for the fleets of a nation. Here were a great number of flying machines of various sizes, all gayly decorated with pleasing colors, and many of them, apparently, waiting for passengers. Thorwald selected one of medium size, and as we approached, whom should we find in charge but our young friend Foedric? In answer to Thorwald's question, he told us that both he and his vessel were at our service, and we proceeded to mount to our seats in the car.

Foedric pulled a small lever, and we began to rise. He then expressed his pleasure to the doctor and me that he had the opportunity of making our further acquaintance.

"We are taking them for the ride," said Thorwald, "and you may choose any course and go to any height you please."

We thanked Foedric for his pleasant words, and then he showed us about the car and explained its conveniences. It was quite large, with a number of apartments and accommodations sufficient for a dozen people both day and night. Besides the ordinary furnishings for comfortable living, we saw air-condensing machines for use in lofty flights, a good-sized telescope, instruments for measuring speed and height, and other scientific apparatus of much of which we were obliged to ask the use.

Although Foedric was so much younger than Thorwald, he was taller and larger every way--a magnificent specimen of a magnificent race. In speaking to Thorwald he showed a proper respect for his greater age, and he bore himself becomingly in the presence of Zenith; but there was not the slightest sign of subserviency, nor anything to show that, though engaged in what might be called a lowly occupation, he was not on terms of perfect equality and even friendship with them. This easy poise of manner would not have surprised us had we known what Thorwald soon told us, and from this experience we learned never to judge a Martian by the work he happened to be doing.

"Foedric is a scholar," said Thorwald, "and is engaged just now in writing a treatise on the color of sounds."

This announcement was a double surprise, for we would have said, if he was writing anything, that it must be something about ballooning--the application of electricity to flying machinery, perhaps. But Thorwald further enlightened us, the talk going on in Foedric's presence:

"He was attracted to that subject by the fact that he possesses in a striking degree the faculty of hearing color, which belongs only to refined minds. We all have this power to some extent, but in this, as in so many other things, there are great differences among us. As an example of this power, if you will excuse me, Doctor, I will tell you that your voice is dark blue, while yours," he continued, turning to me, "is yellow. Foedric, a true son of Mars, speaks red, and as for Zenith, her soft, pink voice has always been to me one of her principal charms, and though it would be folly to deny that she has changed some in appearance (not for the worse, however) since I first knew her, her voice has retained the same tone or color. I will ask Foedric if I am correct in my impressions."

"Quite correct," answered Foedric. "When I first heard your friend, the doctor, speak I thought his voice was brown, but it has changed since to such an extent that I think as you do--that the prevailing tinge is a deep blue. Such cases are not unknown among us, but they are not frequent."

"If the color of my voice sympathizes with my thoughts," said the doctor, "I do not wonder that your quick ears have noticed a change."

"I ought to say," resumed Foedric, "that I have to rely on my friends to tell me the shade of my own voice, for to my ears it is as colorless as a piece of the clearest glass, and this is the common experience."

"I would like to ask about the color of Antonia's voice," I said, "and Avis's, too."

"Antonia's is a beautiful green," answered Foedric, looking with a smile at the fair one, "and Avis, both in song and speech, has your color-- yellow."

"Foedric," said Thorwald, "tell our friends what you and others are trying to discover in connection with the air vibrations. It may be suggestive to them."

"I can claim but little part in the work," Foedric responded, "but it is this. Our ears report to our brain the air waves until they reach a frequency of forty thousand in a second, and we call the sensation sound. When the vibrations of the ether are more rapid than that, we have no sense with which to receive the impression until they reach the great number of four hundred million millions in a second. Then they affect the eye and produce red light, and as they increase still more the color becomes orange, then yellow, green, blue, and violet. Perhaps your limitations are not the same as ours, but our scientists are trying to discover some means by which we can arrest and make use of a small part at least of those waves which strike our bodies at a frequency between forty thousand and four hundred million millions. It is still an unsolved problem, this search for another sense, and we are now looking forward for help in the task to the studies of the civilization represented in our comet."

All this time we were rising slowly but hardly realizing it, being filled with that peculiar sensation, incident to balloon journeys, by which we could almost believe we were remaining about in the same place and the solid ground was falling away from us.

Now Foedric increased our speed and showed us how easily he could sail in any direction and at any rate he pleased, explaining to us the mechanism by which we were upheld and propelled, and also the way in which the current of electricity was generated and applied. They certainly had a wonderful method of producing great power with little weight, and the doctor eagerly drank in the information in regard to it, as if for future use.

It was charming. The atmosphere was as clear as crystal, the air balmy and the motion delightful, and if the Martians, with their purer nature and keener senses, enjoyed the trip that morning more than we earth-dwellers did, then their capacity for enjoyment must have been beyond ours. The ship seemed to be under perfect control; there was nothing uncertain in her movements, and as we went sailing along without fear of harm, in the very poetry of motion, the doctor and I realized over and over again that we had much to learn in this method of navigation.

Now we were riding at a good height, and our vision could take in a wide expanse of land and water. The peculiarity of the surface of Mars was noticeable, the seas being long, narrow inlets, as it were, running through or between winding strings of land, a decided contrast to the great oceans and noble continents of our mother earth. It seemed to me that this was much to the advantage of the earth, and so I was bold enough to say:

"When I used to look at a map of Mars, Thorwald, I remember thinking that the planet was not a handsome one, whatever might be the character of its inhabitants. But I have no doubt you have an answer for me which will give some good reason for the peculiar structure of the surface of Mars and make me ashamed of my sentimental preference for the earth."

"I certainly hope you will hear nothing while you are with us to make you ashamed of your own planet," said Thorwald; "but I must tell you the truth in regard to Mars. How do you like our climate, as far as you have experienced it?"

"We have enjoyed it exceedingly," I answered, "and I have been on the point of remarking several times that we were fortunate in making our visit here at so pleasant a season of the year."

"But," said Thorwald, "you could not have come in a worse season, for we have none worse than this. The temperature varies enough to give variety, hut not enough in either direction to cause discomfort. Each season is quite distinctive from the others, but each has its peculiar charm and all are equally enjoyable. Our telescopes tell us it is not so on the earth, for we can see the winter snow creep well down on its surface and remain there several months, then go away and come on the other hemisphere. We know this means great changes of climate, and as the inclination of the axis of the earth to the plane of its orbit is about the same as that of the axis of Mars, we believe we would have equally violent changes were it not for the fortunate distribution of land and water on our planet. All those narrow seas which disfigure our surface in your eyes, are in reality vast rivers, which are constantly bearing the water from one part of the globe to another. The warm water of the equatorial regions is carried to the cold countries north and south, and the water thus displaced cools in its turn the lands more directly under the sun. Thus the temperature of all parts is nearly equalized. In the summer in this latitude the water that washes our shores is cool and in the winter it is warm, and the strips of land are so narrow that all places feel the influence, making the climate delightful everywhere. At each pole there is a spot of perpetual snow, but these are comparatively small, and the fields are cultivated right up to the foot of the snow hills."

This recital excited the doctor's interest amazingly, and as Thorwald closed he said:

"I rather think my companion did not expect so complete an answer, but I am glad his words suggested to you this statement, Thorwald. It is of great value to us in our study of your remarkable planet. How wonderfully God has adapted everything to your comfort and well-being!"

Thorwald smiled in appreciation of the doctor's final words, but before he had time to speak we were a little startled by the red voice of Foedric, calling out:

"The moon! Look!"

It was nothing new for any of us now to look at our old moon. We had seen it almost every day, had talked much about it, and thought the novelty of its companionship to Mars about worn off. But our present high position and the clear, thin atmosphere gave it quite a changed appearance, as it was slowly coming into view above the horizon. We watched it in silence for a while and saw it mount the eastern sky, and I think all of us except Foedric had the same thought, that it appeared to be much nearer than usual. Foedric had seen it before from the same height, and knew when he called our attention to it that we were going to be surprised.

As the moon rose still higher it appeared to be coming toward us, instead of aiming at a point far over our heads, and our next sensation was caused by Zenith, who mildly exclaimed:

"It cannot be more than a few miles away. Why not go and make it a visit?"

To her surprise, if people of such high endowments ever are surprised, Thorwald asked quickly:

"Are you willing to try it if the rest of us are?"

"Certainly," she replied.

"Foedric," said Thorwald, "what do you say to flying out to the moon and attempting an invasion of it?"

"I say," answered Foedric, "that I am ready. We have provisions enough for several days, and I believe the capacity of our battery is sufficient for the trip." Thorwald learned from Avis and Antonia that they would not object to the trial, and then said:

"Well, we have a good majority, but must not think of deciding on so important a step unless the feeling is unanimous. Let us hear from our friends here, who have had some experience with the moon."

The doctor said pleasantly that he should like nothing better than the proposed experiment, and, as I was the last, I remarked that I could not spoil such an interesting project by withholding my consent. But it seemed to me all the time that the whole thing was a joke and that it would end at once in a laugh. I thought of the cold and cheerless surface of the moon, comparing it in my mind with the delectable world we were leaving, and had no relish for the proposed trip. Something of my feeling must have been reflected in my countenance, for Zenith, who had been looking at me, said in a sympathetic tone:

"Although you gave your consent, you look as if you did not enjoy the prospect of another visit to the moon."

Thorwald heard this remark, and after a glance at me he said:

"You are right, Zenith, and I think we will abandon the idea at once. We started out today for the purpose of entertaining the doctor and his friend, and it would not become us to treat them to more of a ride than they desire."

"You are both excellent mind readers," I responded. "And if I were as honest as you Martians are, I suppose I should have said in the first place that I preferred not to make such an extended journey. I suspect the doctor is willing to go ahead, as he is too sensible to be affected by such a feeling as now moves me. My thoughts turn back to our departure from the earth in a balloon, and I cannot rid my mind of the dreadful fear that perhaps we are now unconsciously bidding a long farewell to Mars."

Thorwald thanked me for my frankness and said they should certainly respect my sentiment. He then stepped to Foedric's side to speak to him in regard to a change of course. At that moment I looked at the moon, which had been rapidly approaching us. What was it that suddenly gave it a deeper interest to me? A flash of intelligence suffused my being like an electric shock, frilling my imagination with the most beautiful vision and making the moon appear to me now as the one desirable place in all the universe.

"Thorwald," I exclaimed, "keep right on! I want to go now. I have changed my mind."

"Yes," he responded, looking at me with a pleased smile, "and I see you have changed your face, too. You look like quite another man. Why this sudden transition?"

"Don't you know? Mona is there."

"Where?"

"In the moon, of course."

"How do you know that? You seem to be pretty confident."

"Why, she must be there. You couldn't find her on land or water, and you know you have no accidents in Mars, so she could not have come to any harm there. I know we shall find her in the moon. She must have been left behind in some way when the doctor and I were thrown off, and now she is no doubt expecting us to come back to her. Oh, let us make haste."

"Well," answered Thorwald, "we were only waiting your consent, and we can now keep on as we are going and try to reach the moon. But I must give you a friendly warning not to let your hope get the better of your judgment in regard to finding your friend."

With this Thorwald and Foedric consulted a moment, and at once our speed increased till we were flying at a fearful rate, but none too fast for me. I knew now why I had been so reluctant to go so far away from Mars. It was because I thought Mona was there; but now, with my present opinion, the moon had suddenly changed its character and become to my imagination a bright and beautiful world. To such a degree does love transform the most unlovely objects.

I was struck with the easy way in which Zenith had accepted the result of what I thought her sportive suggestion, and, not being able to fathom her thoughts, I said to her:

"When we left home, this morning, you did not expect to be gone over night. Have you no anxiety about the house and the children?"

"Oh, no," she replied; "the house will not run away, nor the children either. We do not often stay away from them over night, but we do not hesitate to do so when we have a good reason for it. Our children know us well enough to be sure we have such a reason now, and this faith in us and in our safe return will permit us to stay away as long as we please. As for our feelings, we have no such thing as anxiety, for all our experience teaches us that no harm of any kind can come to our loved ones. I suppose in such circumstances on the earth both the mother and the children would have a feeling of great fear, caused by the fact that there would be in reality some danger of harm, but here we have never heard of such a thing, and even the word 'danger' has little meaning in it to us, because all we know about it comes from our reading." The moon was now well above us, and we were making for a point in the western sky where Foedric hoped to intercept it. We were already so far from the planet that the air was getting weak, so we all put on breathing machines. These were of such perfect construction that our lungs had free play, nor were they cumbersome enough to interfere much with our movements.

By this time the moon had grown so vastly, owing to our swift traveling, that our friends began to be amazed at its enormous proportions. The jagged, mountainous surface was plainly visible, a most uninviting place for people accustomed to the serene beauty and felicity of the planet Mars.

"Remember," said the doctor, "that you are not to judge the earth by what you see of her old satellite."

"Well," answered Thorwald, "we mean to see what we can of the satellite. Foedric, let us point the glass at it and be selecting a place to land."

But Foedric was obliged to let Thorwald handle the glass alone, for his attention was needed just now to manage our craft. He had discovered that shutting off the power did not diminish the speed, and for a moment he was puzzled, quite a new sensation for a Martian of that era. But he soon studied out the difficulty and made the following announcement:

"I find this huge mass that we are approaching is pulling us toward its surface, so that we are using but little power. I expect in a short time we can merely fall to its surface."

This suggested to Thorwald the very trouble that the doctor and I had encountered with our balloon, and he asked Foedric if we could get away again after we had dropped to the moon.

"Yes," Foedric answered, "I am sure we have power enough here to overcome the attraction and get away whenever we please."

Thorwald, who had been intently studying the surface through the telescope, now spoke out with some excitement in his voice:

"Doctor, I begin to think you did not make a thorough investigation of the moon's condition. Did you not report it practically uninhabited?"

"Our means of investigation were rather limited," replied the doctor, "but we surely found no inhabitants except poor Mona, whom, I am confident, we shall never see again. Why do you ask? Are there any signs of life visible? I have no doubt you Martians can see more at this distance than we could when standing on the globe itself."

"Well," Thorwald answered, "either you reached wrong conclusions or else a race has grown up there pretty rapidly. I cannot make out anything definite yet, but there is smoke, I am sure, and I can see some object moving about."

I had great difficulty in restraining my feelings as Thorwald uttered these words, but neither he nor the doctor seemed to realize what significance they had for me.

Both had apparently given up all expectation of finding Mona anywhere, and these evidences of life, so plain to me, were therefore inexplicable to them. I controlled myself and begged Thorwald to let me look through the glass. He adjusted it for me, but before I could get a satisfactory view our swift motion made such a change in the appearance of the surface that Thorwald could not find the same spot again.

As no one said a word to indicate any thought of connecting Mona with the movements that Thorwald had observed, I determined that I would keep quiet also and await the result of our landing. I let my thoughts fly to my love, who, without doubt, had seen the approach of our air ship and was expecting our speedy arrival. What an addition she would make to our party, and how these Martians would study her history as she recounted it in that exquisite voice. But I should claim a large share of her time for myself. How glad I was to think that Foedric had so openly shown his affection for Antonia. Surely I need not harbor the jealous feeling that would arise, for so true a son of Mars could not fall to the level of some earthly men, and be unfaithful to so noble a girl as Antonia. It was beyond all reason, and yet my love for Mona, whom I thought we were soon to find, was such that I undesignedly but still unmistakably made up my mind to keep a close watch on handsome Foedric.

CHAPTER XXIII.
WE SEARCH FOR MONA.

We were indeed approaching the surface with great rapidity, and Foedric was obliged to put on power to prevent us from falling too swiftly. Fortunately he was able to keep our ship under perfect management, and so, without accident or even a shock, he brought us gently to land, not far from the spot where Thorwald had seen the signs of life. It was something new for the latter to show so much curiosity, but he could not be more eager than I was to attempt to find out what we had seen through the telescope. So, leaving the rest of the party, we two started out to investigate. It was kind of Thorwald to take me along, because he could ordinarily walk a great deal faster without me, but my love and hope now added wings to my feet and I surprised him with my agility.

Thorwald's skill in determining locality enabled him to choose the right direction, and after quite a walk we ascended a considerable hill, from which we were delighted to discover in the distance a small column of smoke--a remarkable sight on that sterile shore. We hastened toward it, Thorwald with high expectations of an important discovery, and I with a heart beating with joyful anticipations of a different character.

As we approached the spot of such intense interest for us both, I watched my companion closely to see how he would bear the disappointment which I felt sure awaited him; and this, I think, made it a little easier for me to endure my own grief, for, of course, I was disappointed, too. I ought to have known better than to expect to find Mona out on the bleak surface, when she had such a comfortable home inside the moon. What we found at the end of our journey was merely another party of Martians, who had stolen a march on us and made a prior invasion of the moon.

But so unselfish were they that when they saw our ship afar off they began to make a smudge and smoke in order to attract our attention and give us the opportunity of sharing with them the glory of their anticipated discoveries. They were pleased with our success in finding them, and proposed that we join our forces in a common camp. So, leaving me, Thorwald returned for the rest of our party, and in due time we were all together, conversing on the footing of old acquaintances. The moon had improved somewhat since we knew it, as everything must which remains in the vicinity of the planet Mars, but it was not yet, as far as the outside, at least, was concerned, a desirable place for a long sojourn.

Our new friends had, unlike us, started from home with the intention of making the attempt to land on the moon, and, having come prepared with tools for a little scientific work, had already begun investigating, with a view to finding out whether the moon contained any vestiges of life. They had heard of the doctor and me and the outlines of our story, but now we had to relate to them in detail all our experience on the moon, while I concluded my part of the narration with the statement of my firm conviction that Mona was still in her quiet refuge, waiting for us to return and rescue her. This interested them exceedingly, and they were eager to join us in searching for her.

The members of our party, catching something of my hope, were ready to enter at once upon this task, and it was decided to divide all our forces into two companies, one to be led by the doctor and the other by me, and then to start in different directions to try to find the entrance to that long passage into the interior. As we knew not on what part of the moon's surface we had alighted, we were undertaking a bold piece of work, but its apparent difficulty had no terrors for the Martians, and I should not have hesitated if the circumference of the moon had been a hundred times what it was. As for the doctor, he had too much spirit to suggest any obstacles.

We arranged a code of signals, and agreed that if either party were successful the other should be notified and the descent made only when all had come together. After dividing the provisions we made our adieus and separated, not knowing when we should see one another again.

But, fortunately, our elaborate preparations were not of much use, for before we had been out an hour the doctor signaled to me that he had found some familiar landmarks. This meant that he was sure of discovering what we were in search of, and accordingly we started at once to rendezvous with his company. On our arrival I recognized, with exultant joy, the features of the landscape which had attracted the doctor's attention. We now led the way with complete assurance, and came at length to the crater down whose side Mona had so strangely led us. The wind was not so strong now, but I was none the less eager to descend and enter that dark way, at the other end of which such happiness awaited me. By this time, also, the whole party were becoming enthused over the situation. When they came to see, one after another, features which they had heard us describe, they acquired a personal interest which had been impossible before, and everyone began to share my faith in regard to Mona.

As we entered the tunnel, the doctor and myself still in the lead, I called Avis and asked her to keep as near me as possible.

"I am flattered," she said, "but what do you want to have me do?"

"Sing," I answered.

"What for? You needn't be afraid of the dark, for we can give you light enough."

And at that instant out flashed half a dozen lamps from different members of the party, a timely illustration of the use of their portable electricity.

"No, Avis," I said, "I am not afraid, but I would like to recall something of the sensation of our first descent into the moon, when we were led, as you know, by the sound of beautiful music. And then, as we near the end, Mona may hear you, and that would be a more gentle introduction than if we should burst upon her un-announced. I know she is not subject to fear or the usual emotions to which I have been accustomed on the earth, but still I think she would like to have us come back to her heralded by your noble song."

Seeing how serious I was in the matter, Avis promised to do as I wished, only suggesting that all the rest should join her from time to time. So, without any un-pleasant incident, we traversed the long passage, walking rapidly by the aid of the light and conversing about our interesting situation. It was a rare and pleasing ex-perience for the doctor and me to be showing these wise Martians something new, and we enjoyed the novel sensation of watching their excitement. The fact that we could so satisfactorily entertain our friends after their own fashion with us was something long to be remembered.

But not another one of all the company had the intensity of feeling which filled my breast. Knowing that every downward step was leading me rapidly toward a determination of my fate, I could scarcely control my emotions. Either I was soon to find my heart's life and be raised to the highest pinnacle of happiness, or I was to undergo a disappointment from which I might not recover. For if Mona was not here, where could I look for her? Could I ever regain my hopeful spirits if I should lose her now? I tried to crowd out these dark forebodings by thinking of my love and trying to picture the scene in the midst of which we should discover her.

At length we were drawing near the end. The path was growing wider, which proved to the doctor and me that we should soon emerge into the open village. Indeed, a faint gleam of light was beginning to be seen far in the front. We now pushed on more rapidly, and as we approached the exit Avis was singing at her highest pitch. She stopped suddenly, and then a low and distant strain came to us, sweet even to the ears of our cultured friends from Mars. My heart beat wildly as Thorwald, who was close behind us, exclaimed:

"Hark, hear the echo!"

"Ho!" I cried, "that's not an echo. That's the original, and Avis is the echo. Sing out again, Avis."

A loud, clear note trembled on the air, and brought back to our straining sense, not a repetition of itself but a snatch of varied melody which showed it to be no echo, although evidently an answer. There have been few moments in my life more crowded with happiness than that one. And it was not a passive feeling of enjoyment, but one that spurred me to action. The swift pace which we had all by this time reached was now too slow for me. Seized again by the same fierce passion which took possession of me at my first acquaintance with Mona's voice, I started in her direction on a run, flinging aside everything that might impede me, so overmastered was I by my desire to see her.

But my unreasonable haste brought me a grievous reward. I leaped over the ground with great rapidity for a few minutes, and then, stepping on a treacherous stone, turned my ankle and fell heavily to the ground, my head, thrust forward in running, being the first point of contact with the cruel rocks.

I returned to consciousness by degrees. My faithful ears were, as usual, the first friends to renew acquaintance with me, and the sound they brought was so soothing that I wished for nothing more than to remain as I was, ears only, and listen to it forever. But this was impossible, as I was slowly recovering my other senses and becoming a thinking being once more. I now recognized the pleasant sound as the music of a familiar voice; yes, it was Mona's voice in conversation. I was sure of that, but it seemed so natural that I was not startled. I felt that I must remain perfectly quiet, or the spell would be broken and the music cease. Then I began to wonder where I was and who were with me. I recalled the circumstances of our descent into the moon and my fall as I was running to meet Mona. My mind was active, but I feared that I was physically weak, for I did not seem to have even a desire to move. I wanted to see the face of the dear girl, and it is remarkable that I did not open my eyes at once and call her by name. But I was not in a natural state. The feeling was not sufficiently strong to move me to action. I was just conscious enough to be passively happy, content to lie there quietly and enjoy one thing at a time.

Hitherto I had not tried to distinguish the words, so satisfied was I with the exquisite tones, but now my attention was compelled by this yellow expression:

"So I understand you to say he would not give me up as lost?"

It was the pink voice of Zenith that answered:

"No, indeed. He never faltered in his faith that you would be found. You owe it to him that you can soon leave this worn-out world with us, and we are indebted to him for giving us such a dear friend."

"And he admired my singing?" said Mona in a questioning tone.

"Yes, and everything pertaining to you. He never tired of rehearsing your perfections, and the doctor tells us he loved you from the very first. He certainly seems most devoted to you. I hope, my dear, that you love him."

I was now recovered enough to feel some compunctions about listening further to this conversation, but that is not saying that I had any great desire to stop listening. I knew that in Mona's answer to Zenith's implied question lay my fate, and my moral doubts were not strong enough to make me do anything to keep it back. It has been said on the earth that people who surreptitiously hear themselves spoken of are never pleased, but things must be quite different inside the moon, for, without a shadow of hesitation and in the sweetest air that ever floated from her lips, came Mona's answer:

"Love him? Certainly I love him. Why should I not? I loved him when he was here before, and I should be very ungrateful if I did not care a great deal more for him when I know what he has done for me, and that he now lies here suffering for my sake."

"Oh, Mona," I said to myself, "if this be suffering, let me never know happiness."

Zenith began to speak again, when she was interrupted by the opening of a door. I heard someone walk towards me, and then the doctor's voice broke the silence.

"How is he, Mona? Is there any change?"

"No," replied my beloved, "he hasn't stirred nor shown a sign of consciousness. Cannot something more be done for him?"

I was becoming a little hardened in my guilt by this time, and, although my strength seemed now to be returning to me, I decided to keep still yet longer and hear what words of wisdom the doctor would utter on my case.

"I know of nothing that can be done," he said. "He received no injury except the wound on his head, and that, apparently, is not serious. Time is the great healer in such cases. My chief fear is that when he recovers consciousness we will find his memory is defective, as it was after his plunge into your ocean, Zenith. He will doubtless forget how we ever got into this strange place, and I am almost sure he will not recognize Mona, for that was the direction in which he failed before."

"But you forget," said Zenith, "that Mona herself will be here to sing for him."

"I fear not even that will recall his wandering wits this time. You know he is more badly hurt than before. I dislike to cause you pain, Mona, but I must be frank and tell you that our friend will probably never know you again."

One would naturally expect Mona to have burst into tears at this hopeless prospect, but instead of that she sang out, as joyously as ever:

"Never mind me, Doctor. Only restore him to health and happiness, and it will be of little moment whether he remembers me or not. No one knows better than you do that I am always happy, that's why I am singing all the time."

Such unselfishness as this was more than I could appreciate, and rather more, I thought, than was called for by the circumstances. How could she love me so, and still not care if I never were to know her again? Was she the same Mona, after all, who had so provokingly eluded my love during my former visit? These reflections caused me to decide to come to life, and claim her as mine before she resigned all her interest in me.

So, opening my eyes and looking in her face, I said, as quietly as possible:

"I do remember you, dear Mona, and shall never forget you. Doctor, you see your science has proved false again."

"And glad indeed I am that it has," he rejoined, "since it is so greatly to our advantage."

Then they all gathered around me, and called the others to a general rejoicing over my sudden recovery. My physical injury was but slight, and it was not long before my stupor was entirely gone and I was moving about again. Aside from the finding of Mona, many other things in this place of her abode interested the different members of our party. All were jubilant over the new opportunities for study and investigation, and they promised themselves the pleasure of many more visits to the place in the future. They had now seen enough for once, and all wanted to join in the agreeable task of escorting Mona to Mars and introducing her there. So, without more delay, we ascended to the surface once more, found our air ships in good order, and soon sailed away, leaving the moon without an inhabitant.

Our friends from the antipodes landed with us, and remained some days before reembarking for home.

During our voyage down there was a general agreement to give me plenty of opportunity to remain in Mona's immediate company, though no one seemed to think we need feel at all embarrassed when our conversation was overheard by others.

"Mona," I said, "were you glad to see our relief party when they arrived?"

"I was indeed," she replied, "and yet I was as happy as a bird, living there all by myself and singing for my own amusement the whole day long."

"It is an astonishing thing to me," I continued, "that after the doctor and I had left you so unceremoniously you could go back to your lonely home and be happy there."

"Why, did you think I would mourn for you?"

"Well, yes, I think that would be natural, considering something I know."

"Oh, I should like to hear what you know."

"If I tell you, I shall have to make a confession."

"What is a confession, and how can you make one? Have you anything to make it of?"

"Oh, yes," I replied, laughing. "A confession is an acknowledgment that one has done something wrong, and should be made to the person to whom the wrong has been done."

"Well," said Mona, "if that is it, I am sure I shall never have to make one, for I have never done anything wrong."

This agreed so well with my conception of her that I did not then take in the full meaning of her words, but said in reply:

"But I have, and this is one thing when you were talking to Zenith about me and thought I was unconscious I was recovering, and lay quite still so as to hear what you said."

"And did I say anything to displease you?"

"No, indeed; you said you loved me, and it made me very happy."

"Oh, I remember now. Zenith said she hoped I loved you, and I told her I did. I have always loved you, of course, but I don't see how that can make you happy."

"That's singular," I answered. "I should think you would understand my feeling from your own. But never mind. You and I will be lovers from this time forth, and give the people of Mars an example of devotion worth considering, will we not?"

"You do make the funniest speeches," she replied. "I don't know half the time what you mean. But I am getting tired of sitting so long. Here is Antonia. You talk to her about love, and I'll go over and see Foedric."

The lightness of her manner, when I was so deeply in earnest, gave me a feeling of uneasiness, which was increased when I saw her easy, familiar way with Foedric and heard her merry song as she chatted with him. I was not very pleasant company for Antonia, for I could not prevent a return of that dreadful jealousy. I wondered if this was always to be the history of my wooing--an hour of the supremest happiness, followed so speedily by a period of such anguish. I could not possibly talk on any other subject, and so I said to Antonia:

"They seem well pleased with each other's society. Are you not afraid Foedric will lose his heart to her?"

"My friend," she replied, "we never even think of such things as that. I hope you are not serious in asking the question."

"Forgive me, Antonia," I answered; "I hardly know what I am saying."

And then I rose and followed Mona, and said to her when I came near:

"Well, my dear, what do you and Foedric find so pleasant to talk about?"

"Why, you see," she replied, "Foedric was the first one to find me after you were hurt, and has been very kind to me since, and I have just been telling him I love him. You said it made you happy to hear me say it to you, and I wanted to make him happy too. And then I wanted to see if Foedric would make such funny speeches as you did."

I controlled myself enough to ask:

"And what did Foedric say?"

"Why, his answer made me laugh more than yours did. He said it would make you unhappy to know I had said such a thing to him. I replied that I would tell you myself, and that you were always happy when I said anything to you; and then you came up just in time."

"Now, Mona, do you think it is right to make sport of such a serious matter?"

"I assure you I am in earnest in all I have said."

"Then are you trying to deceive Foedric?"

"Deceive him? What is that?"

"Telling him what isn't true."

"No, indeed. I would never do that."

"It is true, then, that you love him?"

"Certainly it is; isn't it, Foedric?"

I did not wait for Foedric to answer, but continued:

"And still a short time ago you said you loved me."

"Well, is that any wonder, after what you have done for me?"

"But do you love us both at once?"

"I do."

"And do you love Foedric as much as you do me?"

"Certainly. Why shouldn't I? And now let me ask you a question. Do you love me?"

"With all my heart."

"Then why do you bother me so, asking all these questions, and saying things

I don't understand? You appear to be surprised to find that I love Foedric. Why, I love everybody. What am I going to do, if I cannot love people as much as I want to?"

"You shall, Mona," I replied, with a sudden softening of my heart toward her. "I was only going to suggest that, if you love Foedric, Antonia may not like you so well."

Foedric began to protest that Antonia would not care, but Mona went right on with:

"Another complication. What possible difference could it make to Antonia?"

"Why, Antonia and Foedric love each other, you know."

"Oh, they love each other, and therefore no one else can love either of them. Is that it? But you have just been talking with Antonia. Don't you love her?"

"Oh, no," I replied hastily. "Or, at any rate, not in the same way that I love you."

"Not in the same way. That's another remark that I can't see any sense in. I must say for myself that I have but one way in which to love, and that is with my whole heart, without reserve or qualification. I cannot parcel out my love, a little to one, a little more to another, and so on. It all goes out to everyone. I couldn't be happy if I should try to restrain it. I think it must be like this delicious sunlight, which I am just beginning to enjoy, an equal comfort to all who choose to partake of it. I love you dearly. What can I do more? If I love others, I am not robbing you--take all you want, and then there will be just as much left."

"Mona," I asked, as she finished, "where did you get such a heart? You are showing me how utterly selfish I have been."

"Good-by," she exclaimed; "I am going back to Antonia. May I love her?"

"You may love everybody," I answered, as she left me with an exquisite note on her lips.

Foedric and I fell into conversation about her. Foedric praised her to the skies, saying that, if this were a fair specimen, the inhabitants of the moon must have been a remarkable people, and that it was unfortunate that they had so nearly passed from the stage.

When I found opportunity to think over the situation I concluded that I had given my heart to a peculiar being, and what had I received in return? She loved me--that was certain. But what kind of love was this, which had no respect to persons? I knew I could claim no exclusive right to the least corner of her heart, and yet she said: "All my heart is yours. What more can you ask?" I was not able to solve the riddle of her mysterious nature, but as I heard her tuneful voice and watched her beautiful face as she talked with Antonia, the very picture of innocent happiness, I realized with great intensity that I loved her more than ever. And I resolved to be patient, and try to lead her gradually into the way of loving which prevailed on the earth at the time we left it.

In due time we landed on the ruddy planet, and there was great diversion for us all in seeing Mona's continued astonishment and in hearing her varied song.

It seemed almost like home to enter Thorwald's house again, where we found everything just as we had left it. The children did not exhibit any astonishment at our long absence, but were glad to see us back and eager to hear about our adventures.

The next morning after our arrival Thorwald gave us a long ride in an electric carriage to show Mona the country. Returning, we took her about the large house and were all delighted to hear her naive remarks. At length Zenith asked Thorwald if he could not think of something that would interest us all.

CHAPTER XXIV.
THE PICTURE TELEGRAPH.

L et us step into the music room," said Thorwald. "Doctor, what acquaintance have you with the telephone?"

"We think we have brought the telephone to a considerable degree of perfection," said the doctor. "At first it was rather crude, and many preferred to forego its use in order to escape its annoyances. But of recent years great improvements have been made, until its employment is now a pleasure, as well as an essential help in our business and social life."

"Does it minister to any other sense than the hearing?"

"It does not, although I have seen a vague promise somewhere of an invention by which we could see an image of the person we were speaking to."

"If that is all, I shall be able to give you a pleasant surprise," pursued Thorwald. "Just sit in those chairs, and do nothing but keep your eyes open and listen."

We saw him arrange a series of long panels, in which were elegant mirrors, and then, as he gently pulled an ivory knob, there fell upon our ears, very faintly, like distant echoes, strains of the most delicious music. Gradually the tones became louder and more defined, and Zenith, with a quick smile and glance, directed our attention to the opposite side of the room. There our wondering eyes beheld the orchestra with whose notes we were then enchanted. There must have been a hundred players or more, and we seemed to be looking upon them from a distance which would bring the whole group within the bounds of the room. It was not a picture thrown on a screen, but was as if the musicians were actually present. Every motion made with their instruments was in exact accord with the accompanying note, and, wherever this orchestra might have its local habitation, it was certainly playing before our little audience that morning.

As the selection ended the scene faded away under the manipulation of Thorwald, and in a moment the room was filled with a harmony of voices such as I had never heard on the earth. And now the great chorus appeared, crowding this time three sides of the apartment and rising, tier on tier, to the ceiling. We could see the glad faces of the singers and knew how they must be enjoying their work. Brilliant solo parts burst out from one side and the other, and again from the middle throng, but it was impossible to tell from what individual singers these notes came.

When this scene, too, had passed and the music, all too soon, had ceased, Thorwald made haste to answer the inquiry he saw in our faces by saying:

"These concerts are now being given in two cities, both of them several thousand miles east of here, so far that it is now afternoon there. If we desire music after dinner this evening we can make connection with some city west of us, and by going farther west we can invoke sweet sounds to soothe us to sleep. Being connected with all the musical centers, you can see how, by trying either one direction or the other, we can have something worth hearing at any hour of the day or night, with the players and singers themselves employed, of course, only in the daytime. We have daily programmes of every concert sent us by telephone. They are received here, you see, and printed automatically on these sheets."

Zenith had watched us with eager interest during this marvelous exhibition. It was a novel experience, for they had never before had the opportunity of showing this perfected invention to those entirely ignorant of it, and they both enjoyed seeing the pleasure which must have beamed from our faces. I wanted to say something, but could think of nothing fit for the occasion, and was relieved to hear the doctor speak:

"My good friends," said he, "do not try to show us anything beyond this or we shall lose our mental balance. I believe in fairyland now, for I have just come from there. I never paid much attention to music on the earth, and did not feel any shame for it either, but I am now sure it will be to my everlasting disgrace if I neglect it another day."

This speech pleased Zenith exceedingly, and her emotion made her voice and manner more charming than ever as she said:

"If you stay with us, Doctor, you shall have plenty of good music, and you will soon become not only a music lover but a music maker, for every Martian is proficient in this art."

"Do you think," asked the doctor, "that there is the faintest hope that the earth-ly music will ever reach the high standard of that we have just heard?"

"Thorwald has told me something of your history," Zenith replied, "and I share his strong faith in your happy destiny. It seems to me that your race is equal to any achievement you have witnessed here, and even greater things, but it will take much time. Such changes are very slow. As for us, we hope we are still making advancement in music. We have few higher employments, and hardly one in which we are more entirely engrossed. It was given to us at an early stage of our development, and all through our troubled course music has been one of the chief influences for good. It has helped to keep hope alive during the darkest periods of our history, and has always been a mighty incentive toward a higher spiritual state. As your race advances I am sure you will realize more and more the beauty and value of this art, heaven-born and exhaustless."

We all smiled at Zenith's happy assurance that the earth was on the upward path, and Thorwald said:

"You see hope is contagious. But as we have been through all your present troubles and have triumphed over them, it is perhaps easier for us to believe in you than for you to believe in yourselves.

"And now, should you like to see how the telephone works in every-day matters?"

On our replying in the affirmative, Thorwald turned a switch, waited a moment, turned it again, and then there appeared before our eyes a familiar object, nothing less than the ship in which we had made our recent voyage. A number of the men, whom we recognized, were walking about the deck, and one stood apart, near the side of the vessel, conversing with Thorwald, the words of both being audible to us. When they were through, the scene faded away and Thorwald said:

"As soon as the ship reached its dock connection was made with the general system of wires, and the instrument, which is stationed near the place where the man was standing, was ready for use.

"So, whenever we desire to talk to our friends, we summon them to our presence. You see it is not necessary to speak directly into the transmitter. We can sit comfortably in our chairs and converse as easily as when our friends are actually present."

"Let me ask you, Thorwald," said the doctor, "how all the electricity you use is generated? The immense quantity you employ must necessitate a great deal of power to produce it. Is there a huge plant in every city driven by steam?"

"No," answered Thorwald. "We make no use of steam in these days. All the power we need is obtained from natural waterfalls and rapids. This power, which nature has placed ready made at our hand, is so abundant that it can never be exhausted."

"These waterfalls must fortunately be well distributed," remarked the doctor.

"Not more so, I presume, than on the earth," Thorwald made answer. "Every stream that runs in its bed has in it a power proportioned to the volume of water and the swiftness of its current. Think of the amount of water wasted every day in this way--no, not wasted, but unused. We do not need, however, to utilize ordinary streams, as there are enough great falls where power is transformed into electricity to be sent over wires to any distance required. In every city or district large storage facilities are provided from which power can be obtained for all possible purposes. Our beds of coal and wells of oil were long since exhausted, but while rain falls and water runs this power can never fail us."

"Doctor, what is the best metal you have for transmitting electricity?"

"Copper," answered my companion. "Silver is a little better conductor, and a new metal, called glucinium, is better still, but both of these are too expensive for general use. Our telegraph and telephone wires were formerly made of iron for the sake of economy, but copper is now used for these lines, as well as for distributing electricity on a large scale. The copper wire now commonly used for the telegraph has a resistance of something like four ohms to the mile."

"You are making good progress," said Thorwald. "But we have a metal of such good conducting qualities that, without making the wire too large for convenient use, we have reduced the resistance to an ohm to the mile."

"That is an exceedingly valuable metal," the doctor said. "And now let me ask you a practical question. You say you draw your electricity for a thousand and one uses from a large storage plant in each city. Do you pay for it by the kilowatt, or how is it measured?"

"We ask for so many watts or kilowatts, and it is also measured by the watt hour. But are you serious in asking if we pay for it?"

"Why, you surely do not mean it is given away," exclaimed the doctor, "after all the expense connected with producing and transmitting it."

"Yes, I mean that whatever quantity we want to use is ours for the asking. Before we could buy it some one would have to own it, and that could never be. Besides, how could we buy anything without money?"

"What! No money either?" broke in the doctor again. "Well, if you can get along without money, that accounts in my mind for much of your happiness. Just think of that," continued the doctor, turning to me, "to be forever rid of money and all the trouble it brings."

"Of what value would it be to us?" asked Thorwald. "We could not use it."

"Some of our people on the earth," replied the doctor, "have oceans of it which they cannot use, and still they seem to think it is of much value. It is an inherent characteristic of our race to love the mere possession of money or other property, and human nature must change a great deal before we can begin to reach the exalted moral condition which you now enjoy, to say nothing of your spiritual state."

"Your nature will change," said Thorwald, "and do not doubt that the change has already begun. Time is what you need, and there is time enough for everything."

After the midday lunch had been served we were invited to take a walk about the grounds. As the doctor and I were admiring the beautiful lawns and gorgeous beds of flowers, and then stood enraptured at the sight of the noble mansion itself, Zenith watched us eagerly, and finally said, with a smile:

"You discovered my favorite department of art this morning. Now is a good time to learn what Thorwald's is."

"Judging from what we have already seen and heard of your husband," said I, "it seems to me he must be an astronomer, or, if not that, then a theological professor."

"If he has been talking to you on either of those subjects," she returned, "I have no doubt he told you things worth taking home with you, but his pet topics of study are architecture and its sister art, landscape gardening. This house is a creature of his brain, and all the artistic effects in color and pattern, which I know you have the taste to admire, are of his designing."

The simple, unaffected manner in which Zenith showed her pride in her husband's achievements was refreshing, and the knowledge she imparted only added still more to our high appreciation of our friend.

It was now time for Thorwald to speak, and he remarked quietly:

"It is true that I love architecture. It is another occupation of which we can never tire and whose resources we can never fathom. A beautiful, dignified, and truly artistic building is one of the highest possible products of our civilization, and such work brings out all the poetic feeling in one's nature, just as the production of a fine painting or piece of sculpture does. These arts, and literature as well, all have their special devotees among us, but everyone knows enough of all arts to appreciate and enjoy good work in every department.

"We build truthfully, and this helps to make what we build beautiful, for truth is beautiful wherever it is found; and beauty is an object to be sought after for its own sake, an enjoyable thing well worth striving for. Religion and art, using both those terms in a comprehensive sense, have worked together, through all our history, to lift up our souls and fit them for higher and higher duties."

"Thorwald," said Zenith, "I think our friends would enjoy seeing some of our imposing buildings and other works of art while this subject is before them."

That this was not a suggestion that we should start on an extended tour of the country was proved by Thorwald, who said:

"Very well, we will then go into the music room again, if you please."

Here we were shown, by the new powers of the telephone, a bewildering succession of the grandest structures our imagination could picture: churches and cathedrals, college buildings, observatories, museums, music halls and private residences. These were not like pictures or views; but the structures themselves, in full perspective and in all the richness of their coloring, seemed to stand before us. Trees waving in the breeze, people and carriages passing in the streets and occasionally a movement at a window or door, all aided the illusion and made it difficult to realize that we were not in the midst of the scenes we were gazing upon.

Thorwald or Zenith told us the name or purpose of each building as it appeared, and the novel exhibition closed with the presentation of a large and splendid playhouse.

As this was announced I involuntarily exclaimed:

"So you have kept the theater, have you? Some good people on the earth think the drama is demoralizing."

"That," said Zenith, "is probably because you have allowed it to become debased. We read in our histories of such a period here. Indeed, for a long time both the play and the opera were abolished, our advancing civilization having given them up under the impression that the good in them was overbalanced by the evil. But when the era of a more noble personal character had come the drama was revived, and now is not only a source of innocent pleasure but is also a decided help to our growth.

"I recognize the house we are now looking at. It is in quite a distant city, and I see Thorwald has purposely chosen it because at this moment an able company is presenting there one of our most popular plays. Would you like to hear some of it?"

No sooner were these words uttered than we saw Thorwald make a slight movement of the switch, and, lo! the scene was changed to the interior of the building, and there before us was the Martian theater in full play. We sat as it were in the dress circle, with the orchestra and stage in our front. All was beauty and life around us, and the richness and harmonious coloring of the whole interior were simply beyond description. The play was going on in a quiet, dignified manner and every word and gesture were characterized with the greatest naturalness. It struck the doctor and me as a peculiar feature that, while we could hear everything that was said on the stage and even the rustle of the people around us, we ourselves could talk and laugh without being noticed. This effect was produced by an ingenious attachment to the telephone, and the doctor was moved to remark:

"This is an altogether comfortable and satisfactory situation."

"Yes," added Zenith, "we think it is almost as good as being actually present in the theater."

We assured her it was better, in our opinion, and then we thanked them both for the pleasure they had given us. But we began to think their resources for entertaining their friends would never be exhausted when Thorwald told us he would, at some future time, show us specimens of their paintings, sculpture, fine porcelain, elegant furniture, and many other works of art.

One morning, a few days later, as we were rising from breakfast, Thorwald said:

"Well, my friends, I suppose you will go to church with us to-day?"

"To church?" asked we in one breath.

"Yes, this is Sunday."

"Oh, is it?" I said. "I began to think you didn't have Sunday here. It is now eight days since our return from the moon, and this is the first we have heard of it."

"Let me see," said Thorwald, "I believe this is the first Sunday we have spent at home since you came to us."

"Then how long is your week?"

"Ten days."

"That accounts for our misunderstanding," I said, "for our Sunday comes every seventh day."

"That is an odd number," returned Thorwald. "With us the week is the basis of our decimal method of reckoning. We have one hundred minutes in an hour and ten hours in a day."

Of course we were ready to go to church, and when we were on the way, seated in a comfortable carriage, the doctor said to Thorwald:

"If for any reason you do not care to go out on Sunday, I suppose you can all repair to your music room, turn that little switch, and listen to the best preacher and the best church music in the land. But do not imagine by that remark that we have any fault to find with this method of going to church. For my part, I think I prefer it."

"I perceive," answered Thorwald, "that you have a good idea of the capabilities of the telephone, but I shall have to correct you in this case. Our instruments are not connected with any of the churches. But to-morrow we can get, by asking through the telephone, phonograph rolls of any sermons that are delivered to-day. If we preferred we could get them in print, but the phonograph is pleasanter. This instrument is now so perfect that the imitation of the speaker's words and tones is faultless. The works of all our authors can be obtained in this form, and our libraries consist in great part of phonograph rolls. Even the poets of former generations speak to us, and the voice of the singer adds its charm to the song.

"But you will want to ask me why we do not extend the use of the telephone to the churches. We learned long ago that it is a good thing for people to come together for worship and that nothing will take the place of it. We do not go for an intellectual treat nor to enjoy the music, but only for worship, and we try to keep our forms simple yet dignified and as fitting as possible in all ways. Some day I must tell you through what difficulties we have passed in church ceremonies and church government."

CHAPTER XXV.
AN UNSATISFACTORY LOVER.

It was delightful to live in the same world with Mona, not for me only but for every one who knew her. No one could help loving her; there was simply nothing else to do. Others did not make as much show of their affection as I did, perhaps because no one else was selfish enough to claim the same personal rights in her, but I found every new acquaintance she made succumbed to the power of her many charms. The secret of this general homage was her own loving nature, which just worked itself out spontaneously, but the more her love was shed abroad the more she retained for new-comers. At first my naturally jealous disposition continued to give me long hours of anguish, but I happily was able to overcome this to a great extent as I became better acquainted with her marvelous spirit.

Although I was at that time too much under the spell of this fair creature to form an unprejudiced judgment of her, I have since then attempted something of the kind, in comparing her in my mind with Antonia and others whom we met in Mars. Let me say that the Martians are not a perfect race. With our undeveloped spiritual natures we could not, during our entire visit, see any imperfections in them; but, as will be seen further on in this narrative, our good friends Thorwald and Zenith, under whose instructions kind fortune had placed us, were particular to tell us that their race had reached only an advanced state of civilization, to which the earth might one day attain, and that perfection was still a dream of the future. Taking Antonia, then, as a representative of her kind, I can see that she had a solidly formed character. She was what she was, not because she could not help it but because she herself willed it. That is, when she might have done wrong she chose to do right. Her connection with temptation was not entirely through her remote ancestors, whose sins filled such a large page in their history, but she herself had felt drawings toward evil. Yet so slightly had she yielded, and so strongly had her right years of living buttressed her against all kinds of wrong, that she, as well as all of her race whom we saw, appeared to us about perfect. Theoretically she might transgress, but practically it was all but impossible. Hers, then, was a truly noble character, and when she gave her love to Foedric he had good reason to be proud of the gift. Nor did she defraud others of their due, but her heart was open to every proper call.

Such was Antonia, one whom we could in some degree appreciate, although so far above us. But how could we understand a being like Mona, who told us, and we saw no reason to disbelieve her, that she had never known what it was to do wrong? She seemed as incapable of evil as the birds of the air, or, to make the comparison still stronger, as a beautiful rose. She was guileless by nature, and goodness and truth were as much a part of her as her beauty was. She was made to be a joy and comfort to every creature brought within the circle of her influence, and she could no more help loving than the sun can help shining. All who came near her received a share of her gracious beams.

She was unselfish and full of sympathy and every right feeling, not because she had seen the evils of selfishness and meanness, but because these latter qualities were utterly unknown to her. Her high character and perfectly correct life, therefore, were not the result of reason and choice, but were the instinctive manifestations of her pure nature.

I do not undertake to say which of these two presented the higher type of womanhood, and I certainly entered into no such speculations about them at that time, but I never had any difficulty in deciding that Mona was the one I loved. I did not, of course, relish her fondness for others. In that respect I considered her nature altogether too ardent, but I found I must get accustomed to it, as she would not change.

It made me quite despondent at times, fearing I could never lead her to feel any special liking for me. Then when she smiled upon me and sang so sweetly to me, I thought I ought to be happy though I had to share her heart with all the world. Still I did not relax my efforts to make my share larger.

"Mona," I said, one day, "I wish you would ask me to do something real hard for you."

"Why?" she asked.

"So that I could show you how much I love you."

"But you have already shown me," she said. "I cannot think of anything more difficult than you have done. Did you not keep up a firm belief that I would be found, even after the doctor and these wise men of Mars had lost all hope, and did you not, by your enthusiasm, prevail on them to enter on a difficult search for me on the moon? I have heard all about your deep concern for me and how you were affected by hearing singing which you thought was like mine. And now that I have been found, you are so watchful for my comfort and like to be so near me all the time, that I am sure I do not need any further proof of your strong attachment. But why do you pay me so much attention? Why do you not like to be with Antonia as much as with me?"

"Because I do not love her as much as I do you."

"Why do you love me so? Because I took you down to my quiet home and saved you from being blown off the top of the moon?"

"No, the doctor and I are both grateful to you for that kindness, but gratitude isn't love."

"I haven't done anything else for you," she said.

"It isn't for anything you have done that I love you."

"What then?"

"Oh, I don't know. I suppose it is because I can't help it."

"Oh, then you are becoming like me, for I can't help loving everybody."

"I shall never be good enough for that," said I.

"What is love, as you understand it?" asked Mona.

"Love--love," I hesitated; "why, it is the feeling I have in my heart for you. Love is what kept hope alive when you were lost and gave me such joy when I heard your voice and knew we had found you. Love makes every task light that is done for you and every place where you are the brightest spot in the universe. Even this delightful world of Mars is more beautiful than ever because you are here. Love, if mutual, is a precious bond, uniting two hearts and making them beat in harmony. Cannot you and I be joined in heart, Mona?"

"My dear friend," she replied, "I am very sorry I cannot share your feeling, but I do not understand such love as you have been trying to describe."

"Then I fear you do not love me," I responded, with great sadness in my voice.

"Oh, don't say that," she exclaimed. "Indeed I do love you. Now, how can I prove it to you? What is the opposite of love?"

"Hatred; or, in such a case as this, indifference would be about as bad as anything."

"Well, I don't know much about such things, but do I seem like a person who could hate you or be indifferent to you?"

"No, Mona, you seem to be the most loving creature in all the worlds we have ever known, but--"

"Oh, do not spoil that fine speech with a 'but.' I know what you want to say. You think I ought to love you more than anyone else, or in some different way. Now, that desire of yours is what I cannot understand. I love everybody alike because I know of no other sentiment. So it is a matter of course with me, and I do not feel obliged to tell people that I love them. You seem to make too much of it, coming to me everyday and telling me, over and over again, that you love me, just as if I doubted it. Why do you like to be with me so much? Do you think it is right to be so exclusive? You ought to favor the others with your company. As for me, I must say I prefer Foedric's society to yours, because he has so many interesting things to talk about, while you stick continually to one subject and give me little information even on that one. You know I am a new-comer here and eager to learn all I can. Then there's the doctor. I take more pleasure conversing with him than with you, for he seems to know more, or, at any rate, to be more able to tell me things I want to know about the earth. If the doctor were not here and you were the only one to judge from, I should be obliged to think the people of the earth a very curious race. Your companion, however, appears to be a man of considerable sense."

Mona sang all this in her easy, natural way, being perfectly free from any intention of wounding my feelings, but the more innocent I believed her the more incapable I saw she was of entering into my feelings. I began to realize how, in loving everybody, she missed a certain enjoyment derived from a more selfish order of love. It then occurred to me that a world full of such people as Mona must have rather a monotonous time from our point of view, and I asked her if she could tell me about her race in general respecting the subject of our conversation.

"Certainly," she replied, "I can tell you something from my own recollections, but more from our traditions."

"Well, were the men of the moon all sensible, or were they all like me?"

"Oh, I see you have a little sense as soon as you begin to talk in a new direction. In answer to your question, let me say that the stress you have put on our personal relations is something entirely new to me, and I do not see any use or advantage in it. This must be my excuse for speaking so plainly. I should not have spoken so had I not known, in spite of what I have said, that you had too much sense to be offended."

"I thank you," I said. "Do not apologize for your words. I have taken them as a needed rebuke for my haste in appropriating you to myself. But I believe, Mona, that the time will come when you will know the happiness of loving one person so much that your love for all others will not be thought of in comparison. Happy will he be who, in that day, is able to prove the capacity of your great heart."

"Then, in that day," she responded, "shall I prove myself to be the degenerate daughter of a noble race. No, my friend, we were not made of such stuff. We loved everybody, without question and without limit. We could do nothing else, and to love one more than another was therefore impossible."

"Let me ask if everyone was worthy of being loved?"

"Why, as to that, we were all alike. What do you think of me?"

"You know what I think of you, Mona; or, if you do not, I will tell you."

"Yes; you needn't tell me again. What I wanted to say is, that I am no better than the rest of my people were."

"What a world it must have been then," I exclaimed, "and how fortunate that the earth did not discover it earlier. With such an example before us we should have been utterly discouraged."

When Mona had left me at the close of this conversation, I proceeded to take stock of my sensations. I had certainly been seeing a new phase of Mona's character. Could I make such vigorous language consistent with my former conception of her? I answered yes to this question after studying it awhile, for I concluded that she was only just in giving me a lesson that I deserved. Her innocence was only the more evident, and that was the ground on which I built my faith in her. But now came the inquiry whether my love could withstand such a shock as it had received. I was no longer blind to the truth. Mona had no stronger affection for me than for her other friends, and it began to be doubtful if she ever would have, considering her peculiar education in affairs of the heart. If I continued to love her, it must be with the full knowledge that I had not as yet gained the slightest success in my effort to secure her for my own exclusive possession. My exuberant passion had received a serious shock, for I had been plainly told that it was making me appear ridiculous. Then, when there seemed to be danger that my love must grow cold under such treatment, I began to argue Mona's cause to myself, and I bade myself take comfort once more in the old thoughts. She was young and careless, besides being entirely new to our manner of wooing, and I had been too hasty in my approaches and no doubt tired her with my continuous solicitations. But then, on the other hand, I continued, the case seemed much more hopeless than before after such a plain rebuff, and if I had any self-respect I could not continue to pay my court where my honest love was made a matter of jest.

These thoughts passed rapidly through my mind, and I cannot tell to what rash resolve they would have led me had not the music of Mona's laughing voice just then come floating in from another room. As usual, this was more than I could resist, and its immediate effect now was to drive out reason and to enthrone love once more. All my doubt and uncertainty vanished in a twinkling, my self-respect hid itself in a dark corner of my memory, and as I instinctively started to find the fair singer I realized again, with a feeling too strong for argument, that I was still very much in love.

CHAPTER XXVI.
AN ENVIABLE CONDITION.

Our life in this cultured home continued to be as pleasant as were these first days. There was always something new to show us or to tell us. We would walk out every day and often step into a carriage and take a long ride. Our friends were famous walkers but were considerate of our feebleness, and still our returning strength, added to the great buoyancy of our bodies on that smaller planet, soon gave us also remarkable walking powers.

Sometimes the children would accompany us on an all-day excursion, and then the house would be left not only unlocked, but with the doors wide open perhaps. When we remarked on this, Zenith told us that if anyone happened along he would be at perfect liberty to go in and help himself to anything in the house. This was always understood, whether the people were at home or not, and one need not even go through the formality of asking, if he could see what he wanted. This referred not merely to bodily refreshment, of which one might be in need, but literally to everything the house contained; and the reason why there was any sort of comfort living under such conditions was, that the members of that society were all and severally of such ripe characters that it was well known one would not deprive another of anything he was using except for a reason which would be satisfactory to both.

"If we could communicate with the people on the earth," said the doctor to me when we sat alone conversing about these things, "and tell them how the inhabitants here live, they would want to organize an expedition and start for Mars right away."

"Yes, I think they would," I assented. "And yet, if what Thorwald says is true, the earth will one day be as good as Mars. Do you believe it?"

"Well, the fact is," answered the doctor, "I am ready to believe almost anything now."

"Oh, I wish Thorwald could hear you say that."

"I should not object," he continued. "I am sure that some power, not comprehended by our science or philosophy, has operated here to bring these people to the condition in which we find them, and if the same kind forces are at work on the earth, let us hope they will do as much for us, no matter how much time it takes. If a belief in such a power is faith, then perhaps I am beginning to have a little faith.

"I remember I used to hear our preachers in their public prayers ask God that every form of vice and crime might be banished from the earth, and that the time might come when there should be no more sin, but only love and beauty and happiness. I have heard such prayers a hundred times, and never thought much about them. But now I am forced to think, and it seems to me that these prayers would not be made continually unless there were a hope and expectation in the minds of religious people that they would some time be answered. It is not for me to assume that such a hope is unreasonable, drawn as it is from the book which so many believe is the word of God."

I rejoiced to hear my friend talk in this way, but it seemed very odd that he should be preaching my own doctrine to me. I had had the same thoughts, and had been trying to find the right time to offer them to the doctor. I am sure I was thankful that he was coming to such views without a word from me, for he would probably be much more apt to hold to them.

The foregoing conversation was in the evening, and the next morning we were all sitting comfortably in the music room, when Thorwald said:

"The other day I began to give you some orderly account of our history, but you see how it has been broken into by the relation of different phases, in answer to your questions. It seems to me now that it will be more interesting to you if I continue in the same way and take up one subject at a time. And now that we have a little time before us, I wish you would suggest some point upon which you would like to have me talk; that is, if it is agreeable to you."

To which the doctor replied:

"I like your plan very much and I am sure we both have plenty of questions which will keep you supplied with topics. I have desired for some time to ask you about your industrial system. I can see how electricity has relieved you of the most arduous labor, but there must remain much disagreeable work, as we would call it, to be done with the hand. In our busy life there are a thousand such tasks, which I cannot conceive of being performed by machinery, many of them hard only because they are monotonous and awake no interest or enthusiasm in the performer. Men and women are continually wearing themselves out with such work. You must have abolished all that, if everybody here is comfortable and happy. I am very anxious to hear how it has been done."

"In answering your question," Thorwald began, "let me say, first, that I presume we have learned to employ machines in a great many ways which to you would seem incomprehensible. The drudgery and much of the monotony of labor have been removed, as well as its severity. But still, as you surmise, there is plenty of work for all. Our higher civilization does not require less work than yours, but rather more and of greater variety. It is all done quietly, however, without friction or any of the unpleasant features of former times.

"I suspect that the real secret of the change is in the elevation of individual character. This has done more to better our condition than electricity and all the material improvements and inventions of the age. You must believe me when I say that no sort of labor is considered disgraceful, and, further, that one occupation is just as honorable as another. The man who goes into the mine and superintends the machine which gathers the precious metal is esteemed as highly as he who, with an artist's brain and fingers, shapes it to its highest use. The carpenter who works with his hands in the building of the house can hold his head as high as the architect who has spent many years in learning how to create the design. Why not? Both are engaged on the same work, each one in his favorite, and so his best, way. Both are working, not for daily bread or other selfish end, but for the sake of doing something useful. The perfect content and satisfaction we all enjoy in our labor come partly from our abundant health and strength, and largely, also, from our entire freedom from anxiety in regard to the means of maintenance for ourselves and our families. In these respects we are all equally fortunate. We are absolutely unconcerned about what material things we shall have for ourselves or leave to our children."

"Do you then all have equal pay for your work, and that so much that it places you above anxiety?" asked the doctor.

"Yes," answered Thorwald, "we are all paid equally, because we are not paid at all. So, having no wages and owning no property, why should we be anxious? You know I have told you we can have for our use anything that is produced or made without even asking anybody for it. The mere fact that we need a thing makes it rightfully ours."

"But what is the incentive to labor if you get nothing for it, and can live just as well without it?"

"The incentive is in the love for our work and the consciousness that we are doing something to make someone happier and the world a little better. Let me give you an illustration, a personal one, if you will excuse me. A neighbor asks me to make him a plan for a house. He may be a writer of books or he may be a carriage maker, or what not, it makes not the slightest difference. I enjoy that kind of work and, having obtained his ideas in regard to a house, I do the best I can. I cannot conceive that I could do any better if I knew he would pay me for the work, as you say. In like manner he asks other neighbors to build his house for him, and he has no difficulty in finding enough men who enjoy that occupation as much as I do my part of the work, and the principle which governs them in their labor is as high as that which controls me."

"Then," said the doctor, "I should think the poor man--I beg your pardon, I mean the hod-carrier--could have as grand a house as the architect himself."

"I don't know what a hod-carrier is," replied Thorwald, "but I get your meaning, and you are quite right. As an example of just that state of things, I will tell you that the man who tends the digging machine in my garden lives in a larger and handsomer house than this one. Why not? He has a large family, and he and his wife are educated and refined people."

"But with no physical wants to provide against, I should think some men would find existence easier not to work at all. According to your theory they could live in as good style as the toilers and have no one to call them to account."

"No one but themselves. Every man is his own monitor, and he needs no other. He knows his duty, and he has that within him which keeps him up to it more effectually than any outside influence could. In regard to a man's not caring to work, we have been through all that, and we have now no such cases. We found out long ago that it is better to have some one stated employment and follow it. But this does not mean that the work becomes a burden. One can rest as often and as long as he pleases. There is no one to intimate in any way that he should be at work, as the question is left entirely to him. The moment that work ceases to be a necessity it becomes a pleasure and the most natural thing in the world. The multiplication of mechanical inventions has greatly reduced the volume of labor, so that there is really but little for each individual to do; and the truth is, there is never any lack of men. If anything, there is not enough work."

"Your words," said the doctor, "reveal a remarkable condition of affairs, and I fear it will be many, many years before we can begin to think seriously of such a plan, so long as to make it almost hopeless; but there is one more question I would like to ask. With all this freedom of choice, how does it happen that all do not flock to the easy and pleasant occupations, and leave the disagreeable tasks undone?"

To this Thorwald replied:

"Let me ask you, Doctor, if you have not an answer to your question in your own industrial system. Do you not always find men to do every required work, no matter how hard and distasteful it may seem to you? I do not mean that the parallel is exact, but this seems to be governed now, as it has always been, by a dispensation of nature. We are born with different tastes and inclinations. Each one chooses his own occupation, and it comes to pass providentially, just as it did in the olden time, that all do not choose alike."

"Are all equally well educated?"

"No, but all have an equal opportunity. Everyone is given a broad foundation of general information. The mind and hand are both trained and prepared to do good work, and then the choice of occupation is made and the special education begins. But one who has chosen some kind of manual labor as his vocation very often takes up literary or other professional work in addition, and everybody has some kind of study on hand, by which the mind is kept employed. There is no uneducated class among us."

"Before you reached such nobility of character," said the doctor, "that panacea for so many ills, I suppose you had troubles enough. You have already intimated as much to us. I wonder if it would not help us to appreciate better your present condition if you should tell us briefly of your experiences in solving so happily some of the problems of your career. I am thinking now more especially of the difficulties of your social and industrial reformation."

"I will attempt something of the kind," Thorwald replied, "if you are sure I shall not weary you. Remember to prompt me if I do not follow the lines of most interest to you.

"If you should prefer to read you would find the facts you want fully set forth in our histories. The records are especially full and exhaustive on the subjects you have mentioned, for the important changes, or, at least, the changes whose story will be most instructive to you, came in a time of great intellectual activity. Of the earlier days the history is unfortunately less complete, and still further back the records become uncertain and many are merely legendary.

"Let us begin at a time when civilization was confined to a small portion of the surface of our planet. Society was then crude and unformed. It was a rude, selfish age. But the germ of better things was there, for the gospel of Christ had been planted in the world and was sure to spring into life when its time should come. But meanwhile our evil nature was strong and choked the good seed, and made advancement slow and uncertain. Power was divided among many rulers who were despots, whose principal occupation was war. The people were valued merely for their fighting qualities and enjoyed only such rights and privileges as their cruel masters allowed them. Being slaves themselves, they held in a still more bitter slavery every prisoner captured in war.

"Life was mere animal existence for most of the race, without enjoyment for the present or hope for the future. Education being denied them, there was no mental stimulus to compensate for physical wretchedness, and even their meager religious privileges were accompanied with so many superstitious and unnatural rites that life was relieved of but a little of its burden.

"Gradually power was concentrated in the hands of a few autocrats, nations were consolidated, and war began to be a science. Then some attention was paid to the comfort of the people for the purpose of making them better soldiers. Soon it was found that intelligence was the best weapon a man could carry, and so education, in a very stinted form, was encouraged. This was a fatal blunder on the part of the rulers, for as soon as the mind was unfettered the shackles began to fall from the body, and the days of absolutism were numbered. The spirit of knowledge, once released from its imprisonment, became a dominant power in the world, and as time went on the people demanded a voice in the management of affairs. In this way came constitutional government, which for a long time held sway, and under which there came immense benefits to all. Religion and learning flourished, science and art blessed the race with their bounties, and the world began to be a brighter and better place to live in, comparing the times with the ages of ignorance and cruelty that went before.

"And now the stream of liberty broadened, and before long became a flood that swept away thrones and scepters. Personal government ceased, and the people became their own political masters. The right of suffrage was extended and slavery was abolished, while commerce and the spirit of adventure carried civilization to many parts of the world. Then appeared a swarm of mechanical inventions to lighten the labor of mankind, electricity came with its strong arm and great promise, and easier and swifter transportation by land and sea brought the nations and peoples together to the mutual advantage of all.

"Education, once the possession of the rich and powerful only, now shed its benign influence over the whole people. Whereas, in the early times, learning had caused the downfall of despotic power, it was now considered a principal safeguard of good government, and made compulsory. Wealth was accumulated, luxuries multiplied, and great strides were taken in the material welfare of both nations and individuals. It was an age of intense activity. So rapidly did events follow each other, and such possibilities were anticipated, that enthusiasts, whose heads were turned in the mad whirl, prophesied the immediate opening of the millennium.

"Judged by all the race had previously known of freedom, of prosperity, and of happiness, it was a grand age, and that generation might well be proud of their timely birth. But, looked at from our present standpoint, we can see it was still a day of sadness and sin. We understand, what it was more difficult for them to realize, that the revival of pure religion, awakening the conscience of mankind, had brought about all that was good in their condition, while many evil tendencies had only been exaggerated by their material prosperity. So it was still a very imperfect world. Political freedom they had, but there was no emancipation from the powerful thraldom of selfishness. That spirit held universal sway, governing not only individual action but also the policy of nations.

"One of the highest sentiments known to the times, and some writers placed it even above religion, was love of country. Impassioned oratory was fond of declaring that loyalty to one's native land was the loftiest emotion the heart could feel, and no voice was found to rebuke the utterance."

I was a little shocked to hear Thorwald, in his earnest manner, give expression to these words, as though he looked upon such views in a very serious light. I was therefore bold enough to interrupt him with:

"Excuse me, Thorwald, but would not these orators, when their attention was called to their extreme language, acknowledge that love to God was a still higher sentiment?"

"Perhaps they would, for with all the selfishness of the period there was a deep-seated belief in a divine being. But even so, I still would not allow them to be right."

"Why," I asked, "is there more than one motive higher than patriotism?"

"Yes, love is higher," answered Thorwald. "Let me explain. What did love of country mean? At first one's country was a single family, then a tribe, and later a city, when the measure of one's patriotism was the measure also of his hatred for everything foreign. In time a state was formed from many cities and towns, and its citizens were taught to look on all other states as enemies. Then these states that had been fighting each other consolidated into a nation, made up, perhaps, of different races and languages. By this time patriotism became a lofty theme, but it was the same spirit essentially as that which prompts the members of two savage tribes to fight to the death through a blind and unreasoning devotion to their leaders. So do you not think that love to all, which can only come from a generous heart, is more to be praised than love to a part, which necessitates enmity to all the rest? I should think it would have puzzled the people of that age sometimes to tell of what their country really consisted. Was their highest allegiance due to their city, or their county, or their state, or their nation?

"To what did this immoderate love of country lead? To a passion for aggrandizement at the expense of others, and what was this but selfishness with a gloss so bright as to make it look like a virtue? It led to the strangling of conscience in national affairs, so as to make wrong seem right, and, more than that, to persistence in a course when it was well known to be wrong. It taught false ideas of honor and made the world one grand dueling field, where the energy of nations was spent in watching for insults from their neighbors, and where the quick blow followed every real or fancied offense.

"Do not imagine, by what I have said, that I would have advised these people to love their country less. On the contrary, I should tell them to love it so much that they could not see it do wrong; to love it so much that they should have no room in their hearts for bitterness toward others; so much that they should strive to have it lead the world in a march toward universal brotherhood. Love for one's neighbor should not stop at state or national boundaries. Love should know neither caste nor country, but should take in the world, and, I might add for your benefit, other worlds if necessary. Love is a condition of the heart, something within, not without, the man, and when fully developed reaches out to everything that God has made."

"It seems to me, Thorwald," I ventured to say, "that these sentiments, which I can see are admirable, belong to your present high development, while we of the earth have reached only about the condition of the people whose traits you have been describing."

"Then," resumed Thorwald, "you can perhaps understand another evil of those times. It did not grow directly out of love for country, but that too much lauded sentiment prevented the people from seeing its full enormity. This was the practice of attempting by law to protect the inhabitants of one country by shutting out the goods of all others. This prohibition included both the manufactured articles and natural products, and the means adopted was the placing of a high duty on imports. If the political leaders of a people could succeed in convincing them that such a course would raise wages, increase the opportunities for accumulating money, and make them in general more prosperous, then it was forthwith adopted, entirely without regard to the effect it might have on the rest of the world. It is not at all plain to be seen, from reading the history of those times, that the happiest results always followed the passage of these laws, but the experiment was tried whenever a majority felt that there was a fair expectation of such benefits. The only question considered was whether it would be good policy for their particular country. And if one result of this selfish legislation was the closing of mills and the loss of employment to thousands of workmen in some other part of the world, these facts were paraded in the public prints as though they were matter for rejoicing. Men were yet to learn that the maxim which the politicians were fond of quoting, 'the greatest good to the greatest number,' should have a world-wide application to give it any meaning at all."

While my prejudices were receiving another shock, I knew the doctor was really enjoying this part of Thorwald's talk. So, in order to draw him out, I said to him, as Thorwald paused:

"Doctor, I think our friend must belong to your party."

"I should rather belong to his party," replied the doctor.

"Thank you," said Thorwald. "That is a compliment which I appreciate; and now I think I have talked long enough for one sitting. Let us get some lunch, and then go out for a good walk."

Thorwald must have seen that the doctor's mood was softening, but he probably thought it wise not to speak more directly to him at present.

CHAPTER XXVII.
THE CHILDREN'S DAY.

As it was a holiday, the children accompanied us on our walk, and we had further opportunity of observing the easy, natural relations which existed between them and their parents. There was neither undue familiarity nor too much restraint. There was respect as well as affection on both sides, and a scrupulous concern for each other's feelings. Evidently the children had all the rights they could appropriate to their advantage, while there was no abrogation of the privileges or the duties of the parents.

At a convenient time during the afternoon I spoke to Zenith about this happy condition of family affairs, and I was greatly enlightened and not a little amused by her reply.

"It was not always so," she said. "One of the sad chapters of our history tells us of an unfortunate episode in the family life. In the early days the father had complete control over his household, even the lives of its members being at his disposal. But as civilization advanced the law stepped in and protected the dependent ones from too harsh punishment and from neglect. In time sympathy for the weak and unprotected made all corporal punishment unpopular, both at home and at school, and soon discipline of every kind was much weakened. There appeared to be a growing impression on the part of the elders that there could not be any evil in the child's nature, and so if he were allowed to grow up without any particular training he would not go far out of the way. It seemed to be overlooked that this was something new in the history of the race, that the experiment had never been tried of giving the youth their own way, from the cradle up. It had been taught from very early times that the child, for its own future welfare, should receive correction, and the teaching had never before been departed from. The parents might just as well have put the reins of family government in the hands of the children at once, for this is what it came to in the end. The children, released from all restraint, lost first their respect for their elders, and then all regard for their feelings. Instead of love there grew up a careless indifference, and in place of that tender thoughtfulness so necessary to happiness in this relation, parents began to receive harsh and even cruel treatment. As we look back upon it now, it seems strange that the result was not anticipated, and the trend of events changed by a decided stand against such an unnatural course. But the approach to a crisis was insidious and, as I have said, history furnished no parallel from which to draw a warning.

"Two things made it the worst time in the world for parents to become lax in their discipline. One was the growing sentiment in favor of independence which was permeating all classes of society, and the other the great revival of learning among the people. Given a large class of persons highly educated and taught to prize personal liberty above everything else, and still without the discretion that comes only with years, and what could be expected of them when left with no strong hand to guide them? The methods of education improved so rapidly, and there were such constantly increasing opportunities for obtaining knowledge, that there was some excuse for the children in getting the idea that they knew more than their fathers and mothers. This belief would not under any circumstances improve their manners, and at this time it only caused them to despise still more those who seemed willing to withdraw all claim to authority over them. Precocity, which had never been a popular trait, came to the front with no modesty to relieve its disagreeable character.

"But the conduct of the youth of both sexes was not confined to the exhibition of bad manners, nor to the mere passive indulgence of an undutiful spirit. These led gradually to a more serious phase of the rebellion, the inauguration of a series of petty annoyances, to be followed, naturally, by acts of downright injustice and cruelty. It seemed as if the old years of oppression to which, in a ruder age, the children had been subjected, were about to be repeated, with the parents for the victims. You must not suppose that these vast changes came about in the course of one generation. Just as a sentiment in favor of liberty will be perpetuated in a people from one generation to another, and increase with the lapse of years, so this feeling of independence of parental control and this decadence of natural affection were transmitted from one set of children to the next, and matters grew from bad to worse.

"At length the behavior of the young people became so notoriously bad that the matter had to be taken out of the heretofore sacred precincts of home and treated in a public manner. The press tried to work a reformation by ridicule and threats, and when this was seen to have no effect the legislatures took up the subject, and actually passed laws 'for the relief and protection of oppressed parents,' and 'for the reestablishment of rightful authority in the home.' These bold measures so angered the children that they declared they would not submit to such insults, but would take the matter of making laws, as well as all other branches of public business, into their own hands. They started their own organs, which made such silly declarations as this: 'We are young, but in all other respects we are superior to our elders. We have more intelligence, more spirit and courage, we outnumber them two to one, and, what is better than all the rest, we hold them already in our power. So why should we not use that power, and go forward and destroy every vestige of their authority? Let them work and earn our support, and we will do the rest.'"

"And now," asked Zenith, "how do you think the affair came out?"

"I confess," I answered, "that I shall have to give it up."

"Well," she continued, "the problem was solved, as so many others in our career have been, when the needed lesson had been learned, without our being subjected to the extremely dire results which seemed so imminent; and I am happy to be able to tell you that relief came through the efforts of one of my own sex. Just before the last ounce was added to the weight of foolishness and error which was to turn the world completely over, a girl made her appearance with sense enough to call a halt. She happened to be editing one of the fiery journals of her class, when it struck her one day that they were carrying the thing too far. She had the courage to say so, and got roundly abused for it. She persisted, obtained adherents and helpers, and soon a decided reaction set in. Like a house of cards, which a breath will destroy, the unstable structure the children had built fell to the ground, never to be restored.

"The lesson was not forgotten, and the experience, which appears laughable now, has been of great benefit to us at different times since. But the broadening of our minds and the general improvement in our character have long ago placed us beyond the danger of a recurrence of such events. Compared to our present state those were the days of our infancy."

As Zenith closed I told her I had enjoyed her story, and that I hoped the earth would not require such a lesson.

"I trust not," said Zenith.

CHAPTER XXVIII.
BUSINESS ETHICS.

The next day the doctor and I took the first opportunity to tell Thorwald that we were anxious to have him proceed with his narrative.

"Yes," he said, "I shall be glad to do so, for I had not reached the important part when our sitting broke up yesterday.

"I was describing to you a remarkable era in our career, and one of you mentioned the fact that the present condition of your race corresponded in some particulars with that age on Mars. If you shall discover further points of likeness as I continue, it will add a peculiar interest to my story.

"There is a difference of opinion among our historians in regard to those times. Some believe that the whole world was corrupt, that it was an age of material development only, and that, if there were any good impulses at all, they were so smothered with selfishness as to be of no account. But these writers lived long ago, and were themselves more or less under the shadow of that epoch. I strongly hold to the views of the great majority of our scholars, who tell us that, while there was too much evil of all kinds, there was also much good, and many believers in a final happy issue out of all the troubles of the time.

"In a society so entirely given up to the pursuit of wealth and worldly advantage of every sort, those who were trying to hold up the standard of righteousness and to alleviate the lot of their fellow beings should be remembered with gratitude. Among the multitude of inventions were many that were calculated to relieve the laborer of his severest tasks, to mitigate suffering, to ward off disease, and to lighten the load of mankind in various ways. Large sums of money were given for hospitals, charitable institutions, and colleges, and for other kinds of philanthropic work, while private benevolences were not uncommon. There was prosperity, too, of a certain kind, and some people were happy, or thought themselves so. In the records of that as of every period of our history, it is possible to find rays of light if we search for them, and I tell you these things in order that you may get a fair understanding of the situation, for in what follows you will see something of the other side.

"I think I shall not err if I say that the gigantic evil of the times, that from which others sprang, was the inordinate love of money. Even political power, by which the opportunity was obtained of doing public service, was too often sought merely for the better chance one had of making money, as the saying was. In the revolt against aristocratic government, the tendency in our race of going from one extreme to the other was again shown, and universal suffrage was adopted. This would have been wise if intelligence and honesty had also been universal. But the result proved it to be an exceedingly bad policy, for it created a large class of voters who held the high privilege of citizenship so meanly, and were themselves so venal, that they would even sell their votes to the highest bidder. This, supplemented by the immorality of some of the intelligent citizens, made politics corrupt and the name of politician too often a by-word.

"In doing business, by which was meant buying and selling and manufacturing, also financial dealings and commerce, the passion for money-getting was particularly prominent. An astonishingly small percentage of those that went into business, as they said, made a success, if we except the large manufacturers, but in spite of that it was a popular way of earning a livelihood. One thing that made it popular was the fact that there was always more or less speculation in it. The haste to get rich made men too careless of the rights of others."

"Do you mean that all business was conducted dishonestly?" I asked.

"No," answered Thorwald, "not as men looked at it then. There was a great deal of downright knavery in business, but there was another class who satisfied their consciences by being as honest as they could. The thoughtful ones knew the system was wrong but felt themselves utterly unable to replace it by a better one, and feeling no responsibility for it, they were satisfied to smother their sensibilities and drift along. They had their living to make, and, though they were not making it in an ideal way, they did not know that any other kind of work would be more satisfactory to their uneasy consciences."

"Excuse me, Thorwald," I said; "I am dull. What was there wrong in their manner of doing business?"

"Can you see nothing wrong," he answered, "in a system where one man's fortune was built on the ruins of another's, or perhaps a score of others, or where a business was started and increased solely by drawing from another one already established?"

"Why," said I, "that is competition, which they no doubt thought better than monopoly. I can imagine that they argued that a man's first duty was to himself and his family, that one had a right to go into any legitimate business, and that others must take care of themselves. The evil, if there was any, they probably felt was incident to the nature of business and could not be helped. I would like to ask how society could exist with any other business rules."

As I closed it struck me that I had spoken pretty fast and without much discretion, and the impression was not removed as Thorwald answered with dignity: "I am telling you the state of things on this planet thousands of years ago, and it is a sufficient answer to your question to say that society at the present day is not governed on any such principles; still, we seem to exist. It was a favorite saying in those days that 'a man must live,' and one that was used as an argument or excuse for questionable practices. The premise was wrong; it was not necessary to live: death would have been far better for the world and for the individual than a dishonorable life. So with society at large; better a change in the social structure, caused by an awakened conscience, than a state of peace founded on wrong principles. Our history proves that no particular plan of society is necessary to the world and that no order based on selfishness or injustice can long endure. But do not imagine such changes were easy or swift in accomplishment. They came, not by violence nor by the device of crafty men, but only through the universal betterment of the race, whereby a state of things that had been considered good enough, and then endured as the best attainable, became at last positively wrong and was slowly pushed aside by a growing sense of right. "To return to your first question, as to what there was wrong in their way of doing business, I want to say with emphasis that the essence of the wrong was in an undue regard for self and an almost total disregard for the interests of others. There were exceptions to the rule, notably in the direction of charity and philanthropy and in religious work, but I am speaking of the mass of the business community. It was every man singly against all the rest of the world. No man was his brother's keeper. If one did not look out for himself, that was the end of it; there was no one else to do it."

"But the system itself made men selfish," I ventured to say.

"To be sure it did," he replied. "But why did they not then abolish the system before it had brought upon them its long train of evils? It had to go at last."

"But," I asked again, "was not competition a good thing for the large number of people not directly engaged in business? Did it not keep down the prices on all kinds of commodities?"

"Certainly not in the main. It increased prices, because it increased the cost of everything. But let us suppose a case where it had the effect you suggest. Could a man with a heart wear a coat, for example, with any pleasure, if he knew that rivalry between the manufacturers had forced the people who made the garment to accept starvation wages? And this was done, not from humanitarian motives, to furnish the poor with cheap clothing, but for the purpose of getting more business and so of making more money."

I could hardly resist the temptation at this point of asking Thorwald if he had not been reading up on the current history of the earth, but I knew well enough that was not possible, for we had brought no books with us. And then I did not care to tell Thorwald just yet how near he was coming to our experience. But I could not endure having the props knocked from under our social structure without another effort to save it. So I said: "But were not the great majority of business men honest, and were not these instances that you have cited extreme cases?"

"They were the natural results of a bad system. A great many men were as honest as their environment would permit, and they tried to convince themselves that they were not responsible for the environment."

"Were they?" I asked eagerly.

"When they at last discovered that they were, then began a radical change. I am not exaggerating the evils of the times. I am merely setting them forth to show you how our race has improved with its maturity. If my purpose required it, I could detail many good things in the life of that people. One bright point in their character, to which I just now referred, I will illustrate. My boy, who is also my student in drawing, will never be able to make a straight line until he can see that the line he has already made is not straight. His improvement depends upon more than a steady hand. So with this people. Deep down in their being, planted by a divine hand, were the instinct of truth and the principle of growth, and when, in the natural course of their development, they came to realize how unworthy they were of their better nature, they set about the work of improvement.

"But they came to that knowledge through many sad experiences. I have not begun to tell you the number and extent of the evils they endured.

"The desire for money affected all classes. The general prosperity had bettered the condition of the wage-earners, creating many artificial wants which could not be satisfied without good pay. Hence arose a natural and constant effort to obtain higher wages, while competition among the employers operated just as constantly to keep them down, and the result was a sharp and increasing antagonism between capital and labor. The general public shared in the blame for this state of things by reason of the almost universal demand for cheap goods.

"While the introduction of machinery was a real advance, whose benefits we are reaping to this day, other conditions had not become adjusted to it at the time of which we are speaking, so that there was often a surplus of workmen, especially in the lower grades of labor. This had a tendency to reduce wages, of course; and the want of employment, improvidence in the use of small wages, intemperance and other immoralities, ignorance and misfortune, all combined to keep part of the people in poverty. On the other hand, it was a time of great wealth and luxurious living, and these two classes, so far apart in their manner of life but often so near each other in all their selfish aims, seemed to have a strong mutual attraction, for they were always found together, crowding upon each other in every large city.

"One of the most difficult things for us of the present day to imagine is, how persons of refinement and sensibility, living in comfort and without a care, could take any pleasure in life when they knew that within a stone's throw of their doors were human beings who, very often through no fault of their own, were so destitute that a crust would relieve their want, or so friendless that a kind word would make them shed tears of joy. Oh! I cannot comprehend it, and yet the record tells us there were cases of just that nature, where such people, without lifting a finger to alleviate the distress, actually laughed and were happy. Happy! What could they know of happiness? The word must have changed its meaning wonderfully, if we think of what it signifies to-day."

CHAPTER XXIX.
THE INDUSTRIAL PROBLEM.

Thorwald continued as follows:

"The unpleasant relations existing between the employers and the employees created a host of troubles. It was an unreasonable feeling, because the interests of the two classes were identical. But as capital was consolidated and great corporations were formed for extensive operations in transportation and manufacturing, the relation between the two became very impersonal and difficult to control. In order to protect their interests the wage-earners organized into unions, brotherhoods, etc., almost every trade and calling having its own organization.

"When these associations were first formed much stress was laid upon their incidental benefits, such as assistance in time of sickness, care of the families of deceased members, the holding of meetings for discussion and mutual improvement, and the establishment of reading-rooms and libraries. These commendable objects would have been a sufficient excuse for the existence of these bodies, and other legitimate ends might have been sought, but the labor unions did not stop there. They instituted and set in motion the powerful machinery of the strike, as it was called, making it effective by binding their members, under severe penalties, to stop work when they were ordered to do so by their leaders. They also practiced the severest measures of intimidation upon non-union men, to prevent them from getting employment.

"Thus the trades-unions, too often governed by incompetent men, became a mighty power for evil. Strikes and lockouts were common, and were followed by loss of wages and consequent suffering, while the bitterness of feeling between the two classes constantly increased. To meet the rising power of the labor organizations, the employers felt obliged to form combinations among themselves and sometimes also to employ bodies of armed men to protect their property. Then, when a strike came, conflicts would follow so serious that appeal had to be made to the last resort, the military arm of the nation. Here another evil threatened, for the individual soldiers would sometimes prove to be in deep sympathy with the workmen who were making the trouble. At such crises, also, there would appear on the scene the anarchist, who wanted to overthrow society at once in the hope of bringing himself out nearer the top, and who was kept comparatively harmless in quiet times.

"You can imagine something of the disorder and apprehension caused by these troubles. No contract for work could be made without the stipulation that its fulfillment must depend upon freedom from strikes in that particular trade, and no man could start on a journey with any certainty that he would be allowed to finish it in peace and at the appointed time.

"To decide how these evils should be remedied proved to be one of the greatest problems ever presented to the people of that age.

"Political sages had long before promulgated the doctrine upon which society was governed, that every man had a natural right to life, liberty, and his own method of pursuing happiness. Now, both sides in the conflict claimed to be following closely the spirit of this fundamental doctrine. The workingmen declared that they had a perfect right to organize and to induce all their number to join the unions. They said the individual relation between them and the employers had had its day and that experience was proving to them that every concession and privilege they hoped to get must come through their associations, working through the medium of an agent or committee. As independent citizens they could not obey laws and regulations in the making of which they had no voice, and their love of personal liberty would not allow them to accept the wages and hours of service which their employers might, without asking their consent, choose to prescribe. In case of disagreement they asserted their right to stop the whole business, at whatever loss to the employers or inconvenience to the public, and to prevent, if possible, new men from taking their places.

"On the other hand, the employers, while not denying to the workmen the right to form associations for legitimate purposes, insisted that this right was being abused. They claimed that they should be allowed to hire whom they pleased and dismiss incompetent men when it was best for their business, without regard to their membership or non-membership in a union.

"As time went on the trouble increased and society was fast forming itself into classes with opposing aims and mutual dislike. The time had been when a workman, by skill and diligence, could rise above his station and become a large proprietor himself. But with the new order this was hardly possible, and civilization, in this respect, seemed to be retrogressing.

"You may wonder why the lawmakers did not correct the evil at once, but the fact was that the legislatures were made up of representatives from the two classes, and so were undecided as to what remedies to apply. It was proposed by some to enact a law preventing a man from selling himself into slavery, or, in other words, from giving up his liberty of action into the keeping of others, a thing which had caused much suffering. In every strike a large part of the men, earning small wages and with families dependent on these wages for their bread from one day to another, would be obliged to quit work against their will. It was thought, therefore, a fit subject of legislation to enjoin them from binding themselves to strike at the dictation of others, when it was against their judgment. It was suggested, also, to make the intimidation or coercion of non-union men a criminal act.

"When these measures were suggested the cry was raised that the workingmen were to be deprived of their liberty and made the slaves of capital. The labor parties in the legislatures were assisted by a class of politicians who were made cowards through fear of losing the workingmen's votes, and this gave these parties the power to defeat all measures of which they disapproved, and to pass laws in their own interest. They claimed that they should be protected as well as the manufacturer, and so they made it lawful for the government to inspect all industries and to see that the employees received an equitable share of the profits. This was radical action, but they went still further, and took away from every employer the right of discharging men for any cause without the consent of the union; and full power to fix the hours of service and the wages was put into the hands of the government inspectors and the representatives of the trades- unions. The wages were to be based on what the inspectors found to be the profits of the business, and the help or advice of the proprietors was not to be taken. As these astonishing rules governed even the farmer and shopkeeper as well as the manufacturer, you can imagine that there was not much satisfaction in trying to carry on any business.

"The laboring classes were beginning to discover that they were a large majority of the community and that there was a mighty power in the ballot. Their opponents, on the other hand, having lost the control in politics through universal suffrage, now bent their energies still more to the work of combining large interests under one management, hoping to wield in this way a power too formidable to be withstood. Immense trusts were formed in almost every branch of business, and the syndicate gradually took the place of the firm and individual corporation.

"A long time previous to the period of which we are speaking, the people had put part of their business into the hands of the government, with the idea that it would be done with more promptness and also with more economy. A good example of this was seen in the excellent mail service, which the national government conducted much more satisfactorily than it could have been done by private enterprise.

"The local governments, also, had full control of the highways and bridges and the common schools, hospitals, etc., while in large communities, at great expense, they stored and distributed water for domestic and other purposes. As the people had received undoubted benefits from this state of things, there were few to object to it, and even their objection was more for theoretical than practical reasons. It is not strange, therefore, that as the troublous times approached these functions of the state should be multiplied. Besides the gain in convenience and in cost that thus came to the people, they began to rely on the strong arm of the government for protection from the uncertainties and interruptions incident to private control of many kinds of business.

"As the telegraph and telephone came into more general use the government found it necessary to add their facilities to the mail service, in order to give the people the best means of communication. From this point the step was soon taken of assuming control of all the telegraph and telephone lines, in the interest of lower prices and better service. This was attended with such good results that it was thought wise to extend the conveniences of the mail in another direction; and instead of carrying a few small parcels the government took into its hands the entire express business, and it was not long before everybody conceded it to be a good move.

"At the same time, the municipal governments began to exhibit the same paternal character. They first took control of the lighting and heating facilities, and this led in a short time to their furnishing the people with fuel, which was generally brought from a distance, and which, in private hands, always had a way of going up in price at just the time when the poor people were obliged to buy it. For the sake of economy, also, the cities took possession of all street cars, cabs, and omnibuses.

"Affairs had reached this condition when the labor troubles became so serious, and this absorption of private business by the government was so recent and was in general so satisfactory, that men could but think of it in connection with their efforts to solve the industrial problems. The time had now come when some radical measures must be adopted to preserve and extend civilization. The labor party were abusing their power still more in making bad laws, and strikes became more frequent, and were followed by rioting and bloodshed. At length the interruptions to business occasioned by the irregularities in traveling became unbearable. The public demanded better service, but the railroad companies were powerless to render it, being in the hands of the employees, who at the slightest grievance would stop every wheel till the dispute was settled. The trouble generally started with one road and spread to the others by sympathy, and the result was just as disastrous to business whether the men gained their end or not.

"There had always been a party, although at times pretty feeble, in favor of government control of the entire transportation business. This party now argued that that was the only thing that would cure these evils, and they gained thereby many new adherents. When it was considered that government ownership of the telegraph was working well in spite of many adverse prophecies, the people began to entertain the idea that it would perhaps be best to try the experiment with the railroads, especially as it gave some promise of relief from the strikes. To be sure, it would add to the government service immense numbers of men, and increase a danger that had always been threatening, that of making too large a list of civil officers to be managed without great corruption.

"But now it was not long before a large majority of the people asked to have the trial made, and soon all railroads, canals, and steamboats were in the hands of the general government. The employees were formed into an army, with officers of all grades, and put under strict military discipline. At the least show of insubordination a man was discharged, never to be reemployed, and although this caused some hardship in individual cases at first, it put an effectual stop to the strikes and kept business moving. The best of the workmen had been among the strongest advocates of national ownership, and as the movement gained in favor no class were so satisfied with the change as the employees themselves. Work was steady, wages were regular, faithfulness and length of service were rewarded, and the aged and feeble were retired on pensions.

"In this way peace had come in one department of labor, but war still raged among the manufacturers and in the building and other trades. The workingmen literally held the reins in society, but did not know enough to drive away from the rocks. Instead of taking advantage of shorter hours and higher wages to improve their minds and prepare themselves for a better condition, they were too apt to waste their energies in denouncing the capitalists and in trying to force still greater concessions from their unwilling employers. They would loudly demand that every ancient wrong endured by them should be redressed, and then, to show their idea of right, they would compel a builder, in the middle of a contract, where time was more precious than money, to give them higher wages than had been agreed on; or they would boycott to bankruptcy a small shopkeeper who innocently bought goods that happened to be made by non-union workmen.

"But do not imagine that the wrong was all on one side. There were employers who were unjust and cruel when they had the power, unreasonable in argument, and boorish and exasperating in their manners. Many seemed to think they were a different class of beings because they had more money than their workmen, and they resented the idea of the latter rising above the station in which they were born. They raised wages only when forced to do so, and considered any amount of profit made out of their men perfectly legitimate. When want came they would give in charity to the unfortunate ones that which really belonged to them by right. These disagreeable qualities were not possessed alone by such as were employers. There was a class of rich people not engaged in business, and although they had the greatest interest in the perpetuity of society as it was, many of them considered themselves as members of a superior caste, and looked down with disdain upon the majority of mankind, and the real masters of the situation, who had to work for their daily bread.

"It was against this class especially that anarchy was forging its thunderbolt. The freedom of the press and freedom of speech gave the socialist and anarchist the opportunity to promulgate their seditious doctrines, and they looked to the ignorant and depraved portions of the community for adherents. By the successful risings of the people against despotic power the word 'revolution' had gained a certain nobility of sound and meaning, and now these incendiaries employed it to mislead the credulous. They promised an overturning by which all property and money should become a common fund and be redistributed on a more equitable basis, and it is perhaps not to be wondered at that some poor, ignorant ones, seeing the vast inequalities in life, should be carried away with their arguments. The vision of a society where all should share alike and live on the same scale of comfort was intoxicating. But the scheme of the anarchist was not based on love and a desire to promote true brotherhood. Judging from the violent means proposed to bring about the change, it seemed rather to be based on hate. In preaching their doctrine of personal license they were stealing the livery of freedom in which to serve their selfish lusts.

"While the vicious and ignorant thus threatened society on the one hand, the accumulation of enormous wealth by a few fortunate, or unfortunate, men was thought by some to be a menace equally serious. It was argued that this could not go on without making the poor poorer and more numerous, and thus emphasizing and perpetuating the separation of the two classes.

"I need not point out to you a fact that you must realize, namely, that the spring of action with too many men, the one cause of the troubles that really threatened the foundations of society, was selfishness. Can you imagine any danger from all these movements if men could have suddenly become unselfish, really unselfish?

"I hope I have not given you the idea that all the world of people had lost their heads. As in the history of nations of that period war seems to have been the principal occupation, so in the social life of the people the evils and dangers are most prominently seen. But all this time there was a large party of men and women who were alive to the perils of the hour, and intent on seeking the best means to overcome them. This party was made up of many representatives of every class, rich and poor, workingmen and employers, and included the great mass of the intelligent and thoughtful members of society.

"The general and local governments were carrying on, with marked success and without friction, certain kinds of business, while in many other departments there were disorder and possible ruin. Time brought no healing power; the troubles increased and were now truly gigantic. Where should help be found?"

As Thorwald paused here, the doctor, who, I thought, had been wanting to speak for some time, took occasion to say:

"Don't tell us, Thorwald, that this people turned over all their business, both industrial and professional, to the government, and made machines of themselves. I am becoming exceedingly interested in them and hope they found some better release from their woes. I am sure there are a number of methods of relief which they might have tried."

"I am glad you have spoken, Doctor," answered Thorwald, "or I might have talked you to death. We must really break off now and get out of doors."

Mona listened to different portions of the foregoing conversation. It was dull amusement for her, as we could see by her actions, and we wondered at first why she showed so little interest in it. She did not seem to realize the full significance of her unique position in our circle. As the last representative of the race of moon men, she had now the opportunity of learning something of the history of two sister worlds, and one would suppose that she would have been eager to hear every word we said. She had expressed herself more than once as anxious to know all any of us could tell her, nor did she hesitate to ask questions continually--and intelligent questions, too. But she was sympathetic only in certain directions, having a laudable curiosity to hear about any of the pleasant phases of society, either on the earth or on Mars. But when Thorwald talked of the former troubles experienced by his race, or when we compared these with the miseries of our own times on the earth, Mona became an indifferent listener.

She was sitting with us when Thorwald proposed the out-door exercise, and so we all went out together. As we walked, Thorwald said:

"Mona, I fear you have not been enjoying my tedious talk this morning. You would be better pleased, I am sure, with some other topic."

In her sweet accents, so charming to every ear, Mona responded:

"I hope my lack of attention did not give you offense, Thorwald, but I do not understand the things you have talked about to-day."

"Not understand? Why, I know from former conversations with you that such things are not beyond your comprehension."

"Thank you," said Mona, "but I think they are, for I never before heard anything like the ideas you have advanced."

"We shall all be glad to learn, then, how these questions were answered and these wrongs righted by your ancestors."

"They never had any such perplexities," responded Mona.

"Which means, I presume," said Thorwald, "that the race became so far advanced before your time that the records and traditions of their early struggles were all forgotten."

"Oh, no," she sang out, "that's not it. What had they to struggle over?"

"Was it then so easy for them to be just?" asked Thorwald.

"Certainly, and I have been exceedingly surprised to learn by your long talk that there is such a thing as injustice."

We were all becoming thoroughly interested, but left it for Thorwald to continue his questions.

"Mona," said he, "do you mean that your people, even in the remote past, were entirely ignorant of such troubles as we have been speaking about?"

"Yes, and of all other troubles. I am sure there was always only peace and happiness on the moon. Strife and hatred, sorrow, want, and misery are all strange words to me, and entirely unknown except as I have heard them in your conversation."

"Was there never any sickness there?" I asked.

"I don't know the meaning of the word," she replied. "Is it another item in the general unpleasantness of the times you have been describing? I wonder that your race, Thorwald, ever survived those rude days."

"But," asked Thorwald, "what think you of the earth? The doctor and his companion say their planet is now passing through just such a period."

"Well, all I can say is that I am thankful I was not discovered till after the moon had deserted the earth."

"Tell us more about your race," said the doctor. "Were they all as good as you are?"

"Just the same. There were no degrees in goodness."

"And did they all sing as they talked, and in such sweet tones as yours?" I asked.

"Oh, many sang better than I do, and all made music of their words. I never heard speech that was not melodious till you and the doctor came to see me."

"And did everything else in your life there correspond to your charming manner of talking?" asked Thorwald.

"Why, yes, I think so," answered Mona. "It was a delightful world. Everything was bright and joyous, with no shadow of discontent nor anything to cause sadness or discomfort. Do you wonder that I could not sympathize with your story of wrongs and sorrows, the very nature of which was a new revelation to me?"

Mona's notions about the people whom she represented seemed strange and improbable to us, and we attributed them to the influence of her own guileless nature. One so innocent and whole-hearted as she was would naturally clothe her ancestors with at least the virtues and graces she herself possessed. However, we had no means of proving Mona's ideas to be false. We had brought away from the moon no records of any kind by which to study its history, and of that history Mona was as yet our only interpreter. But every word she spoke on this subject only added intensity to the pleasurable anticipation with which these Martians looked forward to their study of the moon and its former inhabitants.

CHAPTER XXX.
ATTEMPTS TO SOLVE THE PROBLEM.

It was not till the next day that we sat down together again to continue the conversation. Remembering what the doctor had said, Thorwald began:

"In sketching for you the history of that age of activity and change in our career, I was in such fear of wearying you with dry details that I hurried along and omitted the very things to which you refer, Doctor. This people did try all the experiments that suggested themselves, and if you think your patience will endure it I will speak of a few of them."

We both assured him that we would gladly listen, and that we considered ourselves fortunate in having such an instructor. He was merely telling us about a certain period in the history of Mars, but if he had known how nearly he had been coming to the course of events on the earth he would not have wondered that we were so eager to hear all he had to say.

"Quite early in the labor difficulties," he resumed, "state arbitration had its day; a short one, however, for the appointment of the arbitrators soon became a matter of partisan politics, and their influence was gone. Whichever side was in power could appoint a board that would be prejudiced in favor of that side from the start, and when the trouble came the other party would not have confidence enough in their judgment to accept their decision.

"Next, laws were passed making arbitration compulsory, but allowing the arbitrators to be chosen at the time of the strike, the employer to name one, the workmen one, and these two to find the third. This did some good as long as only first class men were selected, but a few flagrant cases occurred where the arbitrators, who were allowed to inspect the books of the concern, made public the private affairs of the business, to the great injury of the owners. This brought the law into disfavor, and, as there was no provision for enforcing the decisions, it came to pass that they were often disregarded, and so, before long, this plan of settling disputes was also abandoned.

"For a good many years no other subject so completely filled the public mind as this very troublesome one, and people of all professions were continually suggesting remedies. It was held by many to be a good working theory that the employees in every business, whether industrial, mercantile, or financial, were entitled to some share in the profits over and above their compensation in wages. This was disputed by the large majority of the employers, who claimed that their contract with the workmen was a simple one, by which they agreed to work so many hours for so much pay, and as this was their due even if the business proved a losing one, so they had no just claim to anything more if it were successful the employees had nothing to do or say about the question of profits. On the other hand, where a number of men had, by long and faithful service, a strict regard for the welfare of the business, and loyalty to all of the employer's interests, helped to build up a great industry, an increasing number of people, not only the wage earners but many others not directly interested, felt that the workmen had fairly gained, if not a share in the proprietorship, at least some consideration from the owners. This feeling was especially strong in cases where the laws of the land had materially aided the success of the business, and where the profits were unusually large.

"I want to say, in passing, that it is by such indications as the existence of this sentiment that we can see, all through those troublous times, the gradual improvement of the race.

"As some of the employers came to be impressed with the same thought, they began in a quiet way trying the experiment of giving their men a bonus at the end of the year, proportioned to the amount of wages they earned. In some cases this gave place after a time to the plan of making the workmen regular partners, and giving them a certain percentage of the profits in lieu of wages. But when a time of general depression came and the percentage did not amount to as much as their old pay had been, the men felt as though they had been led into a trap, and after they had endured the situation for a time they were glad to return to the former system.

"Another scheme that was extensively tried was cooperation among the workingmen, both in manufacturing and mercantile business. The argument, which was a plausible one, was that the expense of big salaries for management, together with the enormous profits, would all be available for dividends. The results showed that in the long run the profits, in all but exceptional cases, were not more than a fair interest on the investment, and as to the salaries, it was found that financial and business ability was scarce and costly, and yet necessary to success. The associations of workingmen were willing to put their money into buildings, machinery, and stock, and the men were ready to work hard themselves, but they were not willing to pay for skill in management, and so their failure was inevitable. At the same time they still held to the opinion, which was at the bottom of these experiments, that under the old system the owners and managers of the business got too much of the profits and the operatives too little. Is there anything else, Doctor, that you think these people might have tried?"

"I am not satisfied," the doctor answered, "with their efforts at profit- sharing. It seems to me that that scheme, under proper management, ought to have brought the two classes together by giving them a common interest in every enterprise, and so to have gradually done away with all bitterness and strife. Employers might have used a part of their surplus profits in building better houses for their men, in giving them instruction as to a nobler way of living, in opening libraries and bath- houses and cooking schools and savings banks, in keeping them insured against sickness and death, and in doing a thousand things to show the men that they were thoughtful of their comfort and welfare. If the workmen could discover by such means that the employers were really their friends, I think it must have disarmed their hatred and antagonism. Then if, with these benefits, they could have received in money a small percentage above their usual wages, they would certainly have repaid such friendliness by a service so faithful and an industry so constant as to more than make up, in increased profits, for all the philanthropic expenditures."

"Doctor," said Thorwald, "I am pleased to see you take such an interest in this subject. You talk as though you had thought of it before, and you have outlined almost the exact course pursued by the people of whom we are speaking. Hundreds of such experiments were tried and persisted in for a long time, both before the serious labor troubles began and after. Among their strongest advocates were men of theory in the professions, who were actuated by high motives but did not appreciate the practical difficulties. They were pretty sure they could get along with the workingmen without so much friction. But the profit-sharing scheme also had the aid of many excellent men among the employers, as I have said. However, for one reason or another, the experiments all came to naught. In some cases great expense was entered into to provide comforts for the workmen, and after a few prosperous years depression followed and the proprietors found they had undertaken too much. Several large failures, brought about by such lack of judgment, helped to produce disappointment and discouragement. Then it was found by experience that the evil-disposed among the workmen were not to be converted into honest, industrious, and faithful employees in any such wholesale manner. Making men over could not be done in the block. There never had been any difficulty in dealing with the sober, reasonable, well-intentioned men. The trouble had all come from the vicious, the incompetent, and the shiftless ones. And the more privileges this class obtained, the more they demanded. If their working day was made shorter in order to give them the opportunity of taking advantage of the free facilities for improving their minds, they loudly demanded another hour each day and frequent holidays, with the liberty of spending their leisure time as best suited their tastes. If they were given a share of the profits, they complained because it was so small a share, and thought they were being cheated when the proprietors would not let them inspect the books to see if the profits were not larger than represented. Then as partners they claimed the right to be consulted in the management of the business. Such demands brought on disputes, of course; and the natural result was that strikes were not unknown even in these humanitarian establishments. As the labor organizations were then in full blast the better class of men were drawn into the strikes, which sometimes became so serious that the owners were compelled to give up their philanthropic efforts and go back to the old system of giving what they were obliged to and getting what they could in return.

"In general, employers found they had still an unanswered problem on their hands. An undue spirit of independence had been fostered among a class of uneducated, ill-natured, and thick-headed workmen, and society was rocked to its foundation in the effort to keep them within bounds."

"Will you let me make another suggestion, Thorwald?" asked the doctor. "Why did not all classes approach this difficulty in a businesslike way and work together to remove it? Why did not the state see that the right of private contract was a safe and useful one for all sides, and cease to infringe on it by law? Why did not the public teachers make a combined and continued effort to instill a conciliatory spirit into both sides, and to show how peace and brotherly feeling would be a mutual blessing? Why did not the employers--not one here and there, but all of them-- treat their men as they would like to be treated in their place, make friends with them, talk reason even to unreasonable men, speak kindly to the unfriendly ones, urge the value of sobriety upon the intemperate, teach the incompetent, sympathize with the unfortunate, try to reclaim the vicious instead of turning them off harshly, and in every way strive to prove themselves to the men as beings of the same flesh and blood with them? And why did not the workingmen receive what was done for them with the right spirit--give up their envious and suspicious feelings, improve every precious chance of getting knowledge, work for their employers as they would for themselves, cease to use the power of the unions unjustly, cultivate amicable relations with everybody, and try in all possible ways to make true men of themselves? If the men had worked along this line they would have found they were bettering themselves in every way faster than they could by strikes and conflicts."

"Ah! Doctor," replied Thorwald, "you have now the true solution. Such action would have annihilated the difficulties in a day. But to suppose every employer and every workman capable of following such good advice is to suppose that the world had then reached an almost ideal condition. The very existence and character of the troubles show how imperfect men were. It was a common saying then that human nature was the same as it had been in the earliest days and that it would never change while the world should stand. This was a mistaken view, for there had been a great change. The heart had lost much of its selfishness and had begun to grasp in some slight measure a sense of that distant but high destiny to which it had been called."

"If the world," said the doctor, "was not good enough for these troubles to be cured by kindness, I am anxious to know how they were healed. I am sure you can tell us, for those people were your remote ancestors and you are far removed from such vexations now."

"That is true," said Thorwald. "I can tell you how this social problem was solved, and how our race has found release from the many dangers that have threatened us. It has not been by man's device or invention. But God, whose arm alone has been our defense, has always called men to his aid, and thus, in his own time and way, help has come in every crisis. The most important changes in society have been brought about gradually and without violence, and with that hint I think we had better leave this subject for the present. Some day I want to go over with you briefly the history of the work and influence of the gospel of Jesus in the world, and it will then be fitting to refer again to the period of which we have just now been speaking.

"I am sure you will find it a great relief for me to change the subject, or stop talking."

"We will not object to your changing the subject," said I, "whenever you think it best, but we shall try to keep you talking till we know a great deal more about Mars than we do now."

CHAPTER XXXI.
WINE-DRINKING IN MARS.

I went downstairs the next morning before the doctor was ready, and when I met Thorwald I said, without thought: "A fine morning."

"Yes," he replied, "all our mornings are fine. I do not mean that the sun is always shining or that we do not have clouds and a variety of sky effects, but we know the clouds can be depended on not to give rain till night."

"Do you not lose something by having a perpetual calm?" I asked. "For I understand the rain in the night comes only in gentle showers. In our rough world some of us enjoy the grandeur of the storm."

"How about those who are exposed to its fury?" asked Thorwald in reply. "I do not see how anyone can really enjoy what is sure to be bringing sorrow or even inconvenience to others. Could a mother take pleasure in a tempest if she knew her son was in danger of shipwreck from it? Why should it change her feeling to know her son was by her side and that it was only strangers that were in danger?"

"But," continued Thorwald, "are you and your friend ready for an excursion to-day? If you are, I propose to give you a new experience."

"We shall be delighted to accompany you, and as I see breakfast is ready I will go up and tell the doctor to hurry."

"Oh, I wouldn't do that," exclaimed Thorwald. "You must try to learn to live as we do, and you will remember I said the other day that we are never in haste. If, for example, it were Zenith who was late, I should never think of calling to her to hurry, for I should know she must have a good excuse for staying. Her liberty of action is as valuable to her as mine to me, and however long she might keep me waiting, I should feel sure that her action was the result of right motives and correct reasoning. If the doctor does not appear, we can easily postpone our excursion to to-morrow. There would be no lack of occupation for to-day."

"What a delightful feeling it must be," I said, "to be always free from hurry. It is the commonest experience in our imperfect state for one to start a few minutes late in the morning, and then be on a constant jump all day to make them up. One of the evils of our driving age is the wear and tear of our nerves in what we consider a necessary haste to get there."

"Get where?" asked Thorwald.

"To get anywhere or to do anything that we set out to accomplish," I answered.

"I fear," said Thorwald, "that I have talked too much about Mars and not insisted enough on hearing about the earth. Suppose something should happen to break off your visit?"

"You wouldn't miss much, Thorwald."

"We certainly should regret exceedingly not learning many things that you could tell us," he said.

"Yes," I answered, "but you cannot profit by our experiences, while we of the earth are in a condition where we need all the help and advice you have for us. If we ever return to our home we want to tell all about your advanced civilization and how you have overcome the evils that vex our race. But I wonder why the doctor doesn't come. I think I will go and see, but I promise not to interfere with his liberty of action." I soon returned with my friend, and we all went to breakfast. The doctor said he would not eat much, as he felt somewhat indisposed. Here was something new in the life of this household, and each one began to express sympathy and ask what could be done. The doctor was amused, and I said I thought a good, hearty breakfast would make him all right. But Thorwald insisted that something unusual should be done, although his inexperience was so great that nothing feasible suggested itself at first. Zenith was in favor of all repairing to the library, hunting up the histories of the days when people were ill, and finding out the proper remedy for his ailment. This would have been a logical proceeding, but I thought to myself that they did not understand the value of time in such cases and that the doctor would probably either recover or die while they were at work.

As I did not appear to be any more alarmed than my companion was, the excitement soon subsided. But Thorwald was not satisfied yet, and after some further thought his face brightened and he asked me if a glass of good wine would not be the thing for the doctor. When I replied that it would probably not hurt him, Thorwald told his son to go and bring up a bottle of the oldest wine in the cellar, and soon not only the patient but the members of the family and myself were all partaking. No more was heard after this of the doctor's indisposition, and Thorwald no doubt felicitated himself that he had effected a cure. The situation was rather suggestive to me, and while we were drinking, and eating our breakfast, I could not refrain from saying:

"If some of our friends on the earth could see us now, Thorwald, we would be discredited in all that we might say about your higher condition. It would do no good to expatiate on your ripe character and on your attainments in knowledge and virtue. I fear they would not believe much of it if they knew that you not only drank wine yourselves, but encouraged its use by giving it to your guests."

"Why," said Thorwald, "you could tell them the wine was brought out to be used as a medicine, and that the rest of us drank to keep the doctor company. But when you see your friends you had better tell them the truth at once, that while we all take wine here frequently this is the only instance where I have ever known it to be used medicinally."

"They would tell us," said the doctor, "that you have made one mistake at least, and that it is a dangerous thing to have wine in the house, and especially to give it to children."

"He would have a very gross and imperfect conception of our character," said Thorwald, "who should have the thoughts which you express. I can judge something of the nature of the feeling which you say exists on the earth, however, for only a few days ago I was reading a full account of the different temperance movements on our planet. Few subjects in our history are more interesting. Do not despise the temperance reformers, and if you think they are sometimes too radical you can afford to excuse that for the sake of the absolute good they accomplish. All through the early part of our career there was a perpetual warfare against the drinking habit. At first wine was an ordinary article of food, and in some countries more commonly used for drinking than water. There was much abuse of it, but in general people used it as a matter of course, without thinking they were any more responsible for the drunkards than they were for the intemperate in eating. But the evil of overdrinking increased, and some religious reformers found that the easiest way to check it was to forbid all use of intoxicants. Here is an extreme example that I have read of what one such reformer taught: 'If a single drop of alcoholic liquor should fall into a well one hundred and fifty feet deep, and if the well should afterwards be filled up and grass grow over it, and a sheep should eat of the grass, then my followers must not partake of that mutton.' Could any of your prohibitionists be more radical than that?

"In later times many kinds of strong and poisonous drinks were made, and untold harm was done by their use. Drunkenness was the most fruitful source of crime and misery; it, more than any other cause, filled the jails, the almshouses and the insane asylums; it kept men in poverty and squalor; it scattered families and changed men, and sometimes women, too, into beasts. No class or profession was free from the evil, for it disqualified the scholar and statesman for their duties just as it unfitted the laborer for his daily task. It helped to debauch politics and public morals, while it brought disgrace and ruin to private reputation and character. More money was lost by it than was spent to educate and Christianize the world, and it cost more precious lives than war and pestilence combined. Being a crime utterly selfish and debasing, as well as extremely tenacious of its hold upon the individual life, it was almost the greatest enemy to the spread of the gospel.

"Was there anything in the way of good to be said of the drinking habit to offset all this harm? Men drank to be sociable and companionable and to please their friends, and when the habit was fastened on them found they had lost every friend of value. They took to their cups to drown their sorrow, and found a sorrow more poignant among the dregs. They began the moderate use of stimulants to give strength to the body or activity to the brain, and discovered when too late that their abuse had brought down in common ruin both body and mind. No, it is impossible that anyone should ever attempt to make an argument in favor of drunkenness.

"The more active the age the more prevalent was this evil, but the greater, also, was the determination to overthrow it. When the conscience was quickened by the growth of Christianity and men's lives became more valued, many persistent efforts were made to stamp out the crime of intoxication.

"Numerous societies were organized and good men and women entered heartily into the work. Every argument was used to show the danger of the drink habit and to teach the beauty and value of sobriety, appeal being made both to the reason and the conscience. The power of the state was invoked and punishment administered to the drunkards, while the manufacture and sale of intoxicants were restricted and sometimes prohibited. We see how firm a hold this evil had on all classes when we read that very often public sentiment would not permit these beneficent laws to be enforced. In all great reforms the apathy of a large part of the people has been a most discouraging feature.

"Of course it was never intrinsically wrong to drink a glass of wine, but in view of the enormous amount of sorrow and trouble caused by overdrinking, can it be wondered at that many earnest souls came to abhor everything in the nature of intoxicating drink, and to practice and insist on total abstinence? Oh, I can tell you if I lived on the earth now I should be a radical of the radicals on this subject."

"Notwithstanding which," said I, "here you are sitting at your own table and pouring into our glasses this delicious wine."

As a smile passed around at this remark it was Zenith who said:

"Do you see anything incongruous in that?"

I paused a moment to choose a reply, when the doctor spoke up with:

"Far be it from us, Zenith, with our earth-born ideas, to even seem to pass judgment in this happy place, but I presume my companion was trying to imagine what our temperance friends, who do not know you, would say."

"As for us," said Thorwald, "I trust we shall be justified in your eyes at least, before we are through, but let us inquire about those whom you call your temperance friends. I suppose they would have a poor opinion of a man who was loud in his public advocacy of temperance and yet drank wine at home."

"I think," I replied, "that I have heard some such term as 'hypocrite' applied to men of that class."

"And yet," continued Thorwald, "they would think it perfectly proper for a man to keep razors away from his children, but at the same time have one or more concealed about the house somewhere for his own use. It might very easily be argued that razors were dangerous things under any conditions; the children might find them by accident and do great harm to themselves or others; the man himself, though accustomed to their moderate use, might, in a moment of overconfidence, go too far and inflict a serious injury on himself or even a fatal one; and, further, it might be said that razors are of no real use to men, for nature knows best what is needed for protection, and if hair on the face was not necessary for the well-being of man it would not grow there. This argument could be pushed until, under an awakened public sentiment, the manufacture and sale of razors might be prohibited.

"I have said this to introduce a plea for tolerance of opinion. You were created, I have no doubt, as we were, with different temperaments and inclinations, which, with various kinds of education, produce different opinions. You cannot all have the same mind on any given subject, nor all approve of the same methods of reform, but you will make but little progress in true temperance until you can bury minor differences and all work together. You must learn that everything that has been made, whether produced by the direct hand of God or through the agency of man, has its proper use. Do you say that some people would express the wish that everything intoxicating could be destroyed from the earth, as having no proper use? All the evil in it will surely be removed, but the good will remain. At present it is one of the stubborn obstructions in your thorny path. If your way were to be suddenly made smooth and easy your race would never learn self-denial, the only road that leads to a higher state. Your present imperfect life is a daily conflict, and it is only by battles won and temptations overcome that you will ever be built up into virtuous and God-like characters.

"I said you must be tolerant. I can conceive that a man might feel perfectly safe in the use of wine and have no scruples of any kind against it, and yet be sincere in urging people in general to totally abstain from it on account of the harm some might receive. This man must not be denied a place in the temperance ranks. Another might think it a sin to touch a drop. One might believe the only right way to deal with the subject would be to prohibit the sale entirely, another would think more might be done by some other method of restriction. All that I have read of our experiences goes to prove that the people of the earth will never drive out this evil till all shades of temperance people get Christianity enough into their hearts to unite on a broad platform and work as one army with a single purpose."

"Will you not tell us," I asked, "how the reform was finally effected on Mars?"

"Like all other true reforms," replied Thorwald, "it came about through the sanctified commonsense of the church of God, not suddenly by any means, but gradually and only after many years of severe struggle. A combined effort of all good people, especially women, working with spiritual as well as moral weapons, produced an impression which was lasting. When men were taught from their childhood the dangers which accompany the drinking habit; when one class of people denied themselves all indulgence for the sake of the class who were weak; when drinking became a disgrace, and those who could not keep sober were taken in charge by the state and permanently separated from the rest of the community; when the church awoke to its full duty and the rich poured out their money; when men and women forgot fashion and pride and caste in their love for the practical work of Christianity; when the power of the gospel had strengthened men's will and had begun to plant in every heart a love for something purer than fleshly appetite; when the spiritual part of our nature began to gain the ascendency and to occupy the place for which it was made; then intemperance loosed its hold and soon disappeared, never to trouble us again.

"You see it was a long road with us and I have no doubt it will prove so on the earth, but do not on that account lose courage. And let me counsel both of you to join the ranks of the reformers when you get home.

"Although intemperate drinking has long been unknown among us, as well as all other gross imperfections of character, we still make good wine, and no more danger is felt in drinking it than in using milk. Everybody can have all he wants of it. Our tables may be supplied with the luxuries of every clime, but we have learned that it is best for us to be temperate in both eating and drinking. I am sorry your temperance friends, as you say, would not approve of us, but when you see them I trust you will do what you can to let them understand that such temptations as this of which we have been speaking belong to the childhood of a race, and that the people of Mars have long since passed out of infancy."

CHAPTER XXXII.
A GENUINE ACCIDENT.

M ona did not feel obliged to be present at our conversations after she had explained her position to us, but I saw her many times every day. I tried to respect her feeling and avoid the subject which still occupied so many of my thoughts. I fought against my passion, which I told myself was unmanly, since it was not returned in the good, old-fashioned way. What man of spirit would submit to the enchantment of one who, while professing she loved him with her whole heart, declared in the same breath that she also loved equally well half a dozen others? I tried to make up my mind to shake off the spell and be free. To this end I endeavored to examine my heart with the purpose of discovering if possible the secret of Mona's power over me.

I was sure I could not be weak enough to be held so firmly by her beauty alone, lovely as she was. Her mental equipment did not seem to furnish the ground for such a deep attachment, and I could not believe that I was good enough to be so powerfully drawn to her by the inimitable character of her spiritual nature. What, then, was the attraction? It was not far to seek. What was it that first moved me, before I had ever seen her? What accomplishment was it that always came to my mind first when I thought of her? In short, what would Mona, silent, be? I could hardly imagine. But then, she was not silent, and I knew well enough that, struggle as I night, I never could successfully resist the subtle charm of that voice.

So, as I saw no escape for me, I next began to study how I could infuse into Mona's love for me something more of the personal element. How could I teach her to love me just a little for myself alone? Evidently she had been educated in an atmosphere of the most uncompromising monotony. Where everybody loved everybody what chance could there be for lovers? I wondered what would move

Mona. Some heroic action which should appeal to her sympathies would probably do it. She had been pleased with the part I had taken in discovering her retreat in the moon, and perhaps something else in that line would help me. But what was there one could possibly do in Mars which could be called heroic? I should have to ask Thorwald if he could think of anything I could do to arouse the imagination of Mona and bring her a little closer to me.

Not long after I had been indulging in these conflicting thoughts I had a more promising opportunity than I had hoped for of showing Mona that I could do something besides make love to her.

One morning she came to me and said she would like to go out for a long ride. As I never lost an opportunity of being alone with her I eagerly accepted this one and hurried off with her, lest any other member of the household should appear and propose to accompany us. Mona was as agreeable as ever, and chirruped away in her musical style as we walked down the hill in search of just the right carriage. We soon found one which pleased us, and as I was by this time perfectly at home in the management of these vehicles, we started off at a brisk pace along a road which took us through a charming section of the country. It made me happy to reflect that this pleasant ride was at Mona's suggestion. Although she had peculiar views about my manner of wooing, she did not shun my company, and I could not refuse to believe she really loved me as she said. I turned on more power, and as our speed became exhilarating I said to my companion:

"Mona, they will think we have eloped."

"Excuse me," came out in sweet notes, "you will have to explain."

"Dear me, were your people so very proper that you don't even know the meaning of that word? Didn't they ever do anything wrong?"

"Oh, is it wrong to elope?"

"That depends entirely on the point of view. But I cannot explain further without bringing up the subject which you have forbidden me to speak about."

"What subject is that? I have forgotten that I have ever put you under such a prohibition."

"Why, the subject that is always nearest my heart and nearest my lips, the subject of my great love for you, dear Mona, so different from my regard for any other person."

"Oh, I remember now, but I assure you I had forgotten all about it." And here her voice suddenly lost much of its tenderness and assumed a character which she rarely employed, as she continued, "But let us not discuss that topic again. I already know all you have to say on it, and why should we waste our time with such useless talk when there are so many more valuable things to occupy our attention?"

"Forgive me," I exclaimed. "If you will promise me not to sing in that tone again I will talk about anything you wish."

"I agree," she responded, and never did her accents sound sweeter.

Somehow I was not so much affected by Mona's coldness this time as before, and I was able to recover my cheerfulness at once. I then determined to give her no occasion for another rebuff if I could help it, but to do all in my power to entertain her with what she called sensible conversation. There were many things connected with society on the earth in which she took a lively interest, and I made a great effort to talk myself into her favor, so that she would not say again that she preferred the doctor's company to mine.

We had been riding a couple of hours or more, generally at a swift pace, when, from a high point in the road, we saw we were approaching the shore of the sea or a large lake.

Mona was so delighted with the view that I said:

"If we can find any kind of a boat on the shore we will have a ride on the water."

"Can you manage a boat?" she asked.

"Oh, yes, if it is not too large."

"But it may be some new kind, something you are not acquainted with."

"Then I shall have to study it out. But you are not afraid to go on the water with me, are you?"

"If there is anything in this pleasant world to give me fear it is water in such mass as that," she replied, stretching out her hand toward the sea.

"But I thought you were afraid of nothing," said I.

"You have taught me the word," she responded, "and I hardly know its meaning yet, but I must acknowledge that I shrink from the ocean. Its vastness, so much water, overwhelms me. You know it is many, many years since the moon had any large bodies of water."

"So it is," I exclaimed, "and everything will be new to you. What sport we shall have, and I shall make it my business to see that the water does not harm you."

We hurried down to the shore and found the prettiest little boat I had ever seen all ready for us, as if we had ordered it for the occasion. It was evidently intended for children, but was fitted with both sails and oars, and also, I was glad to find, with a little screw and an electric apparatus to turn it. I was overjoyed with our good fortune, and prepared at once to embark. But Mona plainly hesitated. She kept up her musical chatter and tried to be as cheerful as ever, but I saw she was not as eager for the trip as I was. I did not let her see that I noticed her manner, however, and went on with my preparations. When I had brought the boat around so that she could step into it conveniently, she looked in my face, and asked in a voice which trembled with excitement:

"Are you sure you understand how to manage it? It is all so strange to me."

She wanted to decline to make the venture, I thought, but her courage was too great. Now was the time when I proved myself still a son of the earth, with fallible judgment and a will too much engrossed with self. I had been wishing for an opportunity to do some difficult thing for Mona, something noble which should win her affection, and here, when the chance offered, I did not recognize it. The truly heroic action would have been to respect Mona's feeling and give up the idea entirely, for I knew she had a strong aversion to trusting herself on the water. But it was really my own pleasure and not hers that I was seeking, for in answer to her question I said hurriedly:

"Why, certainly. It is as easy to control as the carriage we have just left. We'll not put up the sails if you say so, and I promise to bring you back all safe and sound in a short time. I am sure you will enjoy the new experience, and then I want to hear how your voice sounds on the water."

"Well, I will go," she said, "on your promise to protect me; but I have the queerest sensation, I don't know what to call it. Do you think it is fear?"

"Oh, no, it can't be that, because there is nothing to fear. Are you ready now? Let me take your hand."

As she stepped in and felt the motion she realized how unstable the water really was, and sank down at my feet, emitting an involuntary note of not very joyful quality. But she showed great bravery and, as I helped her to a seat, she said she would no doubt enjoy it after a while. I now shoved the boat out and used the oars a few minutes, but soon tiring of that exercise, I looked into the operation of the electric motor and found it quite simple. Turning on the power, the screw worked to perfection and sent the boat through the water in good shape.

Mona was now recovering her spirits, seeing that no harm came to her, and at my request she sang some of her native songs. This was delightful, and I resigned myself to the full enjoyment of the occasion. It seemed to me that the excitement she had just passed through added a new and pleasing quality to her voice, if that were possible. As I sat listening and musing, my memory carried me back to the first time I had heard this marvelous singer, and I could not help contrasting the two situations. I felicitated myself on my present happiness, for when Mona was singing I wanted nothing more. I seemed to forget then that she would not listen to my tale of love, or if I thought of it I attached no consequence to it. The voice seemed to be a thing by itself, and a thing which in some way appeared to belong wholly to me, whether Mona was mine or not.

She stopped singing after a while and asked if we had better not start for home. To which I replied:

"I turned the boat around some time ago, and we are now headed directly for the place where we found it."

When she expressed surprise at this I steered about in various directions to show her how easily it was done, and then some mischievous spirit, which. I myself must have imported into Mars, put it into my head to try and see how fast our little vessel could go. My idea was partly to satisfy my own curiosity and partly to treat Mona to as great a variety of sensations as possible. The electric apparatus was extremely sensitive, and a slight movement of the lever made an instant increase in our speed. A little more, and we began to go through the water at quite a handsome rate. I enjoyed it immensely, and if Mona did not like it she had pluck enough not to make it known. This emboldened me to put on still more power, which sent the boat ploughing along at such a velocity that the spray flew all about us and the boat shook so that we kept our seats with difficulty. Not knowing what I might be led to do next, and being in reality terribly frightened, if she had only known what the feeling was, Mona now mildly expostulated with:

"Isn't this a little too fast? Something might happen."

"Don't be afraid," I replied. "I'll take care of you. The doctor must have taught you that last word, as it is not used here. You know nothing ever happens in Mars. Everything goes along in the even tenor of its way, moved by laws which are fixed and certain. This boat, you see, is strong and well able to bear the strain. The water is smooth and contains no hidden rocks, and it is perfectly easy to steer clear of the shore, which you see is some distance off yet. But now that I have given you this little excitement, which you will not regret after it is all over, I will stop the current which produces this great force and bring in an artificial law, as it were, to override the natural law now in operation. Just look at this lever and see how easily it is done."

I seized the handle, intending to shut off the power suddenly, but by some unaccountable mistake I turned it the wrong way. Instantly I saw the bow of the boat jump out of the water and go over our heads, and then Mona and I realized that something had actually happened on Mars, for we were both buried under the boat.

I was the first to extricate myself and come to the surface, and, not seeing my companion, I thought she was surely lost. I might save her yet, though, and was just about to dive under the boat again, when her head appeared insight, only a little way from me, her eyes wide open and, really, a smile on her face.

"Can you swim, Mona?" I cried, excitedly.

She had not the breath to answer or else thought my question unnecessary. But I soon found my own answer when I saw her head sinking again just as I had reached her. I clutched her, and, as I held her head above the water, I began to understand that I had something on my hands to fulfill my promise to take care of her. At this instant I saw one of the oars from the boat floating a little way from us and managed to secure it, holding Mona with one arm and swimming with the other. I now helped my companion to half support herself by grasping the oar, while for the rest she was induced to throw an arm over my shoulder. In this way I was left free to make what progress I could through the water, and I lost no time in swimming toward the shore, since there was no hope of our being able to make use of the boat, which now lay, bottom up, on the surface.

All this was done without a word from Mona, although I had been talking to her freely, giving her directions and assuring her of my ability to save her. As this was her first experience in drowning, she had evidently been trying to sing under the water and had found it so difficult that she had determined to keep her lips closed till she was well out of it. With this thought in my mind I said to her as soon as we were under way:

"Your head is so far above water now that you can open your mouth with perfect safety. You see I can talk, and my head is much lower than yours."

She was so situated that I could not see her face easily, and therefore I do not know whether she ventured to unstop her lips or not, but no sound came from them if she did. Perhaps the water still filled her ears and made her deaf. So I called aloud:

"Can you hear me, Mona?"

No answer in words, but I imagined I felt a slight pressure of her hand on my shoulder. I toiled on, musing over her strange behavior, till it occurred to me to try a subject which had never failed to bring a response from her.

"I hope this will make you more affectionate to me, dear Mona," I said; and then, as she made no answer, I continued:

"If we reach the shore alive and get home safe you will love me more than you do Foedric, will you not?"

I thought this would bring an answer, and I was not disappointed, except in the manner in which it came. Not the faintest note escaped from her lips, but a throb of feeling came along her arm, and her hand grasped my shoulder with unmistakable vigor. I suppose she thought I would understand what this answer meant, but I was puzzled. It might mean so many things. Perhaps her heart was softening toward me and she was so much affected by her love for me, stronger and deeper than she had ever thought it could be, that she dared not speak. With this possibility in view I began to feel very tender toward her and to experience the pleasure of one whose love is returned in full measure.

But then her answer might have quite a different meaning. What if she were telling me that she had determined never to speak another word on that subject, and that my question was an offense to her? Surely she had told me often enough to talk about more sensible things, and perhaps this was only a new and forcible way of repeating the same injunction. I reflected, too, that it was hardly fair to take advantage of the present situation to force upon her a prohibited topic of conversation.

There was another possible meaning to her manner of answering me. Perhaps she was indignant because I had insisted on her getting into the boat with me against her wish, and held me strictly responsible for all that followed. With this view in mind I imagined she was saying to herself:

"I want nothing to say to you. I accept your assistance because I cannot get to shore without you, but when once out of this dreadful water I shall have nothing more to do with you."

To place against the latter theory I had the fact that Mona's face had beamed with pleasure all the time I was getting her fixed so I could swim freely. Dwelling upon this memory my mind returned to thoughts of love, and I felt that I must try once more to start that familiar song. So I said:

"Forgive me, Mona, if I have offended you, and let me hear your voice again. You are too good to punish me so severely for my fault in getting you into this trouble. Will you not cheer me with a few notes while I bear you safely to the shore?"

Again a pressure of the hand but no expression from the lips, and I was left to further conjecture over the strange mood my companion was in. I swam leisurely, so as not to exhaust my strength, and as there was a considerable distance to go I had plenty of time to think after I had found it impossible to induce Mona to enter into conversation. Although so near, my companion seemed far away, and I became extremely lonesome. In trying to determine what had occasioned such a mishap in a world where I had been taught to believe such things entirely out of date, I came to the conclusion that the Martians owe their freedom from many misfortunes to their ripened characters, rather than to anything peculiar in their physical laws. With my imperfect development I had made an error in judgment in taking Mona upon the water, and with my untrained mind I had simply made a mistake when I turned the lever of the electric apparatus the wrong way. The Martians had reached such high attainments in every direction that it was practically impossible for them to make mistakes. Thus had they freed themselves from many of the vexations which harass the people of a younger world.

I was fortunately able to endure the strain of the great task which I had undertaken, and finally succeeded in bringing my precious burden to land and helping her to a place of safety. We were both pretty well fatigued with our exertions, but felt no danger from our wet clothes, because of the mild and balmy air.

Mona's behavior still perplexed me. Her manner was delightfully pleasant and familiar. Now that we were safe she appeared to appreciate the humorous part of the situation, and I was loath to believe that she could or would affect such good nature if she were harboring unpleasant feelings toward me. But I could not account for her continued silence, for as yet no word nor sound of any kind had come from her lips. Her face and hands, however, were continually in motion, and after I had overcome my usual stupidity I discovered that she was actually making signs.

"Why, Mona," I exclaimed, "can't you speak?"

She shook her head.

"Nor sing, I mean?"

Another shake.

"Do you mean to say you have lost your voice?"

A nod.

For a moment a shadow settled upon her face, occasioned, no doubt, by my falling countenance, for I must have shown something of the great shock to my feelings. Mona without the voice of Mona! I could not at once realize the depth of my loss. And now it was her turn to attempt to restore my spirits, as we fell back to our original mode of conversing. I urged her to make an effort to sing, and she told me she had tried many times, and that it had grieved her to be so unsocial while I was toiling so hard to save her life.

"Why, my dear," I answered, "I thought you were angry with me for speaking to you again about my love."

Her reply was a look so full of tenderness that I was almost sure that, if she had had her voice, she would have used it more kindly than before. Still it may have been only compassion.

By this time we had found our carriage and were on our way home, and I am sure that if, on our arrival, our friends had judged from our looks, they would have supposed I, and not Mona, had experienced a great misfortune.

Avis had returned to her distant home several days before this, but Antonia and Foedric were at Thorwald's when we arrived, and I had the unpleasant task of relating to the whole household our sad experience. I did not spare myself, although they were all kind enough to offer every manner of excuse for me. Everybody showed sympathy with Mona in all possible ways, but she herself still exhibited the same sunny disposition as ever, although the house seemed quiet without her bright and happy song.

CHAPTER XXXIII.
THE EMANCIPATION OF WOMAN.

Family life in this model home went forward without a jar. Thorwald and Zenith exhibited not the least sign of restraint before us, so that what we saw from day to day we were sure was their natural and usual behavior. They never worked at cross purposes, were never impatient nor forgetful of each other, but without effort, apparently, to avoid friction, they always did what was best pleasing to themselves, and at the same time what was just suited to each other. This happy state of affairs did not come from a division of labor, by which Zenith should have nothing to do with outside matters and Thorwald nothing to say about how things should go in the house, but it seemed to proceed from their innate love of harmony, their perfect compatibility, and their practical equality. The doctor and I saw there was something here far different from anything existing in the conjugal relation on the earth, but we could not decide just what it was. The doctor was strongly of the opinion, however, that it arose in some way from the higher condition of woman.

"You know," he said, when we were alone, "the civilization of a people on our planet is pretty correctly measured by the position occupied by the women, so that here, in this exalted society, they must be held in high esteem, if there is the same analogy between the two worlds in this as in so many other things."

I quite agreed with him, and took the first opportunity when we were all together to introduce the subject.

"I should like to direct the conversation," I said, addressing our host and hostess, "to a topic of considerable interest, just now, to the people of the earth. I am sure we can learn something of value in regard to it from you, and I will introduce it, if you will pardon my impertinence, with a personal question. Will you please tell me who is the head of this household?"

"Zenith."

"Thorwald."

Two answers in one breath.

"It is very polite of you," I said, "to disclaim the honor and each one give it to the other, but, seriously, is there no head?"

"Why, no," answered Thorwald; "we never think of such a thing, and yet you must admit that things run smoothly without it."

"I will then try again, if you please," I said. "Which of you is the bread-winner?"

To which Zenith replied:

"That question is hardly appropriate, for you know we do not work for our daily bread. The bread would come anyway, whether we worked or not; but then, as a matter of fact, every one does work at some useful occupation, because we have found out by long experience that it is much better for us than idleness. If you reply that you have not seen us work while you have been here, I will say that our time is considered to be well employed if we can be learning anything or imparting knowledge to others, as this is supposed to add indirectly to the general well-being of society. But perhaps what you want to know is which of us does the more to benefit the world, and even this would be a difficult question to answer. Thorwald creates, we will say, an elaborate design for a noble cathedral, and as he watches its fair proportions rise under the hands of skilled men, who take an equal pride and satisfaction in their work, his heart is made glad by the thought that for many years after he has left the body the structure will be used as a place for teaching the way of life, with its graceful spires pointing men to heaven. While I, perhaps--"

"Let me tell that part," interrupted Thorwald. "While Zenith, with just as strong a feeling of responsibility for a share of the world's work, composes a beautiful song and writes the music for it, and then sings it before a vast audience, while the phonograph catches it and holds it for future generations. Is she not doing as much as I am toward earning the bread for the family?"

"It certainly cannot be denied," I answered. "But what I want to find out is, to use a homely expression common with us, which of you two holds the reins in this home?"

"Well," replied Thorwald, laughing, "that is a figure of speech which is not employed here, for we use no reins of any kind; but I know what you mean, and I will answer you by saying that we each hold one rein, and in that way drive as steadily as if we were one person."

"But when disputes arise, which one gives in?"

"Disputes never arise, and if they did we would both 'give in,' whatever that expression means."

"If not your wills, do not your wishes or inclinations sometimes oppose each other?"

"Why, no," Thorwald answered quickly. "It is impossible, and for this reason: each one of us is so intent on trying to please the other that we are saved from all temptation to selfishness, which is the root and source of all differences."

While I was considering what next to ask, the doctor broke in with:

"I think my companion will be obliged to discontinue his questions and accept the truth that here we have found an ideal household, where husband and wife are in reality equal. Let me ask if the women, all over this happy world, are treated with as much consideration as in the case before us."

"Why, what a funny question," exclaimed Zenith, before Thorwald could speak. "Why don't you ask if, all over this happy world, we treat our men with consideration and respect? But, to save you the trouble of asking, I will say that, all over this happy world, a man is held in as high esteem and is as tenderly cared for as a woman, every bit. Your words, Doctor, remind me that I have several times wanted to speak to you about a certain manner which you and your friend have exhibited toward me. No one could accuse you of disrespect to Thorwald; indeed, I think your carriage toward him is excellent, but with me you seem to be a little strained, and your manner is a trifle effusive. Pardon me for the criticism. I know your action is well meant, although it is something I am not accustomed to."

"I suppose," said the doctor, "you refer to our feeble and, it appears, stupid efforts to be polite."

"Oh, then I ought to feel complimented instead of finding fault with you. But why should you wish to be more respectful to me than to Thorwald? He is more worthy your regard than I am, and has as many rights in this house as I have, exactly."

"We have been taught to pay an extra deference to women," answered the doctor.

"Why?" asked Zenith. "Because they are superior beings?"

"Hardly that, I think."

"Then it must be because they are considered inferior, and you seek to hide your real feeling, which is one of commiseration, by a false show of politeness."

"That sounds harsh," said the doctor, "and I believe you are not correct."

"Oh, I do not mean to criticise you personally," Zenith made haste to say, "but the system. It seems to me that you, Doctor, try to be sincere; and assuming that to be so, let me ask you why you are more ceremonious in your manner to your neighbor's wife than to your neighbor's husband."

"Well, let me see. Why do I instinctively make a special show of respect in meeting a woman? I never analyzed my feeling, but I will try to do so for you. I think one principal reason is because it is so very conventional that she would expect it, and think me either piqued or ill-bred if I omitted it. Then, deeper than that is a desire to tell her that I recognize in her and admire those graces and amenities which are supposed to be peculiar to her sex. And I suppose there is, also, a little selfishness in it, as if I were asking her to take note that I knew what were the usages of good society."

"But would you not also tell her in effect by your flattery, if you will excuse the word, that she and the rest of her sex are by birth not quite equal to men, and you are trying to make up the difference all you can by politeness?"

"I am not conscious of such a feeling, I am sure," answered the doctor. "It seems to me that woman is entitled to some extra attention because she is physically weaker than man."

"True," said Zenith; "that is a good reason why she should be protected."

"And should we not maintain and practice toward her the spirit of true courtesy?"

"Most certainly. But women should also exercise the same spirit toward men. The duty is reciprocal. The days of knight-errantry, when men were chivalrous and women were merely beautiful, should not last forever; women, too, should learn to be chivalrous. Do not imagine I would have you less considerate or thoughtful of anyone, or less demonstrative in your feelings, if you will only remember that men and women are equal, have equal duties and privileges, and should have similar treatment. Great respect should go where it is deserved, whether to man or woman. If I were an inhabitant of the earth and a woman, I should try to have some such thought as this: one man of character knows another good man is his equal; therefore as they treat each other so I would have them treat me, for then I would know that they held me, also, as an equal, and not as a doll, pretty and well dressed perhaps, but brainless, nor as a child who must not be told things too deep for its mind."

"I begin to understand you," said the doctor. "You first get me to admit that women are not a superior order of beings, and then you argue that, as we do not treat them exactly as we do each other, we cannot consider them our equals, and therefore nothing remains but that we must look upon them as inferior to us."

Zenith gave a pleasant little pink laugh and answered:

"I see you have found me out. But you do not deny that my logic is correct."

"I have tried to tell you several times," returned the doctor, with a smile, "that, as for me, I do not feel guilty of harboring the least degrading sentiment toward women. But I cannot answer for the opinions of the world at large. This subject promises to be more interesting than we anticipated. I see you know a great deal about it. Have women always been accorded an equality with men, or is it a part of your mature development?"

"Now, Doctor, just see how prejudiced you are. You would never think of asking if the men of Mars had always been the equal of women. It would be quite as natural with us to ask it in one way as the other."

"I will try again, then, by asking if the two sexes have always been so happily equal as at this time."

"I will give you a direct answer to that question. They have not. But I think I have talked enough for once. Thorwald will tell you all about our tortuous course in reaching our present condition, if you wish."

"Not at all," said Thorwald. "I would like to tell it, but this is a topic that Zenith has taken a special interest in, and she shall have the pleasure of talking to you about it."

"Now then!" I said to myself, "here is a difference right away. Zenith says Thorwald must tell it; Thorwald would like to do so, but insists on sacrificing himself for Zenith's sake. Now, what if Zenith should prefer the pleasure of self-denial, and refuse to let Thorwald immolate his desire so readily? What could prevent war in this happy family? Would a quarrel be any less a quarrel because its cause was unselfishness rather than selfishness?"

But if I, with a worldly heart, was expecting a lapse from these excellent people, I was disappointed, for Zenith, with a look of wifely affection toward Thorwald, said pleasantly:

"Very well, since Thorwald is so kind, I will do my best, if you are sure you will not tire of hearing me talk."

The doctor and I expressed our pleasure with the arrangement, and Zenith began:

"I wish to say at the start that, whatever may have been your experience on this question, it is hardly possible that your mistakes have equaled ours, for the folly and wickedness of our race have been stupendous and of long continuance."

"If you will excuse the interruption," I said, "I will suggest that we can sympathize with you, as our history shows the greatest injustice to women."

"Your remark proves to me that you cannot fully sympathize with us. I did not infer, as you seem to do, that the women of Mars had been the only victims of injustice.

"But without further delay let me begin, only do not hesitate to break in upon my story with any inquiries that suggest themselves to you.

"We read that God created man, male and female; that is, there came forth from the hand of the Maker a male man and a female man, and all through that early age of gold they loved each other, and served their God with purity of heart and without a selfish thought. God was their father, they were his children, with equal privileges, equal affection, and equal ability to do faithful service. No evil spirit was near to whisper in the ear of either a suggestion of personal leadership. Ambition, that ambition which would exalt self at the expense of another, was not yet born, and neither of these happy beings could conceive it possible to achieve a higher happiness by lording it over the other.

"So they lived till sin came; and among the woes which sin brought in its train there were few more dreadful than the decree that the man should rule over the woman and that her desire should be unto her husband. For thousands of years our race struggled against that giant evil. During a long period the condition of woman was so low that we know nothing of her, and when she reappears it is only as the servant of man. Made in the image of God as the companion of man and an equal sharer in all his rights and duties, she is now his chattel, a piece of property, held for his selfish use or disposed of for his advantage.

"Even in these dark days individuals of our sex rose out of the general degradation and showed that they were fitted by nature for a higher position. But sin and ignorance kept the mass of them under the heel of their masters. As civilization advanced there came some mitigation of their lot, and where pure religion gained a foothold women began to receive recognition; but their state was deplorable indeed among all those peoples whose religion was only gross superstition and idolatry.

"In the process of time Christ came and brought the light of heaven to this dark world, and from that hour woman can well say that her day began to dawn. One of the sweetest strains in her song of salvation is that evoked by the memory of her resurrection from misery and abasement to a position of honor among the children of men. The change, however, was very gradual, for Christianity itself was slow in gaining ground; but the gospel was ever the friend of woman, as of all the oppressed, lifting her up where she could influence the world and begin to fulfill her destiny. As fast as the nations shook off barbarism and became in any degree enlightened, the unnatural burdens were lifted from the shoulders of woman, although for a long time she was compelled to perform more than her share of severe toil even among people who thought themselves civilized.

"Then came a time when, in nations of some refinement, there was such a reaction against the injustice and degradation to which woman had so long been subjected that she suddenly became an object of sentimental regard among courtly men. Her noble qualities were exaggerated far beyond their merit, and she was set on a pedestal, to receive homage and all the outward forms of respect from those whom she so recently served as a menial. Being so poorly fitted by her long training in serfdom for such exaltation, what wonder is it that her head was turned by the flattery, and that her recovery was slow and difficult? The insincere and superfluous manners of that period remained for ages a vexation to our growing intelligence and a hindrance to our true progress; and, from what you have said, I am inclined to think you of the earth are now going through some such experience as ours.

"After that epoch had been passed, woman never fell back to her former condition, although she did not yet for a long time reach a position that was at all enviable, except as compared with the dark days of her bondage. But she was now where she could take advantage of the general uplifting of the race, and though kept in the background by man as much as was possible, she was constantly growing and learning, preparing herself for a future of which she would then dare not even to dream.

"And now I am coming, in this rapid sketch, to that period of activity and change which Thorwald has described to you in its industrial features. In portraying some of the evils of those days, arising from our almost ineradicable selfishness, he was obliged to make his picture a somber one, a necessity under which, happily, I am not placed. Looking at the times, not as compared with the present era but with what had gone before, which was the only comparison the people of that day could make, there was much room for encouragement. It was, in truth, a bright day, whose beauty, however, consisted not so much in the realization of happiness as in the promise of still brighter days to come. Material prosperity abounded, education flourished, and religion was beginning to creep down from men's heads into their hearts. Wrongs were righted, justice enthroned, and philanthropy sprang into being. Even while there was so much evil, and while some men seemed to be trying all they could to keep back the breaking dawn, the day was surely coming. The brotherhood of man, long preached as a settled principle, now became a living force, showing itself in a multitude of devices for relieving distress, lessening pain, alleviating poverty, and for the general betterment of society.

"Surrounded by such a universal spirit of improvement, woman felt the impulse of new life, and heard the call to a higher service to humanity than she had ever yet rendered. As men's minds broadened and their hearts grew more tender, and as their sympathies reached out to the weak and down-trodden of every class, it was not possible that their ancient prejudice against woman could much longer survive. Her rise from this time forward was rapid. Let us examine the position which, under the influence of this kindly feeling, she soon came to occupy. Protected by many special laws, guarded by all the legitimate forces of society, but exempt from military and police service, honored for her high and noble qualities, respected by all whose regard was of value, and loved with a true affection which scorned the question of individual rights, her lot seemed indeed a happy one. Shielded from the severe struggles of life, freed from the cares of business, released in a great measure from uncongenial work and from the dangers attending exacting labor, with the disagreeable things in life kept from her as much as possible, always seeing the best of every man's character and manners, and, more than all, being supreme in her natural domain, the home, with none to dispute her right, what more could she ask?"

"What, indeed?" I remarked, as Zenith paused a moment after her question. "The picture you have drawn looks so bright, beside your description of her former lot, that I have no doubt she was now contented and happy."

"So you think that shelter and protection and the love of husband and children and the serenity of home ought to be enough to satisfy one who was created with a spirit as restless, a brain as active, an individuality as marked, and hands as clever as those of man?"

As Zenith threw this question at me and waited for me to answer, I realized that I had been caught by her former inquiry, and found not that Zenith was about to take advanced ground on the subject before us. Wishing I had not drawn her attention so squarely to my personal opinions, and yet feeling obliged to stand up for my position, I said:

"It seems to me that woman's surest path to honor and happiness is that marked out for her by nature, a path which she adorns because so well fitted for it, and that to forsake the home and compete with man for the thousand places in the work of the world would be to cast aside the charm of her womanliness and all that makes her what she is, a solace and comfort to all the world. If she seeks for a pleasurable life, where can she find such keen and lasting pleasure as among the duties of home, and if she is ambitious to lift the world to a higher plane, where is it possible for her to have so much influence as in the nurture of the young?"

"So spoke the men of our race in the era I am describing to you," replied Zenith. "It seems as if you must have been reading some of our old writers, so closely do you follow the ideas then prevalent. I have read and reread those histories until I am quite familiar with them, and you shall hear how such views as you have expressed soon became very old-fashioned."

"I am sure your account will closely concern us," I said, "for the age of which you are now speaking must be that corresponding to our own times on the earth. The woman question is attracting special attention, and seems bound to remain with us indefinitely; but I am frank to say I think our women are making a mistake in trying to elbow their way into man's domain, whatever may have been the result of the movement in this favored world."

"I suppose you would have them stay at home where they belong," said Zenith, with a good-natured laugh, which sounded as if she were confident enough of her ability to meet any possible argument."

"Yes," I replied, "out of pure kindness to them. It is an astonishing thing to me that they can think of gaining anything by giving up all that is distinctive in their nature and becoming more like us. I am not so much in love with my own sex as to enjoy seeing our sisters and our wives and daughters trying to make themselves over into men."

I now felt that I had said enough, and so expressed myself to Zenith, but she replied pleasantly that she was glad I had told my thoughts, as it gave her an opportunity to say some things that might not otherwise have been called for.

"You seem to think," she continued, "that woman's supreme happiness is to be gained by self-effacement. I suppose her custom is with you, as it formerly was here, to renounce her own name at the marriage altar."

"It is," I replied.

"And from that hour," resumed Zenith, "she makes every effort to bury herself, to deny her personality, and to lay aside whatever individual desires and aspirations she may have had; that is, if she is what you would call a true woman. If she objects to this renunciation and attempts to make an independent career suited to her talents, then she is strong- minded and is trying to unsex herself. With the world full of work waiting for her nimble fingers and loving heart, she is compelled to suppress all secret hope of doing something to impress her own character on that world, because her only duty is in the home. A man is also called upon to be a good husband and father, but that by no means comprises all he is expected to be and do. To him it is given to strike out into untrodden fields, and, without reproach, to make a name for himself if possible.

"You say work is hard and disagreeable, but is it all dull and uninteresting? Are there not sweet moments of hope in every work, and then the joy of achievement when it is over? Do not men find this joy and the rewards of labor amply sufficient? The more difficult the task, the greater the satisfaction when it is accomplished. Business is perplexing and uncertain, you say, but what of the triumphs of success? Would any man refuse to undertake an enterprise because success was not certain? The very uncertainty adds zest to the business, and makes hope possible. From all this striving and achieving, and from all the satisfying rewards which come with success, woman is debarred. Then there are the professions and the wide range of occupations which require education and special training. What a variety for man to choose from, while you would confine woman to one; and a great many women, not being born good cooks or good housekeepers, cannot fill that one with any credit to themselves. So what can life be to them compared with what it ought to be? Think of the opportunities they might have in these higher occupations of competing for the prizes of life--honor, fame, position, riches, and, above all, the consciousness of doing some good in the world. Oh, it is impossible for you to realize anything of the longing in woman's heart to be someone, to do something, and so to be relieved from the everlasting monotony of the treadmill, which, if men were obliged to submit to it, would make the majority of them insane.

"You see I have put myself in the place of one of my sex in that olden time, and have spoken as she felt when to express her feelings would have been almost a shame to her.

"What I desire to show you is that woman had not then received all that was due her, although men seemed to think she was fully emancipated. But events moved rapidly in that stirring age, and this great question could not be kept in the background in a day when every abuse and injustice was allowed a hearing and reform was in the very air. Even the dumb beasts had such powerful advocates that cruelty and unkindness were greatly checked. What wonder then, as men's sensibilities and consciences became quickened, that they should begin to see, what they could not see before, that a fuller liberty ought to be accorded to woman? But this vision came not without help. Sometimes in our history we have known of a race being deprived of their freedom, and so benumbed by their condition that they desired nothing better, and so perforce waited for a movement for their enfranchisement to come from without. It was not so in this case. Women themselves cried out against their lot. They were not so enraptured with the calm and quiet of their conventional life but that they felt the stirrings of ambition for something different, and they did not fear to raise their voice for more liberty."

"Liberty!" I echoed. "Were they really deprived of liberty?"

"Yes, liberty to choose a calling that would suit their individual tastes and satisfy their growing ambition."

"Excuse me," I again interrupted, "but were not these women who exhibited so much restlessness unattached--that is, without many family ties? And were not the great majority so contented in the shelter of home and so engrossed in the care of husband and children that they were entire strangers to any such disturbing fancies, or ambitions as you call them? And, again, did not this large class of happy and busy wives and mothers resent the action of those self-appointed liberators who were fighting for an image of straw and crying themselves hoarse over imaginary wrongs?"

Zenith smiled again in that peculiar manner which told me, in the pleasantest possible way, that she was perfectly sure I was on the losing side, and with the smile she resumed:

"Your questions are so familiar to one who has studied this subject that they seem like another plagiarism, as it were, from our histories, but I will give you fair answers.

"It is true that the early protests came from the solitary women, unfortunately not a small class at that day, who, being without legal protectors, felt the inequalities of the law and the unjust restraints put upon their sex by society, but the truths they spoke came with added force because of their intimate acquaintance with their needs.

"You are wrong in your supposition that the mass of women were so shallow in mind as to know nothing of those longings for a fuller, more satisfying life. Deep in their nature, planted by the Creator himself, was the same lofty spirit with which man was endowed, and it could not be smothered by marriage. Taking a husband should not, and in reality does not now, change one's ambition or aim in life any more than taking a wife does, but in those benighted days men, after marriage, could go forward with their plans just as if nothing had happened, while the women were supposed to forget their high hopes and aspirations and confine themselves entirely to the trivial round of domestic duties. The men, however, were much mistaken if they thought their wives were forgetting. They but bided their time.

"In your last question you are not altogether wrong, for there were a few unthinking ones who joined with some of the men in ridiculing the whole movement as unnecessary and foolish. But this class had not much influence, and, in spite of such opposition as they offered, the reform made steady progress.

"As a help to obtain what she was striving for, woman asked for the right of suffrage, and thereupon had to undergo a fusillade of cheap criticism from those who would not understand her, and who supposed she wanted this privilege as an end and not as a means. Men were slow to grant the right to vote, but after much discussion suffrage began to be allowed in matters where the women were particularly interested. With the first concession, however, men realized that the force of all their arguments was broken, and before many years the full right was bestowed.

"And now, Thorwald, I am sure our good friends did not come so far from home to hear me talk all the time. The rest of the subject concerns your sex as much as mine, and you had better take up the story at this point."

"Oh, no," replied Thorwald, "I shall not take the narrative away from you now, you may be sure, for what is left is just the part you can best relate. I shall enjoy it as much as our friends from the earth. But I propose that we hear the rest this afternoon, and that, in the meantime, we go out for a drive."

"A drive," I asked, "what do you drive?"

"You shall see," Thorwald answered, as he stepped to the telephone. I thought I should hear his message, but found the instrument had been further improved. In the use of the telephone as I had known it, everybody in the house was much surer of hearing what was said than the person at the other end of the line was, but here the one addressed was the only one to get a word of the communication.

Thorwald talked to us a short time about other matters, and then asked us all to prepare to go out. When we reached the door the doctor and I were surprised to see a beautiful and commodious carriage, to which were attached, with the lightest possible harness, four of the handsomest horses we had ever seen. There were, besides, two fine saddle-horses for the children, who were to accompany us.

Thorwald drove, but without rein or whip, the horses being guided perfectly and easily merely by word of mouth. The animals were also so large and strong that they seemed to enjoy the sport as much as we did.

"Do you mean to say," I inquired, "that such a turnout as this can be had for the asking?"

"Certainly. I just said through the telephone that I would like a carriage for four persons, and two saddle-horses. The man who has the care of the horses is a friend of mine who likes the work better than anything else."

"The horses appear to be well broken," the doctor remarked.

"Broken," said Zenith, "what do you mean by that, Doctor?"

"Why, it is an expression by which we mean that the high spirit with which they were born has been subdued, making it easy to train them to obedience."

"They must be wild, then," spoke Zenith again, "and you are obliged to tame them. The difference here is that the horses are born tame and do not need breaking, and though they have plenty of spirit, as you see, they are so intelligent and have such solidity of character that there is never any danger that they will become unmanageable."

"That must be so," said I, "or you could not be sure of being free from accidents. But tell us, Thorwald, how it happens that we have not seen others enjoying this delightful mode of traveling."

"It is not very singular that you have not seen any horses before," said Thorwald. "They have been entirely superseded in all kinds of business, you remember, by mechanical power, and even for pleasure-riding most people are too tender of heart to enjoy using them. They fear the horses will be fatigued, and they do not like to see them straining themselves in dragging a heavy load, when there is a force that has no feeling ready to do it a great deal better.

"But you can see these horses are not working very hard, and it is a good thing for us sometimes to give up a little sentiment. There is some danger that our sympathies may carry us too far. For instance, it is probably a real kindness to these horses to give them a little work, if we are only careful not to render their service galling to them; and yet there are many people who never drive, on account of the feeling they have for the beasts."

"It would be a good thing if we had more of that sentiment on the earth," said the doctor.

CHAPTER XXXIV.
THE EMANCIPATION OF MAN.

After an exhilarating ride, in which the doctor and I, certainly, were not troubled by any over-sensitiveness in regard to such robust horses, we returned to the house and soon found ourselves seated in the music room listening to one of their famous dramatists reciting his own words through the phonograph. Next we had some music, and then a poem, from the same prolific instrument.

When this entertainment was over, and after lunch, Zenith, at our urgent request, seconded by Thorwald's solicitation, resumed her narrative.

"We read," she began, "that during the time when men were grudgingly bestowing the right of suffrage on our sex, woman was making rapid strides toward a position in society fitted to her talents and aspirations. One occupation after another became available, and it was no longer a disgrace or hardly a peculiarity for women to be earning their living instead of depending for support on their fathers or brothers. This tended to create in them a feeling of independence, and in many employments they had every right to be proud of their attainments, for, with so little training, they often surpassed the men at their own trades. Even then, however, some of the old prejudice against the sex seemed to remain in force, since women were discriminated against in the matter of wages. When they did the same work and did it better, still their pay was less than that of men. But this was a temporary injustice, which disappeared, as it was bound to do, when woman had acquired her full freedom and had been in the field long enough to prove her right and ability to stay.

"The work at which women excelled was that requiring a quick intelligence, nimble fingers, and the faculty of easy adaptability. In the realm of physical strength woman was not a competitor, but there was another field in which she more than made up for that loss, and in which she early began to show great native ability. That was in all pursuits demanding the education of the mind. Here is where she was to look for the greatest of her victories. Nature had endowed man with a superior strength of body and muscle, but woman with a higher order of mind."

"I must interrupt you here, Zenith," said the doctor. "This is assuredly an instance where your race differs materially from that of the earth, for with us man has by nature the stronger mind."

"How do you know?" asked Zenith.

"It has been proved so in all ages."

"Yes, but does not the expression 'all ages' include with you only the ages in which man has been the ruling spirit, and woman has been kept down and allowed but little opportunity to show the strength of her mental faculties? You know our history takes in not only a period similar to that covered by your whole career, but also other ages which we believe correspond with the years yet to come for the inhabitants of the earth. It has been during the latter era, a time which you have not yet seen, that woman has proved the truth of my assertion."

"I wish to make myself understood," said the doctor again. "I am willing to grant the equality of the sexes, as far as natural rights go; that is, that every man and every woman ought to have the opportunity to develop all their talents, untrammeled by any edict or convention of society. Perhaps I would agree with you also in believing it would be better to treat men and women alike, with open-hearted, sincere courtesy, and use equal ceremony in showing respect to individuals of either sex. But it seems to me that there is a vast difference between all that and your latest position. There are many people of our generation on the earth, and their number is rapidly increasing, who believe in the essential equality of the sexes, but I never heard one put forward anything approaching the claim you make, that woman was created with a higher order of mind than man--I believe that was your expression; and this is why I say that in this particular your race differs greatly from ours."

To which Zenith replied:

"I am not so sure of that, my dear doctor. It would seem hardly fair that man should be given both physical and mental superiority. But please tell me again why you think man has the stronger mind."

"Because he has done the thinking of the world. The intellectual achievements of woman, though occasionally brilliant, are not to be compared with those of man. This is true in every department throughout our history--in science and art, in religion, in literature, in government, and in everything that I could name. It is hardly to the point for you to say that woman would have done more if she had possessed a fuller freedom; perhaps it is true, but it seems to me a matter of conjecture. Neither is it a complete answer for you to say that in the years to come woman, being wholly enfranchised, will revolutionize the world by her unexpected powers. We can judge only by what she has done. Excuse me, Zenith, for trying to uphold my point. It is rather discouraging, when I can see by your face that you can demolish my argument in a moment, whenever you choose to attempt it."

We all laughed at the doctor's want of courage, and Zenith answered:

"I beg your pardon; I am greatly at fault if I have any such expression in my face. My confidence, if I have any, is not in any supposed ability I may have in conversation, but in our experience here on Mars. Your history matches ours so well up to your generation that I cannot but think the likeness will continue; and if it does, then woman, in your near future, will prove the truth of my statement. But before I proceed to tell you what she has done in this world, let me ask you if your women have shown any mental peculiarity which distinguishes them from men."

"Yes," answered the doctor, "their intuitive perceptions appear to be more developed than those of men, probably because they use them more. A man may reach a certain conclusion by a course of reasoning, while a woman will often arrive at the same point much quicker by intuition. That is, a man will tell you why he knows a thing, when a woman simply knows it because she knows it."

"Is that faculty akin to anything else with which you are acquainted?"

"Yes, we call it instinct in animals."

"Is not the possession by woman of that quality a silent but powerful suggestion to you of the fact that she was treated like an animal in the dark days of her inthrallment?"

"I had not thought of it," returned the doctor, "but it certainly may be looked upon as a sad commentary on that rude age."

"Do you consider this instinct an advantage to woman?" asked Zenith.

"Certainly; it is a great help to her, often serving with much success in place of other faculties."

"Would it be a valuable quality to add to man's mental equipment?"

"Yes, indeed, if he could retain all his other powers of mind."

"Well, now let me ask you what would come to pass if the women of the earth, possessed already of that quickness of thought, that ability to discern the truth by direct apprehension, should, by thorough education and many years of patient training, acquire the power of reasoning, the judgment, the strength of mind, and all the intellectual powers now held by your men?"

"That is a very large 'if,' and I cannot tell you what would happen," answered the doctor.

"I have only described," continued Zenith, "what actually took place on our planet. When the movement for giving woman a higher education began, men looked at the subject just as you do now. Women were supposed to be of inferior mental capacity, and it was thought to be a foolish thing to attempt to educate them. 'Better educate the boys,' men said, 'and let the girls learn to cook and sew and to play the piano; that is all that will ever be required of them.' But, in spite of every discouragement, the girls improved their opportunities so well that they were soon taking the prizes away from the boys. Broadminded philanthropists of both sexes endowed schools for them, and the highest institutions of learning opened their doors to them. When the young women, almost from the start, began to be successful in competitive contests in different departments of scholarship, it was generally thought that such cases were exceptional and would not be apt to be repeated very often. But this was a great mistake. These instances proved to be no exception. It was found that woman's facility of thought and native acuteness gave her an immense advantage over the masculine mind in mastering any ordinary course of study. But this was surface education. The reasoning power and the solidity of mind for which men were distinguished in mature life came later, but they came.

"At first, only here and there a girl was fortunate enough to be offered a liberal education; but when it was found that in almost every instance they brought great credit on themselves, the number increased with rapidity, until a college course was the customary and expected close of almost every girl's school-days. For it was not the rich only that had this advantage, since by this time education was free, being provided either by the public or by universities richly endowed.

"All this time the boys seemed to find a great attraction in business and the trades, and appeared to be willing that the girls should have a monopoly of the higher education. One circumstance that greatly helped this state of things was the extraordinary furor that prevailed just then in the matter of manual training. This system had received more or less attention from educators for many years, and it had been introduced into schools as an addition to the regular course of study. That was a material age. Men desired first of all to be practical, and the new method of teaching, being eminently practical, became exceedingly popular with the boys. The parents, not dreaming where it would end, and seeing the eager interest with which their sons now crowded into the schools, encouraged them in it.

"Schools of technique, in which the literary branches were entirely subordinate, sprang up on every hand, and two or three years spent in these institutions took the place of a college course. The old universities tried to meet the changing sentiment by paying more attention to science, by giving the students a free choice of studies, and by shortening the course when desired. But the mechanical idea in the new education seemed to be the attraction. The boys were seized with a passion for doing something with their hands, and their inventive faculties were quickened, increasing in a remarkable degree their interest in their work and studies.

"For a long time this movement was thought to be a great advance in education. It was such an improvement on the old way, to find the young men learning something useful, rather than wasting their time over the dead languages and other things they would never need after finishing school. And it must be acknowledged that all this industrial impulse was of advantage to the world in its way. It multiplied labor-saving machinery, added to the people's comforts in many ways, and increased the general prosperity and well-being of society as far as material improvements could do it.

"But there was another side to the picture. So much time could not be given to training the hand and hardening the muscle without detracting from the attention due to the cultivation of the brain. To be sure, the brain was active enough, but it was receiving a one-sided development, which boded it no permanent good.

"I have spoken at such length of this almost universal rage for technical education, because it was a chief factor in turning the world over."

We all smiled at this expression, and the doctor asked:

"How did it overturn the world?"

"By aiding in taking the real brain work away from the men and giving it to the women."

"Did this actually happen?"

"Certainly it did. Not in a day, but in the process of time. How could it be otherwise, when the women alone had been for many years going through that long, patient mind-drilling which is the only preparation for a thorough education? When the young men observed that a civil engineer, a superintendent of a factory, or even a skilled mechanic could earn a larger salary than a college graduate, it took away much of the incentive for the old-fashioned education, and they were perfectly willing to see their sisters take what they had not time for.

"And so it came about that the women began to crowd into the learned professions; and, as there was not one which they could not adorn, the prejudice against them soon wore off, and before many years they were competing with men in all the grandest fields of human action. Even in the matter of government woman's power was felt. Men were so engrossed in the endeavor to develop to their fullest extent the material resources of the planet that they became careless of the higher duties of citizenship, especially after the women began to take control of things. They saw affairs were well managed, and seemed to be relieved to have them taken out of their hands, not dreaming that they were forging chains for themselves which it would take long years to break. Although the world was constantly growing better, it was far from a perfect age. Human nature was still a synonym for selfishness, and with men and women measuring swords on every intellectual battlefield a contest for supremacy was inevitable.

"Man was absorbed in his chosen work, he was indifferent to public affairs, and he was, in his way, proud of the position woman was taking in the world, but he could not let her assume his place as acknowledged leader without a struggle. He said he had given her her rights, and now she wanted to deprive him of his rights.

"There was too much truth in this, for society had not reached a state where the sexes could live in perfect equality. It was admitted by all that there must be a head, both in the household and in the state, and it long remained a question which should rule. But was there ever a struggle of long continuance on the earth in which mind did not triumph at last?"

"I must answer in the negative," replied the doctor, "although I perceive it will help your argument."

"Why, this is not an argument," continued Zenith. "It is simply a story of what has taken place on this planet. If you have any doubt of it, ask Thorwald. You have known him longer than you have me, and, perhaps, would have more confidence in what he would say. He ought to have told this part of the story himself. I know you think I am exaggerating, because you see I am making my sex come out ahead."

Zenith said this in a playful manner, which showed she was as far as possible from being offended, but the doctor pretended to take her seriously, and replied with feeling:

"Do forgive me, Zenith, for my thoughtless expression, and pray do not stop in your narrative at this interesting point. I will tell you how I came to use the word to which you object. While you were talking I was thinking how one would be received on the earth, who should attempt an argument to show the probability that anything like what you are telling us should ever come to pass there."

"Well, how would such an argument be received?" asked Zenith.

"It would probably be passed by without any notice whatever, if you will excuse me for telling the truth," answered the doctor. "It certainly would not be looked upon as serious, and I fear it would not even receive the dignity of being called funny. Even the women would laugh feebly at the extravagant notion, and think no more of it. But we were talking of Mars, not of the earth, and I am exceedingly anxious to know how affairs progressed here, though there is no likelihood that they will ever be paralleled among us."

"I would not be too sure, Doctor," spoke up Thorwald. "Better wait till Zenith is through."

"I shall wait longer than that before I believe the earth will ever go through such an experience. But now I am ready to listen."

"When I speak of woman assuming leadership," resumed Zenith, "do not misunderstand me. Although society was not perfect, still it was not a gross age, and there was no return to the manners of those rude times when women were cruelly treated and men took all the good in the world to themselves. Oh, no, there was no absence of good manners. Women treated men with the greatest courtesy, showing them every mark of outward respect, and being much more polite to them than to each other. And it was not all show, either; for, in spite of the fact that the men were patronized unmercifully, the women really thought a great deal of them, and often remarked to each other that the world would be a dull and uninviting place without them. They admired their robust strength of body, their brawny arms and well-trained hands, as well as their many excellent qualities of mind; and they never tired of telling them in honeyed words how necessary they were to their happiness.

"The women were very considerate also in the matter of laws. The rights of the men were well looked after. To be sure, they were not allowed to vote and hold office, but in their fortunate, happy condition it was incredible that they should care about a little thing like that. Were they not perfectly protected by the law, and did they not have as much to do already as was good for them? The women argued that if the men were given the right of suffrage it would only be the cranks who would avail themselves of it, for the great mass of the men were perfectly satisfied with their condition.

"A man was allowed the right of dower in his deceased wife's estate, and he could hold property in his own right, even after marriage. His wife could not even deed away her real estate without his consent. By this you see how carefully the men were shielded from the liability of coming to want.

"In matters of the heart it was not considered modest for a man to make a direct proposal, but in reality the affair was in his hands, for no woman could make any advance unless she received encouragement from the object of her affections."

"How about the home?" asked the doctor. "Did man take the place of woman there?"

"He did whatever he was asked to do in the home. You must know that at this time domestic duties were quite different from what they formerly were. Men had not given up all their thought and time to handicraft for nothing. The drudgery had pretty well disappeared under the full play of the inventive faculties, so that the home duties were not exacting. What work there was, was shared by the sexes, each doing that which was appropriate. The management of the home was, of course, in the hands of the women."

"Was there no department in which the men were masters?" inquired the doctor.

"Not one. They thought they were in full charge in their peculiar field of labor, but here, as everywhere, the women dictated their terms when they chose."

The doctor was bound to learn all he could about this curious state of things, and asked again:

"What effect did all this strain upon the mind have on woman's physical nature? You have admitted that she was weaker in body than man, and it seems to me she must have been ill prepared for the struggle you have narrated. From the experience we have had in educating women, we believe it is a positive injury to them to attempt to reach that high degree of culture which is easily and safely compassed by men. Our idea is that nature never intended that they should study much, for their minds are really not any stronger than their bodies. Too much brain work has already ruined the health of a good many girls, and when we left the earth the reaction against the higher education of woman had fairly begun. For we believe that her mental faculties can be developed only at the expense of her physical powers, and that if she were to persist in such an abnormal cultivation of her intellect it would be sure to result in the deterioration of her offspring and disaster to the race. So, for the sake of the generations unborn, we--that is, the male men of the earth--who still retain our grip on affairs, have about decided to put a stop to this foolish mania among our young women. We will probably pass laws, setting a limit in the several branches of study beyond which girls shall not be allowed to go, either at school or privately."

We all laughed heartily at this idea, including the doctor himself, who continued:

"Well, what else can we do to stop them? Stop them we must, or we shall soon become a race of weaklings and mental imbeciles."

Thorwald had been getting more and more interested, as I could see by his face, and now broke out with:

"Doctor, you surprise me. I have acquired such a respect for your intelligence that I can hardly believe you serious. If Zenith will excuse me, I should like to answer your question. Hard study did not hurt our young women, and it never hurts anyone. It is careless living and a disregard of the laws of health that do the harm. Physical training was an important part of the education of our women. They could never have accomplished what they did without sound bodies, and it must be unnecessary for me to say that the more highly cultured they became the more our race improved. Learning never made poor mothers. Ignorance does that. Do not keep education out of the home. Keep out folly, low desires, sordid ambitions, uncultivated tastes, narrow-mindedness, envy, strife, wastefulness, inordinate pleasures, and every evil thing that comes from an empty, ignorant mind. Keep out the darkness; let in the light. It is not God's way to give capacity and desire for noble things, and then shut the door to their attainment."

"Many thanks, Thorwald," exclaimed Zenith, "for your good help. And now, Doctor, will you ask anything further?"

"I must admit," answered the doctor, "that your experience gives you more knowledge of the subject than we possess, and perhaps we are wrong. Of course, we want that to come to pass which will be best for our race. But let me ask if the gentler sex, as we call them, did not lose, by such superior culture, their gentleness and their charm. The masculine type of woman is not at all popular with us."

"This question, Doctor," answered Zenith, "shows that you have a poor conception of our condition at that time. This great change in society had been gradual, and I must remind you that by the time it was accomplished the world was much improved in every way, although, as we have seen, it was by no means perfect. In her treatment of man there was none of that domineering spirit which you might expect; and the victory she had achieved was never used harshly. Her reign, if firm, was mild. And woman herself, in the general betterment of things, had improved, even in the direction you mention. Instead of becoming less womanly, in her changed condition, every admirable quality in her had ripened toward perfection, while she had thrown off much that was disagreeable and unlovely in her disposition. In personal appearance the advance had been remarkable. Being relieved of the severe labor and sordid cares which were once her lot, and with her mind set free by high culture and her artistic tastes developed, nature asserted itself by making her truly a delight to the eye and a comfort to the heart of mankind. Whatever charms she possessed in her old life were now doubled, making her indeed a blessing to the world and preparing her for the next great change, which came with the advent of the present age."

"In spite of the sweetness and beauty surrounding them, did not men fret at the firm hand that held them down?"

"At first, yes. But as time went on it came to be looked upon so naturally that it was hardly thought of as a thing which should not be."

"How long did such a state of things continue?"

"It continued until our race had outgrown all such trivial things as selfish ambition and personal strife, until our characters had ripened for a higher service than the old world had ever dreamed of, and until love reigned in our hearts, supreme and unquestionable."

"What makes the situation seem so strange to you is because it is so contrary to your experience. Let me see if I cannot make it look more reasonable to you by epitomizing our history on the subject in this way:

"Our career is made up of three eras. The first was one of brute force, when man ruled by strength of body and subdued the world to our use. Everything weaker than himself, even woman, his natural helper, was made to feel the power of his arm. This age lasted long, but its rigor slowly passed away, and it merged gradually into the second era, which was one of mind. Here, too, man thought to rule, claiming the leadership by right of possession and natural endowment. But woman's sharpness of intellect was more than a match for him when it was given full opportunity, and she won, as we have seen, after a long struggle. The third and present era is a spiritual one. In the realm of the spirit men and women are equally endowed, and hence it is that in this age you find the two sexes living in perfect equality.

"Comparing the words you have spoken with what I have read of our history, I conclude that the earth is now passing from the first to the second era. The struggle is on. Soon your sex will be considering the question of the emancipation of man. You have the sincere sympathy of both Thorwald and myself, and that you may emerge from your trials as happily as we have from ours is our heartfelt wish."

Zenith closed, and the doctor was silent.

CHAPTER XXXV.
AN EXALTED THEME.

The doctor and I had not forgotten that Thorwald still held in store for us a talk on the most important theme of all. We wondered why he did not give it to us, as he had many opportunities in those days of quiet pleasure. He seemed to take great delight in hearing from us everything we chose to tell, asking numerous questions which showed a growing knowledge of the earth and its inhabitants.

It was the doctor who finally inquired when we were going to hear what he had promised us.

"I suppose I have been waiting," answered Thorwald, "for you to ask for it. I could listen to your talk a great deal longer with pleasure and profit. It is astonishing how closely your history matches ours up to your times. The period you have been describing to me as that in which you live corresponds with a similar age here. It was a time of great activity and rapid change, and one whose records make a deep impression on many of our writers, judging from the attention they give to it. It was an enviable time to live in, if you compare it with the previous ages, but chiefly on account of the promise it contained of the glorious day to come.

"Doctor, are you sure you desire to hear about the growth of Christianity in this world and the blessings it has brought us?"

"Most certainly," answered my companion. "I want to learn all I can of your history and present condition, and, as religion seems to occupy a chief place in both, anything you may say on the subject will be listened to with delight."

Perhaps Thorwald was a little disappointed because the doctor did not give a more personal reason; but he failed to show it if he was, and, after calling to Zenith to come and sit with us, he began:

"Fair shines the sun on this fair world. So shines the sun on other fair worlds. Its piercing rays dart out in all directions from the great glowing mass, and as they fly outward they lose in brilliancy and intensity every second. In eight minutes some of these rays are intercepted by the earth and find there an atmosphere well adapted to receive them. In twelve minutes some strike this world, and although they are less powerful than those that fall on the earth, the conditions here are favorable for their reception. At varying distances from the center other rays find other planets as ready to welcome them, no doubt, as ours are.

"As the sun is in the physical universe, so is the Sun of righteousness in the domain of the spirit. Infinite in power, wisdom, and love, he comes wherever there are souls to save, shedding light in every dark spot, bringing life and hope and comfort, and lifting men out of the darkness of sin up to a condition of peace and happiness. Many ages ago he came to this planet, and started into life those forces which have brought us to our present state. Then he came to the earth, and you are at this time beginning to feel more intensely the impulse of his mission."

"Your illustration is a forcible one," said the doctor, as Thorwald paused a moment, "and weakens my former position, which would make it necessary for me to believe that all the rays of the sun, except the few that fall on Mars and the earth, are lost. It seems to me now quite reasonable that some do their beneficent work on other planets also."

"Yes," answered Thorwald, "whenever they are ready to receive them. And now I hope to lead you to see that the same intelligence that made the sun and gave to its rays such power has been present as a personal force in this world, molding it to his use and raising up a people here for his service and glory.

"In the perfect plan of that omniscient being the advent of the Savior occurred at the most opportune moment. Deep in the heart of one nation, firmly grounded in their nature by ages of discipline and suffering, lay the belief in one only God. The other nations of the world, surfeited with sinful pleasure and worn out with a vain pursuit of happiness, were ready to abandon the gods of their imaginations. Some lofty souls among them, following intently every prompting of their better nature, had developed high characters, while of God's peculiar people many pure hearts waited, with joyful expectancy, the coming of the promised Savior.

"He came, the lowly, patient one, and, although the world was made by him, it knew him not. The greatest event in the history of the globe passed almost without notice; but the seed was planted, and in God's own time the growth began, which has filled our happy world with the perfect flower of Christianity.

"The religion which Jesus taught aimed to save the race. It was universal, not only as adapted to all nations, but as fitted to regenerate and perfect the whole nature of man--body, mind, and soul. It would take me too long to tell all the changes it wrought. It found the heart hard and unfeeling, and made it tender and loving. It found men filled with every evil passion and almost without a desire to be better, and it gave them a longing to be free from sin and pure in heart. It found the race in darkness and despair, and brought them hope and light and comfort. Above all, it attacked the demon of selfishness and gave men the promise that in time they should be entirely free from its power.

"Slowly the truths of Christianity spread. The missionary spirit was born and the gospel was carried to remote lands. It was ever God's way to work through the agency of his creatures, whether these be brute forces or intelligent beings. And so through imperfect men the perfect rule of life made feeble progress. But as it was the work of the Spirit, there was never any danger, even in the darkest ages, that the gospel would not triumph over all the sin and degradation of the world, and lift men to a higher plane.

"For a long period the truth lay buried beneath ignorance and superstition. Then came an awakening, and men, with their minds more enlightened and their consciences quickened, began to catch something of the true spirit of the gospel. Christianity now became a dominant power. Under its benign sway civilization advanced, intelligence spread, and Christian nations outstripped all others and extended their power to every part of the globe.

"Soon the ameliorating influences of the gospel were felt on every hand. Government began to be administered with more regard for the interest of the governed, and men came to receive consideration simply because they were men. All the aggravated forms of oppression ceased under the newborn spirit of human brotherhood, a sentiment brought into the world by the founder of Christianity.

"This brings us, my friends, up to that intense age of which I have spoken before, and which you say you recognize as that corresponding with the time in which you are living on the earth. Let me state briefly the condition of some of our affairs of that period.

"The industrial world was in a ferment, as we have seen, and it was only in a general and impersonal way that the Christian religion shed its influence on the majority of the actors in that drama. Individuals, among both employers and workmen, had good impulses and indulged them as much as they could, and I am inclined to think this class was larger than most of our writers admit. But we read that the greater part were moved chiefly by motives of self-interest. Still, Christianity was a growing force among them, and they could not entirely escape its influence. They were born under its elevating power, and, even if they did not acknowledge its sway, they were quite different men from those who lived before Jesus began to preach the law of love. This remark will apply to all the people of that day who were born under Christian skies, and yet acknowledged no personal allegiance to the Savior. They were the unconscious heirs of a priceless inheritance."

"I just want to say, Thorwald," the doctor interrupted, "that I can accept that idea fully now, with respect to the people of the earth, though at one time I should not have been willing to do so."

Thorwald smiled his answer, and without further reply continued:

"Let us look at the business situation. National and local governments had begun to extend their powers beyond what had before been considered legitimate. With one excuse or another they had taken out of private hands many branches of business, and there was a strong tendency toward a continuance of the policy. There was no difference in principle between carrying the mails and carrying freight and passengers, or between giving the people cheap water in their houses and furnishing them with cheap coal.

"It was acknowledged that there were certain things which the city or state could do better than private enterprise, and the difficulty was to decide where to draw the line. While this uncertainty existed in the minds of most people, there was a small but aggressive party who were in favor of not drawing the line at all, but of putting everything into the hands of the government. They would have had the people, in their corporate capacity as a nation, raise and distribute the products of the soil, do all the manufacturing and dispose of the goods to consumers, conduct all the trades and professions, and, in fact, carry on every kind of business necessary to the well-being of society."

Of course, this woke up the doctor, whose practical mind could see nothing attractive in such an arrangement as that, and he was moved to say:

"I trust, Thorwald, that your ancestors did not adopt that crazy scheme as an experimental step in their development. But I beg your pardon for using such vigorous language without knowing whether they did or not."

Thorwald smiled, as he answered:

"You are safe, Doctor. From actual experience we cannot tell what the result of such a trial would be, for the vast majority of the writers, and the people too, of the period were opposed to the plan, and no doubt with good reason.

"But I do not wonder that this idea had a fascination for some right- minded people, in the promise it gave of doing away with the evils arising from competition, to which I have before referred."

Thorwald paused here, as if to invite one of us to speak, if he wanted to do so. I accepted, by saying:

"I wish you would tell us a little more on that subject. Competition is said to be the life of trade with us, an accepted principle of honest business. And yet you speak of it as something that should be done away with."

"If you could know," answered Thorwald, "how repugnant the idea is to us of the present day, you would understand how truly you have voiced my feelings."

"I have no doubt," I said, "that your experience has taught you much on the subject that we do not know, but this is the way it looks from our standpoint: There is born in us a passion for getting that which belongs to others, or that which others are trying to get. In some of us this instinct is developed more than in others, and some are unprincipled enough to indulge it unjustly; but let me ask you if it is wrong to follow the leadings of such a desire if we are strictly honest in all our dealings."

"We might differ over the meaning of the phrase 'strictly honest,' but I will answer your question by saying it is certainly wrong."

"But it seems to be a part of our very nature."

"Do you offer that as a reason for its being right? I never heard you claim that human nature was perfect," said Thorwald.

"Then," I returned, "in our present state, with which you are now pretty well acquainted, is it not possible to carry the principles of Christianity into business?"

"To answer that as I should be obliged to do would make me appear to you too arbitrary, and so perhaps I had better let you find your own answer in the questions which I will ask you. Is not unselfishness one of the first principles of Christianity? Now, the very essence of competition is a regard for self-interest, with no room for thought about the interests of others. In an ideal state of society the rules of life given by Jesus are fully obeyed. In such a state, would a transaction be right where each person was trying to do what was best for himself, although it might be to the damage or loss of another? It might be called honest to own slaves, and probably in the history of the earth a great many sincere Christian people have owned them, but you have now reached that condition, I think, where you can see it is wrong. So your way of doing business may be honest, but in our more ideal state we see that it is not right. Our remote ancestors, through the various stages of our development, did a thousand things with clear consciences which we could not do now. I understand your situation perfectly, and am sure your race will outgrow its imperfections."

I thanked Thorwald for his faith in us, and he resumed his narrative.

"In the age of which I am speaking," he said, "the church was taking a prominent place in the world, but had not assumed the leading position which it afterward reached. Many nations were still without the light of the gospel, and even in nominal Christian lands the actual supporters of the church were in the minority. In the midst of much evil and many discouragements the church was trying to regenerate society, but it had a difficult task, partly on account of the great perversity of the human heart, and partly because the church itself was not free from the imperfections of the age. Its members represented all shades of spirituality, the great majority of them having but a faint appreciation of the glorious cause in which they had enlisted. They called themselves soldiers of the cross, but were so burdened with the ordinary but more pressing duties and occupations of life that they never dreamed of the grandeur of the service, nor of the brilliant deeds of which the church was soon to show itself capable.

"One chief hindrance to the growth of the church and to the spread of its influence was the spirit of division within itself. Theoretically, all believers, the world over, were one body, or church, but in point of fact there were many churches, and in some particulars they were quite sharply opposed to each other. This evil was in full force in that age, but there were signs in the air that it was not to remain forever a stumbling-block to the faith of the world."

"We are afflicted in the same way," said I, "and some of us are hopeful enough to look forward to a really united church. But many think it is a part of our nature to differ, and are not able to see how all can ever come to think alike. They say that if by a miracle all should be brought into one church, and then left to their own inclinations, in a short time there would be as many sects as there are now."

"And so there would," returned Thorwald, "with your present ways. Your imperfect nature must change under the softening influence of the gospel. The differences that cause such trouble come from each individual's selfish regard for his own opinion. All must learn not only to respect but to embrace the opinions of each other when they are right opinions. Two streams may run in parallel channels forever if each persists in following strictly its own course. If one turns toward the other and the other turns away, they will still be kept apart; but let each turn toward the other, and how quickly they come together."

I told Thorwald I could apply his illustration to our condition and we would try to profit by it.

"One of the promising features of the religious situation," he continued, "was the good start the church had made in missionary work. In the zeal with which this was taken up it was quite a new departure for the church, for not long before this time good men believed that if God intended to save the heathen he would do it without any help from man. But now success had come in the work in sufficient measure to greatly encourage the faithful souls engaged in it.

"When I speak of zeal, however, you must understand that this quality was confined to a few people. Nearly all were only half-hearted Christians at the best, doing something, to be sure, but not at all alive to the grand opportunity of bringing the world to the feet of the Savior. Only here and there was one found who was ready to give himself unselfishly to the work, and the amount of money given to advance the cause of Christ, at home and abroad, was small indeed compared to that spent in luxurious living and hurtful indulgences.

"At the same time, it was an age of progress. The ordinary span of life was long enough to show improvement in many ways, and men, seeing the rapid advancement the world was making, took courage and looked forward more confidently for the dawn of a brighter day. Religion was beginning to be more of an every-day matter, and Christians were coming to a faint realization of the real value of the gospel in its adaptation to all the needs of men. Care for the body, better ways of living, and right conduct toward others were all taught, as well as duty to God, and society began to feel the benefit of such sensible teaching."

CHAPTER XXXVI.
VANQUISHED AGAIN BY A VOICE.

We all hoped Mona's affliction would prove temporary, but after a number of days had passed, and no improvement appeared, Thorwald had an expert anatomist come to the house and make an examination of the organs of her throat. Although this was a new way in which to apply his skill, as the Martians of that era were all physically perfect, he thought he might be able to discover the cause of the trouble. The result of this experiment was somewhat reassuring, for our scientist told us there was no defect of organ or injury to any part, closing his report with the remark that the case presented the greatest mystery of the kind he had ever encountered. My companion, the doctor, now expressed his opinion, which coincided with my own. This was, that Mona's trouble was occasioned by the shock to her nervous system when she was plunged into the water, an element which she so much dreaded. Our good friends, including the expert, were utterly unable to understand the meaning of this theory. The remark that Zenith made was:

"Why, but for our friend, and others who pry into these things for us, we would never know we had any nerves."

"Happy will our race be," responded the doctor, "when it arrives at the same blissful ignorance."

"Well," continued Zenith, "if your opinion is the correct one, what have we to hope for in Mona's case?"

"Unfortunately," answered the doctor, "we have no experience to teach us what to expect. We can only hope with you that she may speedily recover her voice, which has seemed to form such a great part of her, and has given us all so much delight."

Perhaps it was imagination, but it seemed to me that Mona's behavior toward me was more affectionate than it had formerly been. She had told me before, to be sure, that she had loved me with all her heart, but in these latter days she appeared to seek my society more and to show other indications that her love was assuming more of the personal element for which I had once so assiduously sought. But how was it with myself? This question forced itself on me, one day, and I was a little startled to find that an answer did not spring up spontaneously. Was it possible that my love was becoming cold? I would not admit it. Just as the poor girl had lost her chief attraction, should I turn from her and forget all my former professions? On the first suspicion that such might possibly be my desire, I said it was a wicked thought and I should never let it be true. But even if I could not force my heart to remain faithful, no one should ever know it but myself.

A little more time elapsed and I discovered that, in spite of my brave resolutions, Mona, silent, was filling less and less of my thoughts, and that I was living on the precious memory of her lost voice. But this discovery did not shake my determination ever to be to Mona herself a true and faithful lover.

At this juncture I was sitting alone, one morning, going over in my mind the strange vicissitudes of my love affair, when, in a far-distant part of the house, I heard a sound which thrilled me. I stopped all motion and listened, my heart, however, trembling with the fear of a disappointment. The music, for it was sweet music to me, came nearer, and now I could not be mistaken. What joy filled my heart! How impossible to forget that voice! I sat still and let it come. She evidently knew where I was and was coming to find me, pouring forth her heart in the way she knew I adored. Where now were my fears that my heart was growing cold toward her? Could it be possible that I had ever doubted my affection for her since I first heard her sing? Nearer it comes, filling my ears now with its familiar melody, a song without words but full of meaning for one who hears aright. She is guided true by the lamp of love and is now in the next room. I cannot wait, but interrupt her song with this cry:

"Come to me, my love, come quickly. I know your voice and the meaning of your song, and my heart responds to yours."

The strain continues, and soon a form appears in the doorway. I spring from my seat and start to meet it, but fall back almost immediately in confusion.

"Oh, Avis," I exclaimed with vexation, "I thought you were Mona again. I supposed you were on the other side of the world."

"I was, but I have come back to sing for you. I heard poor Mona had lost her voice and I wanted to do what I could to fill her place. But I fear you are not pleased with me."

"My dear friend," I replied, "I beg your pardon for the abrupt manner in which I received you. I thought Mona had suddenly recovered her voice and was coming in the fullness of her joy to tell me about it, and you can imagine my disappointment when I discovered my mistake. But now I assure you I am glad to have your sympathy and delighted to know that you are to be near me. Please go on with the song which I so rudely interrupted, and let me hear your voice as often as possible. It is exceedingly fortunate for me to have you here while Mona is recovering. Will you stay till she can sing again, or do you think it is too selfish in me to make such a request?"

Instead of answering me, Avis began to sing again, and in a twinkling I had forgotten my question and everything else in the enjoyment of the moment.

I now wanted little to make me supremely happy. There was Mona herself, with her exquisite beauty and friendly manner, and there was Mona's voice in the mouth of one who liked me enough to go half around the world to entertain me. And, if the truth must be told, my heart inclined more and more toward the voice. This was a startling truth indeed when it first fell upon me, and I fully determined that no one else should know it. Mona should never discover that I loved her less because she could not sing, and Avis should never know that her marvelous song was beginning to make the singer dear to me.

Whenever I found myself alone I could think of nothing but this perplexing subject. As I dwelt upon my situation, I told myself I must be careful, and avoid getting into trouble. Mona was becoming more and more tender toward me every day, and now Avis had come, unconsciously storming the seat of my affections with Mona's own voice. I felt that I was in some danger of embarrassing myself before the rest of my friends, and it behooved me to simplify matters if possible.

First, I must find out to a certainty just how I stood with Mona. Notwithstanding the admission which I had been forced to make to myself, I felt that it must be right for me to continue to devote myself to Mona, even if my heart did not bound toward her as in the days of my exuberant love. I should indeed be unworthy of her to give her up now. When I considered my former depth of feeling, I fairly despised myself for entertaining for a moment the possibility of her becoming less dear to me. But, for all that, I knew deep in my heart that the charm which had held me to her was gone, and I knew of no way to arrest and bring back my wandering affections.

Still, it could not be right for me to let her know I was changing. What would she think of me, and what opinion would Thorwald and Zenith have? I must own that the latter consideration had a good deal of force with me, for I did not want to lower myself and our whole race in their eyes.

So I prepared the form of speech with which to address Mona again on the old subject. It seemed strange that she should begin to grow fond of me just as soon as my love began to cool, and I determined with all my will never to let her know the state of my heart.

Not long after I had made this resolution, I was surprised to have the doctor tell me he was sorry to see I was not so partial to Mona's society since she had lost her voice. I do not remember what I said to him in reply, but I know his remark set me thinking hard. Perhaps other observers had noticed the same thing and were too considerate of my feelings to speak of it. Surely, I must have matters put upon a better footing at once.

As for Mona, she was never happier in her life, if we could judge from her actions. She had now learned to talk so well in her mute language that we all found conversation with her comparatively easy. Her fascinating manners made her interesting always, and in spite of her great loss she was still an important part of the life of the house. I argued to myself that my heart must be hard indeed if I could not continue to love her. To me her behavior was characterized by such a peculiar sweetness that I knew she was ready, on a word from me, to recall some of the harsh things she had said and to own a love quite different in kind from her regard for others.

The opportunity soon came to speak to her, and I embraced it. "Mona," I said, "I want to make a little speech to you. First, let me ask you if I can introduce a subject on which you have more than once stopped my mouth. Perhaps you know what I mean."

"Oh, yes," she replied, "I remember it very well, and you may talk all you please about it now. You must forgive me if I was unkind before and used my voice to vex you. But I am surprised to have you bring up this topic."

"Why?"

"Because I thought from your manner that you did not love me as you used to."

By this time the speech that I had prepared was all out of my head, and I was wondering if it were possible that I had lost so much of my affection for Mona that she had discovered it by a change in my manner. In reply to her remark I said:

"But such a thought has not made you unhappy, Mona, if I may judge from your behavior. I have never seen you more cheerful and full of life."

"No," she responded, "I think it has had the contrary effect. I was rather relieved to find you were recovering from your foolishness, and I thought we would now be able to live in peace, treating each other in a kind and sensible manner. I am disappointed to find that you are still clinging to the old idea, but I will not object to your saying all you please on the subject, for I have my own reasons now for being gracious to you."

"That's the very thing I want to ask you about, Mona. I have noticed your great kindness of late, and have supposed it came from the fact that you were learning to love me in my way; that is, somewhat to the exclusion of others. Isn't it that?"

"I think you will not be pained when I say you have had a wrong impression."

"Why do you think such a discovery will not pain me?"

"Because I am sure you do not care for me now in the same way as before. It was my voice that inthralled you. In all this interview you have not once said you love me, and you know at one time you could say nothing else. But let me tell you why I have shown an extra tenderness toward you recently. It was because I feared you would think I blamed you for my misfortune. I wanted to let you know I had not the least unkind feeling and that, in spite of the loss of my voice, I was as happy and contented as ever."

"Well, after all, you do love me a little, do you not, Mona?"

"Why, of course I do, just as much as ever. And now let us go right along and be nice to each other. We will love each other and love everybody else just the same, and you must promise not to look disturbed any more when I am talking with Foedric; but you have been very good about that of late."

"I will promise," I answered; "but what will you do if you find I am loving another person more than you?"

"Oh, I cannot understand what you mean by loving more and loving less. It is a strange idea to me, and I hope I shall never get accustomed to it. My way is to love everybody with all my heart, and that's an end of it. Don't you see in that way I escape all the worry and vexation which you seem to have in the matter? As to your loving another, you will pardon me if I say it will be a great relief to me for you to do so. I have not been used to being the sole recipient of any person's affection, and I shall rejoice to be freed from the responsibility. If you have thought me happy heretofore, you will now be astonished at my sprightliness. I suppose you refer to Antonia. She is a lovely girl, and--"

"Allow me," I interrupted; but before I could go on with my denial that voice again fell on my ears--so distant and low that I held my breath to listen. At first Mona did not hear it, but it soon increased in volume; and now, as the sweet sounds came pouring upon us, my companion saw how I was affected, and said in her sign language:

"Oh, I was mistaken. Antonia is not the one."

My heart was now all aflame, and, with Mona by my side and gazing into my glowing face, I almost forgot her presence in the approach of one whose song had such power. Was she old? Music like that is never old. Why should not my heart go out to her? She was still beautiful and not so old as I had supposed. And then, of course, people in that advanced condition, did not wear out in a few years as they did on the earth. As for her size, she was rather small for a Martian, and I, living under new conditions, would certainly take a start before many days, and no doubt become as large as Foedric, almost.

These ingenuous sentiments came to me with the sweet accents of that melodious song, and when Avis appeared I had great difficulty to keep from making some foolish exhibition of my feelings.

At my next sober moment, that is, when I was by myself, and out of hearing of that intoxicating music, it was very easy for me to realize my ridiculous situation, but not so easy to tell how I was to escape from it. As to my relations with Mona herself, I was greatly relieved by our last conversation. I certainly need no longer feel obliged to tie my vagrant heart to her. She would not miss it if it never once showed itself again, but how could I hope to preserve any sort of character in the eyes of my other friends? What sport the doctor would make of me if he knew how I felt toward Avis. He little thought that this was the daughter of Mars most likely to bring me to my knees.

And the doctor would have good reason for whatever enjoyment he might have at my expense, for I felt at first that I did not deserve any sympathy. When away from the powerful influence of that voice I was myself, and could see everything in its true perspective, but it is difficult to describe the change that came over me as soon as those entrancing notes fell upon my ear. The music sent great waves of emotion through my being, the storm center generally appearing to be the seat of my affections. My heart would beat fast, going out toward the singer in sympathy and love. The doubts of propriety belonging to my sane moments--hesitation, argument, uncertainty--all went in a flash, and I was almost ready to throw myself before her and proclaim my love without shame or embarrassment. At such times I felt that I could hold my head up in view of all the inhabitants of Mars and prove to them that I was not fickle, but as steadfast as constancy itself in following always one and the same attraction. Was I not as true to the best that was in me, when my heart was ravished by the voice of Avis, as I was when I had loved Mona so tenderly for the same sweet charm?

As day followed day in this delightful home, it was the society of Avis which I continually sought, and I was never quite happy except in her presence, or, at least, within hearing distance of her voice. And it was not long before the constant association of Avis with the music I loved so well began, even when I was not listening to her, to draw my affections toward one who, at will, could exert such power over me.

Mona was still herself, the same friendly, joyous creature as ever, but the knowledge that I could never gain her undivided affection helped to cure my infatuation. And now, with my heart free, why should I not love Avis? The mere fact that she was an inhabitant of Mars proved that she was far too good for me, but I could see by the example of Foedric and Antonia that Avis would never, in consequence of her high development, have any scruples against loving one person more than others.

When I had fully persuaded myself that I was perfectly consistent in my present course, I became quite anxious to know what others would think of me. But I was too much afraid of the doctor's criticism to confide my secret to him. I must try one of the Martians, whose high breeding and true courtesy would not permit them to make light of one's feelings on so serious a subject.

So it was to Zenith that I went for sympathy. She had been more than kind to me, and it is remarkable how easy and perfectly at home she made me feel in her company.

"Zenith," I began, "I want to consult you on a delicate subject, and I will first ask you a rather abrupt question. Will you give us your permission to take Avis back to the earth with us?"

A Martian never loses self-possession and is never at a loss what to say to the most unexpected proposition.

"Well, that is abrupt," Zenith quickly responded. "Do you know, Thorwald and I were talking only this morning about your apparent fondness for the society of Avis. Are you forgetting Mona?"

This was getting into the subject faster than I had intended, and I determined to take my time, so I said:

"Zenith, this province must be the New England of Mars, by the way you evade my question and ask another."

"But you wouldn't expect me to answer such a question offhand. You see, it contains several new ideas. First, I didn't know you thought of returning to the earth. Then I am surprised that you should want to take anybody with you. And, finally, I am more surprised that you should choose Avis rather than Mona. Now that I have explained so fully, may I not ask you again if this means that you are forgetting Mona?"

"Mona is not able to sing for me," I said.

"And do your ideas of what is right allow you to become indifferent to her as soon as she loses one of her attractions? Here her misfortune would tend to make her only more dear to one who really loved her."

To which I made haste to answer:

"I am proud to tell you, Zenith, that such sentiments prevail on the earth, too, and I have been trying hard to hold them in my own breast. But in living with you I am learning to be honest, and it would not be right for me to deny that Mona's chief charm for me is gone from her, and is in the possession of another. The voice of Avis has the same power over me that Mona's formerly had, and shall I fight against my growing fondness for Avis?"

"Is your race so little developed, then," asked Zenith, "that your ears are the only avenue to your hearts?"

Before I could answer, Mona herself came bounding into the room, and Zenith continued:

"There's the poor child now. How can you be so unkind to her?"

"Who's unkind to me?" asked Mona in her sign language.

"Zenith thinks I am," I answered.

"Why, you are mistaken, Zenith; he is just the opposite. We have always loved each other, and I think more of him than ever since I lost my voice, and he has ceased making serious speeches to me that I can't understand. I wish you could see how he enjoys hearing Avis sing."

In this way Mona proved to Zenith that she was not heart-broken. I was going to explain the matter myself, but was glad to have Mona take it out of my hands.

The most difficult task yet remained. I must tell Avis how affairs stood; and yet, was it the proper thing for me to do? I wondered how the delicate subject of making love was handled in Mars, where the two sexes were perfectly equal. Which one was to make the advances? The matter is simple enough on the earth, where women are inferior and dependent. Of course, they must smother their own feelings and wait to be discovered, while the men can make their selection, and if they do not succeed at first can simply try again. That is entirely proper, and everybody knows just what to do; but here things are probably different. I don't want to make a failure in this case, as I did with Mona, not knowing the customs of the moon-dwellers. Perhaps my best way will be to try a little coquetry and pretend I do not care for her nor her singing. That may draw her on to make some avowal to me.

I had gone so far in my deliberations, when I was interrupted by the doctor, who called to ask if I did not want to go out with him. I consented reluctantly, as I preferred to go on with my thinking till I could come to some decision. But the doctor had a purpose in taking me out, and, as soon as a good opportunity presented itself, he said, inquiringly:

"You find Avis a pretty good singer?"

"Excellent."

"And good company?"

"Excellent company. Why?"

"Oh, nothing; only I thought you were neglecting another friend."

"Why, Mona doesn't care for me, and Avis does, or, at least, I think she does."

"Do you mean by this," inquired the doctor, "that you have transferred to Avis the personal interest you had in Mona?"

"Have you anything to say in disparagement of Avis?" I asked.

"Certainly not. I have a high respect for her. But there is one other plain question I would like to ask you, in view of your rather erratic behavior."

"Well, what is it? I'm dying to know."

"It is this. What are you going to do with Margaret?"

"Margaret? Oh, yes, I forgot about Margaret. That is something else I have got to think over."

That night, as I was falling asleep, the same sweet, familiar music came to me from a distant part of the house. Half-thinking and half-dreaming, I let my mind drift where it would. The sensation received through my ears was so delicious and so satisfying that I wondered why I could not rest in it entirely and not think of the singer; but that was impossible. The notes penetrated from my brain down to the region of my heart. I thought of Margaret, but Margaret could not sing like that. Mona could not, now; no one but Avis. Oh, how I loved her for it! I remembered how nice Margaret was, and how much I had once thought of her; but as for loving her now, with this music of Mars in my ears, why, I simply couldn't try to do it. At last Margaret, Mona, Avis, all became jumbled up in my chaotic mind, and I thought they were one superb woman, and I loved her. The conceit was worthy the colossal selfishness of a dreamer. The essence of three worlds was mine. The earth, the moon, and Mars had all given me their best. And she could sing. The thought was soothing. I was asleep.

CHAPTER XXXVII.
UNTIL THE DAY BREAK.

The events related in the foregoing chapter were interesting to us all, in one way and another, but the doctor and I felt that the real purpose of our visit to Mars, if anything so unpremeditated could be said to have a purpose, was to learn all we could of the planet, and especially of its people. And as we did not know how soon our visit might be brought to a close, we lost no time in urging Thorwald to continue his instruction whenever he could find it convenient. Thorwald's answer to this was, that he hoped nothing would occur to hasten our departure, but that it was his convenience to heed at any time our wishes, and he would resume his talk as soon as we pleased. So it was not long before we were seated, and Thorwald began again as follows:

"It is now my privilege to speak to you, my friends, of that part of our history which differs from anything you have experienced, and I anticipate much pleasure in doing so. I must say again that we have found the parallel remarkably close between your career and ours up to the time when you left the earth."

"We have indeed," remarked the doctor, "and that makes us all the more anxious to learn what came to you next and how you escaped the threatening storms."

"There were certainly many clouds upon our horizon at that day," resumed Thorwald. "The people were full of unrest. The worst part wanted to replace organized society with anarchy, but this extreme party never succeeded in their purpose. The world had progressed too far for that. There were too many churches and schools and printing presses. The anarchists should have begun their efforts in a ruder age.

"There was more danger from the jealousies and mischievous tendencies among the great industrial class, because their number was so large. But even here the same influences which saved us from the nihilist had their effect. As time went on, men came to think more, and the result of this was that both conscience and reason began to govern men's actions.

"The workmen had looked about them and had seen many corporations increasing in wealth and power, and individuals rolling up enormous fortunes, and they had felt that they were not getting a fair share of the money their labor was earning. But then a little thought enabled them to realize that these evidences of great prosperity came from the successful few, while a large proportion of all business ventures were failures; and in these the employees received more of the profits than the owners did. Then the wage-earners had the benefit of much of the money accumulated in large fortunes, by having the free use of libraries, trade schools, reading rooms, and an increasing number of philanthropic institutions, which were equipped and endowed by the rich. Such a use of wealth became an ordinary thing, so that it was not a matter of wonder and wide notice when a man spent a liberal share of his fortune in educational or other humanitarian work.

"All this had a great effect on the mass of the people, gradually raising the average of character, and placing before the mind a higher incentive for right living. Ignorance had always been to the race a twin enemy with sin, and the growth of intelligence meant the general elevation of mankind.

"Another chief item in the reformation of men in that age of improvement was the general abandonment of the drinking habit. You will understand, of course, that the mainspring of all these reforms was the gospel of Christ, under which man's spiritual nature was gradually developing. But, at the same time, there was always a secondary cause, and through human instrumentality such blessings came to us. What do you suppose brought about the overthrow of intemperance?"

"I suspect," answered the doctor, with a glance at our hostess, "it was the growing influence of woman, who, by that time, according to Zenith's account, ought to be taking quite a leading position."

"Doctor," said Thorwald, "you take in the situation completely. If there was one thing woman had always been sure she could do, it was the breaking up of the liquor traffic. In the old days, when she had been treated as man's inferior, she had declared that, if she had the power, she would stamp out the manufacture and sale of intoxicating drinks, and make it impossible for men to get them at any price.

And when power came to her I am glad to say she proved that her boast had not been in vain. Not that she fulfilled her threat in any such dramatic way as she had had in mind, but the end was accomplished just as surely by the force of her high character, working itself out in many ways. It was chiefly a crusade of education. The children of one generation after another were taught the value of right habits and purity of body, and in time the change was wrought, a victory for woman more precious to the race than any army of mailed warriors had ever won.

"With temperance came better manners, more self-respect, a kinder spirit, a more tender care for others, and, along with these things, better hearts and better homes."

As Thorwald had invited us to interrupt him as often as we pleased, I took advantage of a pause here by saying:

"I see, Thorwald, you are making the people all too good to leave any fear in the mind of a social convulsion, but I would like to ask how politics were smoothed out. During that period of industrial war, which you described to us, you said the workingmen and ignorant classes found they were in the majority and were beginning to use their power unjustly. We are threatened in a similar way on the earth at this time, and I am anxious to know how the cloud in your sky was dispersed."

"I will endeavor to make it plain to you," replied Thorwald, "but you must remember I am trying to condense the history of a great many years into as few words as possible. It was found that there had been a mistake in making the right of suffrage universal without universal education, and that the ignorant and vicious were so numerous as to make the average unsafe to rely upon in a crisis. It was a difficult matter to remedy this state of things. Some attempts were made from time to time to confine the privilege of citizenship to the intelligent part of the community, but many of the best people thought this was taking the wrong course, and that the only safe cure was in educating all classes up to a full appreciation of their higher duties. There was a growing faith, the world over, in the virtue of the people at large, and wherever they had been given full power to govern themselves, or had taken it from their former rulers, they were exceedingly jealous of any abridgment of this power.

"Here, again, we see the effects of the beneficent influence of woman. The more her dominion increased the more was intelligence diffused, and although she yielded to the subtle temptation of power and reigned alone for a while, yet the world had, on the whole, great cause to be thankful for her signal advancement. With education made compulsory, and with society brought gradually under the sway of woman's finer nature and more lofty ideals, communities were molded to a higher form of life, and saved from the evils which threatened them in their former state.

"Let me tell you briefly how war was banished from our world, that monster whose hideous presence would be so utterly out of place here now. At the beginning of the age I am describing, the foremost nations kept powerful armies and navies, all ready for their deadly work. Wars were frequent and bloody. The best of the young men in nearly every land were forced to bear arms and fight for their country at the command of their rulers, while the conscience of mankind was dulled and stunted by the spectacle or constant menace of war.

"The lives of millions of men were actually in the hands of a few irresponsible autocrats, who were possessed with exaggerated or false notions of national honor. Now came a time when the world stood hushed, as it were, on the eve of a mighty conflict. Every nation had increased its army and strengthened its defenses to the utmost limit. Every day threatened to see the match lighted--a hasty word, a fancied insult, any trivial thing, which would bring on the struggle and put the world in mourning. And what was it all for? No one could tell. It seemed to be nothing but the selfish ambition of the rulers and their innate love for supremacy. As for the real actors, those who were to do the actual fighting, they had no love for their work. However it may have been in the past, the world was older now and better, and war was abhorred with all its accompaniments both by the army and by the people at large.

"It was a time of great inventions, looking not only to the saving of life but to its destruction. Even while the nations were standing, arms in hand, waiting for the signal to begin the conflict, their weapons were rendered useless and the strength of their fortresses reduced to nothing by the working of one man's brain. Yes, by a single invention, inspired by God for the good of his creation, inhuman war received its death-blow and the world obtained a mighty impulse toward its final goal."

The doctor became somewhat excited by these words and asked with eagerness:

"What wonderful invention was that?"

"The perfection of the air ship," Thorwald replied, "by which any required weight could be taken into the air, and carried with ease and certainty by currents of air or force of gravity.

"You no doubt see what such an invention implies. It means that powerful explosives could be dropped from the sky in quantities sufficient to annihilate an army or utterly destroy a city. Experiments were made, and engineers learned, with surprising rapidity, to cast the bombs with great accuracy from any desired height.

"At once every government hastened to build air ships and manufacture explosives. There seemed to be no limit in sight to the production of either, and soon power enough was stored in this way to extinguish half the life of the world, when rightly applied. The entire system of warfare was revolutionized; but, while all were preparing for offensive operations, there appeared to be no adequate plan of defense under the new system. It therefore became apparent that, should the threatening cloud burst, it would be difficult to imagine the extent of the destruction it would bring. This feeling, which filled all hearts with dread, delayed the catastrophe, for no one was ready to assume such an immense responsibility. So matters stood for a long time, the fear of the dire consequences preventing an outbreak, while the sentiment against war was rapidly growing. In nations of the highest civilization, where the Christian character of the people was reflected in the government, some serious disputes had been settled by arbitration, and every time this humane method was adopted a precedent was created which made war appear more and more useless and barbarous. The world was now becoming so much changed that such a good example was contagious, and the result was that the aerial warships and the deadly dynamite did not have to be used.

"Among the legends of the time is the improbable one that, when these air fleets were at their highest point of efficiency, and the world was literally lying at their mercy, one hot-headed young monarch, whose selfish pride had stolen away his senses, gave the command to fire the train which would ram destruction upon his foes, when, wonder of wonders, not a man would obey his order. Angered beyond measure by such an unwonted experience, he seized with his own hand the electric apparatus arranged to give the fatal spark, but with such violence and indiscretion that, instead of sending the current on its appointed mission, it turned from its course and destroyed the angry youth himself.

"This is undoubtedly a myth, but the rest that I have told you is well- authenticated history.

"The abolition of war seems sudden, but it never would have taken place as it did had not the people been prepared for it by a radical change in their character. For many years the spirit of peace had been quietly at work on the heart of mankind, until it came to be realized that warfare and strife, whether between individuals or nations, were bound to die away under the growing appreciation for the higher law.

"It was one of the supreme days in the history of Mars, when grim war passed and became but a memory. The effect was instantaneous. At once the people of the different nations were drawn together to their mutual advantage. Commerce became world-wide, one language was adopted, and the arts of peace flourished as never before. Men began to feel that they were one family, national distinctions were made little of, and the world drifted gradually toward universal brotherhood.

"I must now draw your attention to the work of the church and show you how it was carrying out its great commission. First, to prepare for the highest usefulness, it quite early freed itself from the sectarian spirit. As the magnitude of its mission became more apparent the points of difference between the denominations grew constantly smaller, and, in time, all Christians found themselves united on the fundamental truths of the gospel, and working together to bring the world to the light. With this union fully accomplished, Christianity became more than ever the dominant force in the world, and the church the chief center of all work looking to the elevation of the race.

"The progress of the world was along the line of the brotherhood of man, and that doctrine was the church's own Christianity taught the true socialism, which, however, could not be realized till the heart had lost its selfishness, and each one had learned to care for the interests of his neighbor. Although such a condition was not in sight at that day, there was a mighty awakening which set the current of men's thoughts and desires strongly in the right direction."

"Do you call yourselves socialists now?" asked the doctor.

"No," answered Thorwald, "but you can call us so, if you please. It is a good word, but our condition is much more perfect, since the coming of the kingdom of God in every heart, than any dream of socialism, in the olden time, ever contemplated.

"I was speaking of the increasing power of religion. Where the church had been weak and dependent on a few half-earnest, timid believers, it was now strong and active, and supported by all the self-respecting portion of society. Instead of being forced to beg for its meager subsistence, it now received in abundance the money that was poured out voluntarily. Men did not wait for death, but gave their fortunes away during their lives, and enjoyed the blessing which followed. The church went down to the people, and in so doing lifted them up to itself. It showed them how to make much of life, gave them instruction and recreation and social enjoyment, fed the hungry, clothed the naked, and visited those in trouble. It strengthened family and neighborhood ties, encouraged peace and good- fellowship, and taught men to love each other as a preparation for loving God.

"A local church of that day was not a feeble body of men and women, with an overworked and underpaid man at their head, who was expected to do all the varied work required, except what he could get done by a small number of his members, themselves worn out with the labor and business of life. No, I will acquaint you with a then modern church. It was an institution rich in resources and men, male and female, reaching out into the community in every direction, helping the people in every imaginable way to live as well as preparing them to die, a beauty and a joy to all. It appealed to every side of man's nature, first supplying physical wants, not by indiscriminate largess of money, but by teaching sobriety, industry, and thrift as virtues necessary to a rounded character. Such teaching was not confined to pulpit precepts, but there was no lack of good souls who took delight in going into the homes of the people and showing them by example the best ways of living, and how to make even the homeliest duties a loving and beautiful service. To provide further for the needs of the body, there were gymnasiums, bath-houses, swimming schools, playgrounds, riding schools, and the like.

"More numerous still were the means offered to meet the intellectual and so-cial desires--club-houses, lecture halls, conservatories, museums, picture galleries, libraries, reading rooms, observatories, kindergartens, manual training and trade schools, besides games and sports, spectacular and dramatic exhibitions of a high order, and many other things, designed to compete with attractions of a debasing character.

"Then, rising high over all, both in outward form and inward grace, was the church edifice itself, set apart and strictly preserved for its sacred purpose. In the noble lines of its architecture, in the beauty of its artistic adornment, and in the character of its service, intellectual and musical, it represented the highest culture of the age. The structure included under its roof accommodations for the various departments of religious work, and its doors were always open, inviting every pass-er-by to enter and seek for spiritual refreshment.

"Imagine, if you can, an institution employing all these agencies, every one of them fully equipped and manned, and with streams of money flowing in to their support; no barren appeals from the pulpit for funds to pay expenses, and no auc-tioneer's hammer profaning the sacred aisles.

"This was the church of the period. Can you wonder that God's rich blessing was on such work and that his kingdom made rapid progress? There was an ever-increasing number of God's ministers, men and women, imbued with Christ's own spirit, working in all these various activities to elevate and save their kind.

"In the life of the people there was nothing in all the world that so surrounded them as the church. They could not escape from its influence. It touched them from one side or from another, calling upon them, by every manner of appeal, to lead less sordid lives, and seek the highest good. Whereas in the olden time they seemed to be set in the midst of evil influences, which imperceptibly molded their characters and too often wrecked their lives, their condition was so changed that their environment was now a help and not a hindrance, and so the gospel found easy entrance to their hearts and lives.

"This much the church had done by giving its money and itself, with new-born zeal, to the work of the Master. And from this time you may be sure its victories were rapid and notable.

"While this great change in society had been going on among nominal Christian people, hand in hand had gone the work of the gospel in heathen lands. The faster the money was poured out for the church at home, the more plentifully it was offered for the foreign field. Sometimes it was feared there would be more money than men and women for the work. Then the laborers would come forward in such numbers that the money would be exhausted, which, however, gave no concern, for it was sure to come again as soon as needed. Where one missionary, in the former days, had had the courage to take up the work, now thousands sprang forward and with eager hearts went into the field.

"Going to the heathen in the same spirit of brotherly love and helpfulness which had been so successful at home, the church was almost overwhelmed with the happy results. One people after another threw away their idols, and became followers of the gentle Savior, whose disciples showed so much of his spirit. In every part of the world the gospel was gaining fast over superstition and ignorance. In Christian lands no other news was so sought after by all as the reports of the progress of the cross, at home and abroad. Enthusiasm is a small word with which to describe the burst of genuine interest in this great cause. Nor was it a transient show of feeling, but so steady and constant that there was never any doubt of its enduring till the final victory was won.

"Where now were the dangers that threatened society? What had become of the labor troubles, the schemes of the anarchists, the menace of the unemployed, the risk of a plutocracy, and all the evils that darkened the sky of that former day? How far away, how trivial these things seemed, now that they had passed, and men were learning to dwell together in peace."

CHAPTER XXXVIII.
AND THE SHADOWS FLEE AWAY.

Thorwald paused again, and the doctor felt moved to say:
"Your sketch has been richly enjoyed, Thorwald, and if it can be taken as prophetic, in any sense, of what is to come to pass on the earth, we are to see some happy days indeed. But a question has arisen in my mind which I would like to ask you. When you broke off your former narrative, things were in a pretty serious state among your ancestors. You have now told us in a general way that there was a great change for the better, and that every thing and every body improved until the time came when it was easier to be good than not. I accept the fact, but do not understand the practical operation of the causes that led to such a result. For instance, I would like to know how that industrial strife came to an end. The parties to it seemed to be full of bitter enmity and far enough from ever loving one another. You have perhaps answered my question already, and my stupidity has prevented me from grasping your meaning."

"Let me first ask you a question," said Thorwald. "I have inferred, from some words you have let fall from time to time, that your mind has changed somewhat. Will you admit that whatever advance this world has made has come through the teachings of Christ?"

"It would be rather presumptuous in me," answered the doctor, "to think of denying anything to which you hold so firmly. More than that, in the light of what I have seen and heard here, my own views, so rashly expressed in the first days of our acquaintance, seem to me out of place. They were formed without sufficient study of the subject, and I am free to tell you that I now believe the same influence to which you attribute your growth is the strength and growth of our race also."

"Your words give me great pleasure," Thorwald resumed, "for now I know I have your full sympathy. The troubles to which you refer, and all the clouds of that period, were dispersed by the growth of the spirit of love in the world. Does that seem a vague and insufficient answer to your question? Does the cause appear inadequate to the effect? Perhaps I should have warned you not to expect any new or startling method of removing these evils. The world was not in need of any nostrum for curing sin, nor of any new scheme of the visionary for teaching men how to find peace and happiness.

"No, the old gospel was sufficient. The power was already at work which was to regenerate the world and, in time, to do away with all kinds of oppression and injustice. The gospel did not spend its force so much in attacking special forms of evil. It struck at the foundation of our sinful nature, and, by long and patient effort, won a firm place in our hearts. Then the whole structure of evil passions and low desires fell, and our race began to build, on this new and safe foundation, more beautiful and enduring mansions.

"If we were to be the children of God, it was necessary for us to be like him, to deny ourselves, and to love our enemies. So, with that spirit growing in our hearts, what place was there for greed and anger and strife between man and man?

"One secret of the new power put forth by the church is to be found in the union of all good men and women in its support. Before that period many people of character had stood aloof, giving little thought to religion for themselves, and less still to its influence on the world at large. Some of them were out-and-out unbelievers, but, for the most part, they were careless livers, too much engrossed in the affairs of this world to feel any anxiety about the world to come.

"But now, in the march of events, the time came when the lines must be sharply drawn between the good and evil forces. Iniquity presented such a bold front, and all the foes of order and decency became so threatening, that the moral forces of society had to combine for mutual protection. The church, being the conservator of morals as of religion, was the only rallying point for these forces, and felt at once the impulse of new life. Thus, society, in the hour of its extremity, found the true source of its salvation, and from that day its progress toward a higher state began, a progress which has never yet been stayed.

"Let me urge you, Doctor, to learn a lesson from our history. You acknowledge that, if the earth is to be saved from the evils which threaten its peace, it must be through the gospel. If, therefore, you and others like you wish to help speed the earth in its upward path, you must obey and work for that gospel. To do good to your fellowmen and assist in the regeneration of the world is only one motive for doing this, but it will, I am sure, lead you to that other motive, a desire to please your God. Every consideration calls you to leave your doubts and negations, your neglect and indifference, and join with all the strength of your character in a united effort to free the earth from some of its sin. When this is done, when all the good forces cease their strife and their cold neutrality and come together under the banner of love, you will see a mighty change. Then will the earth grow bright with hope and begin to realize something of the nature of its high destiny.

"Let me continue to describe the effect of such warm-hearted, combined labor among us, and the result on our planet of the great spiritual awakening to which I have referred.

"As men took note of the vast improvement going on around them, for every department of life felt the quickening of the new zeal, they became more and more eager in the overthrow of evil. And they had learned thoroughly the great truth that the way to regenerate the world was for everyone to build up his own character in truth and righteousness. Noble lives, devoted to lofty aims, were the natural result of the change, and our race, emerging from such a state of imperfection as I have tried to outline, began to realize with joy that they were living in a new world.

"I wish I could describe to you in fitting words the wonderful nature of this advancement. All the pride and selfishness, so common to all hearts in our degenerate days, were now driven out and replaced by the spirit of self-denial. Love, the living principle in the gospel, had conquered all its foes and was now enthroned in every heart.

"Do not suppose all this came about in one generation. It is only by comparing one period with another that we are able to see such marked progress. Our development toward the higher life has always been step by step, and sometimes so slow that the people actually living, and in whom the change was taking place, were not aware of any growth.

"But there have been special periods in our history when, after long years of preparation, the race has come to a sudden appreciation of a higher and better condition. The most glorious epoch of this kind came at the close of the period I have just been describing.

"Perhaps you have seen some rare plant, having come to its maturity through a process so slow as to bring discouragement, often, to those who are cultivating it, now suddenly burst into bloom with such magnificence that the disappointments of the past are all forgotten in the enjoyment of its beauty.

"So broke that blessed day upon Mars. None so fair had ever dawned before, and none less fair have we ever seen since.

"While this spiritual awakening was taking place, there had been rapid progress, also, in our material development. The evils that formerly vexed our bodies having disappeared, we were now free from sin and sorrow alike, and so were prepared to enter upon duties relating to our higher condition.

"All nature rejoiced with us, for the world itself was filled with the joy and beauty which came from the knowledge of the Lord. Peace reigned in the animal creation, and such gladness abounded everywhere that it is hardly an exaggeration to say that the mountains and hills broke forth into singing, and all the trees of the field clapped their hands."

As Thorwald uttered these closing words, so beautiful and familiar, I was so impressed with their appropriateness to his narrative that I did not stop to wonder where he had obtained them, but inquired with eagerness:

"And is it true, Thorwald, that instead of the thorn there came up the fir-tree, and instead of the brier there came up the myrtle-tree?"

"That describes the situation admirably," he answered, "and it is literally true."

"Why should that be so?" I asked.

"Because, when sin was banished from our world, it dragged in its train every evil thing and left all bright and joyous behind it. Even the unconscious soil was so improved in character that, whereas in the former time it had brought forth by nature the thorn and brier and noxious weed, there now sprang up spontaneously all manner of healthful plants and fruits."

"But," said I, "we do not attribute moral excellence to the ground that produces our food. How could the absence of sin make it any better?"

"Like everything else," replied Thorwald, "it reflected the spiritual condition of our race. By long and patient cultivation, by a constant use of good seed, and by a persistent fight against every tendency to evil growth, men had so changed the nature of the soil that it yielded only that which was good. Even if left without care the ground did not deteriorate, but the products took on the character of the times and gradually improved. To such a degree had our once sinful world been changed.

"The disagreeable features in nature's laboratory were lost to every sense, while everything that was beautiful in sight or sound, or that was pleasant to the taste, now possessed an added charm. The birds sang in more joyous notes, the flowers glowed in brighter hue, and all created things burst forth in a song of praise to their Maker."

"Is it possible," I asked, "that the growth of love in the heart will so transform a world and make even inanimate things more beautiful? The earth is full of selfishness and I fear will be so for a long time, and yet we think we have a few things that are perfect. I cannot conceive, for instance, how anything could ever grow, sin or no sin, that would surpass in beauty one of our finest roses."

To which Thorwald replied:

"Is this not of value to you, to learn that the roses of the future are entirely beyond your conception? Let me assure you that, with each new advance in your progress toward a higher condition, there will unfold within you new powers of appreciation for the increasing beauties in nature, and new desires for spiritual perfections which are now too high for your mind to grasp. Is it not a pleasure to know that there are many things in reserve for the earth of whose character and perfections you cannot conceive?"

"It surely is," I replied, "and we shall never cease to thank you for this hour's talk. But now let me ask if you were not really in heaven when you reached such a happy state. With both man and nature redeemed from sin, with the tears wiped away from all eyes, with all griefs assuaged and sickness and sorrow forgotten, and with love supreme in the heart, what more was needed to make a heaven? Many of our generation on the earth believe that the earth itself will be our heaven, when sin has been driven out and peace and joy abound."

"Oh, no, not heaven," answered Thorwald. "The earth will be better in a thousand years than it is now, much better in ten thousand years, but it will never be heaven."

"But why?" I persisted. "We cannot understand how there could be any more blessed place than the earth would be if it should ever reach the condition which you have pictured to us as existing here."

"You have just stated the trouble," Thorwald replied.

"You cannot understand. With your present capacities you think a state such as I have described would be perfection; but you--I mean, of course, your race--will come in time to see imperfections even in such a life, and will, with increasing spiritual vision, see still higher things to strive for. Let me urge you to keep your hearts attuned to the heavenly music and your minds open to divine influences."

Here Thorwald was about to leave us, as we remained in quiet thought after his solemn and impressive words. But I kept him a moment to ask if they had solved all the mysteries of God's moral government. "By no means," he replied. "There are still many things unexplained in God's dealings with us, and we think this is well. Life would lose much of its value if the time should come when there would be nothing to learn. We know much of God's character, but are not acquainted with its full depths, and whenever we see or experience anything mysterious in his providences we are content to wait for a fuller revelation of truth in the future.

"We shall see the time when all our questions will be answered--that is, in the world to come--and, in the mean time, we try to strengthen our high and beautiful conception of God's character by referring everything we do not understand to his loving and gracious qualities, which we know so well."

CHAPTER XXXIX.
A SUDDEN RETURN TO THE EARTH.

That night, when the doctor and I were alone, I said to him:

"Well, doctor, what do you think of it all?"

"It would take me a long time," he replied, "to tell what I think. I confess I am beginning to imbibe a little of the spirit of this place. I have spent my life in the pursuit of material facts, which we supposed were the only substantial and valuable things in life Now I find myself thinking lightly of such matters, with my mind held in the grasp of far different thoughts. I realize now something of the substance and reality of unseen things, and believe that man has a spiritual side to his nature, which must be developed if he is to fulfill the high expectations of our friends in this world. Taught by Thorwald's words and by all I have seen here, I have come to that point where I can say I am losing my doubts and acquiring a love for things which formerly did not exist for me. If we ever return to the earth we shall find occupation enough for the rest of our lives in teaching the lessons we have learned here."

"Yes," I said, "if we ever return. But doesn't that seem impossible?"

"It certainly is difficult to imagine how it can be accomplished, but going home ought not to be any more impossible than our coming here. Perhaps we had better bestir ourselves, for Mars is now getting farther away from the earth every day. Thorwald says the two planets were nearer each other at the recent opposition than ever before since their records began, and this is probably what drew our moon here, so fortunately for us. For the return trip we might get these generous people to loan us Demios or Phobos."

"What are they?"

"Why, don't you know? They are the little satellites of Mars, named after the favorite horses of the war god."

"But seriously now," I asked, "how are we to get home?"

"Well, seriously, I don't know," the doctor answered. "Some accident may happen to send us away from here in a hurry."

"You know this is not the right world for accidents," I said.

"I am not able to see," he replied, "how they can be sure that they are entirely free from accidents. They have been so long without them that it seems to me it would not be strange if a big one should come almost any day. One must be due, as we say."

In the morning Thorwald met us with a pleasant greeting, as usual, and then said:

"I have been surprised that you have not shown more curiosity on one subject of vast importance to us. You have not once asked to see our comet."

"We have talked of it by ourselves," said the doctor, "but we have been too much engrossed in studying your history and customs to think much of a topic so far above our comprehension as the comet. Your civilization is much higher than we can appreciate, and I am sure we should make small progress in attempting to investigate a development that is so much beyond yours."

"Your excuse," returned Thorwald, "is as complimentary as it is ingenious. But should you not like to see an object which possesses so much interest for us?"

"Certainly," the doctor made haste to reply; "and just as soon as you choose to take us. You told us it was at the door of a large city. Is it far from here?"

"Yes," Thorwald answered, "a long way in miles, but not far in minutes if we go by the tubular route. But if it is agreeable to you, suppose we take the air line and make a leisurely excursion of it."

We both assured him that we were delighted with the prospect, and I suggested that Zenith and the children should accompany us.

"Yes," said Thorwald, "and in anticipation of your consent to go on the expedition, I invited some other friends of yours last night to share the pleasure with us. And here they are now," he continued, rising and stepping to the door.

The doctor and I hurried forward, and were heartily greeted by Proctor, the astronomer, and Foedric of the red voice. The latter was accompanied by a comely-looking ape, which had been trained to act as his body servant. The animal was intelligent, and quick to understand every word addressed to him, but quiet and respectful in demeanor, and, to all appearance, as well fitted to fill the station he occupied as the servants we had been accustomed to seeing on the earth.

Zenith explained to us that in many households the ape and other creatures were employed for light services, and were exceedingly useful. But as for their own house, she said the work that could not be done by mechanical means she preferred to do herself, assisted by her children. It was much better that every child should have some stated work to do.

It was not long before we were all on our way to the aerial station, where we selected a commodious air ship, managed by one of Foedric's friends.

When we were seated comfortably and were enjoying once more the exquisite sensation of sailing so easily through that balmy air, Thorwald said to the doctor and me:

"We all anticipate a great deal of pleasure in showing you our big natural curiosity and what it contains. We want to see your surprise when you look upon its vast proportions, and your growing curiosity as you try to make out some of its mysteries. Things which baffle our skill may be plain to you, and perhaps you will even be able to do something with that puzzling language."

"Yes," said the doctor, "if it is beyond your skill we shall no doubt be able to read it at sight."

"Well, at any rate," continued Thorwald, "we shall enjoy the novel experience of exhibiting the marvel of our whole world to those who were, until so recently, entirely ignorant of its existence."

"I hope," I said, "that our behavior will not be such as to disappoint you, when we are brought face to face with the object for which you have so deep a sentiment.

"But, Thorwald, the doctor and I have been talking about going home. Not that we are tiring of your society, but we are filled with a desire to tell the people of the earth what we have found on Mars and try to teach them some of the good lessons you have given us. The doctor, who has a monopoly of the scientific culture in our party, can see no prospect of our getting away from your planet. With your more advanced science, can you suggest any way by which we can take a dignified leave of you?"

"We should regret exceedingly," replied Thorwald, "to lose you just as we are becoming well acquainted, but I have no criticism to make on the excuse you offer for wanting to revisit your home. I must say, however, that you present to us too hard a problem to solve. With all our attainments in astronomy and in the navigation of the air, you went one point beyond us when you took passage from the earth to Mars, for we have no means by which to express passengers from one planet to another.

"We consider the circumstances of your leaving the earth and your journey hither the most remarkable thing of the kind ever heard of, and we have nothing in our experience on which we can begin to build any scheme for sending you off on so long a flight through space. If you will only be content to stay here till we have progressed further with our investigations of the high civilization brought to light in our comet, perhaps we can help you. The remarkable people whose exalted condition is there represented may have had powers in this direction of which we cannot conceive. The subject will add even more zest to our researches.

"Why do you desire to leave us so soon? You have seen but few of our notable improvements, and learned comparatively little of the practical workings of our high civilization. And then I have been hoping the doctor would come fully into our belief before he went away."

"If you could hear what he has told me," I said, "you would see that he is already fit to be sent as a foreign missionary from this blessed world to the struggling earth."

"Good!" cried Thorwald. "I am delighted to hear it. If anything could reconcile us to the loss of your society, it is the knowledge that you will both he glad messengers of hope to your promising race. I rejoice that I have had a share in the work of preparing you for your mission.

"And now, suppose we all humor your conceit and give you our parting words, as if the ship were at hand which was to sail the mighty void, and bear you safely to your distant home.

"Come, wife, friends, the day is young and the air delightful. There is nothing to hasten us on our way. Let us ride leisurely along and take a little time to speed these earth-dwellers on their prospective journey with a few words of cheer.

"Foedric, what advice have you to offer them before they take their leave of us?"

Foedric was modest, as we had learned before, but he entered into Thorwald's plan with evident pleasure, and said, addressing the doctor and me:

"My friends from foreign skies, you do not need advice from me after you have been so long with Thorwald and Zenith, but I will send a message to your unfortunate fellow beings who have never had the pleasure of their acquaintance. When you have related your experiences and told them the condition in which you have found us, ask them to call us no longer Mars, but Pax, the world of peace. Our planet is red, but not with war. Its red is rather the blush of the dawn that ushers in the day of universal love. My word to men is to expect the advent of that day, and, expecting, to prepare for it. Useless, cruel, inhuman war must cease, with all strife and hatred and envy and bitter feeling; and then shall you begin to see the full measure of beauty in the song of the angels of which you have told us, and 'Peace on earth' will be a blessed fact and not a prophecy. Thorwald, I have finished."

"You have spoken well, Foedric," said Thorwald. "And now, what wise counsel will you give, Proctor?"

"From what I have learned in regard to the people of the earth," replied Proctor, "it seems to me they will be obliged to have a great deal of war there yet--war against a world of evils, which must be driven out with a strong hand before they can have peace. When each individual has subdued his own spirit, then there will be no more war, and no other enemies to conquer."

"Study the majesty and power of God as exhibited nightly in the starry sky, and learn to revere a being who holds in his hands a million worlds, and not only guides their movements but directs with a heart of love the minutest affairs of all their inhabitants. Look over the broad field of creation, and think of the earth, grand and beautiful as it is, as only one among the vast number of peopled orbs, all swinging in unison, parts of one plan, every one in its day sending forth a song of praise to its maker. So shall your hearts expand and burst the narrow bounds of selfish desire and trivial occupation, and you will begin to grow into the full stature of the sons of God."

Proctor spoke with such feeling that the doctor and I now began to think that these people must be in earnest and were really preparing to send us home in some way, but the latter idea was, as will speedily be seen, an unjust suspicion.

"Zenith," said Thorwald, "will you take your turn, after Proctor's inspiring words?"

"If we were in truth making our farewells to these friends," replied Zenith, "I should feel more sadness than I am conscious of now.

"My message, O men, shall be a plea for purity. If you would seek to make your world the better for your visit here, teach men everywhere to be pure, a hard lesson to learn, but one that will bring a rich reward. First make the fountain sweet. Be pure in heart, and then your lives, and even your thoughts, will be pure. When you can fully obey the command, 'Think no evil,' you will need no other commandment to keep your lives unspotted. Such a requirement no doubt seems too difficult for you now, but the earth must come to its maturity by following the same high ideal which has ever been set before us. There is one law for all worlds, an infinitely pure and holy God commands us all to be perfect even as he is perfect, although to that perfection nor earth nor Mars, nor, perhaps, any other world, has yet attained."

"But, Thorwald, I fear you will not have time to give your farewell words before our friends depart."

"I shall not require much time," replied Thorwald, "but I should not like to lose the opportunity of adding something to what has already been said. I think we have been wise in having this talk, for those who could take advantage of such a novel way of coming to us may discover some means of going home again before we suspect it."

Then, turning to us, Thorwald continued:

"Go back to the earth, my brothers, and tell men to despair not in their conflict with evil; for God reigns, therefore the good will triumph. Tell them you found a race of happy beings here, not perfect, but aiming toward perfection, having escaped many of the perils that belong to an earlier stage of existence. The earth, too, will one day be old. Will it be happy then? Your generation can help to make it so. With our history to guide us, and with the knowledge you have given us of the earth's present condition, we have high hopes of your race, and I venture the prediction that your world will see, in the near future, such an advance as you have never dreamed of. The era of a united effort to overthrow the evil forces is approaching, when all will press with eager, sincere hearts into the work, when money will be poured out like water, when men will begin to lose their selfishness and take each other by the hand as brothers, and when the dark places of the earth will grow bright with the light of the gospel.

"I do not wonder you want to get back there. I hope I should have the same desire if I were in your place. What a time in which to live, with so much good work to do, and such encouragement and sure reward!"

Thorwald's enthusiasm made him eloquent, and we all regarded him intently as he spoke. How well I remember that group of persons: Proctor, the devout astronomer; the stalwart and earnest Foedric; Zenith, the queen of all womanly graces; and Thorwald himself, our friend and brother, the rich fruit of an advanced development.

My companion and I were deeply impressed with the words we had heard, and could hardly realize that these friends were not aware that our life in Mars was nearly over, their farewells were so genuine.

But, hark! Thorwald is still speaking:

"Go back to the earth, I say, and--" a crash, a sensation of falling, a dull pain in my head, a new voice at my ear, saying,

"Why, Walter, are you hurt?"

During the effort to recover full consciousness I said:

"There, Doctor, the accident you expected has certainly come."

And then I opened my eyes and discovered that I was sitting in an undignified position on the deck of a vessel of some kind.

Again the voice, now more familiar and identified with a lovely face, said:

"You must have had that broken chair; I knew it would let you down some time. Don't you know me, Walter?"

"Why, yes, it's you, Margaret, isn't it? But where's the doctor?"

"Oh, how are you hurt?" cried Margaret in alarm. "Tell me, and I will run for the doctor at once."

This conversation had all passed in a moment, and by the time it was finished I had extricated myself from the broken chair with Margaret's assistance, and was now wide awake. I had never expected to leave Mars without the doctor; but now he was gone with all the rest, and I was well content to find myself back by Margaret's side, and to hear her pleasant words, the words of a plain inhabitant of the earth, not too good to love me a little selfishly. A wave of intense happiness in the possession of such a love passed over me. It was a feeling I had never before experienced in my waking moments and it must have illumined my face, for Margaret continued:

"I don't believe you are hurt at all. You look too happy to be in pain. What have you been dreaming about, that makes your face shine so? How thankful I am for this bright moonlight. I never saw you have so much expression before."

"Margaret," I replied, as soon as she would let me speak, "don't you remember you sent me on a quest for my heart? Well, I have found it and brought it back to you."

"How lovely to find it so soon," she exclaimed; "and I know by your looks it's a large one and full of love. But tell me about it. How did it happen?"

"Why, I fell in love with a voice."

"With a voice? Whose voice?"

"Well, it didn't seem to matter much. First it belonged to Mona and then to Avis, and part of the time to both of them."

"You make me jealous," said Margaret.

We were now standing, hand in hand, leaning on the rail of the vessel, in the full enjoyment of our new-found happiness.

"You will not be jealous," I answered, "when you know all about it. I have enough to tell you, Margaret, to occupy a week, I should think. I have seen and heard a great deal, and seemed to be living amid other scenes for many months, and yet I notice the moon is but two or three hours higher than when you left me there in the chair to go and find your book. I shall take great pleasure in relating to you the entire experience when we have time. Perhaps I will write it out for you. I have been stirred as I never expected to be, but I assure you I have brought back my whole heart to you. Only," I added, as a sudden flash of memory startled me with its vividness, "I should like to hear that voice once more."

"Ah," said my companion, "why do you think of that so much? I fear you are not quite heart whole. What was there peculiar about the voice?"

"Margaret, it was the most exquisite music anyone ever dreamed of. I cannot describe my emotions or the intensity of my enjoyment whenever I heard it. First the voice belonged to a beautiful girl whom I thought we met on the moon, and who talked only in the language of the birds. Then she went to Mars with us, and there I heard the same sweet voice also from one of the noble women of that happy planet.

"Oh, what queer things we do in our sleep, and how supremely selfish a dreamer is. I once had a theory that we are all responsible for the character of our dreams, but I hope, my dear, that you will not call me to too strict an account in this case, I should blush to tell you how I loved each singer, and yet I know now it was only the voice that charmed me. I shall seek my pillow with delight to-night, to try and catch in my sleep some faint echo of that song, for I never expect to hear its like in my waking hours. You are laughing at me, and I don't wonder. Let me see. I dreamed that I dreamed that you and Mona and Avis were all one grand, sweet singer. I wonder what would have happened if I had staid there long enough to tell Avis something that was on my mind. Perhaps I never should have come away.

"But forgive me, dear Margaret, for my enthusiasm for simply a memory, and put the blame on my sensitive ears. And now, tell me what you have been doing during these long hours. Did you find the professor and get your book?"

"Yes, but I had to stay a few minutes and hear him talk. I hurried back, however, to be with you, and for my reward found you fast asleep."

"I was only dozing. But what did you do then?"

"Oh, I sat quiet for a while, and then took up the amusement I usually follow when I find myself alone."

"What is that? Pray tell."

"Singing, of course."

"Singing?"

"Why, yes, didn't you know I could sing?"

"Do you mean to say you were singing all those two or three hours?"

"Not all the time, but at intervals. I sang so loud sometimes that I thought I should wake you." "Then," I exclaimed with feeling, "it was you that I heard. You know my ears are never fully asleep. Margaret, it was your voice that I have been falling in love with."

At this Margaret laughed heartily, as she answered:

"You have been a good while finding it out. I knew it all the time. That's what I sang for, and I had my pay as I went on, for every time I began, whether soft or loud, I could see your face light up with the light of your soul, and then I knew my voice was finding its way to some corner of your brain."

"How stupid of me," I said, "not to wake up the very first time I heard you; but I thought it was Mona. Oh, how it did thrill me! And to think I am to hear it again when I am really awake. Come, why do we waste all this time in talking when I have that great happiness still unfulfilled? May I not hear you sing now?"

"Oh, you might be disappointed, after all. My idea is that you enjoyed my singing because all your critical faculties were dulled in sleep, and you heard only through your heart, as it were. Don't you think it would be better to live awhile on the pleasant memory you have brought back with you?"

"Not at all. I can retain the memory, and have the present happiness besides."

"But you said you never expected to hear such music in your waking hours."

"Do not be so cruel, Margaret, as to recall those words against me, although they were really a tribute to you, for it was your own voice that forced me to utter them. But what can I do to induce you to sing?"

"Go to sleep," she replied. "I will sing for you all you please when you are asleep, and you can hear me and think of Mona at the same time. That will be a double pleasure."

"My dear, I prefer to think of you. Mona was a beautiful girl, but she could never love me as you do."

"Why so? Wasn't her heart large enough?"

"Yes, it was too large--so large that she loved everybody, and one no more than another; while you, darling, have chosen me, out of all the people in the world, as the object of your highest and deepest love, and yet in doing that have only increased your power of loving others. Now what will you do to pay me for that speech?"

"Well, I'll relent. But you must at least pretend to be asleep. Come back and find another chair that you can rest in easily, and I will sit beside you. There, that will do. Now turn your head away from me, close your eyes, and promise me you won't open them till I tell you to do so. I intend to have the calm judgment of your ears uninfluenced by your sight or any other sense. If you can manage to fall asleep while I am singing, so much the better."

"Margaret," I replied, "I shall try hard to keep my eyes closed, but there isn't a drug in the ship's dispensary powerful enough to put me to sleep."

"Then keep quiet and think of Mona. That will be the next best occupation for you. Stop laughing, or I shall disappoint you, after all. I should think the memory of the first time I sang for you would be enough to sober you. Now I am going to turn away my head, so that if you do look around you won't see my face."

I said nothing in reply, being too eager to have her begin. And now I had not long to wait for the fulfillment of my oft-expressed desire.

Sweet and low came the first accents of her song, and, with all my anticipations and with the foretaste I had had in my sleep, I was not prepared for the effect they had on me. It was Mona's voice, but with every fine quality so exaggerated that all my faculties, now in the fullest sense awake, were completely taken captive. I made no movement, except to turn my head slightly so that I might drink in the sweet sounds with both ears. As the notes increased in volume my pleasure grew to rapture. Not only was my critical taste fully satisfied, which of itself was almost bliss, but that other and higher effect followed--my heart was enlisted. I had never known love till that hour. We had been introduced to each other years ago and had kept up a cold and formal acquaintance, and in my recent sleep we had made notable progress, but only now did love and I really clasp hands in a warm and lasting embrace.

If I had loved Margaret before, then the feeling I now had was something else, it was so different. But it was nothing else, and, therefore, I was obliged to conclude that I had lived all these years with a false notion in my head. As the song changed now and then, but did not stop, my heart swelled with its strong emotion, and I had the greatest difficulty to keep my promise and remain quiet. At length the music ceased, and I jumped from my chair with the intention of giving Margaret some palpable sign of my new love, when I was arrested by her warning hand and these words:

"Wait, Walter, someone is coming. I can see all you want to tell me in your face."

I was obliged to stop, and reserve for a more private place any violent manifestation of my exuberant affection, but answered quietly:

"Not all, dear Margaret. You will never know all my love." There was now more or less passing back and forth by the passengers, preparing for the approaching landing, but yet we were able to continue our conversation. At Margaret's request I told her more about Mona and Avis, and the principal incidents of what seemed to me a real experience, reserving the graver parts of the story for other occasions. Her sympathies went out particularly toward Mona, and suggested the question:

"Did not the poor child recover her voice?"

"I think she did soon after we left," I replied. "I neglected to tell you that, the morning we started for our last aerial trip, Antonia told me she was teaching Mona the use of the vocal organs, and the results were already such that she believed she would in a short time be entirely successful."

"How fortunate for me," said Margaret, laughing, "that you came away just then."

"Oh, Margaret," I exclaimed as loud as I dared, "I thought I was happy last night, but what shall I call my condition now? Do you have that intensity of feeling for me which is nearly bursting my heart?"

"Yes, my dear, I have had it for years. But my love is certainly increasing now, when I see yours flowering out so luxuriantly."

In such sweet converse the time passed rapidly. Steadily our noble vessel carried us every moment nearer home. And with the last words of Thorwald, "Go back to the earth," still ringing in my ears, we steamed amid familiar scenes--the lights from Long Island, New Jersey, Staten Island, and soon Liberty's torch, Governor's Island, and the great city in front of us. This voyage was ended, but our life's voyage seemed to be just beginning as I led Margaret forth with wonderful tenderness and whispered in her ear, passionately, the magic words, "I love you."

POSTSCRIPT.

E very book should have a purpose. Notwithstanding the popular character of much that is contained in these pages, the purpose of this volume is a serious one.

I acquired the belief in the habitability of other worlds when quite young, and it long ago grew into a settled conviction.

Firmly held by this idea, what is called the astronomical difficulty in theology gave me great concern. When I considered the vast extent of the universe, and saw, with but little imagination, millions on millions of habitable worlds, I felt the force of the old objection, How could our tiny earth have been chosen for such peculiar and high honor as we read of in the gospel story?

Thomas Chalmers, in the preface to his astronomical discourses, states the difficulty in these words: "This argument involves in it an assertion and an inference. The assertion is, that Christianity is a religion which professes to be designed for the single benefit of our world; and the inference is, that God cannot be the author of this religion, for he would not lavish on so insignificant a field such peculiar and such distinguishing attentions as are ascribed to him in the Old and New Testaments."

And then Dr. Chalmers proceeds in his able manner to overthrow both assertion and inference. He shows that it is only presumption for the infidel to claim that Christianity is designed solely for this world, and asks how he is able to tell us, "that if you go to other planets, the person and religion of Jesus are there unknown to them." "For anything he [the infidel] can tell," the writer continues, "the redemption proclaimed to us is not one solitary instance, or not the whole of that redemption which is by the Son of God;... the moral pestilence, which walks abroad over the face of our world, may have spread its desolation over all the planets of all the systems which the telescope has made known to us.... The eternal Son, of whom it is said that by him the worlds were created, may have had the government of many sinful worlds laid upon his shoulders."

In this and in all the rest of his argument Dr. Chalmers, while intimating that the redemption may include other worlds, retains the belief that the actual occurrences related in the gospel took place only on this globe. Others may have heard the story, or, as he beautifully says: "The wonder- working God, who has strewed the field of immensity with so many worlds, and spread the shelter of his omnipotence over them, may have sent a message of love to each, and reassured the hearts of its despairing people by some overpowering manifestation of tenderness.... Angels from paradise may have sped to every planet their delegated way, and sung from each azure canopy a joyful annunciation, and said, 'Peace be to this residence and good will to all its families, and glory to Him in the highest, who from the eminence of his throne has issued an act of grace so magnificent as to carry the tidings of life and of acceptance to the unnumbered orbs of a sinful creation.'"

But, as Dr. Chalmers truthfully says, it is not the infidel alone that raises this question. It is asked by many sincere believers, generally in communion with their own minds, and has disturbed, if not hindered, their faith. These brilliant discourses left me still perplexed on the main point, and I was forced to ask myself again if it was at all likely that one world could be made so unlike all others as to become the only scene of such a wonderful event as the death of the Son of God. And even if this could be made to seem probable, what an infinitesimal chance there would be that our earth would be the one chosen for this exhibition, out of the unnumbered worlds that fill the immensity of space.

As a feeble hint toward a possible solution of this difficulty, this volume is offered. The argument may not be acceptable to a single reader. I do not say that I believe it myself; but the thought has helped to satisfy my mind and may be of assistance to some other soul. I will merely say that, of course, I do not believe the analogy between any two worlds is so close as I have made it, for the purposes of the story, between Mars and the earth.

In my effort to relieve the book of dullness, I have exaggerated some of the situations, as in the treatment of the woman question for example, but the intelligent reader will easily discover whether there be anything of value remaining after the extravagance has been brushed away.

Alvan Clark & Sons, the celebrated makers of telescopic lenses, in view of their recent successes in casting larger object-glasses than was once thought possible, now assert that they can place no limit to the size these glasses may reach in the future. It is only a question of time, skill, patience, and money.

Is it, then, presumptuous to believe that the day will dawn when this world will know whether Venus or Mars is inhabited? And if either or both of them shall be found to be peopled, among the many questions of engrossing interest to be studied it seems clear to me that the most important will be the moral and spiritual condition of the inhabitants.

THE AUTHOR.

The Codes Of Hammurabi And Moses
W. W. Davies

QTY

The discovery of the Hammurabi Code is one of the greatest achievements of archaeology, and is of paramount interest, not only to the student of the Bible, but also to all those interested in ancient history...

Religion   **ISBN:** *1-59462-338-4*   **Pages:132**
MSRP $12.95

The Theory of Moral Sentiments
Adam Smith

QTY

This work from 1749. contains original theories of conscience amd moral judgment and it is the foundation for systemof morals.

Philosophy **ISBN:** *1-59462-777-0*   **Pages:536**
MSRP $19.95

Jessica's First Prayer
Hesba Stretton

QTY

In a screened and secluded corner of one of the many railway-bridges which span the streets of London there could be seen a few years ago, from five o'clock every morning until half past eight, a tidily set-out coffee-stall, consisting of a trestle and board, upon which stood two large tin cans, with a small fire of charcoal burning under each so as to keep the coffee boiling during the early hours of the morning when the work-people were thronging into the city on their way to their daily toil...

Childrens   **ISBN:** *1-59462-373-2*   **Pages:84**
MSRP $9.95

My Life and Work
Henry Ford

QTY

Henry Ford revolutionized the world with his implementation of mass production for the Model T automobile. Gain valuable business insight into his life and work with his own auto-biography... "We have only started on our development of our country we have not as yet, with all our talk of wonderful progress, done more than scratch the surface. The progress has been wonderful enough but..."

Biographies/   **ISBN:** *1-59462-198-5*   **Pages:300**
MSRP $21.95

The Art of Cross-Examination
Francis Wellman

QTY

I presume it is the experience of every author, after his first book is published upon an important subject, to be almost overwhelmed with a wealth of ideas and illustrations which could readily have been included in his book, and which to his own mind, at least, seem to make a second edition inevitable. Such certainly was the case with me; and when the first edition had reached its sixth impression in five months, I rejoiced to learn that it seemed to my publishers that the book had met with a sufficiently favorable reception to justify a second and considerably enlarged edition. ..

Reference   **ISBN:** *1-59462-647-2*

Pages:412

MSRP $19.95

On the Duty of Civil Disobedience
Henry David Thoreau

QTY

Thoreau wrote his famous essay, On the Duty of Civil Disobedience, as a protest against an unjust but popular war and the immoral but popular institution of slave-owning. He did more than write—he declined to pay his taxes, and was hauled off to gaol in consequence. Who can say how much this refusal of his hastened the end of the war and of slavery ?

Law   **ISBN:** *1-59462-747-9*

Pages:48

MSRP $7.45

Dream Psychology Psychoanalysis for Beginners
Sigmund Freud

QTY

Sigmund Freud, born Sigismund Schlomo Freud (May 6, 1856 - September 23, 1939), was a Jewish-Austrian neurologist and psychiatrist who co-founded the psychoanalytic school of psychology. Freud is best known for his theories of the unconscious mind, especially involving the mechanism of repression; his redefinition of sexual desire as mobile and directed towards a wide variety of objects; and his therapeutic techniques, especially his understanding of transference in the therapeutic relationship and the presumed value of dreams as sources of insight into unconscious desires.

Psychology   **ISBN:** *1-59462-905-6*

Pages:196

MSRP $15.45

The Miracle of Right Thought
Orison Swett Marden

QTY

Believe with all of your heart that you will do what you were made to do. When the mind has once formed the habit of holding cheerful, happy, prosperous pictures, it will not be easy to form the opposite habit. It does not matter how improbable or how far away this realization may see, or how dark the prospects may be, if we visualize them as best we can, as vividly as possible, hold tenaciously to them and vigorously struggle to attain them, they will gradually become actualized, realized in the life. But a desire, a longing without endeavor, a yearning abandoned or held indifferently will vanish without realization.

Self Help   **ISBN:** *1-59462-644-8*

Pages:360

MSRP $25.45

The Rosicrucian Cosmo-Conception Mystic Christianity by *Max Heindel*   ISBN: *1-59462-188-8*   **$38.95**
The Rosicrucian Cosmo-conception is not dogmatic, neither does it appeal to any other authority than the reason of the student. It is: not controversial, but is: sent forth in the, hope that it may help to clear..   New Age/Religion Pages 646

Abandonment To Divine Providence by *Jean-Pierre de Caussade*   ISBN: *1-59462-228-0*   **$25.95**
"The Rev. Jean Pierre de Caussade was one of the most remarkable spiritual writers of the Society of Jesus in France in the 18th Century. His death took place at Toulouse in 1751. His works have gone through many editions and have been republished...   Inspirational/Religion Pages 400

Mental Chemistry by *Charles Haanel*   ISBN: *1-59462-192-6*   **$23.95**
Mental Chemistry allows the change of material conditions by combining and appropriately utilizing the power of the mind. Much like applied chemistry creates something new and unique out of careful combinations of chemicals the mastery of mental chemistry...   New Age Pages 354

The Letters of Robert Browning and Elizabeth Barret Barrett 1845-1846 vol II   ISBN: *1-59462-193-4*   **$35.95**
by *Robert Browning* and *Elizabeth Barrett*   Biographies Pages 596

Gleanings In Genesis (volume I) by *Arthur W. Pink*   ISBN: *1-59462-130-6*   **$27.45**
Appropriately has Genesis been termed "the seed plot of the Bible" for in it we have, in germ form, almost all of the great doctrines which are afterwards fully developed in the books of Scripture which follow...   Religion/Inspirational Pages 420

The Master Key by *L. W. de Laurence*   ISBN: *1-59462-001-6*   **$30.95**
In no branch of human knowledge has there been a more lively increase of the spirit of research during the past few years than in the study of Psychology, Concentration and Mental Discipline. The requests for authentic lessons in Thought Control, Mental Discipline and...   New Age/Business Pages 422

The Lesser Key Of Solomon Goetia by *L. W. de Laurence*   ISBN: *1-59462-092-X*   **$9.95**
This translation of the first book of the "Lemegton" which is now for the first time made accessible to students of Talismanic Magic was done, after careful collation and edition, from numerous Ancient Manuscripts in Hebrew, Latin, and French...   New Age/Occult Pages 92

Rubaiyat Of Omar Khayyam by *Edward Fitzgerald*   ISBN:*1-59462-332-5*   **$13.95**
Edward Fitzgerald, whom the world has already learned, in spite of his own efforts to remain within the shadow of anonymity, to look upon as one of the rarest poets of the century, was born at Bredfield, in Suffolk, on the 31st of March, 1809. He was the third son of John Purcell...   Music Pages 172

Ancient Law by *Henry Maine*   ISBN: *1-59462-128-4*   **$29.95**
The chief object of the following pages is to indicate some of the earliest ideas of mankind, as they are reflected in Ancient Law, and to point out the relation of those ideas to modern thought.   Religion/History Pages 452

Far-Away Stories by *William J. Locke*   ISBN: *1-59462-129-2*   **$19.45**
"Good wine needs no bush, but a collection of mixed vintages does. And this book is just such a collection. Some of the stories I do not want to remain buried for ever in the museum files of dead magazine-numbers an author's not unpardonable vanity..."   Fiction Pages 272

Life of David Crockett by *David Crockett*   ISBN: *1-59462-250-7*   **$27.45**
"Colonel David Crockett was one of the most remarkable men of the times in which he lived. Born in humble life, but gifted with a strong will, an indomitable courage, and unremitting perseverance...   Biographies/New Age Pages 424

Lip-Reading by *Edward Nitchie*   ISBN: *1-59462-206-X*   **$25.95**
Edward B. Nitchie, founder of the New York School for the Hard of Hearing, now the Nitchie School of Lip-Reading, Inc, wrote "LIP-READING Principles and Practice". The development and perfecting of this meritorious work on lip-reading was an undertaking...   How-to Pages 400

A Handbook of Suggestive Therapeutics, Applied Hypnotism, Psychic Science   ISBN: *1-59462-214-0*   **$24.95**
by *Henry Munro*   Health/New Age/Health/Self-help Pages 376

A Doll's House: and Two Other Plays by *Henrik Ibsen*   ISBN: *1-59462-112-8*   **$19.95**
Henrik Ibsen created this classic when in revolutionary 1848 Rome. Introducing some striking concepts in playwriting for the realist genre, this play has been studied the world over.   Fiction/Classics/Plays 308

The Light of Asia by *sir Edwin Arnold*   ISBN: *1-59462-204-3*   **$13.95**
In this poetic masterpiece, Edwin Arnold describes the life and teachings of Buddha. The man who was to become known as Buddha to the world was born as Prince Gautama of India but he rejected the worldly riches and abandoned the reigns of power when...   Religion/History/Biographies Pages 170

The Complete Works of Guy de Maupassant by *Guy de Maupassant*   ISBN: *1-59462-157-8*   **$16.95**
"For days and days, nights and nights, I had dreamed of that first kiss which was to consecrate our engagement, and I knew not on what spot I should put my lips..."   Fiction/Classics Pages 240

The Art of Cross-Examination by *Francis L. Wellman*   ISBN: *1-59462-309-0*   **$26.95**
Written by a renowned trial lawyer, Wellman imparts his experience and uses case studies to explain how to use psychology to extract desired information through questioning.   How-to/Science/Reference Pages 408

Answered or Unanswered? by *Louisa Vaughan*   ISBN: *1-59462-248-5*   **$10.95**
Miracles of Faith in China   Religion Pages 112

The Edinburgh Lectures on Mental Science (1909) by *Thomas*   ISBN: *1-59462-008-3*   **$11.95**
This book contains the substance of a course of lectures recently given by the writer in the Queen Street Hall, Edinburgh. Its purpose is to indicate the Natural Principles governing the relation between Mental Action and Material Conditions...   New Age/Psychology Pages 148

Ayesha by *H. Rider Haggard*   ISBN: *1-59462-301-5*   **$24.95**
Verily and indeed it is the unexpected that happens! Probably if there was one person upon the earth from whom the Editor of this, and of a certain previous history, did not expect to hear again...   Classics Pages 380

Ayala's Angel by *Anthony Trollope*   ISBN: *1-59462-352-X*   **$29.95**
The two girls were both pretty, but Lucy who was twenty-one who supposed to be simple and comparatively unattractive, whereas Ayala was credited, as her Bombwhat romantic name might show, with poetic charm and a taste for romance. Ayala when her father died was nineteen...   Fiction Pages 484

The American Commonwealth by *James Bryce*   ISBN: *1-59462-286-8*   **$34.45**
An interpretation of American democratic political theory. It examines political mechanics and society from the perspective of Scotsman James Bryce   Politics Pages 572

Stories of the Pilgrims by *Margaret P. Pumphrey*   ISBN: *1-59462-116-0*   **$17.95**
This book explores pilgrims religious oppression in England as well as their escape to Holland and eventual crossing to America on the Mayflower, and their early days in New England...   History Pages 268

www.bookjungle.com *email: sales@bookjungle.com fax: 630-214-0564 mail: Book Jungle PO Box 2226 Champaign, IL 61825*

QTY

The Fasting Cure *by Sinclair Upton*   ISBN: *1-59462-222-1*   **$13.95**
In the Cosmopolitan Magazine for May, 1910, and in the Contemporary Review (London) for April, 1910, I published an article dealing with my experiences in fasting. I have written a great many magazine articles, but never one which attracted so much attention... New Age/Self Help/Health Pages 164

Hebrew Astrology *by Sepharial*   ISBN: *1-59462-308-2*   **$13.45**
In these days of advanced thinking it is a matter of common observation that we have left many of the old landmarks behind and that we are now pressing forward to greater heights and to a wider horizon than that which represented the mind-content of our progenitors... Astrology Pages 144

Thought Vibration or The Law of Attraction in the Thought World   ISBN: *1-59462-127-6*   **$12.95**
by William Walker Atkinson   Psychology/Religion Pages 144

Optimism *by Helen Keller*   ISBN: *1-59462-108-X*   **$15.95**
Helen Keller was blind, deaf, and mute since 19 months old, yet famously learned how to overcome these handicaps, communicate with the world, and spread her lectures promoting optimism. An inspiring read for everyone... Biographies/Inspirational Pages 84

Sara Crewe *by Frances Burnett*   ISBN: *1-59462-360-0*   **$9.45**
In the first place, Miss Minchin lived in London. Her home was a large, dull, tall one, in a large, dull square, where all the houses were alike, and all the sparrows were alike, and where all the door-knockers made the same heavy sound... Childrens/Classic Pages 88

The Autobiography of Benjamin Franklin *by Benjamin Franklin*   ISBN: *1-59462-135-7*   **$24.95**
The Autobiography of Benjamin Franklin has probably been more extensively read than any other American historical work, and no other book of its kind has had such ups and downs of fortune. Franklin lived for many years in England, where he was agent... Biographies/History Pages 332

Name	
Email	
Telephone	
Address	
City, State ZIP	

☐ Credit Card   ☐ Check / Money Order

Credit Card Number	
Expiration Date	
Signature	

Please Mail to: Book Jungle
PO Box 2226
Champaign, IL 61825
or Fax to: 630-214-0564

ORDERING INFORMATION
web: *www.bookjungle.com*
email: *sales@bookjungle.com*
fax: *630-214-0564*
mail: *Book Jungle PO Box 2226 Champaign, IL 61825*
or PayPal *to sales@bookjungle.com*

Please contact us for bulk discounts

DIRECT-ORDER TERMS
20% Discount if You Order Two or More Books
Free Domestic Shipping!
Accepted: Master Card, Visa, Discover, American Express

www.ingramcontent.com/pod-product-compliance
Lightning Source LLC
Chambersburg PA
CBHW081145020726
47504CB00009B/2001